# ICE CITY BLUES

## A MAX LeBLUE MYSTERY

Published by
ROTHCO PRESS
1331 Havenhurst Drive #103
West Hollywood, CA 90046

Cover Design: Rob Cohen
Photo by: C. David Boxley

Rothco Press is a division of Over Easy Media Inc.
www.RothcoPress.com
@RothcoPress


Ice City Blues
A Max LeBlue Mystery
Paperback ISBN: 978-1-945436-28-4
Ebook ISBN: 978-1-945436-29-1

# ICE
# CITY
# BLUES

A MAX LeBLUE MYSTERY

## Frank Lauria

ROTHCO PRESS • LOS ANGELES, CALIFORNIA

*For Gregory, a mensch among men...*

*"Think where a man's glory most begins and ends,
And say my glory was I had such friends."*
– W.B. Yeats

*"A favor gonna kill you faster than a bullet."*
– Al Pacino, *"Carlito's Way"*

# Chapter 1

I'm back where I started.

New York

Lonely

Paranoid

Drunk.

For me it's a survival strategy.

The only way I can protect my beautiful wife and two-year old daughter is to keep moving. Like a shark.

Now I don't put much stock in philosophy, but I always leaned towards the dark side until the birth of my daughter. Suddenly existence had meaning.

Having been a fugitive since 9/11, I had been tempted to throw in the towel when DEA Director Alvin Delaney caught up to me and Nina in Mexico. Delaney offered me three hundred grand back pay and dismissal of charges if I returned to work for the agency.

My heart wouldn't buy it.

Sometimes I contemplate the evil in the world. The deliberate horrors humans practice on each other with malice aforethought. I tell myself its part of nature: killer whales eating baby seals, venomous spiders, snakes and lizards, man-eating cats and crocodiles, giant cannibal squids – half the damned planet devouring the other half.

Sure I get it, don't fuck with Mother Nature. Which really doesn't cover the ghastly torture-and-kill scenarios humans devise, then inflict, on their fellow man for any number of reasons that have nothing to do with their next meal.

Then I see my two year old daughter Samantha.

And realize that innocence, beauty – and a powerful good – also exists.

Somebody has to stand up for it.

Not for the oil fields, or the mega-corporations, or America's incredible drug hypocrisies. But to stand up for simple human decency.

So I got in the wind.


Nobility doesn't come cheap.

Nina was pregnant and we had built a solid business with a joint called LazyBonz in Zijuataneo Mexico.

Fortunately I had emerged from my last dance with some dedicated psychos, holding enough cash to vanish quickly. And although I left Delaney's big check behind, I took his dismissal of charges with me.

Okay, I admit while undercover I did an enthusiastic amount of drugs and booze. That aside I had the best conviction rate in the unit. Delaney had trumped up the charges because he was banging my ex-wife.

When I found out I went off the grid.

And here I am – twice a deserter in the war against drugs.

My cyber skills keep my identity hazy even in this Orwellian world where we are all positioned, photographed and recorded in real time – whatever that is.

I work in a small computer shop in San Francisco owned by a man called Gavin Kilroy.

That's me.

Mostly I work at home. The shop is also a convenient mail drop for Max LeBlue.

That's also me.

Kilroy is a carefully constructed straw man. If anyone asks I tell them Mr Kilroy is in Florida. He pays me a generous salary and the rest of the profits he sends to my wife.

Nina lives with my daughter Samantha in a condo in Kentfield. I see them four days a week. Stay over most weekends. The rest of the time I ache to be with them.

The condo is in Nina's mother's name which means my visits stay anonymous and I still rent a room in a flat in North Beach shared by two others. I pay the lease holder, an eccentric physicist named Eli Sarfetti, in cash and services. He has three computers and constantly loses files in a cloud of his own making.

Bogus mail drop, no real address.

I hacked the DMV's data base and altered the information on my driver's license, Afterwards I reported it stolen and got a new one with the fresh misinformation.

I'm all about alternative facts.

I also rent an in-law unit across the bridge where I stash a car and some special electronic equipment. I visit once a week just to keep up appearances.

Such are the narrow parameters of my life. But so long as they include Nina and Samantha, narrow is cool with me.

Unfortunately two months ago my parameters expanded at nuclear fission speed—and blasted me into the center of a Black Hole from which no light can emerge...

+     +     +

Only four people have my phone number. Robert Lowell is one.

Lowell is now Detective Captain in the Petaluma PD. He and I go way back, battle-tested comrades in arms. When he called about lunch I was looking forward to some war stories.

San Francisco is a great town for restaurants so his suggestion that we meet at Za, a modest joint which serves fantastic pizza, took me by surprise

"I wanted someplace where we can talk and won't be seen." He said, settling across from me at a table.

That should have been my cue to hail a cab. However I happen to be partial to Za's sweet sausage pie.

"Are we in trouble?"

He squinted at the menu posted overhead on the wall.

"Not really. I have a new associate."

"Associate?"

His sheepish grin was part Gary Cooper part Tom Brady. "I really don't know what to call him. We've been working together for about a month."

"Undercover work?"

"He is. I'm sort of consulting."

I sat back and waited.

"Two days ago I caught a homicide," Lowell said. "At first I thought it was a routine gang shooting. We get about five a year in Petaluma."

He paused to order a sausage pizza and a couple of beers.

"But my Vic wasn't a local. Prints showed he was an American citizen by birth with a current American passport. He had a law degree from Columbia University. He'd also been busted in LA a few months ago for drugs. But the charges were dropped."

"Cartel connection?"

"That's what I thought until we arrested this other guy."

"For the homicide?"

"Stolen car."

Our beers arrived. We lifted our glasses and I took a long, cold swallow.

"When we ran the guy's prints it turned out he's classified, working for the CIA."

"How do you know if he's classified?" I said, reasonably enough. "Could be working for anybody."

Lowell gave me a look that said don't be stupid. "It also turns out he's investigating the same killing. But he doesn't think it's about drugs."

"What then?"

"He couldn't say. Need to know."

Something occurred to me.

"Did he mention why he stole the car in the first place?"

Lowell give me that same look but it wasn't as convincing.

"His car wouldn't start while he was tailing the Vic. He saw him getting ready to leave and hotwired the first unlocked car he found."

"That's what he told you?"

"Uh yeah."

"He was tailing the guy who turned up dead?"

"Yeah."

"How long after you found the body did you arrest this guy?"

"The same night why?"

A tattooed server appeared with our pizza. For the next five minutes we focused on the sweet sausage slices which were delicious. Finally I said, "No professional would drive a hot car any longer than necessary. He claims he was tailing your victim. Did he witness the killing?"

Lowell shrugged, his mouth full. "CIA guy lost him. He was driving around trying to spot the Vic's car when my patrolmen pulled him over."

"And you buy that?"

"Like I said, his prints are classified. He's CIA."

"Truth ain't high on their agenda."

He put his half eaten slice down. "And what's your theory?"

"Don't have one. But based on what you told me, this guy's story is pure bullshit."

A slow smile broke his stern expression. "That's my opinion too. Problem is our Chief is gaga over this guy. Thinks he's the second coming of James Bond."

"Gaga?"

Lowell ducked his head and grabbed another slice. "You know, small town police chief gets in on a big time CIA op. He's given the bastard an office and full access."

"What's his name?"

"Chief Walter Bannon."

"No, the bastard."

"Paul Zallen."

"And he won't say why he was tailing the dead guy."

"Can't," Lowell said between bites, "classified."

I lifted my empty glass and signaled for fresh beers. "What have you got on the homicide so far?"

"Name Fernando Suarez, age thirty-two, got a BS degree University of Arizona, law degree Columbia, busted on suspicion of cooking meth, case dismissed when a witness disappeared."

My inner alarm sounded.

"A chef? Any connection to the Vandals?"

The Vandals were a particularly nasty motorcycle gang that happened to have a standing bounty on me dead or alive – preferably dead – for past transgressions. Such as blowing up their local meth lab while we cracked a human trafficking operation. Lowell had my back during that little caper. He got a promotion, I got a bounty put on my ass.

Lowell shook his head. "First thing I checked out. No ties that I came up with, and I dug deep. Suarez had only been in town a week. He was staying at a motel."

"Which means he was meeting somebody."

Lowell lifted his glass. "Good point."

"Either buying or selling."

"Keep going."

I snatched the last slice on the platter.

"If it's not drugs, it could be guns."

"I knew you were the right guy to consult."

"Want another pizza?"

Lowell patted his stomach. "Usually don't have pizza and beer for lunch."

"Did you toss Suarez's motel room?"

"My lieutenant did." He paused, "Want to give it a pass? Crime tape is still up."

"When?"

"How about tomorrow? We're due to remove the tape about noon. But that's not the favor I need from you."

"Which is?"

He pushed an envelope across the table. "I need you to run Paul Zallen through your magic computer and see if you find anything out of place."

"As in...is he a fraud?"

"I knew you'd understand."

"What I don't understand is why you don't want to be seen with me."

"Paul Zallen has been sitting on my shoulder since the Chief gave him the keys to the station. He keeps showing up in odd places. Like a stalker"

I smiled. "Didn't know there were any odd places in Petaluma."

"I know it's a small town but I keep seeing him where I shouldn't."

I ruled out professional jealousy. Lowell is as ethical as Batman. Which was exactly why I agreed to help him.

"Tell you what, I'll run this guy tonight and if I find anything I'll drive up there and we can take a look at that motel room."

After exchanging a few pleasantries Lowell called for the check. He left the place alone. At his suggestion I lingered a few minutes before leaving.

It was a nice sunny day so I walked down the hill to North Beach. Somewhat spooked by Lowell's certainty that he was being tailed I headed directly to the Café Sappore. It was ideally situated on a corner that afforded me a view of three converging streets. Seated inside I could spot whoever might be following. I ordered a coffee, one eye on the plate glass window. A man walking a dog coming down Taylor. A woman carrying a shopping bag coming down Lombard. Of course the dog routine is damn good cover. I suppressed the thought.

Paranoia is a virus and I have no immune system.

I took the long way home, Lowell's envelope heavy in my pocket.

The envelope contained a copy of Paul Zallen's New York driver's license and his Visa card. It also contained copies of Fernando Suarez's California driver's license and credit card. More than enough to institute a comprehensive search on my Big Mac. Actually I use another PC at the same time. Plus a Microsoft pad. Gives me more dimensions and confounds whoever might be tracking my inquiries.

I usually enjoy difficult cyber projects but Lowell's request spiked my anxiety level. Lowell wasn't the skitterish type. This thing had him worried. Which meant I was worried.

With a minimum of effort I eased past Paul Zallen's Classified wall and delved into his file. Zallen was indeed a liar. He was an ICE agent temporarily assigned to the CIA. Immigration and Customs Enforcement? There were a plenty of undocumented workers toiling on the farms surrounding Petaluma. But the CIA?

Obviously the Agency superseded ICE which suggested Zallen was boots on the ground for a specialized operation. A contractor in somebody's private war.

Digging deeper I found that Zallen had been with the LAPD until his second suspension for using excessive force. Two suspensions were extremely difficult to accrue for an LA cop.

Unfortunately one incident took place in Brentwood the other in Beverly Hills. In both cases charges were brought by white women and corroborated by phone videos. Apparently Zallen liked to rough up ladies driving expensive cars. A serial bully. Probably worse.

The previous suspension was for excessive force. An elderly black man Zallen had mistaken as a suspect in a shoplifting case. The man had come to pick up his granddaughter. Zallen broke the man's arm and nose.

All three cases cost the city significant money to settle.

He was allowed to resign.

A year later Zallen passed the federal test and became an agent with ICE. Ever since then a spotless record. Of course undocumented females had no recourse if detained. Any complaint of excessive force would be brushed aside. Especially these days.

ICE's bar was set at very low. Zallen was in the right job at the right time. He could indulge his sadistic urges on helpless Latinas with impunity.

However I did have problems hacking into his CIA file. I had to take care to route my inquiries through obscure portals in distant lands from Iceland to India, to Indonesia and back to India, a land seething with fellow hackers. This enabled me to get lost in the crowd but it took time.

Finally I popped in. I found that Zallen had contacted the CIA concerning an unnamed trafficker who specialized in smuggling high end clients including suspected terrorists and Mexican cartel dons into Northern California.

All of this was completely unsubstantiated by any hard evidence but given the toxic hysteria drummed up by Trump and his minions, Zallen's assertion was enough to get him temporarily assigned to The Company.

They even gave him a partner. His name was Madison Goldsmith, an experienced agent who like me, had served with the Marines in the Kuwait War. Because of his proficiency in languages he was absorbed into the Intelligence Community. Apparently he had been on at least four top-secret operations since then. These operation were highly classified and would require an investment of risk and time to scale the wall. So I settled for the name, and the knowledge that Zallen had hooked up with the real deal.

The late Fernando Suarez was easier to search but he turned out to be someone I hadn't expected. The meth lab bust was a glaring anomaly in an otherwise stellar young career. The son of Mexican immigrants he was an outstanding student in high school, earned an academic scholarship to the University of Arizona and a paid fellowship at Columbia University Law School in New York. He graduated with honors and went to work for the ACLU.

After successfully defending two high profile cases Suarez moved back to Arizona and began to defend immigrants detained by police or being held for deportation. He also set up centers where undocumented workers were informed of their rights and could receive free legal advice. Within three years he had of cadre of young lawyers manning the centers. He received funding from a number of sources and had begun installing similar legal clinics in San Diego. During that period he married a woman named Selena Martinez and fathered a daughter named Julia.

Out of nowhere he was arrested for operating a meth lab. The warrant had been issued on the word of a mysterious informant named Oswaldo Braggo AKA "Exxon". That had to come from some bright boy drug agent. No self-respecting gangster would adopt the name of an energy corporation. Beer maybe.

It seems Suarez had taken over a building that had been involved in a meth bust three years before. When the smoke cleared the case was dismissed but the agents had confiscated the immigration Center's computers and slowed Suarez's work considerably. Funding was also affected.

Now Fernando Suarez, crusader for immigrant rights was dead. And the immigration agent tailing him for some classified reason, claims he lost Suarez shortly before he was murdered.

The best part was Zallen's claim that he was forced to steal a car in order to continue his surveillance.

Obviously Suarez was a nail in the ICE's jackboot. But assassination? I called Lowell.

"Meet me at that motel we talked about," I said, careful not to say anything directly. "I'll be there at ten."

+     +     +

"This guy Zallen is as dirty as a shithouse rat," I told Lowell over coffee.

He squinted at his muffin and put it aside. "More information than I need over breakfast. What have you got?"

We were sitting in a small bakery in Petaluma. It was nine thirty and I had just arrived. Lowell had wanted a briefing before we checked Fernando Suarez's motel room. I gave him everything I'd pulled from Zallen's file. And the real facts about Suarez.

"ICE huh?" He snorted and shook his head. "San Francisco and Petaluma are Sanctuary Cities. ICE agents are required to let us know if they're operating in the area." He took a thoughtful sip of coffee and looked at me. "Any theories?"

"He could very well have taken Suarez out. But there's something that bothers me."

"Which is?"

"Where's his new partner, Madison Goldsmith?"

Lowell drained his coffee. "Good question. Let's go to the motel and see if he's there."

I had parked around the corner from the bakery aware that the Vandals, the biker gang who have that standing bounty on my head are headquartered in Petaluma. Fortunately I killed all the members who might recognize me.

Which only leaves about two thousand more.

The Quality Inn was an upscale motel featuring a pool, Jacuzzi and a shaded veranda. The whole place seemed brochure-perfect, except for the ominous yellow tape wrapping one door on the second deck.

Suarez's room was large and airy with a double bed, small couch and writing desk along with the usual amenities. It seemed hardly occupied as if Suarez only slept there. A blue suit, blue blazer, two blue button down shirts and a pair of grey flannel trousers hung in the closet. They looked limp and downcast like dogs awaiting the return of their master.

Like many men who travel a lot, socks, sweater, underwear and an extra shirt were in the suitcase on the dresser. Why bother to unpack when you're moving on soon?

We went through every item very carefully. The only thing we found was a book of matches in a shirt pocket with the logo of a bar or restaurant in San Francisco called Pablo's.

I went over to the writing desk. The leather edged green blotter was a holdover from an era when people used ink pens. There was a ballpoint pen on top also rapidly becoming obsolete. But it didn't belong to the Quality Inn. The red letters along its side read San Francisco Hilton. Which suggested Suarez had written something.

There were a couple of blank sheets of stationary in the desk drawer. Nothing else.

"Did your guys check the wastebaskets?"

Lowell frowned. "Not sure."

I bent down and saw an imitation leather wastebasket beneath the desk. My clumsy attempt at pulling it out tipped the basket over. When I crouched down to retrieve it I saw a couple of things.

The basket was empty

A sheet of paper was taped to the underside of the desk.

Carefully I pulled the sheet loose. At first glance it seemed to be a list of some sort.

"Hey dudes can anybody play?"

Reflexively, I reattached the paper and came out from beneath the desk.

A tall, balding man with a sun-reddened face stood grinning at us from the doorway.

Lowell gave me a knowing glance and I knew before being introduced this was Paul Zallen.

"Yo Paul, what's up?" Lowell said with a tepid smile.

"Walter told me you were giving the room a last shot." Zallen said, staring at me.

"Uh Paul this is..." Lowell glanced at me.

I extended my hand and stepped forward. "Max."

His handshake was as limp as his smile.

"Max?"

"DEA – undercover," I confided, "and you?"

Zallen's ruddy skin held the remnants of boyhood acne and sun lines creased his neck. He was taller than me and stocky. His pale blue eyes peered at me as if regarding something unpleasant then darted past me to Lowell.

"You didn't mention the DEA."

I jumped in quickly.

"Suarez was charged with running a meth operation in San Diego. We figure he was here to meet somebody."

He relaxed a notch. I knew he couldn't push my presence there too far. It was Lowell's case.

"So find anything?"

I moved back to the desk and pointed at the wastebasket.

"Nothing there. Drawers either. I was just about to check the bathroom."

"I can do that," Paul said, suddenly eager. He wheeled as if he remembered something he'd left in there.

I motioned for Lowell to follow him then quickly took the paper taped under the desk and put it inside my jacket along with the pen. Then I crowded into the bathroom.

Zallen was crouched over the contents of the waste basket. They consisted to a few crumpled receipts, one of which had been torn. With great concentration he was piecing the torn receipt together,

Lowell stood over him brow furrowed. He glanced at me and shrugged as if to say, see what I mean?

Just to piss Zallen off, I crouched beside him.

"Where's it from?"

He stiffened slightly. "Can't see yet," he said, making it clear I was disturbing him.

Casually I plucked a crumpled receipt and unfolded it, further pissing him off.

"That's evidence," he snapped.

"No shit Sherlock. That's why I'm here with Captain Lowell."

Zallen glared at me, then at Lowell, then turned back to the torn receipt.

Unfolding mine I saw it was a receipt from a San Francisco parking lot. The other one in the basket was for a coffee at Peet's.

I glanced at Zallen who was studying the reconstructed square of paper. "Anything yet?

"It's for a dozen prepaid phones." He reported triumphantly.

"Where were they purchased?"

My question soured his victory. He stood and, turned to leave.

"I've got to run this down right now."

"Hold it Paul."

Lowell looked like John Wayne in a gun duel, drawing his Colt. Except in this case his hand held a plastic ziplock bag.

Same difference.

Lowell's expression left no room for argument.

"Thanks," he said curtly as Zallen deposited the fragments into the bag, "this is still a homicide investigation."

"See you back at the station," Zallen said, glowering at me.

"He made that sound like a threat," I said after Zallen left.

Lowell shrugged. "Most likely he's complaining to Chief Bannon right now."

The phone on his hip buzzed. He ignored it, too busy piecing together the receipt.

"I know this place," he said, "let's go before the Chief sends out an alarm."

We drove to an electronic store in the Designer Outlet district which makes Petaluma a destination for shoppers. Fortunately the store was small by comparison to the trendy warehouses nearby.

Armed with his badge as well as the date and time on the receipt Lowell had no problem gaining access to the security camera archive.

I hit the keyboard and in a few minutes pulled up the image of Fernando Suarez two day earlier, purchasing a dozen pre-paid phones which he paid for in cash. The phones were in boxes and as the clerk packed them into large bags Suarez was speaking to someone who was out of view.

Finally as Suarez took the bags a young woman carrying a child in her arms walked in front of the camera and followed him out of the store. I reversed it a few frames, paused it on the woman and printed out her picture. Total time, roughly fifteen minutes

The manager seemed impressed. "Nice work. You ever need a job look us up."

"You have advanced equipment. Thanks for letting me get a crack at it."

It was true. They had a sophisticated system. And my image would be forever archived along with Lowell's, and the woman in the photograph.

She was young, slim, brunette and from what I could assess, probably a Latina.

"Nobody I know," Lowell said as we drove back to the station. "Maybe we can run her through facial recognition."

I shrugged. "Long shot."

"Only shot we got."

"Let's keep the girl to ourselves for now," I suggested. "You were right about Zallen. He's a fucking pain in the ass."

When we arrived at the station Zallen was hovering like an indignant bird.

"Walter wants to see you right away."

Lowell nodded and ushered me into his office.

"Wait here while I straighten this out."

Lowell's office was remarkably neat. I settled into a wooden chair against the wall and folded my arms. A rustle inside my jacket reminded me of the paper I'd found taped beneath the desk in Suarez's room.

It was a list of names and numbers, written by hand.

I counted.

Twelve names. A dozen pre-paid phones.

I put the list away in time to avoid being seen by Agent Zallen who stalked into the office like a stooped Heron, pale eyes darting around the room until they spotted me.

He perched on the corner of Lowell's desk and cocked his head.

"What's your full name anyway Max?"

I smiled. "Need to know, sorry."

He let it pass. "And you're here because you think Suarez was moving drugs?"

"We've had him under surveillance ever since he beat the meth bust in San Diego," I said using the information I had picked up online. It sounded credible to me.

Zallen didn't buy it. He was about to say so when Lowell entered the office.

He handed the Zip lock bag containing the receipts to Zallen.

"Here's your evidence Paul. Now get the hell off my desk."

Zallen gave him a no-big-deal-amigo grin and scurried out of the office.

When he was gone I took the paper from my jacket.

"This was taped to the bottom of the desk back at the motel."

Brow furrowed Lowell studied the list. From his knotted jaw and tight scowl

I could tell he was still steaming over whatever transpired with his chief.

"Do me a favor make me a copy before the asshole comes back."

"Right away."

While waiting I paced around the small, tidy office, idly examining the orderly stacks of paper on the shelves. I peeked out the window into the parking lot and glimpsed Paul Zallen as he ducked into a blue Malibu and drove off.

"Here the list." Lowell said as he entered, "what do you think?"

"I think they all have pre-paid phones."

"Good point."

"Captain?"

We both turned.

A uniformed patrolman stood at the door. He was young, fair skinned with a blond Mohawk that emphasized his wide neck and beefy shoulders, the result of heavy barbells and too much Creatine.

"There's somebody to see you."

Lowell shrugged. "We're busy."

"A woman."

"So?"

"She's the wife of the homicide victim."

"Mrs Suarez?"

The patrolman's skin flushed and he nodded uncertainly.

"Believe so sir."

"Show her in."

Lowell shook his head. "I hate this part," he said under his breath.

I've been in battle with Lowell but had never seen him appear rattled before. Then again, informing a woman her husband has been murdered is a cop's hardest job.

I recognized Selena Suarez from the print out at the electronic store.

But barely.

As in the photo, she had a little girl in her arms. After that the resemblance faded to a picture of an anguished woman desperately clinging to the shreds of her sanity for the sake of her child. The light in her eyes had been washed out by tears leaving dark hollows that seemed drained of hope. When she spoke her voice sounded like a cross being dragged along Via Dolorosa.

"What happened to my husband?"

"Someone shot him Mrs. Suarez." Lowell said, his manner grave and respectful.

"I want to see him."

"Of course. We'll drive you there."

The word *we* signaled he wanted backup so I tagged along.

Selena Suarez settled into the rear seat of the unmarked Ford, her daughter propped limply against her. She closed her eyes as if relieved of a burden but when they reopened the weight of reality dulled her stunned gaze.

"Mrs. Suarez when did you last see your husband?" Lowell asked as he drove, voice gentle.

It took a while for her to gather the words. "Two days ago. He went shopping. We had...dinner," she added, voice cracking.

Lowell didn't speak. The silence in the car hung over us like a shroud.

"You went shopping? Lowell said softly.

"Cell phones," she droned. "He said he needed phones."

Lowell and I exchanged a quick glance. She was telling the truth.

"Where are you staying Mrs. Suarez?" Lowell asked, easing off the interrogation.

"The Metro, here..." her voice trailed off.

"Why didn't you stay," He paused, "with your husband?"

"He was worried about..." She nodded her head at her daughter who was half asleep in her lap.

Lowell nodded and took a deep breath. The interview was over. It remained quiet until we reached the Coroner's facility. Lowell talked Mrs. Suarez through the paperwork and then escorted her into the morgue to view her husband's body and make a positive ID.

I stayed behind in the lobby with her daughter Julia. In the past being left alone with a two-year old would have terrified me. However since Samantha arrived in my life two years ago I'm less squeamish, even somewhat competent.

She sat very still on the bench, her hands clasped in her lap, head bent as if praying. I noticed her hair was uncombed and her sweatshirt soiled. It was white with a picture of a cat on the front.

"Julia," I whispered.

She looked up, dark eyes wide and fearful.

"Would you like something to drink?"

For a moment she stared at me. She was a pretty girl, with dark pink skin like Samantha's. Then she nodded.

I went to the vending machine and found a juice drink among the toxic choices. I also bought a package of raisins. At the last second I sprung for a package of Oreos figuring the kid needed comfort food.

When I returned Julia was seated in the same position, obviously traumatized by things beyond her understanding. Her daddy was never coming home.

She gulped down the juice and was starting on the Oreos as I went for fresh supplies. I extracted two bottles of water from the machine and drank one while I watched her devour the cookies.

I gave her the water bottle. Nina had nailed it into my head, dilute the sugar content. And by her standards Julia had eaten a week's supply.

Julia grabbed the bottle in two hands and took a couple of swallows.

The cookies seemed to revive her. She sat up and looked around. I could tell she was starting to fidget, anxious for her mother's return.

I smiled and pointed at the image on her shirt. "Do you like kittens?"

Maybe it was my smile or the dumb question but she recoiled slightly before she looked away making it clear she wasn't amused. So much for my child skills.

Julia saw her mother before I did. Still clutching the water bottle she hopped off the bench and ran to meet her.

With effort Selena Suarez managed to scoop her daughter up but she was clearly exhausted. She absently took the bottle from Julia and drank thirstily.

She looked at Lowell. "When can we take him home?"

The question hung in the fluorescent silence.

"Day after tomorrow he'll be released." Lowell sounded hopeful as if Suarez would walk out of his frozen compartment.

"Two days...?" Her voice started to rise.

Lowell lifted his palms. "Please Mrs. Suarez. We're trying to find out who did this."

"Well he can't tell you." She hoisted Julia higher. "Can you drive us back to our motel? My daughter needs to eat."

I liked her already.

"Would you like to stop for something along the way?" I said as we drove to the motel.

She hesitated. "Yes thank you, if it's not inconvenient."

Lowell seemed relieved to be off the hook as the bad guy. "No trouble at all Mrs. Suarez. And if you need anything feel free to call. I'll give you my private number."

Selena didn't answer but the tension inside the car eased considerably.

Lowell pulled into a supermarket and waited. I escorted Selena and Julia inside. I lifted the little girl into a basket and pushed her around the store as her mother shopped. She enjoyed the ride and when she laughed the darkness hovering over her dispersed and seemed to lighten her mother's obvious pain.

We emerged with three shopping bags worth of supplies and drove to the Metro Motel and Café, a quirky, semi-European establishment set off the street. Lowell gave Selena his card and offered to carry the bags but I could see our company only added to her pain. She had just viewed her murdered husband's corpse and was about to collapse with grief.

"That was tough," Lowell said as we drove back.

"She's alone now," I reminded, "Just her and the little girl."

I glanced at Lowell. "Suarez knew there was a good chance he'd be hit. That's why his family is in a separate motel—and why he taped this list under his desk."

"What about the phones? She was with him."

"She told the truth about the phones. Maybe you can show her the list in a couple of days when she's had time to recover."

"Yeah, good idea. Thanks Max, you've been a big help."

"Let's hope Zallen doesn't find out we got to the electronic store first."

"If he doesn't I'll tell him myself. This is my goddamn case."

I gave him a fist bump.

Zallen was striding across the parking lot as we pulled in. He saw us and waved.

"I've got something," he announced.

"What's that?" I asked from the passenger's window.

He gave me a superior smirk and walked off. "I'll show you inside," he said over his shoulder.

I turned to Lowell. "Guess he doesn't know we beat him to it."

"Let's see what he knows. if anything."

In contrast to Lowell's neat, efficient look the décor in Zallen's office looked like a college dorm room. A discarded shirt hung on the corner of one chair and a half-eaten sandwich and a can of Coke decorated his desk. Papers were scattered everywhere including the other chair.

Proudly he dropped a print-out of Suarez and his wife next to the sandwich.

"I want this woman," he said. "How do we find her?"

"She's holding a baby, probably his wife." Lowell suggested.

"All those bitches have babies," Zallen snapped. "They pump them out like roaches."

That did it for me. Lowell too.

"Let me know if you turn up anything," he said, following me out.

"Slimeball," I said under my breath. I felt The Preacher begin to stir from a deep sleep. The Preacher is my name for the blind, black rage that consumes me when confronted with cruelty in all its forms, be it murder, rape, slavery or child labor. He has a special hard-on for racists.

Thing is, the Preacher causes more problems than he resolves. However he'd been asleep for a long while and I preferred it that way. He has a way of getting me hurt.

"That prick wants to hold Suarez's widow overnight and leave her little girl with strangers. After her husband was murdered. Maybe by him."

Lowell sighed. "Sooner or later "I'll have to tell him,"

"Either way he'll be pissed off so it may as well be later."

Lowell shrugged. "Maybe."

It turned out to be sooner.

Zallen stalked into Lowell's office, still holding the print out.

"Why didn't you tell me Suarez's wife was here?"

"She came to claim the body."

"I had to hear that from one of your clerks. Where is she?" he demanded before Lowell could answer.

Lowell stonewalled him "After she ID'd her husband and signed the usual papers she left with her child."

"Where would she find a cab out there?"

"I believe she called an Uber," I said.

Zallen narrowed his eyes. "Somebody must know where she's staying."

"She had to leave an address with the Coroner," Lowell said, sounding helpful.

"Yeah right." He turned on his heel and went off to make the call.

"Bannon will go ballistic when he finds out."

"Trust me – he won't. Get the coroner and ask him to stall Zallen for thirty minutes."

"Okay," he reached for the phone.

"Oh, and lend me your car. I'll leave it parked at the bakery where we met."

He tossed the keys on the desk. As I hurried out I heard him talking to the Coroner.

As I drove back to the Metro Motel I called Nina.

"Max, when are you coming home? Samantha's been asking about you."

"I'll be home soon. But I might have company. Think you can handle it?"

"Just tell me what's going on."

I gave her the short version and she grasped the gravity of the situation.

"Of course Max I'll be ready. Does this mean we'll see you tonight?"

"Absolutely, that's my reward."

"You mean our reward. Get home soon. We need you too."

My warms feelings were short lived.

"I don't believe you," Selena Suarez told me flatly, arms folded. "It's a trick. You people are all the same."

"Look, about thirty minutes after I leave and an agent from ICE name Paul Zallen is going to take you back to the station for questioning. You'll be separated from your daughter for at least twenty four hours."

Despite her exhaustion Selena's spirit broke through like a lightning flash. She picked up Julia and locked her eyes on mine.

"How do you know this so precisely?"

"I arranged for the coroner to delay giving your location so I'd have time to warn you."

"And why does this Immigration agent want me so badly?"

I took the print out from my inside pocket and showed it to her.

"You were photographed while buying a dozen pre-paid phones. The immigration agent has this picture."

"This proves nothing."

I took Suarez's handwritten list from my jacket. "There are twelve names on this list."

Her eyes widened. "Where did you get that?"

"It was taped to the bottom of a desk in your husband's room. The ICE agent doesn't know it exists

"And you, I suppose you take me somewhere safe and I tell you about the names. Is that how it works?"

I slowly shook my head. "I have a daughter about Julia's age. This is how it works. I take you somewhere safe until you can claim your husband's body with a lawyer at your side."

She relented a notch but remained unconvinced. "I know all about you people. You hounded Fernando for years. You'll do anything to get what you want."

I lifted my hands in surrender. "Okay, we're running out of time. If you don't want to believe me..." I took out my phone and punched the speed dial.

"Nina? I need you to speak to Mrs Suarez."

I handed Selena the phone.

She looked at it as if it was a grenade. "Who is Nina?"

"My wife."

For the next few minutes the conversation was in rapid Spanish. I understood her saying something about 'your husband' but I lost the rest. After a prolonged conversation Selena handed me the phone. Nina had disconnected.

"You want to take me to your home?"

I shrugged. "We have a daughter about Julia's age, and we have an extra room."

"Why are you doing this? To get information?"

"To protect you from this immigration agent. He was following your husband the night he was killed."

Selena let that sink in a few minutes.

"Tell your lawyer when you call him but please don't reveal the source. Look – if you're leaving it will have to be now. I don't want to be here when Zallen shows up. Do you understand?"

"Yes," she said softly, "I'll pack some things." She gently lowered Julia to the carpet. Then she looked up at me with a tortured gaze. "I pray I'm doing the right thing."

The Metro Motel is quite eccentric and Selena's room was L shaped with a full kitchen in front and a living area and bedroom in the rear. I waited impatiently while she gathered her things. It took longer than I estimated. Finally we headed out to the car with me carrying two suitcases and a shopping bag full of the food Selena had bought earlier.

As we pulled out of the parking area I thought I saw Zallen's blue Malibu in my rear view.

We switched cars near the bakery which made Selena suspicious. I had to patiently explain that our present vehicle belonged to Police Captain Lowell before she agreed to the move.

Selena sat with Julia in the back seat of my '94 Mercury Sable. It was an improved replica of my original custom Mercury, better known as the Green Ghost. This because it looked like every other car on the freeway, Honda Toyota, whatever. Except for the thick layer of hard rubber on the front and rear bumpers it was featureless to the point of being invisible – which suited me fine.

The inside was another story. Like the previous model my interior designer and weed dealer Len Zane had installed two hidden panels, one under the dash big enough for the Taurus .45 that lived there. The other panel which he put overhead could hold a large dictionary, or a kilo of my drug of choice. At the moment it housed a loaded Glock 9 and two magazines.

Paranoid?

Always.

Press a button inside the glove compartment and my twin computers fanned out from beneath eager for action. Len had also made a couple of improvements over the old model. He had lined the door panels with Kevlar making them bullet resistant. He did the same by installing thick, shatter proof glass. Both choices added a minimum of weight.

Actually I had destroyed Green Ghost 1 myself with a high velocity .45 slug shot from my Taurus. It embarrasses me to admit that my car had been stolen. While in hot pursuit on a motorcycle I put a bullet in the Mercury's gas tank and it burst into flame before tumbling into the Pacific like a sparkling pinwheel.

For this reason I asked Len to put a layer of Kevlar over the tank. All of these innovations added very little weight to the Mercury which could compete with anything on the road due to Len's major overhaul of the engine and suspension.

It cost a bundle of cash but no matter what ride I chose, be it a Mercedes or Mustang, my man Len would have to customize it. And I liked driving an innocuous car that is no longer being manufactured.

Commuter traffic was heavy and twenty minutes into the slow drive home both Selena and Julia were dozing, the little girl with her head in her mother's lap. Crawling along the freeway as the sun went down, shading the brown hills with streaks of gold against a dramatic red sky, the only sound the motor's low drone, created a warm, peaceful lull within the car. A momentary bubble of tranquility in a violent sea.

It popped when I pulled in front of the house.

"Daddy, daddy!"

Nina was on the deck with Samantha, both of them waving.

Julia woke up and announced, "I'm hungry mommy."

I helped Selena Suarez with her bags and when I reached the top of our redwood stairway Nina was in my arms and Samantha had attached herself to my left leg.

The arrival was noisy with Nina and Selena talking rapidly in Spanish, Samantha telling me something about her rabbit and Julia needing to go potty.

I carried the bags to the guest room dragging Samantha who still held tight to my leg.

Our home in Kentfield is California Natural. Nestled off a narrow road and surrounded by trees, it could be in Big Sur or Laurel Canyon. It's a duplex with the top floor set slightly behind the bottom creating a deck for the master bedroom. It has three bedrooms, two and a half bathrooms and a large, sunny kitchen. As an added perk my car can't be seen from the road,

Nina had prepared the guest room and laid out sliced chicken, cheese, bagels, salad, wine and milk in the kitchen should anyone be hungry.

And everyone was starved.

The conversation around the table was muted. Samantha and Julia eyed each other suspiciously, Selena two days a widow, was polite, grateful but still wary and I hadn't told Nina the full reasons for giving the Suarez family sanctuary.

After the meal Selena took Julia to the guest room for a much needed rest. Nina, Samantha and me took the wine bottle and curled up for some family time. I put on a Miles Davis CD and we talked.

Samantha told me all about her stuffed rabbit. I promised to read to her and she ran to her room to choose a book.

As soon as she left Nina said, "Tell me why we're doing this Max."

I gave her all the details including Agent Zallen and the phones.

"Immigration had obviously targeted Suarez with his work with Latino communities. Since the Great White Hope took office ICE has been making raids without authority. Agent Zallen wants to detain Mrs Suarez for at least twenty-four hours and interrogate her about the phones her husband bought. When I asked her she told me straight out he bought them. No hesitation. No lies. Big fucking deal. But Zallen doesn't care that she still hasn't buried her husband. Or that little Julia will be more traumatized than she already is. He's out to get bad hombre's—or in this case hombritas."

I had gotten a bit wound up. When I looked at Nina she was smiling,

"Max,"

"What?"

"Come here."

And she kissed me.

Just then Samantha reappeared with a copy of *Where The Wild Things Are*.

Later that night Nina revealed her own wild side.

Domestic bliss.

Didn't last long.

Shortly after nine the next morning I was awakened by my cell phone. I looked around. Nina wasn't there.

"Max?"

It was Lowell.

"Yeah, what."

"Make sure you steer clear of Petaluma. Zallen's burned about Mrs. Suarez, taking off. He's sure we had something to do with it and threatening all kinds of shit. And he has the Chief worked up about it. He even called me into his office."

"What did you say?" I knew Lowell wasn't much on lying.

"What could I say? After we dropped Mrs. Suarez off I came back to the station."

"Yeah so?"

"The Chief and Zallen want you to come in for debriefing."

"Tell them they can debrief my ass."

I switched off.

After a shower and change of clothes I went down to the kitchen looking for Nina. The place was empty, nobody around.

I found warm coffee in the pot and dropped some bread in the toaster. I took the coffee out to the kitchen deck and saw them coming down the road, Samantha and Julia skipping and giggling like old pals while Nina and Selena solemnly walked behind, their arms crossed, their heads down, like nuns. The sun was streaking through the trees and the kids' chatter sounded like birds but there was so mistaking their measured, funereal steps.

Men die. Women weep. I knew what Nina was feeling. I felt it myself.

Odds were three to five Nina would be a young widow like Selena.

And unlike me Selena's husband worked at a non-violent profession.

Theoretically that is, until Trump decided Latinos were a threat to civilization – just like refugee children, CNN and *Saturday Night Live*.

So U.S. Immigration and Customs Enforcement hired an army of ill qualified thugs to carry out their grab and go policy. Thugs like Zallen.

I had the bastard as likely for Suarez's killing.

The kids ran past me to Samantha's room. The ladies came up the stairs slowly, talking in low tones.

"I'm going to help Selena make arrangements," Nina said quietly."

"Make sure she contacts a lawyer. When she shows up they'll pounce."

I stood on the deck, a bagel in one hand, a coffee cup in the other, contemplating my next move.

You've done your good deed, I told myself. It was time to think of Nina and Samantha. Tomorrow you'll take Selena to Petaluma and get out of the line of fire. You can consult with Lowell from a neutral zone.

Selena had decided to have her husband's body shipped to San Diego for burial. The cost for the hour long flight might have been exorbitant but she knew a pilot, a family friend who agreed to pick up the body and fly back to San Diego with Selena and Julia.

Case closed right?

Lowell handles the homicide case and I slip behind the curtain again.

Dream on.

The arrangements concluded, Nina prepared lunch. Despite the heavy circumstances, the atmosphere was decidedly lighter.

"My lawyer will meet us at the Metro parking lot," Selena told me.

"Very good," I said, "don't forget to tell him Zallen was following your husband."

She met my eyes. "You and your wife have been most generous and kind. Please forgive my rudeness earlier."

I started to wave her off but she went on.

"I think you should know my lawyer, Sidney Kingman, is one of the names on the list you found."

"Your husband gave him a phone?" was all I could think of to say.

"Fernando never got the chance. Those phones are probably in the trunk of his rented car."

"It's been impounded. I'll call Captain Lowell."

She nodded absently as if it didn't matter. In the sunlit kitchen, her natural beauty was evident beneath the cobweb of grief, shock and crushing responsibility crossing her youthful face.

"Thanks for telling me about your lawyer."

She shrugged. "Of course. If you'll please excuse me I'm exhausted. With your permission I'd like to take a nap."

"Please do. Uh, I'm curious about something."

"Yes?"

"What were all those phones for?"

She smiled sadly. "Fernando was organizing a legal task force. To fight the mass deportations."

"My cousin George was caught up in one of those sweeps," Nina said, her gold-flecked eyes bright with anger.

Selena heaved a deep sigh. "All Latinos, legal, illegal, citizens...we're all targets."

As if realizing what she said, Selena left the table and hurried to her room.

Nina and I cozied up in the den, listening to the kids in the other room.

"Max?"

"Umnn what?"

"You know it's a wonderful thing you're doing for Selena. Her husband must have been a fine man. But so are you..."

I kissed her lightly. "I hear you. Look, I did a favor for Bob Lowell, helped some good people but now I'm out. Back to the boring world of computers, and us."

She wasn't convinced. "I know you Max. You don't do boring very well." She kissed me, not so lightly. "Remember I believe in you whatever happens. "Just be careful okay?"

"Okay," I said.

But I don't do careful very well either.

That morning Nina insisted we all have a big breakfast under the Jack Reacher theory which is 'you never know when you'll get a chance to eat again'. Facing possible detention Selena took her advice.

Julia also displayed a hearty appetite. She looked clean and rested. Her hair was brushed and she was wearing a dark blue dress. Selena had chosen a dark blue suit for her appearance, her black hair pulled back in a severe bun. While still under stress she seemed prepared to meet the challenge.

Just before we left Samantha presented Julia with one of her Beanie Babies, a gesture which broke my heart.

We drove to Petaluma in relative silence. This time Selena sat in the front. A small sign of trust.

Turning into the parking lot I noticed two cars of interest.

One was a blue Malibu.

Another was a Mercedes convertible, top down, driver's door open to allow a pair of red and black cowboy boots to rest on the asphalt in all their glory. Their owner lolled in the front seat smoking a cigarillo while he perused a folded newspaper through rose tinted glasses. A gold and ruby ring on his pinky gleamed in the sunlight.

He was about forty, with a beautiful head of silvery black hair and a craggy face featuring a prominent jaw. A pencil thin moustache underlined his long Roman nose. He wore a black slim cut suit and one of those Colonel Sanders black string ties.

"There's Sidney," Selena said.

Why was I not surprised? If you googled Sleazy Mouthpiece, Sidney's picture would pop up first.

I stopped so Selena could get out and talk to him. Julia jumped after her, one hand clutching her Beanie Baby. As I parked I watched them in my rear view.

Sidney Kingman tossed his paper and cigarillo aside, took off his rose shades and got out of his car to meet her. I gave him a few points for courtesy. They didn't hug. Instead he grasped her shoulders and said something.

Selena nodded.

Then he bent and lifted Julia in his arms, his expression morphing from gravely concerned attorney to beaming uncle. Kingman stood taller than me and his lean body moved smoothly. When I approached, he half-turned and extended his hand.

"You must be the gentleman who's been so kind to Mrs. Suarez. As her counselor and family friend I thank you. I've known Fernando Suarez since we worked for the ACLU in New York. I was best man at their wedding."

That gave me pause. I shrugged and took his hand. "I hope we can have a talk after you assist Mrs. Suarez."

His grip was firm and his voice cultured.

"You can be sure I will do everything in my power to help bring Fernando's cowardly assassin to justice."

I couldn't top that sound bite so I looked at Selena.

"Do you want to go to the coroner now?"

"Please give me a few minutes to go to my room. Julia needs to freshen up."

I took that to mean, go potty. At any rate I looked forward to having a few minutes alone with Kingman.

"Uh, are you staying in Petaluma Mr. Kingman?" I asked as they walked to the motel lobby.

He looked at me as if the idea was preposterous.

"Here, no. I have a country place in a little town called Healdsburg."

Kingman's 'little town' had grown to be one of the most affluent communities in the wine country. Pronounced Heelsburg it was known as Beverly Healdsburg by the locals.

A shouting female cut off my next question.

It was Selena. Instinctively I bolted for the lobby.

I stopped short when I saw Paul Zallen, his face bright red, pulling Selena roughly by the arm, who was half dragging Julia behind her.

"You have no right to do this!" Selena yelled. "Stop, you're hurting me! My daughter!"

I stepped in front of Zallen and lifted my arms. "Whoa," I said as if trying to calming a horse. "Let the woman go. What do you think you're doing?"

"What the fuck do you think?" Zallen snarled trying to shoulder me aside.

"I think you have no probable cause and no warrant."

He smirked and leaned into my face "You didn't get the memo asshole. ICE doesn't need warrants anymore."

His breath was stale enough to piss me off. But when he put his hand on my chest he woke the Preacher who struck with the speed of a viper. I snatched Zallen's thumb and bent it back towards his wrist.

Surprised, Zallen grimaced, face deep red.

"Let her go now," I said, in low, measured tones. "Or I break it."

I kept my voice low. I might have been discussing the weather.

He released Selena who immediately ran to Kingman's side, clutching Julia in her arms.

"I'm charging you with assault on a federal officer, mister," Zallen hissed – and the woman with resisting arrest."

"I don't think so."

We both turned. Kingman was holding up a large screen phone.

"I shot a video of the confrontation," he said calmly. "It's clear the evidence shows an unlawful arrest on a widow and her two year-old child. I predict this will be big news on social media. Could even go viral."

I thought Zallen's head was going to explode. His face seemed to swell up as if being pumped full of air and his pale blue eyes bulged with rage. He brushed past me and marched off to his Malibu.

A thought fluttered like an alarmed bird. I didn't need my mug plastered over social media.

"What are you going to do with the video?" I said, trying to sound casual.

He gave me a wolfish grin. "I was bluffing,' he said, coal black eyes sparkling with mischief. "Never got to my phone in time. I barely know how to send a text anyway."

My initial aversion shifted an inch. I could get to like this dude.

"My compliments on your handling of a most unpleasant situation," he added, inching closer to my good side. "I take it you know that agent?"

Nice try counselor but not until we exchange information.

"Why don't we discuss this over a drink. I'll be in Captain Lowell's office later while she makes her statement. This way the man from ICE won't have her to himself."

He smiled, revealing even white teeth. "I like the way you think Mr...?"

"Max for now."

"As you say Max." He reached into his tailored suit, pulled out a black business card embossed in red, and handed to me with a flourish.

"Until we see each other at the station then. Adios amigo."

Did he really say that? I thought, watching him walk away.

"You were right," Lowell said when I entered his office, "the phones were in the trunk of Suarez's rental. Nobody considered them as evidence first time we looked." He pointed to two neat stack of boxes against the wall.

"Does Zallen know?"

"Not yet why?"

"He tried to forcibly bring Mrs. Suarez in. I convinced him to let her go."

Lowell tried to suppress a grin. "Thought something was up, I could hear Zallen yelling from the Chief's office."

"Her lawyer is bringing her to see you after she makes the arrangements."

"Will the funeral be here?"

"No," I said examining one of the boxes. "A pilot friend is flying from San Diego and taking them back with the body."

"Ten to one Zallen will claim it's a criminal conspiracy."

"Make it twenty," I said, replacing the box. Nothing unusual there, just your everyday prepaid phone preferred by tech savvy criminals everywhere.

"Mrs Suarez said Fernando was setting up a legal task force to fight illegal deportation," I said, settling in a chair. "Something must be up or ICE wouldn't be here."

On cue Zallen bustled into the room. "Where is she?"

"Mrs Suarez will be here with her lawyer for an interview," Lowell said calmly.

Zallen waved the printout as if it was an imperial decree. "The bitch is going to tell me what happened to those phones."

Lowell pointed to the boxes stacked beside me.

"The phones are right there Paul."

Zallen glared at the boxes suspiciously. "Well I need to know why he bought them. And she's going to tell me."

Lowell sighed heavily and stood.

"Actually she's not going to tell you anything, because you won't be here."

"What the fuck are you talking about?"

"This is my homicide and you are in the way. Not only that, you're at the very least a material witness— and at most, a prime suspect. Therefore you are not permitted to interview anybody. And if you use foul language in my office again I'll throw you out bodily."

Zallen's eyes bulged as they had when I bent his finger.

"A suspect? I told Walter..."

"Chief Bannon isn't in charge of this investigation – I am. Try to interfere again and I'll charge you with obstruction of justice."

Zallen's scalp flushed bright red making it seem that his thin hair was on fire. Fists clenched, he marched out.

"Foul language?" I said softly.

Lowell squinted at me. "His language dehumanizes Mrs. Suarez and all the Latinos he deals with. He's also homophobic."

I heard that.

As it happens Lowell is gay.

"So it's official? Zallen is a suspect in Suarez's killing."

"At present, he's my only suspect. C'mon Max, I'm a small town cop but I'm not stupid."

We didn't have to wait long for Sidney Kingman's grand entrance.

The attorney strode into Lowell's office radiating confidence, as if he had solved the case. Selena followed, Julia in her arms. Her expression as stoic as Kingman's was aggressive. She smiled and nodded when she saw me.

Julia waved.

I waved back.

Lowell was quick to provide a chair for Selena. "Can I get you something? Water? Coffee?"

"Nothing thanks," Kingman said, "we'd like to do this as quickly as possible. My client has the difficult task of burying her husband. But I must warn you, any attempt to hold my client will result in a subpoena to show Just Cause, followed by a lawsuit." He punctuated the statement by jabbing one finger in the air.

"My client has already been subjected to an attempt to forcibly detain her. For which we are considering further action."

Lowell glanced at me. I spread my palms.

Lowell smiled diplomatically. "I can assure you that we do not consider Mrs. Suarez a suspect. However we are anxious the find the person who murdered her husband."

"Of course, of course, we are at your service. We all share the same goal."

I noted how quickly Kingman put Lowell on the defensive while being cooperative.

The rest of the interview did not reveal anything we didn't already know. Selena accompanied her husband to the electronic store where he purchased a dozen prepaid phones. The phones were for a legal task force formed to fight mass deportation sweeps by ICE. Suarez insisted Selena stay at a separate hotel fearing retaliation for his work.

That night they had dinner. It was the last time she saw him.

"I found out he was dead on Spanish language radio," Selena said, voice cracking.

"Fernando was an important figure in the Latino community," Kingman put in hurriedly, patting her shoulder. "For the record I am part of that task force. I hope that information will be confidential. Until Fernando's killer is apprehended we are all in jeopardy."

"So you think this is related to your task force?" Lowell said, pouncing on the idea.

"Cui bono?" Kingman declared, one finger pointed skyward. "Who benefits Captain Lowell? Answer that question and you'll solve your case."

Suddenly the ball was in Lowell's court. Slick.

"If you have no further questions Captain, may we be permitted to leave? My client has to see to the needs of her daughter."

Lowell looked at me helplessly. I shrugged.

"I guess that's it," Lowell said, "please let me covey my deepest condolences for your loss. I promise we'll do everything possible."

"Thank you Captain," we'll be flying back to San Diego in the morning. If you need anything..." he produced his black business card "...I am at your service."

It could have been an exit by Zorro.

Lowell and I looked at each other as they marched out. A few moments

later I remembered something and charged after them.

"Mr. Kingman."

He paused and smiled politely. "Yes Max, what is it?"

"Since you're leaving tomorrow, it's important we meet later today."

"Important." Kingman glanced at Selena who nodded.

"Alright then Max, meet us for dinner at Graziano's. Say six thirtyish."

I turned and saw Zallen hovering nearby. He gave me a buddy-buddy smile, like a white shark about to strike.

"They mention anything about a secret cartel?"

By that I took him to mean the legal task force.

"You mean like drugs?" I said, playing dumb.

"Maybe." His smiled grew wider and his voice lower. "We need to get together on this. We're both working the same side of the fence."

"Not really." I started to move away. "You're a prime suspect remember?"

I paused and looked back. "Did you really steal a car?"

Graziano's restaurant is classic home-style Italian, and at six-thirty the regulars were at the bar talking sports and the older patrons sat in booths having the early bird special.

Everyone was in the house except Sidney Kingman. It became clear six-thirtyish was a relative concept. I sat alone in my red leather booth, nursing a bourbon and watched the door. At seven it opened.

Everyone in the room turned to look when the two men entered. I had expected Kingman to cause a stir and he didn't let me down. He had exchanged his conservative black suit for a black western jacket with sequined lapels, a red shirt open to show a gold chain, and black Levis over his red and black cowboy boots. The only thing missing was a guitar.

The man with him was no less colorful with his long white hair, blue shades wrapped around his weathered face, and equally weathered fringed leather jacket. Faded blue Levis and alligator boots completed the look.

Kingman spread his arms in a gesture of apology.

"Forgive me please. Berto ran into a little bad weather."

"Wind squall off Catalina," The white haired man said, "had to take a detour. He sat down heavily. "I could use a drink."

Kingman ordered a martini, Berto a double Patron. My kind of drinker. As it turned out I overestimated my status.

"Have you looked at the menu?" Kingman said, "They tell me it's authentic."

"Are you a pilot Berto?" I said, trying for casual conversation.

The waitress arrived with our drinks. Kingman lifted his martini .

"To my colleague and comrade Fernando Suarez – who died a hero."

"Berto took off his shades and knocked back his tequila. Then he regarded me with remarkably clear grey eyes that seemed to scrutinize the smallest detail of my untidy person.

"Had my ticket since age eighteen. Flown everything from crop dusters, to Hueys in the Gulf War, to Lear jets and transports like the old Queen Air I got now."

I knew from experience that Huey helicopters were used by the medical units in Kuwait. Flying unarmed in a war zone to ferry wounded men is my idea of heroism. I tossed off my watery bourbon in a silent toast.

"Berto is an old friend," Kingman put in, "he too attended Fernando's wedding to Selena."

The waitress appeared and Kingman ordered an array of appetizers and another round. I switched from bourbon to tequila. Never a good idea.

The Patron went down smoothly until it hit my belly and caught fire, igniting my brain cells. Tequila has vague psychedelic properties probably related to the Algarve cactus' close cousin, peyote.

"I didn't know Petaluma had an airport," I said.

Berto and Kingman exchanged glances. There was something there, but knew better than to press it. Yet.

Kingman too, bided his time. We had almost finished the appetizers and were ready for more drinks before he said,

"You seem to know the agent who tried to detain Selena."

I shrugged. "His name is Paul Zallen. He's an immigration agent up here on some classified assignment. You should know Zallen was tailing Mr. Suarez the night he was killed." In deference to Lowell I left out the stolen car part.

Kingman sat back and eyed me shrewdly. "Are you sure of this?"

"Captain Lowell has all the facts. Including this."

I produced Suarez's list from my jacket.

"Your name is on here. Care to explain?"

He studied it for a moment and smiled.

"First tell me where you acquired it."

From his expression my little drama backfired. Now I had to explain.

"I found it in Fernando's motel room. It was taped to the bottom of his desk. Captain Lowell has a copy."

"And the agent Zallen?"

"He doesn't know it exists."

Kingman took a thoughtful sip of his martini. "I recognize Fernando's handwriting. I believe you Max so I'll tell you. All the names on that list are lawyers. Criminal, civil rights, immigration, financial, we cover the spectrum.

We're a task force organized by Fernando, to fight the illegal deportation of hundreds of people at a time. In many cases without cause. You don't know what it's like to be Latino these days."

I knew. Nina mentioned it often. But I didn't want to bring her into it. The less anyone knew about me the better. I came back to the point.

"And the famous pre-paid phones? There's one for each of you."

Kingman popped a calamari into his mouth. "Exactly. Fernando felt his was targeted by ICE. This Zallen, do you think he had something to do with this?"

"That's Captain Lowell's department. It's his case."

"And you Max?"

"Consultant."

To his credit he let it slide and signaled for more drinks.

I tried to work the conversation to his side.

"These mass deportations, are they rounding up migrant workers on the local farms or..."

"They're targeting everybody!" Kingman slammed his palm on the table, eyes blazing. "From San Diego to Santa Monica to Santa Rosa they have ICE agents at traffic checkpoints with local police. Men go out to buy bread and milk for their children and never come home. ICE agents raid whole neighborhoods sweeping through homes without warrants. Families are being destroyed wholesale. That is why we formed our task force. San Diego, Santa Rosa, these are Spanish names of saints, but today this corrupt administration treats the Latino community like untouchables, the lowest caste. And allows an equally corrupt enforcement agency to spread fear and violence among my people."

As he said this his voice while not louder seemed to expand in tone and intensity. A strand of hair fell across his broad forehead and for a moment, string tie and all he might have been a sequined Abe Lincoln delivering the Gettysburg Address. I could see Sidney Kingman was a persuasive lawyer.

Until now Berto had been quiet, munching appetizers and drinking shots. He leaned on the table and shook a thick finger at me.

"Private charter companies are making a fucking fortune."

"How's that?" I said, not getting his drift.

"They got big fat contracts with the Feds to fly deportees to Mexico. They round people up, put them in these immigration centers and then send them across the border by the planeload. There's at least one flight every night."

"From Petaluma?"

He nodded and speared a fried calamari. "Almost every fucking night. I know a couple of the pilots. Like I said, everybody's getting rich."

"That's why Fernando called us here," Kingman said. "To stop this gross abuse of authority." He shook his head sadly.

Immigration centers, it reminded me of Trump's inept press secretary Spicer referring to Nazi Death Camps as 'Holocaust Centers'. Are we fucked up or what?

At this point I was about to shoot a fourth Patron and had reached a level of philosophical clarity. Of course the CIA would be involved. It was their kind of party. People get shipped out, who knows what gets shipped in.

"I suppose these planes have top-level clearance," I said aloud.

Berto snorted. "Bet your ass. Like I said people are getting rich."

"Profiting on the blood and sorrow of the entire Latino community," Kingman said, signaling for more drinks. "You are a good man Max. I will make sure to follow up on this Zallen matter."

Good luck I said to myself. This operation gave the bastard a cloak of invincibility.

Kingman paid the tab which was just as well because by that time I had trouble counting.

"Max it has been a great pleasure. Believe me I will visit Captain Lowell first thing in the morning."

"Just don't mention who told you."

"Privileged information my friend." He handed me a card. This one was white with a number printed in ballpoint. "My personal mobile."

"Can we drop you somewhere?" He said as I stared blankly at the card.

"Uh no thanks, I think I need some air." I looked at Berto. The stocky pilot looked as fresh as when he arrived. "Tough keeping up with you."

"Hey you were neck and neck pardner," he held out his hand. It was as hard and tight as a vise.

"Did you know Petaluma is the arm wrestling capitol of the world?" I remarked retrieving my fingers.

Berto grinned. "Matter of fact I entered one year. Didn't make it past the second round."

My idea was to walk off the booze for a while, maybe have some coffee before I got back to my car and drove home to Nina.

The small town was shut down for the night and a lone man walking through the dark, tree shrouded streets of the suburban hood could arouse a negative reaction by a nervous citizen, so I stuck to the well-lit commercial section of Petaluma. Which only covers four city blocks, leaving me adrift in closely inhabited patches. I decided to risk a DUI and turned back to where I had parked my car.

As I did I glimpsed something move about fifty yards away, and heard a low rustle. Ever paranoid, a spurt of adrenaline cleared my numbed brain.

Possibilities:

Assassin

Mugger

Raccoon

Probability: Raccoon.

I took a deep breath and continued walking to my car, alert for anything ahead.

A flash of pain slammed me to the concrete. My gut exploded spewing an acid fountain of half-digested food and booze.

*"If you're not at the table,*
*you might be on the menu."*
*– Ruben Gonzalez*

# Chapter 2

It was no fucking raccoon going through my pockets.

Much later when my mind was clear enough to register the severe agony in my belly where I had been kicked, and the piercing throb in my skull, I doubted the mugger probability. Whoever rolled me was quick and professional.

I lay there until the stink of my vomit acted like smelling salts and forced me upright. If you could call it that.

I was half bent and started walking crab-like to my car. The shoe that deflated my stomach felt as if it was still lodged there, and my ribs vibrated pain like mad piano strings.

My wallet was missing as well as my phone, but the car keys were still there. My assailant didn't get much, maybe sixty bucks. I always travel with fake ID and a pre-paid phone.

My real fake ID is in the Green Ghost's glove compartment. Alternative facts are a criminal's best friend.

The drive home was a bitch. Forced to sit behind the wheel at an awkward angle my limited focus was on staying between the white lines and avoiding those revolving red and blue lights in my rear view.

I parked in the driveway and phoned Nina to prepare her for my battered appearance.

"Max what happened?" Nina said when she opened the car door.

"I got coldcocked. Bastard took my wallet."

"You were mugged?"

"Maybe." I tried to slide out of the car but a sharp, deep pain lanced my stiff torso. Despite my gritted teeth I groaned, which alarmed Nina

"Stay there Max, I'm going to get Samantha."

"What for?"

"I'm taking you to the ER and I'm not leaving her alone."

While she ran back upstairs I slowly got out of the car and holding onto the hood for support moved hand over hand to the passenger's side. With my wife and daughter in the car I was taking no chances.

Nina came down with Samantha and a car seat. After Samantha was secured she slipped behind the wheel.

"Jesus Max it stinks in here," she said, starting the car."

"My air freshener copped out on me."

She didn't laugh.

During the short ride we got our stories straight. I was an out of town relative who got mugged in San Rafael. I gave them the fake name on my stolen ID and Nina handled the financials under her real name.

The intern told me nothing was broken, patched up my bloody skull, gave me some downs and told me to expect to be uncomfortable for a week or two.

"Max what did you get yourself into?" Nina said on the drive home.

"Don't know, except it's big."

"Can you get out?"

"Can't say, all they got was a fake ID." Then a light went on inside my soggy brain. "Son of a bitch."

"What?"

"If the bastard or bastards were smart they would have hung around and followed me to the car. Checked my plates, maybe even tailed me."

"Maybe you're a little paranoid right now," she said hopefully.

I closed my eyes. "Maybe. But my ribs tell me otherwise."

When I got home I popped a couple of painkillers and washed them down with scotch. Then I rolled a joint and went out on the deck to smoke. It was dark and quiet outside. I wondered if someone was lurking behind a tree.

The air smelled clean and heavy. As the pills and scotch took effect the pain faded and I took a few deep breaths. Back inside I felt good enough to climb the stairs to our bedroom. The moment my euphoric head hit the pillow I fell into a dreamless sleep.

It was late when I awoke.

I lay there trying to get sorted out.

Nina appeared at the door. "Finally. Come down and I'll fix breakfast."

"Where's Samantha?"

"I took her to day care. How do you feel?"

Gingerly, I rolled to my feet. "Felt better when I went to bed."

Resisting the temptation to reach for the pain pills I took a long hot shower and finished with cold forcing blood into my injured cells. Whatever, I felt better than when my eyes first opened. I capped the routine with four Advil and followed the aroma of coffee and bacon downstairs

"So what did you decide?" Nina asked, sitting down while I devoured my hevous rancheros."

"About what?"

"Are you in or out of this?"

"I have to find out what they know about me."

"They...?"

"Look whoever clocked me was a mugger or some-body with a motive. Right now the only motive out there belongs to the ICE agent who tried to detain Selena."

She sighed. "Logical but it doesn't help me deal with this."

"I'm sorry. But these people are dangerous. They might have already murdered Selena's husband."

"What about my husband?"

I put my arm around her. "I have to make sure you and Samantha aren't involved. Suppose they followed me?"

"Max okay, I know it's a savage planet but our mar-riage has to live in it."

Then she kissed the large bump on the side of my skull. "I'm sorry Max. You know I trust you. Do what you have to do."

Before leaving I swept the car for tracking devices. The Green Ghost was clean which relieved my worst fear. But there were still a lot left.

There was also a sour scent in the car, a remnant of the previous nights festivities. I drove with the win-dows rolled down.

On the way to Petaluma I called Lowell. He told me to meet him at the bakery. I suspect he had a thing for the pastry.

Sure enough as soon as he got there he ordered a blueberry muffin. He patted his zero-fat belly.

"I have to stay out of this place."

I gingerly patted my belly.

"I've been on the kick-me diet."

His look of concern made me regret the remark. "Max I'm sorry I got you into this mess."

"Easy man. You've had my back too many times."

He nodded, but the look was still there.

"Who do you think did it?"

"Not sure. But this thing might be bigger than we thought."

I gave him what Berto told me about the charter flights.

"Jesus no wonder the CIA is up here," Lowell said.

"I thought we might visit the airport and see Mrs. Suarez off."

Lowell wolfed down his muffin. "Good idea. I'll drive."

Petaluma Municipal Airport was located in Sonoma County on Sky Ranch Drive. It boasted two runways, the Two-Niner Diner at the end of runway 290, and not much else. Storage facilities and aircraft hangers lined the runways and one or two planes could be seen in position for take-off. One was a Fed Ex transport slowly rolling onto the tarmac.

The other plane wasn't moving and there were a number of people standing around as if waiting to board. I recognized Julia first, then Selena, Kingman and Berto. Next to them was a black casket on a gurney.

Sidney met us as we approached. "We have a problem," he said, suppressing his anger. "Agent Zallen wants to search the plane and open the casket, or he won't give us clearance to the plane leave."

"Open the casket...he's fucking insane," I blurted, outraged by the cruelty.

"He ordered the air traffic controller to hold the plane until we comply."

"Did he have a subpoena?" Lowell said, his jaw knotted.

Kingman snorted. "Apparently ICE Agents are beyond the law at airports.

"Where is he now?"

"The controller is in that building next to the tower." Kingman said. "Then he looked at me. "Max, what the hell happened to you?"

"Tell you later," I said and followed Lowell to the controller's office.

His determined stride told me he was as angry as I was. More perhaps because the airport was his turf.

The controller was about forty, tall with receding blond hair. He wore aviator shades and one of those brown leather WWII flight jackets you see advertised in magazines. They have a map of China printed on the lining, should you get lost on your way to the Great Wall.

Camouflage cargo pants, black T and black boots completed the paramilitary ensemble. He was seated feet up on his desk, head bobbing to the beat of his head phones.

He didn't notice when we entered. Without preamble Lowell yanked the headphones off. Startled the guy nearly fell off his chair.

"Yo...What the hell's your problem man?"

"You're the problem," Lowell flashed his badge. "Why is that plane grounded?'

The controller straightened his jacket. Making an effort to regain his poise.

"Hey look I have authority..."

The Preacher stirred. I took a menacing step closer. One glimpse of my thousand-yard stare and the newly found poise dissolved.

"...Uh authority from Special Agent Zallen, with Immigration and Customs."

"Did he show you a warrant?"

"Uh, no but..."

"Did he show you a memo any paperwork at all?"

"No but..."

"Then the buck stops with you Mr...What's your name?"

"Uh Warren. Harold Warren." He took off his shades. a worried expression on his face. "What do you mean the buck stops with me?"

"Well Mr. Warren," Lowell said calmly, "you have a bereaved widow and two year old child stranded on the tarmac with a murdered man's casket on your authority, without any legal documentation. If that wasn't bad enough, the widow is accompanied by her attorney. When his lawsuit hits the media you're going to be on the hook for all charges. Not to mention your own legal expenses. And if that isn't enough I'm arresting you right now for obstructing criminal investigation, as well as aiding and abetting a suspect. Am I making myself clear?"

"Uh, yessir."

"Then get that plane loaded and in the air. Now."

"Yessir uh..."

"What the hell is it?"

"We've been instructed to cooperate fully with Immigrations and Customs."

"Well at this moment you're cooperating with Detective Captain Lowell of the Petaluma Police. If Agent Zallen objects tell him to see me. So what is it Warren the cuffs, or ready for take-off?"

Warren took off. He even helped load the casket.

As we watched the plane liftoff I turned to Lowell. "No wonder they made you Captain."

He didn't smile.

"I'm going to take Warren's statement."

My ribs were telling me to lie down and rather than take the Oxy I brought along for emergencies, I opted for the joint in my other pocket. In deference to airport rules I stepped to the side of the building and lit up.

Halfway down the J the painful tension in my chest eased. It tensed again when I spotted a blue Malibu coming in my direction. It came to an abrupt stop in front of me and Zallen stormed out of the car, leaving the door open.

"Who the fuck let that plane take off?" He blared. Then he paused and squinted at me. "What happened to you man?"

He was a bad actor.

How did I know? I saw my vomit crusted on the side of his shoe.

Then he made it worse. "Is that marijuana? I could bust you for that."

The Preacher stirred. Righteous anger drew his from a long nap.

="Medical." I said, and held out my hands. "But you can cuff me if you want."

Confusion wiped away his little smirk.

"Hey, I didn't..."

I snatched his polyester lapel and spun him hard against the wall.

"Now motherfucker, I want answers."

"Easy! Easy! You're..."

I should have known when his stricken expression morphed to triumph. A second later cold steel dug into my skull. It wasn't a shovel.

"Let him go," a voice said softly.

Never argue with a gun. I lifted my hands.

"Who the fuck are you and why are you assaulting a federal officer?"

"Your federal officer is a murder suspect and he assaulted me last night."

"Bullshit!" Zallen said, taking a step closer.

"You were busted in a stolen car – Is that bullshit?"

The gun backed off my head allowing me to turn.

The owner looked like Brad Pitt. If Brad was black. He was taller than me and his caramel features were battle hardened. A thin crooked scar ran from his eyebrow to his red blond hair.

"And who are you asshole?"

"It's Max asshole to you. DEA undercover. We've been watching Suarez since the bust in San Diego, "I said, sticking to my story.

"Then Suarez turns up dead and Zallen steals a car. What would you think?"

His orange-freckled pupils regarded me with contempt. "I think you're out of your depth asshole."

"Let me take a wild guess. You're Madison Goldsmith."

I braced as he cocked his arm but his surprised expression was worth the punch. He glanced at Zallen as if to ask 'Did you say something you dumb shit?'

"Problem here Max?"

Lowell stood there, seemingly relaxed. I knew he carried a .38 but it remained out of sight.

Goldsmith lifted his arm slightly, his Glock dangling from one finger.

"Special Agent," he said tersely, obviously upset. "Check my ID, captain."

Lowell lifted his eyebrows, seemingly impressed.

"You know who I am but I don't seem to recall meeting you," he said stepping closer. He carefully plucked the Glock from Goldsmith's finger. "Federal regulations about firearms in an airport."

Goldsmith shrugged. His expression was one of stoic resignation but his knotted jaw and clenched fists told me he was furious. Probably about being outed. Until now Lowell hadn't met Zallen's CIA partner.

"You're going to take me in? Really?"

"Maybe. Let's have the ID."

Zallen stood stock still, eyes darting from Goldsmith to Lowell as he took the wallet and examined its contents. He handed it back.

"Welcome to Petaluma Mr. Goldsmith. Can you tell me what you boys are doing here? Maybe I can be of help."

"Sorry classified."

"Can we go now?" Zallen put in.

"Captain Lowell do you happen to have an evidence bag with you?" It was a rhetorical question. I knew Bob always carried basic investigative tools.

"Yeah I do, why?"

"If you could scrape a little of that crud from Agent Zallen's right shoe and test it along with my DNA..."

Zallen's face flushed. "That dog shit are you crazy?"

"...then we could clear Agent Zallen as a suspect in last night's assault." I concluded, doing my best to keep the Preacher calm.

"This is ridiculous," Zallen blustered.

Lowell produced a plastic bag. "All we need is a small sample. Won't harm the shoe. Only take a second."

"Hold it Captain," Goldsmith drilled Lowell with a steely stare. "Unless you have a warrant any evidence is unacceptable in court."

Zallen regained his shaky composure. "Yeah right."

The plastic bag hung in mid-air before Lowell put it in his pocket. He gave me a regretful shrug.

"Good point counselor."

"What about him?" Zallen said, pointing at me. "The bastard assaulted me. In front of a witness. Right?"

Goldsmith tried to stay cool but I could see being a witness in open court wasn't his idea of something to do.

"Hey forget it, okay?" His sharp tone cut Zallen off. "I'm tired of this shit. Let's go."

Then he paused. "Lowell...you're the gay cop right?"

I wrestled to keep the Preacher in his cage as they turned to leave.

"Hey! Someone yelled. "Who the hell does this belong to?"

Warren the airport flight controller stomped into view, arms waving at the blue Malibu parked sideways, door still open.

"You're on my tarmac. There's a plane coming in right now. We could lose our fucking license. Get it out now!"

Zallen took a step but Lowell put a hand on his chest.

"You mean it's a federal offense to park there?"

"You're damn right. Now move it."

Lowell produced a pair of cuffs. "You better do the honors Goldsmith. Zallen here just committed a federal crime and I'm going to have to detain him."

They locked eyes. Frustrated, Goldsmith broke away and trotted to the car. He had an athletic stride. I made a note to step up my workouts.

"And since you are now under arrest, any evidence obtained is legal and admissible in a court of law," Lowell said, snapping the cuffs on Zallen's wrist. "Please hold still a moment."

He took out the evidence bag and knelt down. With a small knife he scraped the brown pasty crap from Zallen's shoe and placed in in the bag. He carefully sealed it, and stood.

"You're released under your own recognizance," he said, unlocking the cuffs. "I'll see you back at the station. Bring Goldsmith with you."

"Fuck you both," Zallen muttered, face nearing tomato red. I thought he might have a stroke. Instead he marched stiffly away to the Malibu which Goldsmith had parked near the control tower.

"That seemed to go well," I said.

Lowell didn't answer. He started to follow Zallen. I trailed behind.

As the Malibu pulled away Lowell went into the tower. He climbed the stairs to the control room. Warren sat in front of a bank of computers wearing a set of earphones. He held up a finger when he saw Lowell and returned to his screens.

A few minutes later a twin engine plane touched down on the runway and taxied to a stop.

Warren removed the headphones. "Okay, what do you want now?"

"Your statement. Everything that happened here, starting with Zallen ordering you to detain the flight."

While Warren laboriously wrote out his statement under Lowell's stern direction I watched five passengers debark from the plane onto the tarmac. Three women and two men. One of the men carried a satchel, the other man had two of the women by the arm. It looked as shady as a stickup.

"Did you see that?" I asked

Lowell studied the statement Warren had signed. "See what?"

"Five people just got off that plane."

"So?"

I looked back at the controller who was back at his console. "Hey Warren, where did that plane depart from?"

He kept his eyes on the screen. "Mexico."

"Is that the deportation charter?"

After a pause he gave me a narrow eyed glance, wondering what I might know. That glance told me plenty.

"Yes. We call it the *Iceman Cometh*, get it?"

I wanted to stuff the name down his throat. Instead I asked, "What time does it leave?"

He ducked his head behind the screen. "Eleven forty five every night."

I checked the landing time, eleven forty five.

I looked at Lowell.

"We done here?"

Lowell was steaming all the way to the car. "Five people got off that plane from Mexico," he said, as if talking to himself.

"Yes. One of them had luggage. A satchel."

And they walked off, no customs, no ID check."

"No need. They get undiplomatic immunity from ICE, who runs the charter."

Lowell stopped. For a moment the pent up outrage he'd nursed since Goldsmith' gay remark, burst to the surface. His chiseled features darkened, shifting from square-jawed athlete to someone you don't want to fuck with. Made me glad I was on his side.

"Son of a bitch!" Was all he said, but his voice rumbled with primal ferocity. Like a lion who'd picked up a rival scent.

He took a deep breath and started toward the plane.

I reached out to stop him.

"Leave it for now Bob. Let's get that statement filed first."

One thing about Lowell, he kept his head under pressure.

"You're right. The statement gives me probable cause."

"Do me a favor."

"Sure Max, what?"

"Let's drop the sample at the DNA clinic first."

I had my own stash of pent up outrage.

The DNA testing center was less a clinic than a mail drop. It mainly catered to couples with babies who needed to determine parenthood for the purposes of child support, and convicted criminals on probation or parole who had to register their DNA with the national data base.

How it works, you filled out a form, someone in a white lab coat takes a swab of saliva with a tongue compressor, puts it a pre marked envelope with your own code. He does the same with the baby. The guy in the white coat then mails both envelopes to the actual testing lab somewhere in the Midwest.

A week later they send you the results by Email. If they match, congratulations you're a father.

In my case it meant matching my saliva to what was likely dog shit.

"Investigating the deportation charters could have gotten Suarez killed," I said as we waited our turn. "Gives Zallen a serious motive."

Lowell nodded, but I could tell he was still fuming. He stayed that way all the way to the station.

While waiting for Bob to file the report I saw Zallen and Goldsmith huddled in the parking lot. Zallen turned and headed back inside. Goldsmith started off on foot. On impulse I decided to follow.

Zallen was coming in as I left.

"Leaving already?" He said hopefully.

I shrugged him off. "No such luck."

But his sly smile worried me. He knew something I didn't.

*"I don't understand people but they interest me."*
— Lt. Joe Kenda, Homicide Detective

# Chapter 3

Lowell made sure he did everything by the book before filing his report. Long ago he'd learned that half of police work was in the bureaucratic details.

There was no book for the other half.

Routine drunk driving arrests that turned into shootouts or dangerous chases were far from rare. And as a homicide detective he'd seen more than his share of senseless tragedies. As for plain human cruelty, so far as he was concerned, it came with the planet. Lowell couldn't explain it or even try to, he was no street philosopher like Max. Just a cop.

And a damned good one, he reflected, still not over the anger the CIA agent stoked with his deliberate remark. Lowell had always kept the fact he was gay on the down low. Few people in the department – if any – knew. Not that he stayed in the closet. He just didn't make a big deal about it.

His partner Steve lived in San Francisco where being gay was part of the culture. To keep his private life private, Lowell spent most of his free time in the city.

"Captain Lowell?"

Rookie officer Tim Ferris stood at the door, a pained expression on his usually cheerful face

"I was just about to call you. What's up?""

"Chief wants to see you ASAP."

"That soon?"

Ferris didn't find it funny. "That's what he said."

Lowell left his chair and handed his report to Ferris.

"File this ASAP. Got it?"

"Got it, sir."

No doubt this had to do with Zallen. The man was a craven snitch, always whining to Bannon. And of course Brannon accommodated him, awed by the power of the CIA.

Judging from Goldsmith, Lowell thought, the CIA is heavy with assholes.

+     +     +

Walter Bannon, head of the Petaluma PD, had plans. There was an election coming up next year and he intended to run for state assembly. After that, perhaps even congress.

Congressman Walter Winston Bannon. He liked how it sounded.

However Captain Lowell was proving to be a significant obstacle. Bannon himself agreed with the new guidelines on immigration. He had no problem shipping illegals out as soon as they were detained. It was the law. A law he favored.

Zallen and Goldsmith had assured him that they were on the verge of breaking an international cartel. It could be his ticket. With a major case under his belt he was sure to be nominated as a law and order candidate. Which was very popular here in this part of the state. Not like San Francisco where they tolerated degenerates and flaunted the president's executive order by protecting illegal immigrants.

In fact he was due to meet the District Attorney for dinner that night. Jim Kearny was a tough prosecutor who had fired one of his law clerks when he discovered the clerk was gay.

Of course he had found another reason for dismissal but Walter knew Jim didn't tolerate homos or blacks in his department. And old Kearney had the family connections to back his new political career all the way to DC.

Granted, Captain Lowell had an outstanding record, including a citation from the FBI for breaking up a big-time smuggling operation. He suffered a leg wound in the process and when he recovered was promoted to Captain. Actually his rapid rise had made Bannon uncomfortable. The news that Lowell was gay eased his concerns.

Bannon opened his desk drawer and pulled out the pocket mirror lying next to a bottle of Dewar's scotch. He carefully examined his reflection, taking notes along the way as if checking his weapons inventory.

Good teeth but his blue eyes could use a little lift. Strong chin, a bit jowly, need to lay off desserts, start putting in time at the gym. Best feature, a full head of silver hair, just like the Vice President. All in all an impressive candidate.

There was a knock at the door and it opened. Bannon dropped the mirror in the open drawer. He saw the glass crack as he shut the drawer. The accident sparked a flash of annoyance.

Lowell entered, further fueling Bannon's anger.

"You wanted to see me, sir?"

"Yes. Sit down."

His tone was far from friendly.

As Lowell sat, he braced himself.

He knew it was about the incident at the airport, but Walter had never been so obviously hostile.

"Something wrong Chief?"

"Wrong is an understatement. You and your DEA pal interfered with a federal operation today."

"They had no warrant and no probable cause."

"The fucking CIA doesn't need probable cause. Lowell, this is way over your head. I'm recommending a thirty day suspension until you cool off."

At first it didn't quite register.

"Might I remind the chief that Paul Zallen is a prime suspect in the Suarez killing?" Lowell said.

"There's absolutely no evidence of that."

"And there won't be if you won't let me do my god-damned job."

"Like I said, you are way over your head on this. I'll need your badge and your gun."

The reality sunk in and as Lowell removed the Beretta from his shoulder holster his anger turned to indignation.

"I'm taking this to the review board."

"Your kind always does."

"What the hell does that mean?"

Bannon backed off. If the review board thought this was about Lowell's sexual orientation things might get messy. Especially with the liberal media.

"Look Bob, because of your record I'll give you a choice. You have vacation time coming right?'

"Thirty days," Lowell said, not swayed by Bannon's conciliatory tone, "you saying I should take it?"

"Your choice."

Lowell shrugged. "Fine, I'll put in the paperwork."

"I knew you'd understand. And uh Bob..."

"Yes?"

"I'll still need your badge and your gun."

Lowell wanted to lean over Bannon's desk and shove the gun in his nose but he laid it carefully on the Chief's desk and put his badge alongside it.

Bannon gave him a curt smile. "There, now you're officially on vacation."

Lowell stormed back to his office. The Petaluma Homicide Unit consisted of three people: himself, Detective Lieutenant Jake Boone, and their administrative assistant Tim Ferris.

Currently Boone was working on a two-month old gang drive-by that left one boy dead, another wounded. Naturally the survivor knew nothing. Lowell had to move off the case when he caught the Suarez killing.

He made a copy of the murder book, the thin investigative file he'd compiled. Then he went to Boone's small office, actually not much larger than a storage room, and closed the door behind him.

Boone looked up from his computer.

"Whatever's up, please make it fast, it gets stuffy in here."

"Then you best open the window Jake."

Boone was lantern-jawed and wide-bodied as befitting a former all-state high school linebacker. Technically he made second team but he was no less proud and mentioned it often. He lifted himself out of his chair with difficulty and moved to the small window. He attributed his stiff gait to a back injury sustained wrestling down a suspect who tried to flee arrest.

Lowell suspected it was an old football injury but didn't question it. Boone was a good, solid homicide investigator and if his stiff back qualified him for disability payments so be it.

Despite the open window both men were perspiring when Lowell finished telling Boone what happened.

Boone listened silently, head down, occasionally nodding. Then he looked up his expression both sympathetic and resigned.

"That stinks Bob."

"No shit. At least I haven't been suspended."

"Walter's letting that honcho from ICE jerk him around." Boone snorted derisively. "Thinks he'll break a big case and be on FOX news with a flag stuck in his ass."

As it happened, Boone's wife was Muslim. Rezan was an Iranian born MD who completed her medical residency at the UC Berkeley Surgical Center.

He leaned closer to Lowell. "Rumor is he's gonna run for office."

"Bannon? He's an empty suit."

"What I hear. Okay so, tell me what you need. I'll cover until you get your badge back."

"Keep me in the loop. Lay off the Suarez killing for now. Let Zallen think the heat's off. If he makes a hinky move call me. Especially if he tries to get a look at the murder book."

"But the murder book's already on our computer right?"

"Not all of it."

Boone grinned showing square, white teeth.

"Smart. What if he gets into your computer?"

"I've got hard copies. Which reminds me, I need a favor right now."

"Name it."

"Bannon will probably want to make sure I'm not taking anything with me when I leave."

"Most likely, yeah."

Lowell handed him the manila envelope containing the Suarez file. "I'd like you take this over to the bakery. I'll meet you there in about fifteen minutes."

"Enough time to gain another few pounds," Boone said, taking the envelope. "Oh, one thing Bob."

"Yeah?"

"What the hell is hinky?"

Lowell made a big show of clearing his office. As he left he was met at the door by the desk sergeant. Marty was a veteran close to retirement. Since he'd been assigned to desk duty he'd become testy.

Now he inspected Lowell's briefcase carefully and seemed disappointed when he found only a blank yellow legal pad, a few ballpoint pens and two chocolate protein bars. He even riffled through the papers in the legal pad to make sure they were blank.

Boone was waiting at the bakery, a take-out coffee and pastry in from of him. The envelope was beside him. Lowell ordered a coffee, resisting the apple turnover. The two men talked about sports and exchanged office gossip. When Boone finished his coffee he left the bakery, leaving the envelope behind.

A few minutes after his departure Lowell called Max.

# Chapter 4

Against his wife's wishes George Medina went to the local 7-11 for milk, cereal, bread, donuts and cigarettes. The cigarettes were for him, the groceries for his wife and two children.

He drove the short distance carefully, aware of Immigration's increased presence in the area. Although he had lived and worked in the area for seventeen years, paid his taxes, had a driver's license and registration he was still at risk without a green card, visa, or proof of citizenship. None of which he had. So far he'd gotten by on his driver's license and credit card.

George used his card to pay for the groceries.

"Be careful driving at night," Alberta, the cashier said in a low tone, even though the store was empty. "They're stopping everybody out there."

"I don't live far. And I drive safe. But thanks."

As he picked up his packages he looked up. "Where were they when you got robbed last month?"

Alberta nodded vigorously. "I heard that."

Outside he paused to light a cigarette. As he smoked he reflected on Alberta's warning. After overstaying his migrant visa George had gone to work for a landscaper. He had a feel for the soil and growing things, and in time had been able to start his own business and build a nice list of clients. He raised a family, his kid were Americans, and he never had any trouble. But lately it was like an old TV movie he saw about WWII Nazis. Everybody getting stopped and forced to show ID. His kids had told him their schoolmates had been pulled off the street and taken away.

When he was finished he started his car, turned on the lights, fastened his seat belt and slowly pulled out of the parking lot. Before turning onto the street he turned on his directional, checking both sides of the empty street.

George kept the radio off as he drove, his complete attention on the road. He stopped at the intersection, looked both ways, and turned right. Before he reached the next Stop sign he saw the flashing red and blue lights in his rear view mirror. Immediately he pulled over.

Nothing to worry about, he told himself. License and registration were in order. He rolled down his window as the patrolman approached.

The patrolman beamed his flashlight around the interior of George's Toyota.

"Good evening sir. May I see your license and registration?"

They're so polite before the drop the hammer, George thought handing over his ID. While he waited he kept both hands on the wheel.

He wanted to call Carlita, his wife, but he knew that often police 'mistook' a phone for a gun. Many times they shot first and checked later.

The patrolman appeared at the widow.

"Do you know why I stopped you?"

"No officer."

"You left rear tail light is out."

George kicked himself mentally for neglecting it.

The officer handed George a ticket. "Get it fixed and bring proof to your local police station. They'll sign off on it."

Gratefully George took the ticket along with his ID.

"Excuse me, sir."

George squinted. A man stood beside the officer. He wore a dark suit.

"Immigration," he said, showing a badge. "I need to see your driver's license."

George's heart sank. When the ICE agent checked his ID in the Immigration computer he'd see George Medina had no green card or visa. His heart pumped faster and his mind raced ahead. He'd need to get a lawyer. More money. He'd call Carlita and tell her to get someone. He hoped they wouldn't hold him overnight. His best client Mrs. Holbrook, insisted that he have her gardens ready for her big party. Maybe his son Alex could finish the job.

"Okay George, step out of the car."

Numbly George complied, resigned to the inevitable. He was trapped in the system and it would take money and time to come out the other end. He knew the routine, having heard from others over the years.

Twenty one years, he thought, that's how long he had been in California. There must be some way to find amnesty.

"Can I call me wife?" he asked when the agent took his phone.

"Not now," the agent said as he took George's wallet and keys and put them in an envelope. George saw the agent write his name on the envelope.

The agent walked him back to a waiting car. A black man sat in front. The agent handed him the phone before cuffing George and putting him in the back seat.

Carlita was probably worried by now, George thought. He'd call her from the station.

He never got the chance.

First, they took him to a motel where one of the rooms had been converted to an office. They sat him down and the black agent questioned him. He asked George what he knew about the Cartels, and about drug trafficking in the area.

"I'm a gardener mister," George said warily. "I have a landscape business. That's all I do. You can see my taxes. I think those people make more money than me."

After a few more questions by the black agent the white one took over.

"How many people work for you?"

"Nobody. Sometimes my son helps out."

"You expect us to believe that?"

George shrugged. "It's true. I can't afford any steady help. Sometimes I get a guy for the day, off the street corner. You know the one on the boulevard by the supermarket."

The man sneered. Up close his skin was pink. "We know the one and they're all illegals, like you."

"Been here twenty years mister and..."

The agent leaned closer. George smelled bad breath.

"Okay, okay. You let us know where we can find some real illegals and we can help you," he said, voice low and oily.

A wave of disgust stiffened George's resentment. They treat me like an animal and expect me to sell my soul, he raged.

"I don't know about any real illegals mister," he said. "I got to go to the bathroom."

They put him in the bedroom, which had a bathroom. Almost an hour later he overheard them talking in the other room.

"That's nine," the white man said. "Let's take him over there."

George was relieved. At the station he could make a phone call.

"We need three more."

"I've got someone on it. Let's go. I need something to eat."

So did George.

But they didn't take him to the police station. Instead they drove to the airport and locked him in a room with eight other men. As they talked he learned that all of them had been picked up in similar fashion: traffic stop, immigration officer, visa check, arrest. None of them had been allowed to make a call. At least four had been in California over ten years. Only one, a kid called Valentine had been arrested before.

The room had a picnic table and was lit by three metal ceiling lamps. There was a small toilet at the end of the room. It was probably a workshop of some sort before they turned it into a jail, George speculated.

Outside the locked door was a single uniformed policeman. George assumed this was some kind of special jail. He wondered if he'd be there until morning. It was already after ten.

"Amigo."

George looked up.

Valentine smiled. He looked to be about twenty-two, with the usual fade haircut and tats. Would be gang banger.

"You got a smoke?"

George realized he still had the pack he had gone out for earlier.

Fucking cigarettes.

"Take them all," he said, tossing the pack, "I just stopped smoking."

# Chapter 5

I stared at Lowell, drink an inch away from my lips.
"They pulled you off a homicide investigation?"

"Take the suspension or take a vacation. Not much of a choice. He made it seem like a favor."

"Bullshit. The bastard wanted to avoid an official hearing on your suspension."

Lowell gave me a mysterious grin. "I do need a vacation."

"Seriously?"

"So I can stay on the case without Zallen tracking every move I make. With pay."

We slapped palms.

As I sipped my drink I remembered something. "Who was the arresting officer when Zallen stole that car?"

"Good question. That would be Sergeant Berry. He's on night patrol."

"Alone?"

"Petaluma can't afford two-man patrols except at traffic checks. Lately ICE has been recruiting cops to help them pick up illegals. It's against local and state law but Bannon sanctioned it."

I drained my scotch and was about to signal for another when Lowell said,

"But Agent Paul Zallen wasn't at any traffic stop the night Suarez was murdered. He was busy stealing a car."

"Fucking Incredible. Another round?"

"I've got some work tonight."

"Work?"

"I'm going to take a pass at the airport. Check out the night flight."

"In that case I'll have a coffee."

"Better eat something, the flight lands at eleven forty-five."

We were in Graziano's, where I had my ill-fated dinner the night before. Advil and weed helped deal with the head bruise but the stiffness in my torso had settled in for a long visit. Rather than risk hurling another fine Italian meal I ordered the All-American special, a burger and coffee.

"Maybe we can talk to Sergeant Berry while we wait," I suggested. It was about nine pm and the airport was a short drive.

Lowell looked up from his ravioli. "You read my mind. I call him after we eat."

I was on my third coffee when he called. Lowell has to polish off his pasta with dessert.

"He can meet us after his shift."

"Good. What do we do until then?"

"There's a diner at the airport that serves a great apple pie."

"Do you ever stop eating?"

"Sure, when I sleep."

The Two-Niner Diner was located in a low building at the end runway 290. However the diner is named after the 29.92 reading on the altimeter considered an ideal flying condition. The interior is a tribute to aviation with photos of airplanes papering the walls and models of WWI aircraft dangling from the ceiling.

A bi-winged Sopwith Camel was my personal favorite.

Counting us there were only five people in the place: a short-order cook, a counter girl, and the air traffic controller Harold Warren who didn't look happy when we came in.

Warren sat at the counter. Without consulting each other Lowell and I sat on either side of him. That really made him anxious.

"Good evening Mr. Warren," Lowell said, "taking a dinner break?"

"Uh yeah," Warren said, trying to smile and failing. "Something like that."

"What's good here?" I said, scanning the menu which was peppered with aviation terms, such as the whirlybird breakfast burrito.

"Good burgers."

"Just had one. How about the apple pie?"

"Wouldn't know." He kept eyeing the kitchen area as if in a hurry.

Bracketing him had been a good move. I could tell he felt squeezed.

"Good evening boys, what will it be?"

The waitress was on the wrong side of fifty, hefty but not fat wearing a tight hair bun and a no-nonsense expression.

"Apple pie," Lowell said.

"Coffee." I turned to Warren. "How about you?"

"Oh his order will take a few minutes." The waitress said. "That's a lot of burgers."

Warren kept his face blank but his shoulders hunched lower.

"Maybe he has a big appetite," I said.

"If he can eat a dozen burgers God bless him."

Lowell and I looked at each other. Warren continued to stare straight ahead.

Our order came right away. Lowell attacked his pie pausing only to tell us it was really good. The coffee wasn't bad.

We had finished both when the cook came from behind the divider carrying two large bags.

"Here you go twelve cheese burgers. Ketchup, mustard's in there. Okay Greta, I'll be shuttin' it down. Shouldn't be open this late anyhow."

"Why are you open late tonight?" I said, sliding a twenty across the marble counter."

"Usually, we close about four. But there's been a lot of traffic lately and the airport asked us to stay open for a few weeks," Greta said ringing up Warren.

"Let us help you with that," I said, reaching for one of the burger bags.

Warren snatched it away. "No worries I'm fine."

He walked out quickly and we were right behind him.

Once outside he whirled to face Lowell.

"You ain't got the authority to hassle me like this." His chin was set but his lip trembled a bit.

Lowell gave him his aw shucks smile. "Hey Mr. Warren I'm not here to hassle you. This is a municipal airport and I'm a municipal cop. That simple."

Warren started walking. "Well I got a lot of heat for letting that plane take off."

Lowell stayed in step, I trailed close behind.

"Believe me if you didn't you would be in a shitload of trouble right now. You'd be looking at a million dollar lawsuit. You don't think the airport would pay your legal fees do you?"

Warren paused "What do you mean?"

"I mean they'd say you acted without their authority. Period. Anyway you got off easy. The ICE people don't fill out your fitness reports right?"

"Right. All the bastards do is treat me like their fucking butt boy."

Lowell had hit a nerve. By the time we got to his destination he and Lowell were commiserating about ICE's arrogance.

"They practically took over the department," Lowell confided.

"Yeah, well they got one of your guys on duty tonight. Two of these burgers are for him."

"The rest are for you?"

"One is. The rest are for the people on the charter flight."

"Why didn't they eat at the diner?"

"They're deportees. ICE has them locked up in Hanger Seven."

I could feel the Preacher yawn awake and scratch at the anger Chakra at the base of my spine.

"Oh yeah of course," Lowell said casually, as if he knew.

I could see Lowell's low key technique was getting results so I put the Preacher back in his crib and hung back.

When we reached Hanger Seven I recognized the uniformed police officer who stood outside the door. It was Lowell's young assistant.

"Evening Tim. We brought you dinner."

Hunger overcame Tim's confusion and he eagerly grabbed his cheeseburgers.

"Thanks Captain. Hey, I heard you took vacation."

"Not yet. What are you doing here? I thought you were working with Boone."

Tim Ferris nodded. "I am. Chief Bannon authorized this night detail. And I could use the overtime."

"Shit," Warren said, "unlock the door and open it slow. They come at you like animals."

"Here I'll help," I said, taking one of the bags. This time he let me have it.

I saw what he meant. Except it wasn't animals who gathered at the open door but desperate humanity: hungry, lost, confused and totally fucked. Herded into an empty room with only a toilet to separate it from a cattle car.

The detainees formed a ragged line and as I handed out the burgers I noticed one man trying to get my attention. Not with words but with his eyes which were wide and pleading.

Warren was passing out food as quickly as possible his aversion to the flock obvious in his body language. He flinched whenever one of the poor bastards got too close.

I instead took my time inserting a word of Spanish here and there.

"I gotta get back to the flight deck. They'll be coming back with the rest anytime."

I gave him a military salute which seemed to please him. When he was out of range I approached the wide-eyed man.

"Please mister one phone call please. My wife doesn't know..."

He was short and broad, with a sun-creased face and hard, leathery hands which suggested he was either a farmer of some kind or a construction worker.

I glanced back. Officer Ferris was talking to Lowell.

I passed him my phone. What the hell it was a burner.

"Rapido." I said.

The man's face came alive.

As he punched in the numbers and murmured his wife's name I had an idea.

I checked the door again. Warren had gone and Ferris and Lowell were still deep in conversation.

+    +    +

"You saw him?" Lowell said, "You're sure."

Ferris nodded vigorously, his mouth full of cheeseburger.

"Most definitely," he said when he swallowed. "Zallen was at your desk looking at your computer."

Zallen hurried out of the hanger. Lowell saw Max still inside talking.

"Son of a bitch. Where was Boone?"

"Out of the office."

"Make sure you let him know."

"Yessir." The young officer's eyes flicked to the still open door.

Realizing Max was up to something Lowell tried to distract Ferris.

"And whatever you do don't tell Zallen I was here." He leaned closer. "Remember he's a suspect in my homicide case."

"Sure, right sir." His second burger half-finished Ferris moved to check the door.

Just then Max appeared. "Those boys were hungry," he said, his tone steely, "What about water?"

"Supposed to be coming with the next batch. They need seven more to fill the plane."

Lowell saw the expression on Max's face.

"Hey we better go now Tim. See you when I get back."

Before Max could add anything Lowell herded him off to the car.

"No sense waiting for Zallen to see us here." He muttered.

"Think you can trust the kid?"

"He's green but he's solid. I don't think he likes Zallen any more than you do."

Once in the car he told Max what Ferris had seen.

"The bastard was trying to get into my computer. Maybe he succeeded."

Max snorted. "Zallen couldn't open an envelope. When we get to my ride I'll Take care of it."

Then he leaned back in his seat, held up his phone, and gave Lowell a shit eating grin.

"This will really piss Zallen off."

# Chapter 6

Back at the Green Ghost I locked Lowell's computer against any unfriendly intrusion.

"That will prevent Zallen from spying while you're gone," I said, as my own computers slid back under the dashboard.

"What did you get on your phone – pictures?"

"That too."

"And..."

"The names and numbers of all the poor bastards in there. Wasn't enough time for all of them to make a call."

"Now what?" Lowell said with a touch of admiration. I could tell he was enjoying this.

My fingers were already punching in numbers. "Now we call Sidney Kingman and ..."

"Who is this?" Kingman said taking the call.

"It's Max. Is this a secure line?"

"Yes, why?"

As I texted him the list of names and numbers, along with a few grainy photos, I told him how we acquired them. I also mentioned getting  mugged after our dinner.

"It was an inside job," I said, "maybe you need a bodyguard."

"The old mafia Don Frank Costello never had bodyguards. He claimed they're the first people your enemy bribes. Et tu Brute."

He was flamboyant even over the phone.

"What will you do with the list?" I said.

"Distribute it to our legal team. We also have lawyers in Mexico. Do you know where the charter is headed?"

I turned to Lowell. "Where is that plane supposed to land?"

"I'll find out."

He called Harold Warren who spent a few minutes complaining about the flight delay. "If they ever take the fuck off, they land in the airport outside Tijuana."

"Thank Max," Sidney said when he heard, "I'll have a couple of lawyers there to meet them. And I'll call these numbers in the morning and inform the families."

"In the morning?" Nina said indignantly when I told her. "Fuck that. Give me the phone."

After hearing the events of the evening my lovely Latina bride became fired up. In a way her passion took the pressure off my lack of family duties over the past week.

The next day I biked to the ferry and went into town to open up my small shop. City traffic had become worse since the mass gentrification of San Francisco and I was constantly in danger of being swiped by some demented driver. Still it beat trying to park.

After attending to the monthly bills, I took my phone apart and methodically smashed the chip and other components to powder. Then I pulled a fresh one from the large box on my shelf and charged it. Among other things my shop sold pre-paid phones.

I called Nina and Lowell with my new number. Then I locked up and strolled to North Beach. Along the way I deposited the remnants of my old phone in an outdoor trash bin. I'm a devout paranoid.

Mario's Bohemian Cigar Store is an ideal hangout. Tasty food, strong coffee and a hip location. Beer and wine if you're so inclined.

I took an outdoor table facing Washington Square Park and took a deep breath. On a sunny day the park blooms with activity: Dogs shagging Frizbees, kids playing tag, slackers avoiding work, pretty babes working on their tans, and lovers sharing dreams. Which made me think of Nina.

It was still early so I decided to stop off at my town house, namely the room I share in a North Beach flat with two other eccentrics.

The flat belongs to Eli Sarfetti, a bohemian physicist with royal ambitions. Eli is often invited to various scientific conferences so he's away much of the time. When he's home he spends much of his time shooting out insulting emails to his colleagues who insult him back. Some sort of high IQ pissing contest.

Since the apartment was empty so I assumed Eli was out of town. I gave his four computers a run through to make sure they were working properly then retired to my room and turned on CNN. The talking heads were parsing Trump's latest tweets which are Shakespearean, full of sound and fury, signifying nothing.

In the midst of the babble I dozed off. Later that afternoon I woke up to the sounds of anguish coming from Eli's office.

Eli had converted his spacious living room to a commend center, with Macs, PCs, and iPads everywhere amid messy stacks of paper, books and correspondence.

Standing in the center of this messy universe was Eli, his pale shin mottled red as he kept shouting.

"Goddamn Stanley. He should be shot!"

I was slightly surprised by the outburst as Eli is usually soft spoken.

"What's up?"

Goddamn Stanley. He should be shot."

"So I hear. Who is Stanley and what did he do to deserve capitol punishment?"

"Stanley Kubrowski, he's a well know astrophysicist at Stanford. He deliberately sent me a computer virus."

"Why would he do that?"

Eli tugged at his white beard. "I called him a peabrained fraud. But he called me a sophomoric narcissist first."

I had a tendency to agree with Stanley but Eli was my client and landlord.

"Macs don't seen affected," I said after a brief inspection. "It's located in your PC."

Eli fretted over me as I worked, cursing under his breath.

It wasn't much of a virus. More of a diversion, like a stink bomb. The virus sent all commands to a defunct site. It took all of twenty minutes to reconvert, and another ten to erect a defense.

"That's it Eli, all better."

As I rose Eli was almost in my lap eager to get at the keyboard.

"Do not email Stanley," I said sternly. "Repeat do not..."

"Okay, okay Stanley... but why?"

"When you don't respond Stanley will think you didn't get his little virus and he'll resend it."

"If he does..."

"If he does I've programmed your computer to send it back, like a tennis ball that lands in Stanley's court."

Eli gave me a wicked grin. "Brilliant Max. You should get an award."

He was still cackling with glee as I left.

Having earned my rent I hiked back to my shop, picked up the bike and cycled through a gauntlet of angry drivers to the Ferry building. The boat to Corte Madera cast off in fifteen minutes and along the way I grabbed a coffee and bagel for the voyage.

I was home in time for dinner and later I read Samantha a bedtime story. She loved *Where The Wild Things Are* and demanded to see every illustration.

She fell asleep before the book was finished.

Later Nina and I snuggled in front of the TV lazily watching the Warriors demolish the Cleveland Cavaliers in a pre-season NBA game. When Steph Curry juked LeBron, left him flatfooted, and drove in for the score, we came to and cheered.

I went to sleep holding Nina and dreaming of my long ago basketball days.

It was our last peaceful night together.

Shortly before noon Lowell called.

"You won't believe this."

"Convince me."

"Zallen killed someone last night. In front of witnesses."

# Chapter 7

Lowell was right. I couldn't believe it.

Apparently there was a neighborhood ICE sweep with Zallen leading the charge. Except he blundered into the wrong house. One belonging to Carlos Canseco, a bona-fide citizen with two sons and a wife. In the ensuing confusion Carlos Canseco was shot.

"While Boone's investigating, Paul Zallen is free."

That was the part I couldn't believe.

"Let me get this straight. This sonofabitch is on the hook for two homicides and he keeps his gun and his badge. But you they tell to take a vacation."

Lowell nodded sadly and cut into his pancakes,

"What is Boone investigating? There were plenty of witnesses."

"Zallen claims he was in fear of his life."

Fear of his life. The new Fifth Amendment. If you fear for your life try selling insurance – don't swear to protect and serve.

"He did have a fucking gun," I reminded, trying to keep the Preacher sedated.

Lowell shrugged. "Reason has nothing to do with it."

We were sitting in a breakfast all day joint and I was working on my third coffee while I watched Lowell polish off a full stack including bacon.

He carefully placed his fork on the table. "You ready to go?"

"Sure, where?"

"We never had a talk with Sergeant Berry. The officer who arrested Zallen in the stolen car.

+     +     +

"Shit, I swear the dude was drunk."

Sergeant Miles Berry shook his bald head. He was a hefty African American with greying hair and a beer belly.

"He refused to take breathalyzer, and when we got to the station the whole thing disappeared. Like I didn't arrest anybody. No blood test, no nothin'."

"Try no homicide," Lowell said.

"Fucking Bannon. This shithead walks and he shoots somebody else. Guaranteed he was drunk."

"I'll ask Boone if they took a drug test."

"What makes you think he was drunk?" I said.

Berry looked me up and down.

"Bob tells me you're in law enforcement." Meaning the only reason he tolerated my presence was on Bob's say so.

"DEA."

"Well after twenty two years you can spot a DUI even if their driving five miles an hour. Like this asshole Zallen was. He said he was looking for parking when I stopped him. But he was sweatin' through his shirt and his breath stank."

That jibed with my own experience with Zallen.

"Like I said he refused a test. I ran the plates and sure enough the car was hot. That's when he claimed he was CIA. Demands I call Chief Bannon. Like he's a personal friend.'"

"Did you?"

"I booked him first. Made damn sure to file a report on the stolen car. Then I called the Chief. Near three

A.M. and Bannon takes the damn call. Tells me to put the perp in his office until he gets there."

I looked at Lowell. "No wonder you're on vacation."

Berry finished his drink. "What the fuck?"

My sentiments exactly. We were in a local bar called the Buckhorn with a pool table in back and deer heads on the wall. I signaled for another round.

"Shit you know how many times I've been passed over?" Berry said.

Lowell shrugged. "At least twice. I wrote the recommendations."

"That's right. And both times I had higher scores on the damn test."

Our drinks came and I lifted my glass. "To protect, serve and get fucked."

For the first time Berry regarded me with something other than suspicion.

"Got that right," he said, downing half his beer. "But the one really getting' fucked is that kid Ferris."

Lowell perked up. "Fucked how?"

"You didn't hear? Ferris was on that raid when Bannon's butt boy shot that poor bastard by mistake."

"Yeah, and?"

"So initially he told Boone the Vic was unarmed. Then later he tried to change his statement but Boone knew it was bullshit. Now they're saying the kid maybe over-reacted and put him on medical leave. By the time they're done they'll be sayin' he's the damn shooter."

I saw Lowell's knotted jaw and knew he was angry. Normally an easy going dude, it takes a lot to piss him off. But when he's finally there he's dangerous.

As for me I wrestled to keep the Preacher down. I needed a clear head. Immediately I called Kingman and told him what happened.

"Where are you?" he said.

"A joint called the Buckhorn."

"I know it. I'll be there in an hour."

He arrived forty minutes later and ordered a martini.

I could see Berry was skeptical of this long haired dude dressed like Johnny Cash in a black western shirt, black jeans and bolo tie. Five minutes into the conversation however Berry was a fan.

"We already have people on the ground at the Mexican airport and a team here in Petaluma working your homicide case." He tilted his glass toward Lowell. "But they say you're on vacation."

Lowell nodded grimly. "Lieutenant Boone's got my back."

"We also have a second team ready to investigate the Canseco shooting."

"They won't get much from Chief Bannon but Boone is a good cop."

"Problem is the Sonoma DA. Kearny doesn't like migrants, marijuana or meddlesome lawyers. And your Chief plays golf with Kearny."

"FBI?" I ventured.

Kingman shook his head and signaled for another round.

"Right now civil rights are low on their priorities. Our man in Sacramento is going to the Governor's office. We want the state Attorney General on this killing."

"That's the way to go," Berry said. "You people got your shit together."

I wondered if this wasn't my cue to ease back into anonymity. There would be a lot of eyes on Petaluma and sooner or later they'd turn my way. There was already one CIA agent with a hard on for me.

To that end I made sure Lowell and Kingman had each other's contact info so I would no longer be middle man.

+    +    +

When I returned home Nina went to tuck Samantha in for the night and didn't return. When I peeked into Samantha's room they were both asleep, my daughter safely curled in Nina's arms.

I left them there and poured a scotch to help me sleep.

It didn't work. Two drinks later I was still staring blankly at some TV wildlife show, brain sifting through the lethal events of the past few days. Being focused on the recent death of Carlos Canseco, I had forgotten to ask Kingman about Mrs. Suarez. In his zeal to deport illegal migrant workers Zallen was leaving a trail of widows.

Finally I dozed off. It seemed like only ten minutes later when the phone woke me. Actually it was six hours. Still a bit numb from the booze I became alert when I heard Lowell's voice.

"Max, it's Sergeant Berry."

"Something happen?"

"He's dead," Lowell said. "They say he shot himself."

+    +    +

It was nearly dawn when I arrived at the address Lowell gave me. I didn't want to get out of the car. In the short time I spent with Miles Berry I had come to like and respect him.

And I definitely didn't pin him for a fucking suicide.

Finally I sucked it up and walked to the small house where Berry lived – and died. Lowell met me at the door.

"We're not supposed to be here."

Neither was Berry but I caught his drift.

There was a lone detective covering the crime scene, a tall, lanky dude name Jake Boone. He gave me a tired smile and shook my hand.

"Bob tells me you brought down the Vandals' human trafficking operation. Nice work."

Apparently Lowell had done some pre-publicity, which made my fugitive nature uncomfortable. I gave him a just-doing-my-job shrug.

"Thanks Jake, but Bob was there too. What happened here?"

His smile turned mournful. "Sergeant Berry was a friend. He was over our house for dinner a few times since he broke up with Jasmine, that's his ex-wife."

"Was he depressed?"

"Angry, yeah. But no more depressed than you'd expect. Drank a little maybe."

"I noticed last night."

Boone squinted at me. "Oh yeah?" You mean at the Buckhorn?"

I assumed Lowell had already told him the details but my anger blurted out.

"Yes, and there's no fucking way he was suicidal."

For a second it was quiet. Lowell's tensed expression seemed to be warning me to shut up. Boone continued to study me as if looking for clues to my outburst."

"You a psychiatrist?" he said calmly. "Bob said you're DEA."

"No offense," I mumbled, walking it back. "Just my field experience talking."

He nodded. "The body's in the living room."

Boone's craggy face was impassive as we gathered around the easy chair where Berry corpse sat watching the large screen TV, which was still on, the sound having been muted.

Miles Berry was leaning to the left, the right side of his skull now spattered over the lamp shade and shag rug. His service revolver was gripped loosely in his dangling hand. On the table next to the lamp was a bottle of bourbon and an uncapped bottle of pills.

"I left everything the way I found it," Boone said. Meaning don't touch.

The dawn light streaming into the small house competed with the flickering images on the TV and brain-smeared lamp light to amplify the surreal quiet shrouding the scene.

In death Sergeant Berry's beefy vigor had been deflated, his sunken cheeks and grey skin making him seem oddly frail—and much older than the feisty lawman drinking beer with us a few hours ago.

Finally Lowell said, "Who called it in?"

"Neighbor. He was out on his regular four a.m. run, came back and was mixing a protein drink when he heard the shot. Guy went over, the door was unlocked, found Miles like you see him. He called us right away. When I got here the body was still warm. So I figure time of death to be about four forty five, best estimate."

"Were forensics already here?" I ventured.

Boone snorted. "You're looking at them." He lifted his iPhone. "Pictures, video of the scene, my recorded notes, that's it. Since Bob was sent on vacation, the new kid Ferris on med leave and now...well let's say we're short-handed."

"What about the coroner?"

"He won't be here for at least an hour."

"Did you find anything unusual?" Bob said.

"Only the fact that Miles happened to be a lefty. And the gun's in his right hand." He turned to me, face deadpan. "I'm inclined to agree with your friend Max.

Problem is you're not here. And this conversation never happened."

"Of course it didn't," I said. "And I'm not looking at a left-handed corpse."

+         +         +

Frustration and rage chafed at me like two sticks making a fire. Lowell on the other hand retained an air of calm acceptance which I agreed was the more professional approach.

The tension and broken sleep also turned up the volume on my bruised ribs and belly. We were sitting in a booth at a local diner and I kept shifting position to ease the ache, without success.

Lowell was eating his way through a stack of pancakes with bacon and eggs while I made do with orange juice, toast and coffee. Seeing Berry's corpse had dulled my appetite. My smoldering anger didn't help.

Three dead in ten days. One outright murder, one 'accidental' homicide, and one questionable suicide. Two directly connected to Paul Zallen. Which made me think of something.

"This pretty much quashes the stolen car beef."

Lowell stopped eating and nodded thoughtfully. "That's right. Jesus you don't think..."

"I can't help it. My mind is twisted."

"Boone is a good detective."

"He's already found one clue."

"Clue?"

"Right handed shot by a lefty. I'd say that qualifies as a serious clue."

"Boone is a good detective," Lowell repeated.

"As you personally know there's only so much he can do. This shit is way above our pay grade."

Lowell shook his head. "We can't just walk away."

"Who said walk away? We just don't want to walk into something we can't walk out of."

"Like Berry."

For a few minutes we went silent, Lowell toying with the remnants of his breakfast until his phone buzzed. As he looked at the screen a quiet smile slowly erased his grim expression.

"Are you ready for this Max?"

"I was born ready."

"Your DNA matches the crud from Zallen's shoe."

*"I need him like the axe needs the turkey."*
– Barbara Stanwyck, *"The Lady Eve"*

# Chapter 8

I squeezed my glass so hard it cracked.

"That motherfucker," was all I could muster. I carefully placed to damaged glass on the table, grateful it hadn't speared my hand.

"Easy partner," Lowell said quietly. "This isn't the time."

It made sense but the Preacher was light on logic. Once he was loose it wasn't easy to push him back into his cage. And he was definitely off and running.

"The bastard needs to go."

Something in my voice alarmed Lowell.

"You go this route you ride alone."

"You called me, remember partner?"

It was low but so are the Preacher's ethics.

Lowell sighed. "Shit, okay I've got your back." Then he leaned forward and met my eyes. "But not like this. Revenge is a dish..."

"...that's best eaten cold. Thanks Godfather but how many more get killed while the lasagna cools down?"

He shook his head in exasperation. "I hear you. But not until we come up with a damn good plan—which doesn't include murder."

"How about assault with a deadly weapon?"

"I can live with that."

We both broke out laughing which shrank the Preacher down to manageable size and he retreated. Thinking clearly I realized I had to come up with a foolproof strategy to take Zallen off the board anonymously. However I have a character flaw.

I'm not an assassin.

I've killed men but always in self-defense of one sort or another. At least that's how I see it.

The laughter sharpened the ache in my ribs which renewed my fierce dislike of Zallen. Still I needed to devise a trap of some sort. And fast.

The body count was mounting.

+      +      +

It was still early when I left Petaluma and I ran into rush hour traffic.

Two lanes of cars crawled south like a gleaming metal worm. Resigned to the pace I turned up my sound system. Marvin Gaye singing *What's Goin' On* reflected my dour thoughts. As I hummed along I glanced at my side mirror and went silent.

Three cars behind me was a blue Malibu.

It could have been anyone's Malibu but I've always subscribed to William Burrough's axiom "there's no such thing as coincidence" so I kept the Malibu in sight. Commuter traffic may as well have been on a conveyer belt, which made it easy for me–and him.

The drive was slow but the Preacher's motor was revving like a Formula One Ferrari, all ferocious power driven by a relentless death wish. While I reveled in the rush it worried me. It erupted too easily despite my domestication as a family man.

It didn't even know if the Malibu belonged to Zallen, or a bank clerk on his way to work and yet the Preacher was eager for blood.

Exactly the sort of self-righteous bullshit that gets you dead in a hurry.

Or leads to killing the wrong man.

So I took deep breaths and convinced myself not to be like Paul Zallen. Still the idea that he might even be within five miles of my family had me fuming.

If it was Zallen behind me he had already run my plates but I had that covered. The most he'd get was my last name and last address. If the Malibu was clean I would drive to my pad in North Beach and take a nap.

At Novato the freeway expanded to four lanes. The Malibu stayed on the right so I jockeyed to the left, trying to get a glimpse of the driver in my rear view.

No dice. The Malibu dropped back out of sight behind a semi.

Intentional? Maybe. Paranoid? Oh yeah.

It stayed that way until well past my exit. Approaching the Golden Gate Bridge I saw the blue Malibu nose into the next lane then drop back again.

Making sure I was there?

The truck took the Marin City exit, which finally left the Malibu exposed.

Slowing down as I eased onto the bridge, I caught a decent look at the Malibu's driver.

It wasn't Zallen at all.

The face behind the wheel belonged to Matthew Goldsmith.

+      +      +

In the midst of the thick traffic my brain juggled the possibilities. A: He was out to kill me. B: He needed to know more about me before he killed me. C: He needed to find out what I knew about him before he killed me.

D: All of the above.

I also became aware that the Preacher had a new pal. An odd exhilaration I recognized from my days with the Marines in combat.

Senses on full alert I scrambled to devise a strategy.

There was plenty of time. It took fifteen minutes to cross the Golden Gate Bridge and by then I had a plan. Actually more of a route than a plan.

The Malibu stayed three cars behind until I darted into a surprise gap on my right. I needed room to wiggle free of the hook.

It wasn't enough. Every time I checked my mirrors the Malibu was there.

Once past the toll booth cameras, I switched on my sound system and activated the hidden panel beneath the dash. The sight of the Taurus .45 tucked inside soothed my nerves.

I had already decided how to shake Goldsmith loose but as traffic crept past the rust red dome of Palace of Fine Arts it occurred to me that it would only delay my death, not prevent it. Sooner or later the CIA bastard would hunt me down.

No, I had to confront Goldsmith on my terms.

A shoot-out in the streets of San Francisco was ill advised. The most efficient way would be in a secluded, confined space – like his car.

Fast and nasty.

The more I mulled it over the better it looked. Certainly the Preacher admired the idea. I just had to figure out how and where.

The pace picked up and as I turned onto Lombard heading towards Russian Hill it came to me. Driving aggressively i.e. like an asshole, I managed to get two more cars worth of separation.

At Van Ness traffic split in two directions and I continued slowly onto Lombard. I say slowly because halfway up the hill was the tail end of a line of cars, all waiting for their turn to go down our city's famed "crooked street."

It's nothing more than a double S shaped narrow brick road between Hyde Street and Leavenworth with a brilliant view of North Beach below, but tourists from everywhere flock to the quaint, old world patch of San Francisco,

On either side of the crooked street are sleek, expensive Mediterranean homes with picture-book flowered terraces. I often wondered if the occupants feel trapped inside, like rare animals in a zoo teeming with gawkers crawling over their cages.

Of course I had no intention of going down the crooked street. Instead when I reached the corner I turned right onto Hyde and looked for a parking space. At that hour in the morning parking was no problem and I found a spot a few hundred feet away.

Given that Goldsmith was at least six vehicles behind, it gave me time to position myself across the street among a herd of tourists, their iPhones held high, snapping everything in sight. I had put on an old ball cap I found in the glove compartment and shades. Not much of a disguise but Goldsmith would be looking for my Mercury, not me.

I had made it easy for him, leaving the car at angle, bumper out, as if I'd parked in a hurry.

A few minutes later the Malibu appeared. It wavered in the center of the street until Goldsmith spotted my car. He made a hard right and spurted ahead. Seeing the Mercury was empty he pulled into a space about two cars ahead.

I was already moving. Quickly crossing the street I came up on him as he started to get out of the car. His face registered confusion just before my Taurus whacked the side of his skull.

Stunned, he slumped down behind the wheel. I slipped into the back and, after making sure nobody was taking a video, jammed the Taurus against his neck and patted him down. He was carrying a Glock 9, an iPhone and a thin wallet. I took them all.

Time: less than two minutes.

Goldsmith groaned. "Motherfucker..."

"Start driving."

I punctuated the command by digging the Taurus into his ear.

Still groggy he started the car.

I knew there wasn't much time. When the ringing and numbness in Goldsmith's brain subsided, odds were he'd make a play. However I knew a secluded street just a few blocks down the hill.

"I got blood on my suit..." he mumbled.

"Keep driving."

At Hyde Street, Broadway becomes a narrow lane that forks around the Broadway Tunnel below. One side is bordered by the tunnel wall itself. Traffic on the lane is sporadic and a car parked against the wall attracted little attention. Added to that was the fact the loud noises in the tunnel below were amplified so the few neighbors were used to loud pops. The tunnel was an ideal place to get major audio from a Cherry Bomb as the local fireworks dealers knew.

When Goldsmith parked I leaned over and took the keys from the ignition. He sat up as if considering a move. But by then I was back out of reach.

"Why the tail?"

It took a moment for the question to register in Goldsmith's pounding brain.

"Serious? You've been all over our shit since you showed up. Nobody knows who the fuck you are except your cop pal." He pulled some tissues from a box next to his seat and mopped his head.

"Your pal Zallen jacked my ID. You must have run me through the system."

Goldsmith snorted. "Yeah, runaround you mean. All we got is a last name and a phony address."

I tried to calm the Preacher. I had a need-to-know motive for not slamming Goldsmith again.

"We know about the charter flights," I said, trying to sound like I was part of an organization instead of an adrenaline fueled lunatic. "Why did you kill Sergeant Berry?"

Goldsmith was good. He had recovered his poise and answered my question with an award-winning look of surprise.

"Who the fuck is Sergeant Berry?"

"The officer who busted Zallen in a stolen car," I said.

Then I hit him again. I used his Glock this time.

He reacted the same way.

"Motherfucker..." he said, throat tight with rage..

"I'm not playing. Who wanted him dead?"

His eyes were bright with pain. "You don't know who you're playing with asshole. Your faggot buddy is already history."

Hitting him again would be counter-productive. So I shot him.

The blast inside the car was deafening.

I used his Glock and the 9 mm bullet plowed his thigh and punched through the door. That really got his attention.

Goldsmith's angry eyes burned through the cordite fog like orange lasers.

"You're fucking crazy!" He grabbed a bunch of tissues to stem the bleeding staining his pants.

"Right about that. Now who wanted Berry killed?"

The bastard was good. He flung the bloody tissues in my face and grabbed the gun. For a few grunting seconds we arm wrestled. Then the gun went off again, muffled this time because Goldsmith's half-bent body deadened the shot.

He went slack in my arms and fell back.

"Jesus I'm hit."

By then he was bleeding from his head, thigh and abdomen.

"Who told you to kill Berry?"

"Fuck you," he said squeezing the words through pain locked teeth.

I held up his phone.

"Two choices Matt. You tell me what I want and I call 911. Second choice, I let you bleed out and walk away."

He didn't answer right away. But as the blood drenching his belly and groin began to pool over the floor mats he gave it up.

"Bannon. Chief Bannon," he said.

"Because of the Zallen bust?"

"Running for office. Can't take...scandal."

"Why didn't Zallen hit Berry?"

Goldsmith managed a coughing laugh. "Stupid bastard...turn in his gun after...shot...the spic."

It was unanimous. Zallen was a stupid bastard.

"You said my gay pal is already history—what did you mean?"

He half snorted. "I said faggot...motherfu..."

I held the phone close to his face. "Your choice, 911 or you die in a rented car."

"Child porn..." He said, voice weak as he slid into shock.

"What about child porn?"

"Planted...computer..."

About then he passed out. I was sorely tempted to break our deal but I got out of the car, called 911 and walked quickly away.

+      +      +

I had a small window of time.

When Langley found out one of their agents had been shot they'd immediately put a trace on his missing phone. I raced to my shop, made a safe copy of the contents then later dismantled the phone and threw the chip into the rear of a passing pickup truck.

I also got rid of the Beretta. Acquiring a gun is no problem in America.

Goldsmith's wallet contained four hundred dollars, two credit cards, a New York driver's license, and an Agency ID card with a hologram.

With the help of my advanced equipment and the blank plastic cards I keep around for just such a situation, I replaced Goldsmith's picture on the both ID's with my own. The fake hologram would be a problem only if I tried to break into CIA headquarters, wherever that might be in northern California. My guess was Sacramento, the state capitol.

After disposing of the credit cards I walked directly to Spec's bar in North Beach. The formal name is Spec's Twelve Adler Museum Café and it's nice and quiet in the afternoon. The establishment boasts wall to wall memorabilia. honest drinks, and a disreputable clientele.

I sat in the corner and nursed a double scotch while I came down from my adrenaline jag. The Preacher was pissed that I didn't finish the job. There was a chance Goldsmith would survive. In that case he'd be looking for me when he recovered.

At least a few months from now, I reminded. Which meant Zallen was alone.

The tussle with Goldsmith had reawakened the pain in my ribs and the Preacher was screaming for payback. I finished my scotch and went to retrieve my car.

It was still early enough to find parking in North Beach. I walked to my pad and called Lowell. I didn't mention Goldsmith instead I focused on the attempt to frame him as a pedophile. Not only would his distinguished career be demolished but for the rest of his life he would have to go house to house declaring his sins.

"Those fucking bastards," Lowell said, his voice heavy with disgust. "How did you find out?"

"I'll tell you later. Right now I need all your personal computer passwords. I've already locked up the PC in your office so they can't hack you there. And while you're at it give me Chief Bannon's email address."

"Going to send him a message?"

"Something like that. Listen I strongly suggest you find another place to stay while you're on vacation."

"I guess I could stay with Koop in the city."

By Koop he meant Steve Kooper, his partner. Good choice. Completely anonymous as long as he used a prepaid phone.

"Better leave the iPhone at home."

"Roger that. Call me when you're done."

Roger that. The all-American fighter pilot.

I intended to sweep Lowell's computer before making it bullet proof to insure nothing had wormed its way inside. Where does the CIA get its child porn anyway? Do they have a special file handy labeled DIL for destroying innocent lives? I think of myself as a professional cynic but in this game I'm a rank amateur.

Lowell's PC was clean but vulnerable. I shut all the doors and installed locks. Bob would have to consult with me before he could open his Apple again.

I used my flat-mate's equipment, three desk PCs and a Mac Pro laptop. It belonged to Eli, a dotty physicist who was away in London. In return for a room in his apartment I maintained his three desk computers and a Mac pro laptop. Ideal for routing my handiwork to the far corners of the earth

I also buried a little grenade of my own. If anyone tried to plant something in Lowell's computer it would bounce back to Chief Bannon's email.

"You can really do that?" Lowell said over drinks.

"We'll know soon. I plan to monitor Bannon's computer."

He had driven into the city and we were having dinner at Tutto Qua, an Italian restaurant across the street from the a strip joint and the Beat Museum.. His partner was tending bar and Lowell was waiting for his shift to end. The food is excellent at Tutto Qua and it's noisy enough that we could talk about personal matters, like killing people, without being overheard.

Lowell leaned closer. "Nothing yet about Goldsmith. You think he's...?"

"I think he's in the CIA, so alive or not, very few people will know. Most likely Zallen."

"Boone says Zallen hasn't been seen since the accidental shooting."

"He'll come around to see Bannon as soon as he hears about Goldsmith. Tell Jake to look for signs of extreme stress."

Lowell chuckled. Then his expression clouded and he shook his head.

"Miles Berry was a good man, and a good cop."

He raised his glass and drained it. I did the same.

"The funeral is tomorrow."

"No point telling you to stay away."

"Miles was my friend."

I nodded. My situation was slightly different. If Goldsmith had somehow fingered me as his assailant I'd be shot on sight.

"Watch your back," I said. "They've already got plans for you. Might even make a move right there at the funeral."

"They? You mean Zallen? Goldsmith's gone."

"The minute he's identified as CIA, his replacement, maybe two, will be on a plane. Make no mistake, it's them or us now."

"I'll be in uniform. Still have my sidearm."

"Best case scenario, Goldsmith doesn't make it."

Lowell squinted unhappily.

"Kind of cold Max."

I met his eyes.

"Berry's murder was cold – Goldsmith was an accident."

+          +          +

For all my tough talk I didn't sleep easily, if at all.

I've killed men. All in self-defense, the heat of battle. Each of them took a chunk of my soul with them. I toasted them all, one by one, in the empty apartment. Sitting at the kitchen table with a bottle of Laphroaige scotch, a bag of weed, a water glass, an ashtray and my Taurus .45, now a constant companion.

I was on full red alert.

Even if Goldsmith didn't recover Zallen would finger me and Lowell as suspects. It was one thing to have the DEA on your ass, but the Agency?

Like them or not the bastards are ruthless.

And relentless.

Eventually they'd be able to tear down the cyber walls protecting my anonymity. Which meant my family would be exposed.

I swore to myself I would never let them be harmed. But my oath echoed hollow in the dark, empty flat.

# Chapter 9

The Golden Hills Memorial Cemetery was located on Magnolia Avenue, a leafy stretch of road not far from the Petaluma police precinct building. Lowell arrived early, having skipped the church service.

The police department had 95 employees, including the Chief, one captain, nine lieutenants, ten sergeants, and forty five active officers. Lowell was the sole captain having been awarded the rank after he helped Max break the Vandals' human trafficking and drug smuggling operation a couple of years back.

Now we're down to nine sergeants Lowell thought, walking between the tombstones.

He had driven from San Francisco where he'd spent the night with Steve. Waking up in his partner's Castro apartment was a far cry from his quiet cottage in Petaluma. Steve had worked the late shift at the Park Tavern, an upscale bar and restaurant in North Beach. But he was awake when Lowell was getting into his dress uniform.

Steve made a face. "Do you really need the gun?"

Lowell adjusted the holder for his Glock. "Regulations. See you when it's over."

"Remember I'll be working tonight," Steve shouted after him.

While trying to locate the gravesite Lowell saw a couple of officers he didn't know coming over a ridge behind him and his hand instinctively moved closer to the Glock.

Easy now, he thought as the men nodded and moved past him, you're as paranoid as Max. He instantly regretted the thought. Berry's murder showed a sociopath's indifference for human life. And as Max had once told him, 'better tense than past tense.'

A small group of uniforms had already gathered at the gravesite. Tim Ferris was one of them. He smiled uncertainly when Lowell approached.

"Chief Bannon suspended me," he blurted out as if confessing a crime.

"I heard. But it was Zallen who shot the man."

Ferris nodded. He looked like a high school kid wearing his dad's uniform. "I never saw anyone get shot before. He died in front of his wife, kids...I went outside and threw up."

"Is that why Bannon suspended you?"

Abruptly the man in Ferris emerged, resolute and strong. "I wouldn't change my report that say that the victim attacked Zallen. Then Zallen claimed that I bolted outside at the first sign of violence."

His clear blue eyes flared and his voice trembled with compressed fury. "I am not a coward sir,"

Lowell patted him on the shoulder. "I wouldn't believe a fucking thing Zallen says. Have you been to the Review Board yet for a hearing?

Ferris furrowed his brow. "Uh no, uh not yet. I thought..."

"Then do it. You speak to Susan Hawthorne. She's vice chairperson on the board. Tell her I recommended you speak to her. In fact I'll call her myself."

"Thank you sir. Susan Hawthorne. Uh, but is it okay to go over Chief Bannon's head?"

"If you don't your head is on the block. At best Zallen's report will go on your record. Worst case, you're finished. Remember, we've got rights."

The resoluteness returned to the young patrolman's face. "Thanks sir. I'll get right on it."

"Just tell Susan exactly what happened, including the request to alter your report."

Before Ferris could thank him again a large contingent of uniformed officers led by Chief Bannon came into view. Apparently the church service was over.

At the same time a hearse carrying Berry's casket rolled up to the curb.

When Lowell saw the casket being lifted from the hearse and set on a wheeled dolly, depression fell over him like a heavy cloak. He recalled Berry's vitality and gruff sense of humor the last night of his life.

About forty people had gathered for the burial service. Most Lowell recognized from the precinct. He heard later that Berry's ex-wife and son were in Atlanta and couldn't make the funeral.

The sum of a man's life, neatly boxed and soon forgotten, Lowell thought as the coffin was slowly lowered.

Chief Bannon was there in full dress, looking somber. Lowell spotted Zallen hovering at the rear edge of the mourners. A spike of anger cut through Lowell's emotions when Bannon threw a handful of dirt on the casket.

You murderous hypocrite, Lowell railed inwardly. Suddenly he was glad Max shot Goldsmith. He got the confession and now they knew who ordered Berry's murder.

And there he is less than twenty feet away and there's not a damned thing I can do about it Lowell fumed, his face expressionless.

Then he saw Zallen move to Bannon's side and whisper excitedly. From the expressions on both their faces Lowell surmised that Zallen was relaying the news about Goldsmith. Max called it right, he thought.

Realizing that any contact with Bannon or Zallen was pointless, he worked his way through the group of uniformed mourners until he was standing next to Lt. Jake Boone.

"Any news?" He said through the side of his mouth.

Boone too, stared straight ahead. "Isn't this enough? Bannon is rushing me to call it suicide and close the book."

"And you?"

"I only fight when I think I can win. All I've got is Miles was left handed. Not nearly enough."

"I've got something."

"Yeah what?"

"Our chief ordered the hit."

Boone's bony features remained impassive behind his shades but Lowell felt the homicide detective's body tense.

"You serious?"

"Serious as this funeral. Watch your back partner."

Lowell edged away from Boone's side and threaded through the scattered groups of uniforms starting to leave the cemetery. The birds chirping in the sun streaked trees did little to lighten his gathering depression.

Like blood coagulating, his mood darkened. Ignoring his hunger, he got into his Mustang and drove directly to 101 South. I'll eat something when I get into the city, he decided, maybe have lunch with Steve.

As he neared San Francisco he called Steve to confirm. Then he called Max.

He never noticed the black Ford that had been tailing him since he left the cemetery.

+      +      +

The driver of the black Ford Taurus was new to the Bay Area.

Tom Boutilier had been in Los Angeles assigned to a human trafficking operation involving young Asian women and the Russian mob, when he diverted to San Francisco.

He had contacted ICE agent Paul Zallen and advised him that his new partner from the Agency was in critical condition, the victim of a shooting.

Zallen seemed shaken by the news, immediately accusing a police captain Lowell and a DEA agent named Max LeBlue of having something to do with Agent Goldsmith being shot.

Boutilier tried to switch on the radio and got the AC instead. He groaned aloud. Just off the fucking plane and he was in a rented sedan tailing Lowell on Zallen's directive. The ICE agent mentioned Lowell was gay. A "deviant homo" as he put it, whatever that meant. Boutilier's younger brother was gay.

In his opinion Zallen was a few cards short of a straight himself. Something about how he got pink and sweaty when he heard the news about Goldsmith.

Boutilier didn't like being dropped in the middle of a potentially lethal situation where he knew none of the players—or the game. All he knew was that a fellow agent had been shot and he was ordered to cover for him in an ongoing investigation.

It's a shit assignment, Boutilier thought. And he knew why he got it. His handlers in Los Angeles didn't think he was a "team player." His mother had been born in Haiti and his father was French. His copper skin color enabled him to pass for anything from a Muslim to a Latino. So he stayed on the street most of the time. What the office boys didn't grasp was that no "team" existed out there. Just him and his ability to improvise.

The bitch of it was he was just getting closer to Petrov. The Russian billionaire had managed to elude the FBI, CIA and IRS for five years. Drugs, extortion, gambling, prostitution, money laundering, guns: they knew Petrov profited from them all but he was too far removed. However he had a fatal weakness. Very young girls.

The Russian was involved in a human trafficking operation and that weakness exposed him as a high lever player—and an avid customer.

By becoming a regular on the LA club scene Boutilier had managed to build a passing relationship with a bouncer named Hugo who was one of Petrov's enforcers.

Boutilier's agency handlers expected bi-weekly reports, preferably by the afternoon never realizing his peak business hours were between midnight and five a.m. So he wasn't a "team player" and instead of helping to lock up Petrov, he was chasing a small town cop who may or may not have something to do with an assault on an agent.

He was also very hungry. There had been nothing but coffee and peanuts on the plane. The first signs of a headache were coming on.

The scenic crossing over the Golden Gate Bridge was lost on him, but when Lowell stopped in North Beach, Boutilier was relieved to see the abundance of cafes and small restaurants. The only problem was finding a parking space.

He strolled slowly after Lowell who was walking briskly to the corner. Boutilier assumed he was going to the park across the street but instead he ducked into a corner café called Mario's something. He couldn't see because he was busy keeping tabs on Lowell and trying to find a place to park.

The car behind him honked. In desperation he pulled up in front of a hydrant, hurried to the café and peered inside. Lowell was at a table by himself. Bouilier glanced back at his illegally parked vehicle and went inside.

I can watch the car from the counter, he thought, if a cop comes I'll run outside.

He observed Lowell sitting alone for a few minutes. The police captain was tall, perhaps six two, and looked like a clean cut athlete or a cowboy. Not the type to shoot CIA agents. While at the counter Boutilier ordered a pastrami sandwich and a double espresso.

Lowell checked his watch and said something to the waitress.

The sandwich came and Boutilier attacked it, keeping one eye on his car and the other on Lowell.

Halfway through his sandwich a man entered and sat down at Lowell's table. The man was shorter, perhaps six feet, with closely cropped hair and deep set green eyes. In contrast to Lowell he was far from clean cut. He was dressed neatly enough in a black leather jacket, black jeans and plaid shirt but he had the thousand yard stare common to combat vets and career criminals. Boutilier guessed he was Max LeBlue but to make certain he snapped a couple of pictures with his phone.

The man sat at Lowell's table for a few minutes then got up and walked past Boutilier on his way out. Shortly after that Lowell stood and left the café through the back door. Still holding his unfinished sandwich Boutilier dropped a twenty on the counter and went after him.

He followed Lowell and saw him sit on a bench in the park across the street. Realizing he'd left his car unattended he walked back just in time to see a traffic cop tuck a parking ticket under his windshield wiper.

At least I got their picture, Boutilier thought, consoling himself, when I get to a motel room I'll run the photo through my computer.

But when he pulled up to the Holiday Motel in Petaluma and opened the trunk of his car his stomach dropped.

His suitcase was gone. Along with his computer and weapon.

I'm seriously fucked, was his only thought.

# Chapter 10

Lowell squinted at me in disbelief.

"You're sure."

"Yes, don't look over there."

"He's at the counter?"

"At the end, where the cook works."

Lowell lowered his gaze to the carrot cake in front of him. I was having a cappuccino.

"You saw him following me?"

"All the way from your car. I was across the street watching the whole thing. When you went in here he parked in front of the hydrant outside."

"Who do you think he is?"

"I intend to find out."

"You're not going to shoot him?"

"If I have to."

"He looks Indian, maybe Latino."

"I said not to look."

"Relax. I just glanced. Anyway, he's not looking over here. He's eating a sandwich."

"Good, finish your cake."

"What's my hurry?"

"You're leaving soon."

"Where am I going?"

"Out the back entrance behind you. Just stroll out the door and across the street to the park, and sit on a bench."

"Okay, I'll move when you say the word."

"I won't be here."

He sighed in exasperation. "Then how do I know when to go?"

"Check your watch. Exactly four minutes after I leave through the front door, you exit through the back door."

My plan was simple. The guy tailing Lowell would follow him out the back giving me enough time to boost his illegally parked car. If it went as planned I'd be gone in sixty seconds.

The fool made it easy for me. In his haste to keep tabs on Lowell he'd left the car unlocked. I swept the car, opened the glove box, took the rental agreement inside, and then popped the trunk.

Jackpot.

The man's suitcase lay there, with tags fresh from LAX. Next to it was a backpack with a laptop and a Glock inside. I grabbed them both, and walked quickly across the street.

I found an empty bench on the far side of the park, opened the laptop and disabled the GPS function before I went back to my North Beach flat. Once there I made a copy of the man's hard drive.

My paranoid instincts had been vindicated, Thomas B. Boutilier was a CIA operative assigned to Petaluma from LA. He attended college on a Navy ROTC scholarship and served three years as an intelligence officer, two of them in the Persian Gulf. After discharge he entered the agency. He was barely twenty six years old. Green as clover.

Zallen probably put the poor bastard on Lowell at the funeral. Now he was sitting in a motel room in Petaluma wondering if he could get a job in night security. However I intended to take him out of his misery.

I had caught a glimpse him taking pictures with his phone. Last thing I needed was my profile in a CIA file.

So in exchange for the use of his phone for five minutes I would return his laptop and weapon. I already had his hard drive and the weapon was useless to me.

His voice registered surprise when I called.

"How did you get this number?"

"Rental agreement was in the glove box. For a secret agent you leave a lot in the open."

"What do you want?"

"It's about what you want. I have your computer and your Glock. Are you in San Francisco?"

"No."

"Get in your Ford and drive back. If you're lucky you'll make it in less than forty minutes. When you arrive take the same seat you had at Mario's. I'll be in touch."

I got myself ready and forty minutes later I saw him sitting at the counter of Mario's. I called him from across the street.

As soon as he answered his head swiveled 180 degrees, trying to pick out who was talking on their phone. At the moment I counted nine, including myself. But even if he made me I wasn't worried.

All he would see is a guy in a Hawaiian shirt, with long, salt and pepper hair. a gray Van Dyke beard and a fanny pack. I had the disguise left over from a previous psychotic escapade.

"Listen carefully," I told him, "leave your phone on the counter and walk across the street to the liquor store."

"Are you crazy...?"

"Look if you want the laptop and Glock do it. You have my word when you get back to Mario's the phone will be there."

While talking I crossed the street, strolling in his direction.

A few moments silence then a grudging, "Alright, how do I get my stuff?"

It was all about timing. I had left a Levi shopping bag in a bar called Rogue under the table where I had just consumed a beer. I figure it would take five minutes for him to get there and find the bag, and about three to four minutes to get back. Enough time for me to switch the chips on his phone.

I gave him my instructions, and as Boutilier was leaving Mario's I came in through the side door and headed straight for the seat he had vacated.

Shit. The phone wasn't there.

I gave the lady behind the counter my best smile.

"I think my friend left his phone behind."

"Oh right, I just picked it up. " She handed the phone to me. "Can I get you anything?"

"Cappuccino."

Having performed the operation at least two hundred times before, I removed the old card and installed in a new one before the coffee – or Boutilier – arrived. I left a twenty and the phone on the counter and strolled outside feeling almost relieved.

For the moment my face was not in the CIA database. But they would be hunting my ass for years to come. What the fuck, join the club.

+     +     +

Boutilier's hard drive turned up nothing unusual except for the occasional peek at YouPorn. His pay grade was too low for any startling revelations. No mention of how Paul Zallen had convinced the Agency to partner up with him.

However I now had access to his computer and phone.

Feeling good about the whole thing I smoked a cele-bratory J and felt even better. Then my phone buzzed. It was Lowell.

"Goldsmith is in critical condition at St. Francis Hospital."

"Who told you?"

"Jake heard at the precinct."

I didn't know whether to be relieved or disappoint-ed. I went with disappointed. As soon as the bastard got on his feet he'd be gunning for me.

"Has he been talking to anybody?"

"Not yet."

"His replacement is called Tom Boutiiier. Fresh out of boot camp. After what happened he'll be eager for your ass."

"I hear you."

"Better lay low for a while."

"What about you?"

"I'm going to pack some hardware and reconnoiter."

"I'm going with you."

"Don't you want to know where I'm going?"

"I think I already guessed

+          +          +

I was grateful for the company. At best surveillance is boring.

We picked up five of Za's signature pizzas along the way and sat there in the dark eating slices.

"You shouldn't be here," I said, surveying the area with night vision binoculars.

"What about you?"

"I don't have a career in law enforcement."

"You call errand boy for Bannon and Zallen a career?"

"Good point."

We were at the Petaluma airport, sitting in my car watching the now familiar hanger where the deportees were stored before being whisked off to Mexico, no questions asked or answered.

I was prepared should an opportunity present itself: tiny microphones (cameras were no use in the dark) and a few disposable phones.

We got lucky. About an hour into it, when all twenty Latino immigrants had been herded inside and locked up, Zallen left Boutilier in charge and walked towards the diner. When he was safely past the car I grabbed the four uneaten pizza boxes stashed two of the phones inside the boxes, donned a disguise which consisted of a ball cap and shades and sauntered over to the hanger where the hostages were stored. Boutilier was out front. He was wearing a sports coat and khakis, talk about disguises. And he looked nothing like the fresh, smiling Navy ensign I'd seen in his photos.

He looked bored, exhausted and miserable. But I expect he had to hurry back to Petaluma after he retrieved his things. Maybe have time for a shower before he joined Zallen in his nightly round up. I saw him check his watch twice as I strolled closer.

He became alert as I neared.

"Pizza delivery," I said.

He frowned. "Who ordered pizza?"

"Guy called Zallen." I jerked my head toward the hanger. "For the guys inside. Most every night," I added as a touch of authenticity.

Still frowning he opened the top box and peered inside. Now I was tense. If he went a box lower he'd find a phone.

Instead he reached in and took a slice. "Hungry," he said, half apologetic.

Then he unlocked the door. Fortunately he stayed outside.

I couldn't blame him, the air inside was heavy with the smell of sweat, fear and despair. In the dim light shadowy faces looked at me with a mixture of curiosity and hostility.

I carefully placed the boxes on the floor and opened the box containing the phones."

"Be very quiet," I said in Spanish. A few men approached warily. Most hung back fearing a trick. Seconds later they were clustered around the boxes I slipped a business card to one of the guys who was trying to shake my hand. It had Sidney Kingman's number.

"After you call your families make sure you call this lawyer."

Then I left. On my way out the door I bumped into Boutilier who was still eating his pizza.

"Sorry man."

Mouth full, he just waved me on.

I returned to the car feeling like all four Musketeers.

"You look pleased with yourself." Lowell said as I slipped behind the wheel.

"It shows huh?" I said, fiddling with the radio. I found some static and left it there.

"What's up Max?"

"I planted a mike on the kid."

We waited nearly a half hour the static on low.

I saw Zallen come around a corner accompanied by a uniformed officer. I handed the glasses to Lowell.

"Do you know the cop?"

"Gibbon," Lowell said, "a rookie like Ferris."

A flat, electronic voice came over the speaker. I turned it up.

"Everything good?" It was Zallen.

"When is the plane due?"

I saw Zallen look at his watch.

"Four minutes. Officer Gibbon, watch the door okay?"

Zallen walked Boutilier around the corner out of sight.

"When the plane lands we get all these shitbirds boarded , call it a night," Zallen said. "Here take it."

"What's this?" Boutilier said.

"Your cut kid. You got damn lucky with this gig."

"There's a lot of money here."

"One thou a head. Twenty grand a load, every night."

"Are you shitting me?"

Zallen's response was interrupted by the sound of an approaching airplane. The runway lights blinked on. A twin engine cargo plane dropped out of the sky and made a smooth landing, coming to a stop in front of the hanger where the men were being held.

As we watched three men debarked and walked across the tarmac to a waiting car. Then Gibbon unlocked the hanger door and helped Boutilier escort the ragged line of deportees to the plane while Zallen stood at the door checking off names on his clipboard. When the doors were shut and the plane began to taxi for take-off Boutilier's voice came over my car speaker.

"Listen this ..."

"Yeah, what?"

"It's a lot of money."

"Fuckin' A, it's a lot."

"I mean, who's paying...?"

Good question, I thought.

"Who? Uncle Sam that's who."

"I don't get it."

"The charter company charges Uncle Sam ten grand a head to fly the beaners over the border."

"That's two hundred thousand a flight."

"And we get thirty percent."

There was a long pause. "Who gets the other twenty grand?"

Another good question. The kid knew how to count.

"That we don't discuss."

After that there was nothing but static.

I switched off the audio.

"Out of range. Let's get back to the city."

The runway was dark and the area deserted but I rolled out of there with my headlights off.

+        +        +

"Now we know why the bastards were so hot to kill Suarez and Berry."

We were having a late snack but Lowell wasn't touching his food

"I was at Berry's funeral this morning."

I sipped my beer.

"Knew Miles a long time," he said, almost to himself.

"Bannon ordered the hit," I reminded, "Goldsmith talked."

Lowell lifted his head, eyes like blue ice. "I'm going to take him down Max."

"Correction, we're going to take him down. My guess is that mysterious ten percent is going into Bannon's political war chest. Six hundred grand a month. I'm going to dig into his finances."

"Then what? Why not just shoot the scumbag?"

I sensed Lowell was close to profound depression. Not only over the death of his friend and fellow officer, but because he had been blindsided by the deep corruption destroying the institution he had sworn to uphold.

It was a grim and lonely place. I knew because I had lived there for years.

Problem was, it might motivate him to do something crazy and get himself killed, maybe both of us. I couldn't let him do it.

Crazy is my job.

# Chapter 11

Boutilier woke up feeling like shit.

Since leaving LA his life had descended steadily into the sewer. While on routine surveillance his computer and gun had been stolen. Whoever did it also had his mobile number. Then he discovered his assignment was to help round up and deport a quota of undocumented Latinos, lock up the poor bastards in a room with no food, water or decent light, and then herd them onto a plane bound for Mexico.

A modern version of the Nazi boxcars, he observed, stepping into the shower. And then there was the fucking money. He didn't even know what to do with it. The envelope was in the pocket of the rumpled suit hanging in the closet.

It made him feel dirty. Corrupt. He lingered in the shower trying to wash away the stink.

I didn't sign up for this, he told himself. Toweling himself dry.

By the time he was dressed Boutilier knew what he had to do.

He went directly to the nearest bank and opened a checking account. He also rented a safety deposit box. He placed the twenty thousand dollars Zallen had given him in the box along with a dated memo, detailing how he received the money.

If I learned anything in the Navy, he thought as he left the bank. It's to always cover your ass.

Feeling better he found a café and ate a big breakfast before he met with Zallen to go over their night's
'agenda.'

+ + +

Rosa Canseco woke up feeling the weight of every
minute of a long, difficult life.

At the age of nine she migrated north with her parents. Rosa remembered the long, arduous journey from
their small village to the border. She endured exhaustion, hunger and thirst on the march across the desert.
The fear was always there beside her, a constant companion on the lonely trek through the chill blackness.

When they arrived it was only slightly better. They
had a room and kitchen, a place to sleep and a chance to
make money. Her parents worked the crops; traveling
between vineyards, strawberry fields, apple orchards,
farms, wherever someone needed cheap labor.

Rosa was left alone much of the time. Alone and
afraid. She didn't speak more than a few words of
English and she was aware of her illegal status. Her
mother had taught her to read and they had picked up
a book in Spanish at a milk farm. The book was about
a girl who loved a beautiful horse. Rosa read the book
over and over even though she understood only half of
it.

Rosa's parents said she was too young to work in
the fields so they sent her to a private school. One run
by one of the wives of the migrants called Marta who
taught the eight or so children in her care basic English
and arithmetic. Marta would also read them stories.

Marta also had a few books in English. One of them
was about a girl who loved a horse called *Black Beauty*.
Rosa realized it was the same book she had read in

Spanish. In fact she had read it so much she almost had it memorized. So when she read the book in English she was able to translate in her head.

In a short time she spoke English so well she became the family translator. Marta took a special interest in her and convinced her parents to put her in a regular school that had a special program for children of migrant workers. After passing a test she was put in the eighth grade. There Rosa was exposed to more books than she had ever seen. Books on geography and strange places, books on nature and strange animals, books on the lives of great men and even great women. At that tiny public school in Alexander Valley California, a world she had never imagined opened up to her.

When Rosa grew older hard reality punctured her book dreams. She entered high school and did very well in the classroom but soon realized that she, and the other migrant children, were despised by the other students.

While she excelled in her studies as she matured the scorn took on a sinister tone. The boys that noticed her beauty were disrespectful and threatening. She had heard what happened to other girls. How they had been raped by white students and the police did nothing. So despite the pleadings of Marta, and her math teacher, Rosa dropped out after her sophomore year.

At first she went to work with her mother and father on the nearby farms however she soon found that her talents as a translator, letter writer and amateur accountant were in great demand. Before the year was out she was earning twice as much as she could in the fields.

Although her maturing beauty attracted many potential suitors Rosa remained aloof. Barely sixteen she had no intention of tying herself down before she had seen a bit of the world.

Ironically, it was during her first trip away from home that she met Carlos.

Her friend Julia convinced her to take the six a.m. bus to San Francisco where they would spend the day and catch the ten p.m. bus to Santa Rosa, where Julia's brother would pick them up and take them back to Alexander Valley,

However while they sat dazzled at Fisherman's Wharf trying to decide if they should ride on the Cable Car, a young man overhead them and offered his help. He was tall, with broad shoulders and smiling white teeth. His hair and eyes were brown but the in the sunlight his pupils were dark gold.

His name was Carlos Canseco and he was from Petaluma, not far from Alexander Valley. In fact he knew her barrio quite well since he often hired workers from that area. Carlos was a contractor, he explained as they rode up the steep hills on the cable car.

The streets were lined with fine houses that gave way to the tall glass buildings in the downtown area. Rosa walked the aisles in the biggest stores she had ever seen filled with wonderful clothes, perfumes, watches, even candy.

Then Carlos treated them to lunch at a real restaurant and Rosa had Italian food. After that he escorted them to the Mission District where Rosa felt more comfortable. They went to Dolores Park, stopped at an outdoor café, saw the original Mission, then went for tacos at a place where Carlos knew the owner.

Best of all Carlos drove them all the way home in his new Chevrolet. It was the best day of Rosa's young life. And she was dazzled by the older man who took such interest in her.

The next day Carlos called on her and Rosa introduced him to her parents. He began to visit her regularly for months. Her family was impressed with the handsome young businessman, her neighbors were impressed, and so was Rosa.

Carlos was thirty, Rosa seventeen when they married. He took her to Disneyland on their honeymoon and then to Hollywood. It was the first time she stayed in a real hotel.

They had barely been married a year when Rosa became pregnant with her first child, a boy named Carlos after his proud father. Then came Amanda and a few years later, Julia.

Carlos was a good husband and excellent businessman. He liked to brag that he was related to the famous baseball player. Carlos had a green card and through his various contacts procured a work permit and driver's license for his wife. She even had a bank account and credit card.

Rosa's cottage business had also expanded through his contacts who often needed documents translated.

The family prospered and bought a small home. Of course like any man Carlos had faults. He gambled and drank too much, a dangerous combination. At times he would fall into debt but always he managed to come up with one deal or another. People said Carlos could sell heaters in hell.

There were rumors of womanizing but Carlos had always been devoted to his family so Rosa kept her feelings locked inside.

Between raising a family and work, the years passed quickly. Rosa had high hopes that her children would go on to college. Carlos Jr. was in his third year of high school, on the baseball team and near the top in academics. Amanda wasn't near, she stood at the very top of her freshman class.

Things changed with the new president. Suddenly the immigration people moved into the area in force. Their small Latino community went into hiding, terrorized by the ICE sweeps and sudden disappearances of family members and friends. The once thriving barrio became like the walled ghettos Rosa had seen on TV shows about WWII.

As usual Carlos kept his head above water, wheeling and dealing with the authorities. He had a good reputation, kept his word and knew where to grease the wheels. However the same could not be said for the men Carlos had to do business with.

One in particular made Rosa's skin crawl. She had only seen him twice.

The first time he was parked near their house talking to Carlos. She couldn't hear what they said but she got a good look at him. The man behind the wheel of the blue Chevy had thin blonde hair and blotchy red skin. He glanced at her and said something to Carlos.

Her husband stiffened as if to wave her off but Rosa had already turned and headed home, disturbed by the man's presence. Later Carlos let it be known that the man was an agent. And he was paying the agent off to stay in business.

The second time was worse. She had been shopping at the supermarket when she ran into Carlos in the parking lot. The man was there too, leaning on his blue car. He turned to look at her, his gaze both lewd and hostile, pale eyes flat, like some demonic white serpent.

Rosa pretended not to see them and hurried to her Honda. She drove directly to the church crossed herself with holy water and said three Hail Mary's. Tragically, it did no good.

Less than two weeks later Carlos was dead. Shot in his own home with his wife and kids watching.

They had all been gathered around the basketball game on TV when the door burst open. Stunned, she watched them as policemen and agents filled the small living room. Then the man she recognized came inside, pointing a gun. Carlos got up to greet him but the man yelled a warning and shot.

The blast fogged the room with smoke and deafening confusion. The girls were screaming as Rosa fell to her knees beside her collapsed husband. Carlos died in her arms while the agents ransacked the house.

After they took his body away she remained kneeling there for a long time.

Rosa knew her husband had been murdered but was powerless to accuse his killer. Without the protection of her husband's green card Rosa had to remain silent for the sake of her children. Despite being born in California, their future was bleak.

They were now strangers in a land that hated them.

# Chapter 12

As soon as I opened my eyes I turned on the TV news.

Three minutes later I turned it off unable to stomach the blatant lies being spewed by our current CEO. Instead I switched on some music, rolled off the bed and stretched my still aching bones.

It was still early so I went for a run along the Embarcadero, my sore ribs protesting. However in a few minutes the pain dulled and I was focused on my breathing. I've run with the flu and with injuries and I've noted the body suspends the symptoms during heavy exertion. A vital cog in our survival mechanism.

Of course you pay double when you stop exerting. Over coffee and a breakfast sandwich at Mario's, my ribs screamed that it was way too soon for extreme sports.

They also reminded me of Paul Zallen.

Motivated by brute anger I went back to my flat and dove deep into Walter Bannon's life. The money was stashed somewhere. I also took another look at Zallen.

I came up with nothing.

No off shore accounts, unusual deposits, large credit purchases or real estate. Every dime neatly accounted for.

Too neatly.

Frustrated, I rolled a J and took it for a walk. One of the benefits of legalization is that one can find a quiet corner in the shade and smoke a joint without fear of the police swooping down. Getting high outdoors puts it all in perspective.

However the missing possibility continued to elude me despite a strong cup of espresso at Café Trieste. As I watched the grizzled ghosts of San Francisco past shuffle in and out, Lowell phoned.

"I just got a call from Sidney Kingman."

"Yeah?"

"He wants a meeting. Says it's important."

"Where?"

"His place, Healdsburg."

"He called directly? How'd he get the number?""

"We all had dinner together remember?"

My ribs certainly remembered. And those puke stained cordovans held a special place in my memory book.

"I'll pick you up."

Once a rural community of farms, vineyards, small outdoor markets, a one screen movie house and honest diner food, Healdsburg morphed into a surreal mix of excessive boutiques, pompous restaurants, overpriced real estate and luxury SUVs. All in the midst of unspoiled forests and secluded hiking trails. Northern California's answer to the Hamptons.

Kingman's home was modest by local standards. There was a dusty black Honda parked next to Sidney's Mercedes when we arrived. Sidney greeted us at the door and ushered us into his study.

It was more a sanctum, with high, beamed ceilings, a large window overlooking a verdant flower garden, a full wall bookcase filled to capacity, a massive carved mahogany desk that held an Apple PC on either side, leather armchairs, a long plush couch and a brick fireplace the size of a New York studio.

A few paintings graced the redwood walls. I recognized one by Frida Kahlo. To his credit, there was no gallery of framed photos showing him posing with the rich and famous. Instead there was only one. A picture of Sidney in a Brooks Brothers suit standing next to President Obama. They were both laughing. Probably at the suit.

Later I learned that Sidney hardly ever used the rest of the seven room house except to sleep and shower. The rest of the time he operated from his magnificent command center.

"Welcome," he said, "mia casa e su casa."

He was wearing a red and black checked flannel shirt, black jeans and work boots in contrast to the singing cowboy outfit he wore in public.

"You boys hungry? Mrs. Canseco is heating up some food."

"Con gusto." I said, taking in the impressive décor.

"Please make yourselves comfortable. He moved behind his desk and sat down. Lowell and I took the armchairs.

He gave us a grave stare. "We have a serious problem."

I glanced at Lowell. "You think?"

Kingman wasn't amused. "We have two murders in the space of a week connected to one man."

"Three murders," I said, "and it's not just one man it's a fucking conspiracy involving Paul Zallen, a CIA agent named Mathew Goldsmith, and Petaluma police Chief Walter Bannon."

Kingman sat silent, his expression shifting from outrage to admiration and back to outrage. He looked at Lowell.

"Is this true?"

"I'll vouch for everything Max said."

"Tell me about this third murder" Kingman said, leaning forward on his desk, eyes intense.

When Lowell and I finished giving him the details of Berry's faked suicide, big money charters hauling undocumented Latinos, Bannon's political plans and the five figure payoffs, the lawyer was sitting back in his chair, shaking his head.

I neglected to mention how I acquired the confession. Self-incrimination is un-American.

"The worst part of this bloody conspiracy is that wolves are in the barn." Kingman said in measured tones. "This administration leaves us no recourse."

The conversation was interrupted by a woman carrying a tray of steaming food. The spicy fragrance nudged my hunger.

Lowell didn't need nudging. One look at the burritos and tacos on the tray and he broke into a wolfish grin.

However the woman bearing the tray wasn't smiling.

Kingman rose. "Gentlemen this is Mrs. Canseco. Her husband was killed by Agent Zallen."

We both got to our feet. Mrs. Canseco nodded. "This is left over from my husband's funeral," she said. "Please eat."

Awkwardly I took a plate and speared a burrito, aware of Mrs. Canseco's stoic presence beside me. She was a handsome woman, tall and straight, with large intelligent eyes that regarded the world warily. Her weathered hands and taut body suggested that she was used to hard work.

When all our plates were filled she left the room. In a few minutes she returned holding a tray with six bottles of beer and three glasses. She put the tray on the desk and sat down on the couch, slightly out of our circle.

We ate in silence. The cold beer went a long way in easing the sense of tension generated by Mrs. Canseco's presence. I sensed her ferocious pent-up rage, and her consuming grief. .

"He shot my husband right there, in front of me and my children," she said abruptly, quiet voice sounding disembodied, as if from a distance. She showed no expression, eyes half closed in reverie.

"Please Mrs. Canseco," Kingman said gently, "tell our friends exactly what happened that night."

"We were watching TV. The Warriors game. Carlos always watched with the family. He wouldn't admit it but I know he bet on the game. Julia was making popcorn..." She began to rock back and forth..."I heard a knock. I said who's there and everything went crazy. The door crashes open, two men, one white one black and a policeman come in yelling, then this Zallen runs in holding a gun. I recognize him. So does my husband. Carlos starts to say something to him, Zallen yells watch out gun and he...he shoots."

She took a deep breath. "Watch out gun...there was no gun, only his – the coward..."

She shook her head in disgust. We all did.

"Carlos died right there in my arms."

She paused, rocking back and forth as if in prayer.

"Did Carlos...say anything?" I ventured.

"It didn't make sense."

"What didn't make sense?"

"There was so much noise."

"What didn't make sense?" I repeated gently.

"He said...see bite money...I think."

I glanced at Kingman and Lowell. "see bite money?" They both shrugged.

I knew from bitter experience a dying man's last words had a tendency to wander, ranging from calls to mother to rants at invisible visitors. However the word money gave Carlos' words a certain gravitas.

"Thank God my youngest Julia was in the kitchen and didn't see her father killed," Mrs. Canseco said. "I hoped Carlos junior and Amanda could go on to college." She lifted her head and looked at Kingman. "Now I don't know if we can even stay in this cursed country."

Sidney met her eyes, his expression grim. "You will stay—for as long as you wish to stay." His steel tone made it a contract.

She bowed her head in thanks.

"Mrs. Canseco..."

She looked at me reluctantly. "Yes?"

"You said you recognized agent Zallen."

She glanced at Sidney, then back at me. "Yes. About a month ago I saw them talking near my house."

"Saw who talking?"

"Zallen and Carlos. Zallen was in the car and I saw his face. Pale white like death's own face."

I was about to probe a bit more but Kingman motioned me off.

"Thank you Mrs. Canseco, if you're tired you can return to your room."

Lowell and I stood and she solemnly shook each of our hands before leaving the room.

"I have a question," Lowell said, voice lowered.

"Yes?"

"Do you know who the third man is?"

Kingman seemed confused by the question.

"We know the uniformed cop was Tim Ferris, the black man probably Matthew Goldsmith – so was the white man who broke in before Zallen?"

Fair question and Kingman answered it.

"Oh yes, the name on the police report is Harvey Platt, a junior agent with Immigration. He confirmed Zallen's version. At least in writing. No one has questioned him yet." He paused and looked out at the peaceful scene beyond the window. "And probably no one ever will."

I made a mental note to squeeze Harvey Platt and see what came out.

"We have people, lawyers, some lawmen even..." Kingman nodded at Lowell ... "placed strategically in this area. However this administration has contempt for the law. And so far they have trampled it. Which brings us here – faced with these blatant murders, this incredibly corrupt human trafficking system ..."

Sidney's voice started to rise and his eyes blazed. "... operating under the umbrella of the police and the CIA. Leaving us nowhere to go."

"We go underground," I said.

"I say we go into the wild blue yonder."

I looked up and saw Kingman's pilot friend Berto stride into the room.

"Am I too late to get a beer?"

He was wearing his signature fringed jacket and alligator boots. The only change was that his long white hair had been pulled back into a ponytail. It accentuated the hard edges of his face just under the layer of friendly fat.

Kingman left his chair. "I'll get us a fresh round, you know everybody."

"I'll help, we'll need more than a round." I rose, bumped fists with Berto, and followed Kingman.

We walked through a dining room than seated at least twenty, filed around a huge carved mahogany table, into a spacious, sunny kitchen. Than we loaded up two trays with beer bottles, a bowl of chips and some cheese and cold cuts Sidney found in the refrigerator.

I decided to be direct. "Uh Sidney, do you know of a safe house in the area?"

"Why Max, did you do something you shouldn't have?"

"It's what I'm about to do."

Since hearing Mrs. Canseco's story, the Preacher had been trashing in his cage like a bull elephant in musk, His outrage was biblical.

As was my vengeance.

Kingman gave me a long, searching look, then shrugged.

"There's a small guest house about fifty yards behind here. It even has a small private road. But I don't know how safe it is. The feds have me tapped and tailed at least half the time. Goes with the territory."

"I can handle it if you can."

"I'll show you the place later. Let's drink our beer while it's cold."

We returned to the kitchen a few more times as day faded to dusk, finally ending up there, the four of us seated around a big wooden country table.

"I've got a forty-eight hour layover," Berto said, "so I've got time for a hangover."

After four beers I was trending towards something sharper, like scotch. I settled on a J. Kingman and Berto joined me enthusiastically. Lowell looked on with bemusement.

"We get regular drug tests," he explained. "One of chief Bannon's ideas. Testing positive for marijuana is grounds for dismissal."

"I'd take that case to court," Kingman said, between puffs. "It is now legal in California."

Lowell shrugged. "It's not a big factor in my life. Being a cop is."

I could attest to that. A few beers and Bob was done. An all American poster child for clean living.

"What's your next flight Berto?" Lowell asked, changing the subject.

Sidney passed the J and Berto took a hit. "I fly out of a small airstrip about an hour south off 101. Courier run. Private."

It was clear Berto wasn't volunteering much so the conversation turned back to the problem at hand. We sat around bullshitting for a couple of hours without reaching any solution.

However I privately formed a rough plan.

Before I left Kingman showed me the guest cottage behind his house.

"It's small but it's cozy," he said, leading me along a path through a thick grove of trees.

Actually it was idyllic.

Set back far enough from the house that it was isolated, the cottage had an eat-in kitchen, a sitting room and a large bedroom. Ideal for a hermit or a fugitive. Perfectly suited for me.

"Thanks Sidney, I owe you," I said.

Kingman shook his head. "You don't owe me anything Max. I don't forget what you did for Mrs. Suarez, or those men who were denied representation or communication with their families."

His voice began to rise as he warmed to the subject. I lifted my hands in surrender. "Yeah, I'm the second coming of Lancelot."

Sidney tossed me the keys. "It's yours as long as you need it."

I hoped I wouldn't need it at all but that was wishful thinking. If Goldsmith regained consciousness, I'd be hunted by three agencies and the police. Which would give me a very little chance of staying alive.

It also meant Nina and my little girl would have to move to a neutral zone, like Tibet.

Still the Preacher's ferocious need for vengeance drove me on. I was in this for everybody.

It being commuter hour I risked a DUI and became part of the metal worm crawling below on 101 north. When I passed the Corte Madera exit I was strongly tempted to turn off and catch a glimpse of my family. However the stakes were too high at this point.

I couldn't discount the possibility of a surveillance drone.

Two hundred grand a night feeds a lot of predators.

It occurred to me that I might use a drone myself if need be. I was full of bright ideas.

However when I reached my computer shop, I locked the door behind me and hit the couch in the back room for a disco nap.

+        +        +

At eight thirty that night I was on the road back to Petaluma.

I picked up Lowell along the way.

"Where to?" he said as he settled in.

"Where else?"

"The airport again?'

"Seems to be where the action is."

"They must be looking for us."

"We'll be out of sight. But we need to get there early and set things up."

Although the airport seemed deserted, I had to assume we were being watched. To that effect I wore classic Bank Robber Chic: hoodie, ball cap and shades.

I parked a block away and proceeded on foot while Lowell stood watch.

It took less than five minutes to plant three small microphones around the hanger Zallen used to house his prisoners. I ambled back to the car, turned on the radio, and settled in for a long wait.

"You going to hear it with the music playing?"

"Not coming through the radio, coming through here." I showed him a recording device no larger than a box of kitchen matches.

"It has speakers too. We'll get everything that bastard says."

I spoke too soon.

As the time neared for the plane to arrive, the airport remained as silent as a cemetery.

"Where is everybody?" Lowell said. "You think they canceled the flight?"

"Not at these prices."

Shortly before the plane was due to arrive, headlights briefly swung into view then blinked out of sight behind the airport hangers.

I activated the recorder. "There's our hosts for the party – but where are the guests?"

"Maybe their housing the deportees somewhere else,"

"Maybe I planted the mikes in the wrong place."

"Patience Max. We'll get something."

It took a while. We heard the approaching aircraft long before Zallen's voice came over the speaker.

"Just make sure you take Mister Z wherever he needs to go. If you're stopped for any reason flash your credentials."

"Who is this guy and why the escort?"

I recognized Boutilier's voice from our intimate phone conversations.

"Far as I know he's NSA. Look it's over my head. Like I said in the car, our schedule is changed, but the money's the same."

"And I just drive him where he wants to go."

"Simple assignment."

"Is that why you rented the Lincoln?"

"I couldn't find a Mercedes on short notice."

The sound of the plane's engine grew louder and the runway lights raked the darkness.

I grabbed my night vision field glasses and stepped out of the car. Lowell followed.

"What about the recorder?" he said, voice low.

"It'll keep working without us."

I watched the plane slide out of the night sky and skim the runway. It rolled to a stop not far from the hanger ICE had been using as a holding pen. The door opened and a short ladder dropped to the tarmac. In the strobing lights I saw three men emerge from the plane and start walking towards the hanger.

The first man out was tall, with white hair. His lean body was draped in a sleek dark suit. The two who followed were very large. One was black with a Mr. T Mohawk, and the other seemed Latino with a shaved head and a black goatee. The Latino sported some sort of designer ink on his wide neck. There was no mistaking their role as bodyguards for the white haired gent.

Mr. T wore a maroon leisure outfit and carried a large leather suitcase. The other bodyguard carried an identical suitcase. He was dressed completely in black from his boots to his leather jacket.

Abruptly the lights blinked out.

The trio walked towards a car parked beside the hanger. Using the night vision glasses I zoomed in on the lead dog. When I focused, the face in the lens slammed me like a head butt.

Stunned I stared at the crooked teardrop scar at the edge of his eye.

NSA my ass. I had met the man before.

Exactly four days after I died, to be precise.

+ + +

Two or three lifetimes ago, while still a functioning addict working for the DEA, I made contact with a high level drug and arms dealer. I was looking for military hardware: AK47s, machine guns, hand-held missles, plastic explosives, det cord, grenade launchers, land mines, mortars – everything you need for a major atrocity.

As a sign of good faith I sold this dealer two ounces of pure heroin. He told me his name was Byron "like the poet."

But before I could worm my way back to Byron's source and set up a bust, I quit the DEA and got myself a steady job. I crossed into Canada, established a new identity, forged a green card and came back to the States as Max LeBlue, mild mannered computer troubleshooter.

I had actually spotted Byron in North Beach some years back. My reaction then was to take a vacation in Mexico.

This time I didn't have that option. A new killer had dropped into the game.

And he had a CIA parachute.

# Chapter 13

Behind his impassive expression Boutilier was fuming.

He sat stiffly behind the wheel of his Lincoln staring at the road. Occasionally his eyes would scan the rear view if only to fix the description of his passengers in his memory.

The leader had a distinctive scar at the corner of one pale blue eye. He spoke with a trace of an accent and was very polite. The other two were thick-necked, wide-bodied goons. One had a shaved head, a trim beard and a prominent neck tattoo, a flaming skull with a knife clenched in its teeth. The other was a surly black dude with a Mohawk who resembled Suge Knight on crack. Nobody spoke during the short ride to the hotel but the black dude kept shifting in his seat, looking in all directions as if anticipating an ambush.

He made Boutilier nervous, which in turn made him angry.

This is fucked, he ranted inwardly, now the bastard has me ferrying thugs carrying God knows what in those fat bags.

Boutilier had dispatched a carefully worded memo to his section chief Tip Jenkins days before only to be reminded his assignment was to assist Zallen. Now he had doubts about Jenkins and suspected he was the designated fall guy in a bigger scheme. .

His destination was outside Petaluma, a posh hotel in the Sonoma Valley. When he reached the courtyard of the Fairmont Mission Inn the two bodyguards wordlessly left the Lincoln and scanned the area before they took the bags from the trunk.

Only then did his Alpha passenger emerge. Mr. Z half turned, murmured a thank you and strolled behind his burly escorts to the hotel lobby. Boutilier started to pull away then changed his mind. He parked just outside the ornate courtyard and took off his jacket and tie, even as he told himself what he was doing was stupid.

His indignation won over reason. He was tired of being treated like a flunky and frustrated by his section chief's seeming indifference to any hint of wrongdoing.

They'll spot you as soon as you walk in, Boutilier thought. He had a pair of sunglasses but instead went for the plain reading glasses. The shades attracted too much attention and cut down visibility. Especially at night. His only other change of dress was to roll up the sleeves of his white shirt.

Boutilier had finished first in his training unit at Langley and he had excelled at surveillance. He had a knack for blending in.

I'd better be fucking invisible, he observed as he approached the brightly lit canopy that led to the lobby.

The place was huge and ornate. The busy lobby made it easier for him to browse. It didn't take long.

He spotted Mr. Z talking to someone at the elevator. His two bodyguards stood a respectful distance behind so that what he was saying to his new companion couldn't be overheard.

At the risk of being recognized Boutilier angled closer for a better look.

One of the bodyguards turned his way. He was wearing sunglasses. Vision dimmed, no problem. Boutilier took a few steps closer.

The elevator doors opened and Mr. Z motioned for the men carrying his bags to enter first. Mr. Z and his companion followed. They turned to face the lobby just before the doors closed.

For a moment Boutilier got a clear look at Mr. Z's friend.

His stomach clenched as the doors slid shut. He recognized the cherubic face smiling at Mr.Z. It belonged to Petrov–the elusive crime lord he'd spent ten months trying to bring down.

Seething with conflicting emotions Boutilier made his way to the bar. He had just ordered his second vodka martini when he saw Mr. Z's white bodyguard stalking through the lobby.

His first instinct was to follow but tempered by the martini he figured the bodyguard was on an errand and would soon return. The second martini mellowed his tensions until the body guard walked into the lobby accompanied by a small entourage .

Four females in tight dresses and high heels followed him to the elevator. A very large, very hairy man with dark glasses loomed behind them like King Kong with a beard. One of the females looked to be about seventeen or eighteen. The others would have a hard time proving they were sixteen.

Despite their party attire the girls seemed subdued, scared even.

Petrov. He was infamous for his appetite for young girls. The vodka turned sour in his stomach. Mellow fermented into rage.

Boutilier considered pulling his weapon from the Lincoln and executing all five men. Then he gathered himself and considered his options.

He had none.

Short of his initial reaction there was nothing he could do except go back to Petaluma. Depression smothered his anger and he left the bar. When he reached the car he paused to reconsider the first option. His Glock was hidden under the front seat. He visualized bursting into their hotel suite and blasting the bodyguards first. The fantasy only deepened his depression.

His murky frame of mind blurred his usual instincts.

It wasn't until he unlocked the car door that he became aware that someone was close behind him. Before he could turn he felt something hard press against his skull.

"Keys please," a calm voice said.

Shit. This is all I need, Boutilier thought, a fucking hijack. Then he realized it could be much worse. Petrov had probably spotted him at the bar.

The figure behind him opened the rear door "Get behind the wheel real slow Mr. CIA man," the voice said quietly.

Boutilier felt a cold blade of fear slice his belly. The other bodyguard, he thought. Sober now, he got into the car. The man took the rear seat and tossed him the keys. "Now drive."

This is it, Boutilier told himself, you're dead you dumb fuck.

*"Life is a business. The only thing that
changes is the merchandise."*
– Teresa Mendoza

# Chapter 14

I had no trouble tapping into the Fairmont Mission Inn's data base but when I got there I faced a slight problem. There were two guests registered under foreign passports. One was a Russian called Alexander Petrov, the other was a Serbian national called Zsa Zsa Berlinski. Both had reserved suites. I was looking for a scumbag who called himself Byron. Although I had the passport numbers, cracking the foreign data bases would be a full day's work.

I had tailed Byron & Co. from the airport and was on the computer in my car when I saw Boutilier come out, park his Mercedes in a remote corner, and go back inside the hotel. I figured he was either taking a meeting, checking in, or doing some snooping on his own. I decided to wait and see.

Some twenty minutes later a white van pulled into the lot. It stopped but no one got out. At the same time a familiar figure came into view. I watched Byron's bald bodyguard enter the van before it backed out of the lot.

In less than a half hour the van was back. The side door slid open and six people poured out. One was a hairy hulk, the others were four girls who looked much too young to be out that late. Trailed by the hulk they followed the bald bodyguard into the hotel, walking unsteadily on their high heels.

Apparently it was party time. What was it with these neo gangsters and their ostentatious perversions? Whatever happened to the dignified Dons who maintained respectable family lives between killings?

My philosophical ramblings were interrupted by the appearance of Boutilier walking slowly to his car. His careful gait suggested he'd imbibed a drink too many. Which suited me just fine.

He didn't notice when I came up behind him until I pressed the barrel of my Taurus against his head.

"Get in," I said, slipping into the rear seat directly behind him.

"Now drive."

"Where to?" He said wearily.

"I'll let you know. And if you move for that weapon you have stashed I'll smoke you now."

"Now or later, what's the difference?"

He sounded resigned and I realized he thought I was a hit man. I decided to keep him guessing.

"Nice and slow," I said as the car rolled out of the lot.

We were in farm country and the main road was poorly lit and mostly deserted at that hour. Just in case there was an ambitious cop about, trolling for a DUI I looked for someplace more private. In a few minutes I spotted an unlit side street.

"Turn here."

The darkened houses had plenty of space between them so the narrow road was basically isolated. It was near pitch black, the only illumination coming from a dim porch light in the distance.

"Pull over and turn off your lights."

I heard Boutilier sigh heavily. "Look I stuck around for a few drinks, is that a goddamn crime?" he said, voice tight.

I dug my Taurus into his neck. "Your goddamn crime is taking payoffs on the backs of poor bastards trying to make a living for their families while you're chauffeuring international drug dealers."

He half turned. "Who the hell are you?"

"Never mind that. Don't look at me."

"Whoever you are you've got it all wrong."

"We'll see. Who's the scumbag that got off the plane?"

"I don't know his name."

I cocked the Taurus. It made a loud click. "I won't ask you again."

"They told me his name is Mr. Z. That's all I know."

"Who told you?"

"Zallen, the ICE agent in charge."

That squared with what my mikes had picked up. But there was still the matter of the payoffs.

"So what were you discussing with Mr. Z back there?"

"Nothing. I followed them back in hoping to get a line on why they were there."

"And so?"

"So he met with a major slime called Petrov."

"How do you know this Petrov?"

"He was the target of my assignment in L.A. until they pulled me for this shithole duty."

Petrov. Which meant my boy Byron was the Berlinski on the hotel register.

"Tell me about Petrov."

Boutilier's outline of Petrov's criminal resume was the usual: arms dealer, drugs, prostitutes. Textbook Russian gangster right down to the White House connections. The new normal in American politics.

"His specialty is underage girls," he added. There was no mistaking the anger in his voice.

My sentiments exactly. I felt the Preacher stirring in his sleep I tightened my hold on the gun a notch.

"But you don't mind those fat payoffs do you?"

"Yeah I mind—and I can prove it."

'How's that?"

"You're the guy who stole my phone."

I nudged him with the gun. "Let's stay on point. I've got you on tape taking money."

"Collecting evidence."

"Bullshit."

"I can prove it."

"Yeah how?"

"Meet me at the Chase bank in Petaluma. Ten a.m."

"Right. And you'll be waiting with a swat team."

"Look if you want to nail these bastards you'll have to trust me. Either that or shoot me now. Your choice."

He had me there.

"Alright," I said finally, "Ten a.m. Now put your phone on the seat and get out of the car."

"What?"

"I'll leave it at the hotel."

"That's a long walk."

"Call Uber." I said, starting the motor.

Along the way I found the Glock under his seat. As a precaution I removed the bullets.

+        +        +

I spent half the night trying to get a fix on everyone's finances. Zallen, Bannon. Petrov, Berlinski: they all eluded my cyber skills. Professional pride ruffled, I drove to Petaluma in the morning, arriving at seven. Always get there early to avoid a set up.

The streets around the bank were empty. But that didn't prove anything. I found a space with a good view of the bank and settled in with my take out coffee.

Petaluma is essentially a small town so foot traffic remained sparse.

I wasn't convinced.

As a professional fugitive I knew the postman up the street could have a shotgun in his mailbag. Or maybe the young mother strolling by had an UZI in her baby carriage. Even the schoolkid on his skateboard might be a very short cop.

Paranoid?

Twenty four seven.

At ten I saw Boutilier approach the bank and stand outside for a minute or so. I called his mobile.

"Get your evidence and go to the Starbucks behind the Copperfield book store and wait."

"How'd you get this number?"

"I stole your phone, remember? Be there."

The alley next to Copperfield's book store opens onto a small mall housing a tattoo parlor, gift shops and boutique clothing stores, It is also home to teenagers in various stages of development: Goths, hippies, skateboarders and nubile groupies, all sporting tats, piercings or oversized ear studs. The local Starbucks occupies the far corner.

There are three streets that lead to the coffee shop and I covered them all before approaching. Boutilier was seated by the window, three thick, padded mailing envelopes stacked on the table in front of him. I grabbed a coffee and sat across from him. He picked up the top envelope and pushed it in front of me.

Boutilier was thorough. It was all there: dates, cash amounts, passenger lists, flight numbers – the whole enchilada. Each item was accompanied by a detailed memo.

'What's in the other envelopes?"

"The cash. A hundred grands worth. All itemized and accounted for."

"Have you reported this to your section chief?"

Boutilier snorted. "He didn't want to know. Told me to be a good boy and cooperate."

"They could be setting you up to be the fall guy."

"Why do you think I'm keeping meticulous records?"

"Yeah well, watch your back. They've already killed three people."

"So I'm alone here."

"You can trust Captain Lowell. But watch out for Bannon."

"The police chief? He's in on this?"

"Up to his eyeballs."

Boutilier paused and looked away. "I met with Zallen this morning."

"And?"

"Tonight's flight."

"What about it?"

He met my stare. "It's all women this time."

I felt the Preacher blink awake, deep in my belly.

"Bastards. Well I'll be there."

"Zallen wants me to stand down."

"I'll take care of it."

"Not without me."

I looked at him. His smooth copper features were knotted with anger. But despite his grim expression he still seemed like a high school basketball player.

"You're taking a big risk."

"That's what they pay me for."

I gave him a short smile. I was starting to like this kid.

"Tonight then. I'll call you about nine."

+        +        +

I was at the airport at seven, nosing around.
Nothing.

At eight I came back and saw two uniformed cops hanging around the hangers Zallen used to warehouse deportees. One of them wandered off in the general direction of the Two-Niner Diner. Probably on a burger run.

At nine I checked again and saw the uniformed pair standing dutifully in front of one of the hangers. I took a position near the entrance. As I was calling Boutiler a pair of buses pulled up and a line of women slowly get out. Zallen was with them holding a flashlight. He waved the policemen over.

I watched Zallen and the cops usher the women to the hangers. As they straggled inside the women looked haggard and hollow-eyed, like POW's after a grueling battle. A few were teenagers. One wore a high school T- shirt that read "Go Knights." I took it as a sign.

Boutilier's voice came over the phone. "Max?"

"Yeah they're here."

"I'm close. See you in five."

"I'll be in front of the diner."

The next person I called was Lowell.

Ten minutes later the three of us were standing in the darkened parking lot.

Lowell nodded at Boutilier then turned to me. "What's the drill?"

"Zallen's got two uniforms in front..."

"Negative," Lowell said, "I just took a pass. There are two cops hanging around their squad car. A couple of goons are at the hanger."

My instincts went on full alert. Walking quickly, I headed for the hanger.

Boutilier hurried behind me. "Back me up," I said over my shoulder.

As we neared the hanger I slipped the Taurus from my waistband and held it close to my side. There was only one guard at the door, a wide-bodied Neanderthal with a pony tail.

I lifted my free hand as we came closer. "Where's agent Zallen?"

"Inside," the Neanderthal said with a knowing smirk. "He's busy."

The butt of my Taurus slammed into his skull just above his ear, erasing the smirk. He toppled like a chopped tree."

"Watch him," I said quietly, and opened the door.

The scent of sweat and fear spiced with perfume was thick inside the dimly lit hanger. At first all I could see were shadows. As my eyes adjusted to the gloom I saw a group of women against the far wall, huddled like frightened sheep. I heard the low, pleading moan and turned.

I saw Zallen in the rear of the hanger. He was holding someone by the shoulders. His pale skin shone like a fish in the low light. Stepping closer I saw it was the girl with the high school T shirt except the shirt was gone. She had her hands crossed over her bare breasts. Behind them was a tall, thin figure. He appeared to be grinning.

Hugging the wall I crept closer. A sharp object jabbed my bruised ribs rousing the dormant pain–and the Preacher's rage. I looked down and saw it was a metal lever. Without thinking I jerked it upward and the overhead lights flooded the hanger.

Momentarily blinded I blinked furiously until my sight returned. The tall guy was rubbing his eyes with one hand and reaching back for what I assumed was a weapon. Zallen was holding the girl by her arm and fumbling with his other hand.

"Max LeBlue you dumb bastard," he yelled. "this isn't DEA business, Get the fuck out!"

I neglected to mention I was no longer with the DEA. "Leave the girl alone you fucking perv," I said instead.

Zallen's face was red under the harsh lights. "Goddamnit shoot him Goose."

Goose was no *Top Gun*. While his Glock searched for my kill zone, my Tauris ripped a hole in his thigh. The impact of a .45 slug traveling at eight hundred thirty feet per second sent him spinning back like a figure skater, arms upraised. He fell heavily, his Glock clattering across the floor.

The blast filled the cavernous space. The women squealed and crouched back in the far corner. Through the gun smoke I glimpsed Zallen pointing a .38 at me. His other hand clutched the girl's arm, trying to pull her close. Her struggles to get free threw him off balance momentarily.

"Alejarse! Alejarse!" I yelled in Spanish, "Move Away!"

Zallen fired a wild shot, still struggling with the girl. I ducked, not willing to risk hitting her with return fire.

Suddenly the girl wrenched free and ran towards the others.

Maybe it was the painful reminder of my still bruised ribs, maybe the fury generated by seeing a helpless young girl violated, whatever it was amplified the Preacher's mad rage and I went for the kill.

My bullet hit Zallen square in the chest lifting him six inches off the ground.

His back hit the floor and he lay still, eyes staring up at the ceiling and gaping wound spewing blood and smoke. The women's squeals were now low screams and they remained huddled, hands covering their heads.

"Correr!" I shouted in Spanish. "¡Sal de aqu!" "Run! Get out of here!"

They stayed where they were, confused, uncertain. Boutilier came through the door.

"Get them out!" I roared, expecting the cops to appear any moment.

"¡Sal de aqui!" I repeated, and the women started to move, herded by Boutilier.

As they rushed out I turned off the lights.

"What the fuck." Boutilier said when I got outside. "You okay?"

"Zallen's dead. You better get lost before the cops come."

The women had filtered out and were dispersing into the shadows. I ran to my car half expecting to be shot in the back. I made it to the parking area before the flashlights showed up. As I started the motor the runway lights popped on leaving me exposed.

I stepped hard on the accelerator. Tires screeching I fishtailed out of the area heading for the street. As I turned out of the airport a pair of headlights lit up my rear view.

Rather than head for the freeway I looped around local streets until the mirror went dark then hastily parked the Mercury and doused the lights. A few minutes later a police car sped past me.

As the adrenaline drained, exhaustion dropped over me like a blanket. I sat in the dark, hands trembling, head pounding and sweat running down my neck. I had done it this time.

I had killed men before in the heat of battle. Their weight continues to burden my weary soul and mocks my attempts at sleep too many nights. I even regretted Goldsmith's accidental shooting although if our positions were reversed he would consider it a job well done.

But I had little remorse over killing Zallen. One, he shot at me first, and two – he fucking had it coming.

However I had shot two government agents in as many weeks. No way would I be allowed to walk. Which meant I couldn't see my wife and daughter until I figured out an alternative existence.

I had lost my California privileges.

The realization drenched me with cold depression. Without thinking I started the car and headed for the city.

# Chapter 15

Sleep was out of the question.

Finally I gave up and started gathering the equipment I'd need. At nine a.m. I called Sidney Kingman.

"Jesus Max, you really stirred up a shit storm. Santa Rosa is crawling with initials..."

"Initials?"

"ICE, FBI, ATF, CHP, they're all here."

And the CIA wasn't far behind. I felt like a chicken at a barbecue.

"How did you hear so soon?"

"Mrs. Canseco. Her niece is one of the women you turned loose."

"Is Berto around?"

"I'll get him. He's sleeping last night off. And Max..."

"What?"

"Thanks. Mrs. Canseco told me Zallen was abusing her fifteen year-old niece. Do you have somewhere to lay low for a while?"

"That's why I'm calling Berto."

"After I made my arrangements with Berto I called Lowell.

Same story.

"Max, you are in deep shit. Chief Bannon's got every cop in the state looking for you."

"How did he ID me?"

"The guy you shot in the leg. He heard Zallen yell your name. And Max...""

"Yeah?"

"The guy is a Vandal."

Great. Just what I needed. The Vandals motorcycle gang already had a quarter million dollar bounty on my ass from previous sociopathic encounters.

"Maybe you should leave town. San Francisco will stay red hot for a while."

"I've been thinking the same thing."

Actually I was holed up in my country estate, a small in-law unit in Corte Madera in Marin County. The unit is conveniently located behind a house that belongs to a character known as Organic Phil, a local health guru. I pay the rent in cash and maintain my lifestyle off the grid. Totally anonymous.

"Damnit Max I'm sorry."

"About what, Zallen?"

"I got you mixed up in this."

"Forget it. It was my choice."

Sounded good. A manly response. Actually however I was a bit pissed. I wouldn't be seeing Nina and Samantha for a long while.

I said, "Stay close to Boutilier. I'll be in touch."

I put off making the next call. Instead I made sure to pack the equipment I needed. As I was putting my bags in the car Organic Phil came out of his house.

"Max you don't look so good," he announced, what have you been doing?"

"Work related stress."

"You need to eat better. Come on I'll make you breakfast."

I followed him inside. The centerpiece of Phil's home is the kitchen. Larger than most it's equipped with a number of devices: Cusinart, two pro blenders and an industrial sized juicer. No microwave. When it came to cooking Phil disapproved of artificial short cuts.

Phil immediately started chopping vegetables. "What work is giving you this stress?"

"I'll tell you if you tell me how old you are."

Phil laughed and continued chopping. It was well known that Phil doggedly avoided disclosing his age. With his thick shock of pure white hair and weight trained body he could have been sixty but clues he dropped over the years put him closer to eighty.

"You should think about settling down," he said, "and raising a family."

Tell me about it Phil. I had thought of nothing else for days.

After much whirring and crunching he produced a tall glass of greenish brown liquid and handed it to me with a flourish. "Carrots, apples, celery, parsley, spinach and crushed almonds," he said proudly. "It will make a new man out of you."

I was still the same old fugitive after I downed it but I had to admit it was refreshing.

"I saw you putting bags in the car. Taking a trip?"

"Portland," I lied.

"Rains too much there. Business or vacation?"

"Bit of both. I'm setting up some computer generated effects for a movie shoot."

His eyes lit up as I knew they would. Phil was always trying to break into show business

"Really? Are they looking for anybody? I've been taking acting classes."

"Don't know, that's another department. I'll let you know if they're still casting."

"Do that Max. I can fly out there in a few hours."

Satisfied I had diverted Phil's curiosity I checked my watch. "Time to go. I'm on a schedule. Thanks for the health drink."

"Let me know if you need my picture and resume." Phil called as I left.

I had told the truth about being on a schedule. One out of three wasn't too bad.

I drove a few miles to a small garage located behind some warehouses on the other side of 101. The proprietor Len Zane shared my enthusiasm for anononynity. He was also the best mechanic on the West Coast, and the genius who had created my custom Mercury, the Green Ghost.

As I entered Len was bent inside the hood of a '69 Dodge. He emerged and wiped his hands with an oil stained towel. When he saw me he fished a Camel from the pack tucked inside the rolled up sleeve of his soiled T-shirt.

"Max," he said, shaking his head, "what the fuck is up with you? Word is you're the new *Dirty Harry*."

"Bad news travels fast."

He lit up and blew some smoke my way. "You can't kill an ICE agent and shoot a Vandal without stirring up bad publicity."

"Ever wonder what the fucking Vandals have to do with ICE?"

"They say he was just passing by."

"You believe that?"

Len is tall, lean and hard, and when he smiles his craggy face shows deep creases.

"Don't believe anything you hear and only half of what you see."

"Good advice. I need a favor or two."

He peered at me and took a long drag. "Okay, what's the first?"

"Take care of my car while I'm gone."

"Gone is a good idea, you're as hot as a third degree burn. What's the second?"

"Drive me to the airstrip outside Novato."

"Gnoss field? I didn't think anybody used that strip anymore. When do you want to go?"

"Now."

He dropped his cigarette into a nearby can. "Let me clean up."

Along the way I filled him in on what was happening.

"Damn, this country's going sideways." He muttered, "I sure didn't sign up for this shit." He paused and glanced at me. "Maybe you did the right thing but you'll be paying for it a long time. Matter of fact the Vandals upped the bounty on you to a cold half million."

I didn't know whether to be flattered or alarmed. That kind of money was extremely tempting.

When we reached Gnoss Field I saw a twin engine plane at the end of the strip.

"Looks pretty big for this runway," Len observed, "it's built for single engine jobs. I hope you brought along a parachute."

Not exactly reassuring. As we neared the plane I saw Berto in his fringed jacket standing next to the fuselage.

"That's him."

Before I left the car Len said, "Happy landings Max, Let me know if you need anything else."

"Thanks. When things cool down I'll give you a message for Nina."

"She might be bugged."

"Tell her you're coming over to repair the car. She'll know what it means." I gave him a fist bump and headed to meet Berto. Along the way I noticed the tarmac was cracked and pitted. I even spotted some potholes.

Berto tapped his wristwatch as I neared. "Good, right on time. Sidney told me what happened. Who was that in the old car?"

"No worries, he's cool." And the 'old car' is my custom beauty.

Berto scrambled aboard and pulled me inside. He stashed my bags and pointed to the co-pilot's seat. "Everything else is occupied."

One of the percs of flying private is you can bring a friend. In this case my Sig Sauer. The Taurus was also along for the ride.

As I strapped in Berto settled behind the controls. "Don't want to sit here too long. Attracts attention."

He revved the motors until they were screaming. The plane shook and one wing was trying to wave goodbye."

"Have to get a good head of steam on this short strip," Berto yelled over the noise. There's power lines over the trees there."

They looked damn close as the plane shot forward and bumped across the cratered tarmac. Watching the trees rush closer I had a serious case of fugitive's remorse.

"Hold on baby! Berto called joyfully as if we were on a carnival ride.

A second before we smashed into the tree line Berto leaned back and the plane nosed straight up. Suddenly it was quiet and we were airborne.

When my stomach dropped back to my abdomen I took a deep breath. "That cut it close."

Berto nodded cheerfully. "We're a bit overweight."

I looked around but a curtain walled off the back of the plane. However I picked up a familiar scent.

"What's our cargo?"

"Weed," Berto chuckled, "about a ton."

What the hell. I was looking at life in the slam anyway.

As we gained altitude Berto tilted the plane and made a left turn.

"Where are we headed?"

"Chicago. You're gonna need some breathing room."

"Maybe I could use some anger management."

"Not as far as I'm concerned. That bastard Zallen killed Suarez in cold blood."

"Do you know why?"

He gave me a hard look. "Suarez was winning too many cases in court."

"There must be lots of other immigration lawyers."

"Not really. Immigration courts are different. They're not required to provide an attorney. There's ten year old kids being tried without representation. Suarez and his pro bono team were out to change that. And they were doing a good job. That's why they hit him with that phony meth charge."

I settled back in my seat feeling slightly better. "Can this buggy make to Chicago non-stop?"

"This is a De Havilland twin otter. Best crate in the air." Berto said proudly. I installed an extra gas tank to increase its range. We should make it."

"Should? Have you done it before?"

"First time," Berto said, lighting a J. "But I'm confident."

That made one of us.

"Yeah can you believe it? Kids on trial, no lawyer, no English, no chance. Detention, deportation, maybe worse... Hell I didn't risk my ass in 'Nam for this." He passed me the joint. "You did the right thing."

I had done hard time myself in Kuwait to save our democracy. Or so I thought. But it was all about oil then. And maybe still was. "This ICE scam is right out of the Nazi playbook," I said exhaling a cloud of smoke. "Problem is the fix goes up to the top."

"How far?"

I passed the joint. "Don't know yet."

"Might be too big for one guy."

At the moment I had no choice. If I ever hoped to draw a free breath I had to nuke their operation. My main weapon was Boutilier – If he lasted long enough.

I thought about Selena Suarez flying back with a young daughter and her husband's corpse. And Mrs. Canseco left to raise a family on her own. I thought about Zallen, Goldsmith, Bannon and the others who imposed brute tragedy on innocent lives for no other reason than profit. Then there was Petrov and Berlinski, arch fucking criminals with ties to the White House. Talk about a swamp.

But where was the bloody cash? I still hadn't found it.

I remembered what Mrs. Canseco said. Her husband's dying words, "...find bite money".

And I had an idea.

"This is very good pot," I said.

Berto grinned. "Humboldt's finest."

"Should bring a nice price."

He gave me a shrewd look. "Sidney says you're DEA."

"Retired. Anyway weed is practically legal."

"Nine states. Twenty nine have Medical Marijuana. They've even got the ex-Speaker of the House on the board of a new Cannabis corporation. But they're still busting black kids. Fucking hypocrites."

"Hypocrisy is America's leading export."

"You a philosopher too?"

"Just an observer."

"A third of the profits here go to the AFJ."

"Which is...?"

"Attorneys For Justice, Sidney's team of pro bono warriors."

"Good cause."

"Least I can do. Sidney got me out of a jam few years back."

I didn't ask for details. If they caught up to me I doubted I'd ever see a courtroom.

For the next few hours Berto busied himself with piloting the Otter, occasionally pointing out places of interest below.

"Get ready for a bumpy landing," Berto said presently.

"Can't be worse than the take off."

Berto grinned. "At least back there we had a tarmac."

"Where are we setting down?" I said, trying to keep my voice calm.

"Small field northwest of Chicago crop dusters use."

In fifteen minutes the plane began to circle an area the size and shape of a block of postage stamps. Alarmingly, as we rapidly descended those stamps didn't get much larger. Berto came in fast, threading a space between six tiny corn fields. We touched down hard, wheels squealing when he braked.

I heard the slap of the wings slicing stalks of corn as the plane lifted and slammed back onto the dirt gap, throwing me forward against my seat belt and snapping my neck. Abruptly the wheels screeched and the Otter nosed to the ground, threatening to go belly up before it skidded forward and stopped.

Suddenly four men emerged from the corn field and ran towards us. Dazed, I thought it might be a SWAT team. They went to the rear of the plane and silently began unloading the cargo. As I climbed out a dusty truck drove up behind us followed by an SUV.

Berto left the cockpit and motioned me over to the SUV. He told the driver to join the loaders and got behind the wheel.

"Where to?" Berto said.

"Any motel that takes cash."

Berto sighed. "Okay, I've got a safe house in the city you can use for twenty four hours. After that it's booked. But it has everything you'll need."

When I used the key Berto gave me I saw what he meant by 'everything you'll need'. The tiny two room flat had a bed, a TV, a glass, a half bottle of scotch, and in the refrigerator, a bag of weed. I bought a pizza and coke from a joint up the block and settled down for the day.

I switched on the news and was so disgusted I almost threw up my deep dish pie. The administration had set up internment camps for kids forcibly separated from their immigrant parents.

The new Auschwitz.

For children.

To numb my outrage I began working on the scotch. I fell asleep with the TV on and woke up to the sound of the door buzzer.

It was Berto. He held up a large paper bag.

"I bought you breakfast and bad news."

I opened the bag. Inside was an egg and bacon sandwich, two large containers of coffee and a couple of jelly donuts.

"So what's the bad news?" I said as I wolfed down the sandwich.

"You've got an hour to vacate the premises."

"Any good news?"

"How'd you like to make twenty grand?"

"Doing what?"

"Drive a load of weed to New York."

I was headed that way anyway and I had left most of my money with Nina.

"Truck?"

"Brand new Escalade with a hundred kilos in the panels."

"Lot of money for a driver."

"At five grand a pound wholesale, you do the math."

After coffee and a quick shower I left the flat and found Berto waiting in a shiny, black urban assault vehicle. The Escalade was luxurious but I missed the tight suspension and special amenities of my custom Mercury. Especially the stash panel for my Sig Sauer.

Along with the keys Berto gave me a business card.

"Go to this place and deliver the car to Manny. Nobody else understand? He's got your money."

I understood the money part very clearly. After dropping him off I was on my way east to the Big Apple, the city where I died on 9/11.

+      +      +

Traveling across *Reefer Madness* states with a hundred kilos and a loaded gun requires diplomatic driving.

For this reason I confined myself mainly to commuter and business hours on the road when there was less chance of a cop stopping me out of sheer boredom. However I wished Berto had chosen a vehicle less identified with hip-hop gangsters. Still, the car was roomy and comfortable even if it would be worthless in a police chase.

I headed northeast for Detroit and stopped at a motel that accepted cash. Early the next morning I drove to Boston. I had elected to come into the city from Massachusetts rather than Philly. There was good reason for taking the circuitous route. It's well known that law enforcement lies in wait on the Jersey Turnpike for unsuspecting mules carrying drugs up from Miami.

Along the way the radio news was mostly bad. Kids in cages, alienating our close allies, tearing apart the country's social fabric, blatant corruption: there seemed to be no end to the cynical abuses of power. After a while I opted for easy listening.

I rolled into New York without incident and went directly to the address Berto had given me. My destination was a grimy auto repair shop on the lower West Side, in a neighborhood which had successfully eluded gentrification. It was located next to an industrial yard with a large sign that read Red Ball Demolition.

When I pulled up to the repair shop a short, muscular man wearing greasy overalls came out to greet me. He had a shaved head and a flat, unfriendly stare. He was trailed by a tall, thin punk type with spiked hair, holding a crow bar. His white T-shirt and skinny black jeans were spotless. Obviously an executive.

They watched me warily as I climbed down from the Escalade.

"Manny here?" I said, using the name Berto had given me. Berto's instruction had been short but strict.

The muscular man stepped closer. The red, script letters stitched on his overalls spelled Nacho.

"Manny ain't here. I'm in charge until he get's back."

"When will he be back?"

"Two weeks." The exec said, moving closer. "He's on vacation."

I smiled. "Well I guess I'll come back then."

The short man gave me that nasty, you're-my-bitch stare. "Look I'll take care of the car. Like I said, I'm in charge."

After the long road trip the Preacher was surly and easily riled. Still, I kept smiling. My motto: never commit a misdemeanor on your way to committing a felony.

"That's cool," I said. "Only one problem."

The short man shrugged. "What's the problem?"

"What about my money?–the deal is C.O.D."

The two men glanced at each other. The exec tapped the crow bar against his palm and stepped closer.

"Hey pal we're wasting time here. Just leave the fucking car and Manny will pay you off when he gets back. He's good for it, no problem."

"I don't know..."

As I spoke the exec stepped even closer.

Too close.

I snatched the bar from his hand and tapped him hard across the cheek. He didn't fall but gaped in stunned amazement.

Behind me I heard the raspy slide and lock of a shotgun being cocked.

Fucking overalls. You can conceal a SAM missile in those floppy pants.

Without hesitation I spun, whipping the iron bar shoulder high, and swatted his shaved skull. He dropped to his knees then rolled to the ground.

I took a quick look around. The street was deserted.

I picked up the shotgun and gestured to the exec. "Grab his ankles and get him inside."

A bit wobbly, the thin dude dragged his unconscious buddy into the garage.

"Okay let's start over. Where's Manny?"

"We told you Manny's on..."

I slapped his shin with a crowbar.

He yowled and began hopping on one foot.

"We can do this all day, where's Manny?"

"Okay, fuck okay He's in the pit."

I hefted the bar. "Where?"

"The pit." He pointed wildly to the rear of the garage. "The fucking pit."

"Show me."

He hobbled to the back and stood beside an old-fashioned grease pit. At the bottom a large man sat against the wall, hands and feet bound and his mouth taped.

"Cut him loose."

With exaggerated effort the exec crawled down and began untying the man's feet. Then he untied the man's hands and helped him up.

The man was big, maybe six-five, with a fringe of long, black hair around his bald dome. His hefty torso filled out his overalls. For a moment he stood, swaying from side to side. Suddenly the big man whirled and unleashed a powerful right hook that caught the exec smack on his jaw. The thin man crumpled nose down, smearing his face and white T-shirt with black grease.

Then big man ripped the tape off his mouth and glared at me. "And who the fuck are you?"

"Friend of Berto's."

His glare dissolved into a broad grin. He vaulted out of the pit and extended a thick hand. "Nice going friend. Where's the other one?"

"Sleeping it off." I gesture toward the entrance.

"Let's get him inside." He went over to the unconscious man, dragged him back to the pit and dumped him inside. "They'll keep until my boys arrive. You got a name?"

"Max."

"Okay Max let's get you squared away, then I'll deal with those assholes."

"He one of yours?"

"Who?"

"The guy with the shotgun. Nacho."

"That ain't Nacho. That's Nicky Melons. He put on the overalls when you got here. Dumb bastard thinks he can take over my turf. The other shithead is my brother-in-law, if you can believe it."

He led me into a small, messy office. As soon as we entered he picked up his land line phone. I noticed a grey metal device shaped like a cigar box next to his phone. I recognized it as a sophisticated scrambler. Not CIA grade but very good.

"Nacho? It's here. Bring the crew. And call Carmine. We got a roach problem."

He gave me a big smile and reached down. His brow furrowed in concentration as he fumbled with something under his desk. I heard a metallic squeak and a few minutes later he emerged with five banded stacks of cash which he tossed on the desk.

"Twenty five grand delivery fee."

"Bert said twenty."

"The extra five is for saving my ass. Who knows what those dumb bastards were planning. Anything else you need?"

"I could use a place to crash."

He picked up the phone and punched some numbers. "Joe? It's me. I'm sending a guy to stay for the night. Get the place ready."

He wrote down an address and gave it to me. "It's two blocks away. Come back tomorrow and I'll have something better. Leave the shotgun here."

Before handing the weapon over I wiped it clean of prints.

Manny gave me an approving nod. "You must be a pro. See you mañana."

The Spanish word made me homesick. I took the address and hauled my bags to the new digs.

The short walk left me weary. After a long drive and an adrenaline spike I was ready for bed.

The building looked as if it had been around since the Dutch owned the real estate. When I was buzzed in however it became a new era. Surveillance cameras dotted the hall above a carpeted stairway that led to a steel door.

"Who's there?" A voice squawked over an electronic speaker.

"Manny sent me over."

I heard a bolt slide and the door opened.

Standing there was a slim brunette, perhaps twenty five and extremely attractive with straight black hair that framed her blue eyes and pouty red lips.

"Is Joe here?" I said.

"I'm Jo without the 'e'. Who are you again?"

I extended my hand. "Max. Manny said I could crash here tonight."

She took my hand briefly and gave me a penetrating glance.

"Yeah, okay. Just for the night. You want some coffee?"

Without waiting for an answer she bolted the door and headed for the kitchen. Bags in hand I followed. She set two cups on the table and took a pot off the stove.

"So what's your story?" She said, pouring the coffee.

"I just drove in from Chicago."

She brightened. "Which means I'm real busy tomorrow."

"Hey don't worry. I'll be gone in the morning."

"No worries. I meant I'm really real busy tomorrow. I'm Manny's elite boutique.'

I understood. Jo was one of Manny's distributers.

"More of a salon really," she mused. She was wearing a paint-splotched T-shirt and torn jeans that probably cost five hundred bucks.

"Jay-Z will be over in a shot once I call him. Maybe Beyonce too."

"Well give them my best. I'll be long gone by then."

"Lots of cool fun," she said, making it sound like an invitation.

I shrugged. "I'm booked."

"Yeah, who's your agent?"

"Life." I sipped my coffee. It was excellent.

I said, "This is good coffee."

"You've got taste. I'm a coffee gourmand."

"I come from coffee heaven." I immediately regretted the remark. True, San Francisco has two or three cafes per block but it was unique that way. Jo picked up on it right away.

"Chicago? Coffee? I thought it was deep dish pizza."

"Seattle." A man in my position couldn't afford to be candid. "You an artist?" I said, changing the subject.

She waved a self-deprecating hand. "I try. My friend says I have talent."

"Who's your friend?"

"Schnabel. He's a good client. By the way are you holding?"

"Just my personal stash." I reached into my flight bag and came up with the weed Berto had given me.

Jo expertly rolled three joints. She lit up and took a deep, contemplative drag.

"Tastes nice." She passed the J. "A hit?"

It seemed rude to refuse.

Top grade weed will get one high on one or two hits and after my third I declined a fourth. Jo too set the J in an ashtray from Hong Fat's Chinese restaurant.

"This is superb bud," she said, voice low and respectful. "Is this what you brought Manny?"

"Don't know. But it's from the same source."

"New York will be happy."

"Could you show me where I crash? It's been a long drive."

"Oh. Sure." She sounded disappointed. "I've got a small guestroom right off my studio."

Jo's studio was large, sunny and cluttered. There were two easels with paintings propped up on them. I had to agree with Schnabel. Both works displayed strong, sure lines with classic grace blended with a modernist's sense of color and surprise.

I was equally impressed with the small, windowless guestroom. It had all the amenities including TV and an adjoining bath.

The first thing I did was take a long, hot shower. Right after that I hit the sack. My last thoughts were of Nina and Samantha. When I woke up it was dark.

I checked my watch, two a.m..

For the rest of the night I stared at the ceiling watching home movies of my family. When I can't sleep I count my mistakes instead of sheep.

I was up and out by seven. I found a greasy spoon that opened early and lingered over breakfast while I read the papers.

The news was all bad. The administration was waging an all-out blitzkrieg on the truth while children lay in cages, separated from their families for the crime of seeking refuge.

Jeff Sessions even quoted the Bible to justify the action.

In desperation I turned to the sports section.

When I arrived at Manny's garage I was surprised to see the thin, spike haired guy there. He was sporting overalls and a large blue contusion on the side of his face. He glared at me and vanished in the rear of the shop.

"He's still working here?" I said to Manny.

He spread his big hands. "What can I do? Like I said he's my brother-in-law. Don't worry, after he saw what we did to Nicky Melons he'll be a good boy, know what I'm sayin'?"

I shrugged, not wanting to know.

"So what do you need? Manny said briskly, "After yesterday I owe you."

"Still could use a place to stay."

He squinted, studying me with bemused curiosity, like a gorilla regarding an armadillo.

"Jo's ain't good enough?"

"She's a nice kid but I need privacy."

"I know what you mean. Jo likes her social life."

He reached into his overalls and took out a set of keys. "This my own personal man cave. If anybody asks you're my cousin from Milwaukee. It's rent controlled."

He dangled the keys. "A month tops. When you go leave these on the kitchen table."

Man Cave was an apt description of Manny's tiny second floor walk-up on the fringe of the lower west side. Kitchen, living room, bedroom, in that order. Flat screen TV in each room, racing forms, and *Playboy* magazines scattered about, I was pleased to see a Mac computer on a small desk in the corner of the bedroom. I opened the fridge and found assorted cold cuts and three six packs of Fosters. The cabinet above the sink housed a bottle of Laphroaig single malt scotch. There were ashtrays on each table. I put my bags in the bedroom, sat on a sagging easy chair and took a deep breath aware of a strange exhilaration.

I was back in New York.

It was crisp, sunny morning so I decided to take a walk. I headed east through the heart of Greenwich Village. Bleeker Street, Mac Dougal Alley, Sullivan Street, Prince Street: they all evoked memories. I stopped to watch a basketball game at the outdoor court on Sixth Avenue. Some of the best players in the city came to that court. I played that court myself while I was point guard for Columbia University. It was there I scored my first pound of marijuana which I sold in the dorms.

Eventually I was busted and kicked out of school. A sympathetic judge gave me a choice – jail or military service. I chose the Marines. To my disappointment they assigned me to computers after Parris Island. I had majored in computer engineering at Columbia but I was young, dumb and read too much Hemingway. Using my computer skills I finagled my way into a combat unit.

The sight of my first mangled, charred body tamped down my enthusiasm. I left the Corps a devout cynic.

It turned out to be a long walk, taking me all the way to the East River. Watching an ancient barge crawl through the sun streaked water I came up with a crude plan. Its only downside was that it required me to walk straight into the lion's mouth. If I guessed wrong the jaws would snap and I'd be doing life. Which in my case meant less than a year in the slam before some amped up Vandal parked a shank in my belly.

On my way back I stopped for a meatball hero at a pizza joint that had been there since 1940. Cutting through Tompkins Square Park the air was alive with the chirping of children at play. I couldn't help thinking of Samantha and my mood darkened. I stopped a few times to pick up supplies and arrived at the apartment in the early afternoon.

It was dark when I finished setting up my equipment. I had piggy-backed on Manny's system which seemed to be mostly for gambling records and porn. I poured a celebratory scotch. Tomorrow would be the beginning–or quick conclusion–of my new life.

I awoke the next morning with a slight hangover and made a mental note to pick up a fresh bottle of Laphroaig. Manny's supply had been considerably diminished.

After a long shower climaxed with a burst of ice cold water, I dressed and went out for breakfast. Three coffees and two bagels later, I began to walk uptown.

I dawdled along the way, like a schoolboy on his way to the principal's office to answer for a grave offense.

Finally I arrived.

I took a deep breath and marched into the Northeastern Headquarters of the Drug Enforcement Agency.

# Chapter 16

There were two assistants at the computers and a receptionist at the door to the outer office. All female.

Director Alvin Delany always did have an eye for the ladies.

Including my ex-wife.

I smiled at the pert blonde receptionist. "Would you tell Mr. Delaney Sam Devine is here to see him?" I said, using the name that died with me on 9/11.

She seemed disconcerted. "Do you have...?"

"No appointment. But I'm sure he'll want to see me."

Despite her doubts she called anyway. To her credit the only reaction was a slight lift of her brows when she heard Delaney's response.

"He'll see you Mr. Devine. I'll show you..."

She started to rise but I was already past her desk. "I know the way thanks."

As I ambled to Delaney's office I went over what I would say. When I entered he was standing with his back to the door.

"Shut it behind you." he said.

He turned slowly, extending his hand. Except it wasn't a handshake. He had a snub-nosed .38 pointed at my chest.

"You're under arrest. Let's see your hands."

I waved him off and sat down. "Put it away Alvin. There's a reason I'm here."

"Yeah, you're a fucking lunatic. He dropped the gun in his pocket and moved behind the desk. "I just received a priority dispatch that claims a rogue DEA operative called Max killed an ICE agent who was performing his duty. You are top banana on Homeland Security's hit list."

"You mean Langley hasn't called?"

"Matter of fact they did. They threatened me with a senate investigation."

"Let me guess. Was his name Jenkins?"

He squinted suspiciously making him look like a cross between a bulldog and J. Edgar Hoover.

"How did you know?"

"He's dirty. So is the agent I shot. This goes all the way to Capitol Hill."

I gave him the details: Lowell's request, the Suarez killing, the fat payoffs, the murders of Berry and Canseco, how I shot Goldsmith, the Berlinski connection and the circumstances when I killed Zallen. I didn't mention the degree of Kingman's involvement.

It took a while. Halfway through Delaney took off his suit jacket and began pacing the floor.

"Jesus – what the fuck did you get me into?"

"You? I'm the one marked for extinction."

"And I get all the fallout. ICE is Washington's fair haired child, huge budgets..." he paused at the chair where he'd hung his coat "...they'd eat us alive and spit me out into forced retirement. And those senate hearings get nasty."

He dipped his hand into his coat pocket and came up with the .38. No, it's better all round if I turn you in."

"Don't be stupid Alvin. What happens when they find out you listed me as deceased on 9/11 and married my widow and a shitload of death insurance?"

He flushed. "Still not over it are you?"

"Actually I am but the press and politicians will never get over it. You'll become a catch phrase like 'I got Delaneyed'."

I watched the .38 lower to his side.

"I think I have a way that covers us both."

Delaney put the gun back in his pocket and sat down. "I'm listening."

"Hire me on a six month contract starting two days ago."

He drummed his fingers on the desk. "On what basis?"

"Those pricey ICE cattle cars are flying in every night from Mexico. No sign of customs."

"Drugs?"

"That's the least of it. And we can bring it down."

"We? If I do this you're still on your own. You know that."

"I never doubted your disloyal ass for a second Alvin. And while you're busy not helping me check out this Berlinski character. He's come up in the world."

I hung around until the formalities were completed then left the building with a signed contract that gave me the right to bear firearms.

Retroactive.

Which covered my indiscretions over the past few weeks.

Walking back to Manny's I stopped at a men's clothing shop and selected a blazer, shirt, tie, and grey flannel trousers. My evening destination required a dress code.

The first thing I did when I got back to the pad was unpack my Sig and stash it a convenient location. The long walk and my dealings with Delaney had tired me out so I lay on the couch and switched on the TV.

It was night when I woke up. The digital clock on the cable box read 9:47. Good timing. Deacon Weary's salon doesn't open its doors until well past eleven.

Shortly before midnight, dressed in my newly acquired outfit I went out in search of a cab. The necktie was uncomfortable but showing up in my usual black T and Levis wouldn't do. At the Deacon's you might run into the mayor, a senator, the occasional Cartel don, movie stars, newscasters, high end call girls, various criminals, all sorts of power brokers and, of course, slick lawyers. For me, the necktie was a neat disguise.

My new look was no help in finding a cab. Despite gentrification New York cabbies are still reluctant to go to Harlem but a flat fee of forty bucks convinced my driver.

Out of respect for the Deacon's privacy I had the cab drop me a block from Weary's townhouse.

As I approached I saw a couple of men leaning against a parked car. I knew they were there to make sure the limos waited somewhere else.

The three-story townhouse stood in the middle of the block. A short stairway led to a well-lit door. But that wasn't the way inside.

Shadowed by the front stairs was a set of steps that went down to the service entrance.

I rang and after a few moments the door opened onto a steel cubicle armed with security cameras and metal detectors. As I stepped inside, the door clicked shut behind me. I waited while I was photographed and scanned, knowing that if I didn't pass muster I wouldn't be allowed to leave.

Deacon Weary didn't tolerate gate crashers.

I earned my all-access pass years back in a situation similar to the one I had recently experienced with my new friend Manny.

Some time before my premature death on 9/11, while still an undercover employee of the DEA, I arranged a heroin buy from a dealer called Big Benny. My contact was a junkie called Cuda aka Barracuda.

Cuda set me up. Instead of two keys of smack Benny came up with an UZI.

When the smoke cleared Big Benny was dead and I found Deacon Weary handcuffed in the back of Benny's Mercedes, with an attaches case full of cash in the front seat. I freed Weary and sent him home with his money. After that I became one of Weary's elite associates. As his influence grew so did mine. For a DEA agent his contacts were invaluable.

Weary dubbed me Angel and the name stuck. I didn't mind.

You can't have enough aliases in my business.

The Deacon met me at the elevator door. Except for the grey streaks in his hair he hadn't changed. Tall and loose limbed he carried himself with regal grace. He wore and elegantly understated suit but as I glanced around the room I realized my fashion sense was out of date. Two thirds of the guests were dressed in California casual. The rest were mostly in black.

Weary's gold-flecked eyes gave me a quick pat down. "Damn Angel. You look great."

The three ages of man: *youth, middle age you look great.*

He grinned and moved in for a hug. "Where you been all this time, a health farm?"

Actually, Marin County is the world's biggest convalescent home.

"I just dropped my bad habits."

"Well it worked brother. Make yourself at home. Let me know if there's something you need."

"Perhaps we could take a meeting."

"No problem. Let me take care of my guests first. The bar is over there, food's over here. And if you decide to revisit some bad habits, Terry's over there."

On my way to the bar I scanned the room. Terry was deep in conversation with a tall, older man with slicked back silver hair. If she noticed my entrance she made no sign.

Just as well. We had a history.

The knot of young people at the bar had the hand moves and exaggerated body angles of dedicated hip hoppers. They gave me a cursory glance and turned away.

To them I was just another necktie. I ordered a scotch then moved on.

Weary was nowhere in sight, obviously holding court in his private den. I nursed my drink and looked for a spot to sit it out while I waited my turn. Then I saw Terry waving me over.

The years had favored Terry. Honey skin, aqua eyes and a body by Corvette, she was still stunning by any standard. And she still had the same bad habits.

Terry was a boutique coke dealer who supplied premium blow to a select clientele.

"Angel baby, where have you been hiding? I've missed you."

"I've been out of the country."

I kissed her cheek and settled beside her.

She leaned closer. "Have you been cheating on me?"

I inhaled her musky scent. It was full of tempting memories. "Cheat on you? Never."

"I want to give you something." She whispered.

Coke? Sex? Back in my drug and alcohol heyday I'd be there, but I was a family man now.

I was bailed out by the serious young man wearing rimless glasses who came up to me and leaned into my other ear.

"Deacon Weary will see you now."

"Sorry Terry, business," I said quickly.

As I got up I felt a tug on my sleeve. Terry extended a red business card. "My number." She said, her aqua eyes locked on mine, "Use it soon."

I took the card and followed my escort to Weary's sanctum.

It hadn't changed much.

Weary sat in a plush leather chair behind a large mahogany desk. I remembered the chair and the desk. The only new item was a signed photograph of Weary seated beside President Obama at a black tie dinner. The Deacon headed an important tax-free ministry that could deliver key districts in times of need.

His hands were pressed together, prayer like. When I sat down he spread his palms and smiled.

"So my friend what brings you back after all these years?"

"Actually, the same thing as last time. You introduced me to a client. I lost touch and need another introduction. Back then he used the name Byron."

Weary nodded thoughtfully. "Byron's stock has climbed considerably since you met."

"Of course," I slid a five grand stack across the desk. "No problem."

He slid it back. "You already took care of the introduction. What I meant was that Byron is more difficult to contact. He's frequently in D.C."

"Sounds promising. "

Weary leaned forward and lowered his voice. "Step carefully Angel. The man is said to be a psycho."

"Aren't they all?"

"This cat is of another stripe. Takes things to the extreme."

"Thanks, I'll bear it in mind."

Weary fished a phone from his desk and pushed it towards me. "You'll get a call. When you do lose the phone."

I scooped up the burner. "I know the drill."

"Don't forget the cash."

"Thanks Deacon, let me know if you need anything."

"You always were stand up Angel. A rare quality these days."

Praise ringing in my ear I went back to the bar thinking I'd have another scotch and leave.

The rappers were still ignoring me. I turned and saw a vaguely familiar man staring at me. The older dude who'd been chatting up Terry. He nodded and lifted his glass. I nodded politely.

A mistake.

He jumped on the nod like a hungry shark and came closer.

"Hello I'm Georgio."

"Angel."

"That Terry is something, isn't she."

I shrugged. "Haven't seen her in years."

"Oh, been away?"

Georgio was beginning to annoy me. I drained my scotch and gave him a terse smile.

"Yes, Europe." I turned away hoping to avoid further conversation. To my surprise one of the rappers gave me a friendly nod. "What's up dog?"

"Not much. Actually I'm on my way out," I added, loud enough for Georgio to hear.

He grinned, revealing gold incisors. "Y'all roll safe now, heah?"

Grabbing the cue I moved directly to the elevator. Once outside I began walking in search of a cab. Three blocks later I hadn't seen one.

As I walked I became aware of two men a short distance behind me on the other side of the street. I stopped to light a cigarette. They paused. That convinced me.

I was being stalked.

Cursing, I braced myself. My ribs were barely recovered from the late Paul Zallen's kick.

An SUV came up beside me. The window rolled down and the driver smiled at me. I recognized the gold incisors. In the street light he looked like a bionic vampire.

"My man. Need a ride? Hop in."

I climbed into a cloud of weed. I sat next to my host. The rear was occupied by a huge black dude with blonde dreads who was smoking a joint the size of a small cigar. He passed me the J.

"Mos got y'self jacked," he noted gently.

I took a hit and was instantly high. "Those two across the street? Maybe."

Both my new pals chuckled. "I'm Snappy Jack," the driver said, taking the joint, "my man back there is King Bong."

"They call me Angel."

"Okay Angel, where we goin'?"

"West twenty third, the Chelsea Hotel."

The J was passed again. Jack pressed a button and a sinuous industrial beat filled the car. Someone started rapping in a deep drone.

"How long you know that cat Georgio?"

Jack's casual question filtered through a haze of smoke and sound.

Never saw him before. You?"

"I seen him around."

His tone carried a hint of scorn.

"Friendly guy."

The big man snorted. "Yeah real friendly."

I realized it was his voice rapping on the sound system. We rode the rest of the way in silence except for King Bong's big bass drawl over the lazy beat.

"Catch you on the rebound Angel." Jack said, as I exited the car.

"Yeah, later."

I waited until he was gone then took a cab to Manny's hideaway.

You can't be too paranoid.

+        +        +

About noon the next day the Deacon called. "You're a popular guy Angel. Three people inquired about you this morning."

"Really, who?"

"Terry of course, Georgio Amanti, and Snappy Jack."

"Quite a range."

"Byron was most anxious to hear from you."

He gave me the number and hung up. I called Berlinski, aka Byron immediately.

"Angel, my old friend I'm glad you called. Can we meet tonight?'

"Very good. When and where?"

"I'm having a party. Please be my guest."

He gave me a Park Avenue address. One more night in a suit.

That done, I went out for a late breakfast. New York was enjoying Indian Summer and the balmy weather lifted my spirits. The holidays were near and the city was out in full force. I drank a third coffee and watched the world roll by.

Then I saw a young couple, the man carrying a little girl piggyback on his shoulders, and my psyche went into free fall.

My wife and daughter were three thousand miles away and I had no idea when – or if – I would see them again. I spent the rest of the day staring at the tube, a scotch in one hand, a joint in the other.

When I arrived at Berlinski's little party at his Fifth Avenue penthouse I was in a foul mood. I had even brought along my Sig Sauer.

A tall, Nordic type with shoulders that stretched his pale blue suit opened the door and looked me over carefully.

I nodded and moved past him

The place was crowded and noisy. I spotted Byron across the room chatting up a couple of young ladies.

I headed directly for them, the blonde dude close behind. He elbowed me aside and took a position between me and my host.

Byron seemed annoyed. "Andre, what the fuck."

"Mr. Berlinski, he's packing."

The two ladies edged away.

"Really?" Byron, said calmly. "Is that true Angel?"

"Of course. Is that a problem?"

Byron smiled. "Only if I see it."

The blonde man decided to be an asshole. "I can hold it for him Mr. Berlinski." He said, blue eyes fixed on me."

"You've been very efficient Andre, but it won't be necessary. Angel and I are old friends." He patted my arm and steered me towards a wine bar but I could feel Andre's eyes on my back.

The bar was attended by a pretty redhead who didn't look old enough to drink.

"Please forgive Andre. He's young and eager. Champagne my friend?"

"Why not."

The wine came in a crystal flute. As I sipped I scanned the room which was decorated in white Deco, reminiscent of a Fred Astaire movie. The men were older and reeked of success. The girls sleek and very young. Everything in the penthouse was expensive: the wine, the white furniture, the girls, the fucking suits.

"So Angel, we meet at a good time"

"How so?"

"I have need of your special product."

"Which one?"

He leaned closer and I caught the scent of expensive cologne. "Heroin, a kilo."

I made a quick calculation. "Three hundred K."

He gave me a disbelieving smile. "Expensive."

"Isn't everything these days?"

"I assume it's pure."

"Always."

He lifted his glass. "Nothing is always my friend."

He was smiling but the threat was clear.

I said

"I'll call with the details."

"No. Better details now. No phone talk."

"Good. You remember our first meet?"

"Yes. P.J. Clarke."

"Meet me there Friday at noon."

"That's the day after tomorrow."

"Do you need more time to gather the cash?" I said, just to needle him.

It worked. His smile dropped and his chest inflated. "I can give it to you now."

"I can wait."

I mistook his sudden grin for humor until I saw it was directed at a willowy blonde model behind me.

"Excuse me," he said curtly and hurried to join her leaving me to finish my champagne and get a refill.

I began to wander. Out of habit I checked for security cameras. There were four. I recognized the pattern. Berlinski had installed commercial equipment, very easy to disable.

As I paused to examine a splashy painting by Leroy Neiman I glimpsed a familiar face. My favorite coke dealer, Terry. I caught her eye but she turned away. The I saw the tall, silver-haired man trailing her as she threaded through the crowd. Georgio.

I wondered what Terry saw in the oily motherfucker. Of course like politics the drug business breeds strange bedfellows.

A loud, rough laugh drew my attention. I turner and saw a bald, burly man smack a tall brunette's skinny ass. To my surprise the brunette's only reaction was a vague smile. I edged closer and saw her pupils were pinned. Dilated from some opioid or another.

Then I saw Georgio weaving his way in my general direction and took it as my cue to leave.

Andre was still lurking near the door and when I approached our eyes collided like Summo wrestlers. He smiled and nodded and I did the same but we both knew we would meet again.

# Chapter 17

Delaney hated to fly.

Which was why he was sipping coffee in the dining car of the Acela express train headed for Washington D.C.. Plenty of leg room, no annoying shoe searches, comfortable lounge chairs, and the train deposited him in the center of the city at Union Station.

Normally he would have enjoyed the scenic trip. But today he was on his way to being grilled, chewed out or possibly fired by his boss, National Director of the DEA, Carter Osborne.

And all because of Max.

I should have shot him when I had the chance, Delaney thought glumly. Then I'd be heading for a promotion instead of a dressing down.

Problem was Max wouldn't have come in unless he had something solid. Personal fuck ups aside the bastard was the best in the business. And he was honest.

Which made him a liability, Delaney reflected. Or an ace in the hole. Either way, he had forty days before the axe fell.

"Forty days!"

Carter Osborn III looked like he had swallowed a grapefruit. "Are you freaking insane?" he said, voice strangled and eyes bulging.

Delaney examined his knuckles, waiting for the tirade to blow over.

"Do you realize what's happening? Osborne went on, "our budget is being cut to..." He struggled to find the right word "...to crap!"

Osborne was a Mormon and frowned on swearing. He was also a self-righteous prick, Delaney observed calmly. His boss had never been a field agent. He came from the administrative side – a numbers cruncher who had never heard a shot fired in anger. Consequently, he did not share the same code as a combat vet in the war against drugs.

The son of a two-time Senator, Osborne grew up in the halls of power. Following graduation from Princeton he joined the DEA, rose rapidly through and the ranks and it came as no surprise when he was named head of the agency.

Delaney came from Mission Hill, a tough Boston neighborhood. After graduating from Boston U he became a cop. After a few years on the street he joined the DEA and distinguished himself as an undercover agent. When he helped bring down Alphonso Sosa, a cartel kingpin, he was finally appointed section chief. Years later he was named Northeast Director. A slow, hard climb.

"You need to bring your boy in and turn him over to Homeland," Osborne was saying.

Delaney looked up. "First of all he's not my boy he's our boy. And even if we turn him in today the Agency winds up with a black eye the size of Brazil."

"We have no choice."

"Actually we do. Our boy has evidence of a corrupt operation being run by ICE and a faction of the CIA. If he's right we'll end up with a citation and a healthy budget bump."

"Or a massive cut. We can't..."

"Look, we know our Moron-in-Chief is pouring money into ICE, Border Security and the ATF trying to build his own private Gestapo. The bastards want to militarize Homeland Security. Either way we get nothing unless we break a case big enough to make the six o'clock news. So which is it, sure black eye or a shot at redemption?"

After a long silence Osborne nodded reluctantly.

"Forty days. If this thing blows up our jobs blow up with it."

You mean my job, Delaney thought.

Later on the train back to New York Delaney wondered how he had become so fucking stupid. He had deliberately put his own head on the chopping block. And Osborne was itching to swing that axe.

Had been for years, Delaney brooded. They had butted heads often over the years. Mainly over Osborne's favorite topic.

The almighty budget.

He drained his second glass of wine and ordered another, trying to stave off depression. He had risked his career on a quasi-criminal defector from the Agency—who held a grudge against him. Why the fuck did he do that?

Years back he had an affair with Max's wife and later married her. In the process he had Max brought up on charges. True Max's wife was estranged, true Max was heavily using drugs.

But that didn't change jack shit. He had back-stabbed a comrade in arms.

It did solve the riddle however Delaney mused, staring unhappily at his empty glass.

Guilt.

Fucking guilt will make you as stupid as a concrete wall.

But if Max stumbled.

Even a half-step.

Delaney would turn him in to Osborne quicker than a hiccup.

He wasn't that stupid.

# Chapter 18

Delaney agreed to my request without argument.

Which made me suspicious.

Keeping one eye over my shoulder I picked up my package at an Agency drop, a seedy Bodega on the Lower East Side. I gave the clerk the code number and took a shopping bag from below the counter.

I took a circuitous route back stopping to buy two pre-paid phones.

Once home I examined the merch.

Heroin was never my specialty. In the old days I was merely a dabbler, known in the trade as having a 'chippie,' mainly to offset the coke. But in my role as a professional dealer I was obligated to inspect the product.

The H came in a tightly compressed brick encased in clear plastic. Using a sharp paring knife I cut a small slit in the plastic and drew out a sample.

I dropped the powder on my tongue.

It was very bitter. And slightly grainy.

It also left my tongue a bit numb.

There was a speck of white on the tip of the knife. Absently I snorted it.

For the next three hours I sat in front of a blank TV screen, the remote in my limp hand.

When recovered I certified it as primo grade smack.

Later I activated one of the fresh burners and called Byron aka Berlinski.

"Angel here."

"Angel you have a new number."

"Every week"

"I like that. Wise man."

"Right now I'm bearing Frankincense."

"Good. Tonight. Same place." He hung up.

I didn't like it. Too many cameras around his place. I lit a J and tried to come up with a simple plan.

The weed perked up my appetite. Still pondering I built a sandwich from Manny's cold cut collection. I took a shower and while toweling off noticed a first-aid kit on a shelf. Problem solved.

I arrived at Byron's penthouse early hoping to avoid a crowd. But when Andre reluctantly ushered me in there was a healthy quorum of guests, mostly female.

Andre eyed my small bag suspiciously. I eyed him back.

"Tell Mr. Berlinski I'm here."

When he put down his phone I said, "Where's the restroom?"

He sneered and pointed, "Servant's quarters right over there."

I followed his dismissive finger to a closed door at the end of a short hall. Beyond was an alcove, bedroom and bath. It didn't seem that anyone lived there.

There were two cameras in the bathroom. Using the band-aids from Manny's first-aid kit I put them to sleep. Then I stashed the goods behind the shower curtain.

When I came out Andre was there.

"Mr Berlinski wants to see you now."

His emphasis on 'now' annoyed me but I trailed him through three large rooms to a double door. Along the way I noticed there were very few men at the party, just a surplus of languid young women who looked like they were in a perfume ad.

Andre opened the double door and I stepped into another era. Unline the slick décor of the rest of the penthouse the immense room resembled the library of a Victorian lord. Floor to ceiling bookshelves covered one wall complete with books and a rolling ladder. Oversized club chairs were arranged in a semi-circle around a massive carved wood desk. There was even a fucking fireplace. I half-expected to see medieval tapestries on the walls.

A pair of brawny louts lounged in the club chairs. They regarded me with ill-disguised contempt as I entered.

Berlinski sat behind the big desk, baronial in a bespoke blue pin stripe. He looked at me with surprise. "I thought you were bringing me a gift."

"Who are these people?"

"It's alright, I trust them."

"I don't. Please ask them to leave."

He shrugged and waved a dismissive hand.

The goons lurched to their feet and headed for the door.

Andre stayed behind.

I turned to him. "I took a quick shower in the servant's quarters."

His brow furrowed and he looked questioningly at his boss.

"Go check." Berlinski barked.

He shook his head. "Why Angel? I thought our appointment was at Clarkes."

"In this business never be predictable." He chuckled. "And you just left the goods in that room?"

"It was empty."

"From time to time my guests use the rooms here."

"Like a brothel?"

"That doesn't interest you."

It did but I let it go.

"I unlike unnecessary risks."

"And I don't like fucking cameras."

Andre bustled in. "It's here Mr. Berlinski."

I smiled. "Where's my money?"

"Of course, of course. Why don't you have a drink, enjoy the party. I'll have it for you in fifteen minutes."

Annoyed by his cavalier attitude I took a spin around the penthouse to cool down. In the drug business the accepted mode of payment is C.O.D. A lot can happen in fifteen minutes. I snatched a glass of wine from a passing tray and wandered through the plush digs.

It had a rec room with pool tables, a spacious deck with an outdoor grill attended by two chefs, a mini aquarium, plenty of bad art – think Hugh Hefner meets Kanye West. The languid young ladies seemed more animated, due perhaps to the wine, or the influx of well-dressed men. As I circled back I saw a familiar pair of aqua eyes.

Terry didn't seem happy to see me. Which made us even.

I lifted my glass and nodded, intending to move on but Terry stepped in my way.

"Surprise to see you here."

"Makes two of us. Actually I was heading out."

She gave me a sexy pout. "I was hoping we could talk."

"Sure is tomorrow…"

"Tonight." Her sudden smile came out of nowhere, like someone who knew they were being watched. "Call me in an hour, I'll be home."

"Yes alright but…" Still smiling she kissed me lightly on the cheek. "Please don't forget," she whispered, and walked away.

The brief encounter amped up my state of paranoia. Senses bristling I went back to Berlinski's lair.

Andre stood outside the double doors posturing in front of two skinny young ladies, probably models. He was wearing a shiny grey suit with those corny cloth covered buttons John Gotti favored.

We ignored each other as I moved past into the office. Berlinski was on the phone. He lifted a finger as I sat down as if to say don't talk I'm busy.

Still unsettled by my encounter with Terry I drifted around the library examining the books on the shelves. They were the usual leather bound classics: Dickens, Dostoevsky, Celine, Proust, even Arthur Conan Doyle. Odds were high they'd never been cracked.

"That was my meter reader," Berlinski said, "my compliments Angel."

"Now that I have your approval what about my fee?"

"You shall have. Well deserved. Now please turn, and face the wall."

It was either a silencer or a safe. I accommodated him, killing me here would be too messy.

"Alright."

When I turned I saw a black crocodile bag on the desk. Berlinski stood behind it arms spread, beaming like a magician celebrating his trick.

"Nice bag", I said.

"It's a Hermes," he said proudly. My gift to you."

"I didn't care if it was a Target, so long as my cash was inside."

I made a quick inspection. I had to admit it was a handy bag, roomy, and the zipper worked. It also had a shoulder strap. Three hundred and fifty grand in twenties weighs about forty five pounds. I made a quick count or tried to. Fortunately half came in hundred-dollar packets but it still took ten minutes.

"Seems to be right," I zipped it up and hefted the bag. "I'll be on my way. Thanks for the gift."

Berlinski nodded and checked his phone, "My pleasure. I hope to see you soon."

I walked out into a growing swarm of guests. The music and the conversational buzz had become louder. Obviously Byron's library was soundproof. No silencer required. I caught a glimpse of Georgio in the next room and moved smartly to the exit.

The front door was monitored by an Andre clone, shorter, darker, but with the same vacant eyes. I filed him away for future reference.

Outside the first signs of winter sliced the night air. The cabbie drove with the windows wide open and I was chilled when I got back to my pad. I had a quick scotch to warm up then transferred the cash to my backpack. Finished, I poured another scotch and called Terry.

"Angel. I was getting worried. Thanks for calling."

I knew Terry to be many things. Worried wasn't one of them.

"No problem. What's up?"

I'm at Melon's. Can you meet me?"

"On my way."

Rooted on upper Third Avenue, Melon's is a classic New York bar; heavy drinkers, heavy players. Terry and I played there sometimes in the old days. She was sitting at a table in the back room. Her smile was one of relief.

"Angel you're here."

"Of course. What's up? You seem stressed."

"Stressed?" She punctuated the word with a hollow laugh. "Fractured is more like it."

"Somebody moving on you?"

She shrugged. "Look I know it's been a few years but...I need a favor."

"Sure, what?"

"I need to stay at your place tonight."

Luckily the waitress came. While I ordered I considered my options.

Actually I had none.

A lifetime ago, on the run, I had taken sanctuary at Terry's apartment. Street code of honor and all that crap that gets you killed.

"Yeah mea casa e su casa. What's the problem?"

She looked away. "Long story. How long have you known Zsa Zsa?"

"Zsa Zsa?"

"Berlinski."

"Not long. I met him briefly some time back. Quick deal. He's blown up since?"

"He's a fixer; drugs, guns, women, crooked judges... they say his connections run all the way to the white house.

"What's his deal with you, blow?

Her face tightened and her mouth clamped shut. The drinks came and I raised my glass. "To old friends."

She made a visible effort to smile. "Not too old, I'm in my prime."

It was true. On the cool side of forty Terry could pass for twenty-five. Her body was slim and firm and her skin was as smooth as polished copper. A turquoise necklace set off her clear, sea blue eyes.

"I won't deny that fact," I said trying to be polite without seeming to hit on her.

The remark appeared to relax her and we started making small talk; who's still around, remember when, that kind of thing.

"Who's this guy Georgio? I ventured.

I felt a chill. The waitress came and I ordered another round to warm up.

"He's Berlinski's bag man..." she said finally. There was a long pause.

"...and his procurer." She spat out the word.

"As in prostitutes?"

"As in he traffics in young women. The younger the better."

I flashed back to the Latino women held captive inside an airplane hanger in Petaluma. Deep inside the Preacher yawned awake.

"What about the party girls?"

"They service the clients. Belinski keeps most of them strung out on smack."

Suddenly the enormity of what I'd done by selling him the fucking heroin came crashing over me like a tsunami.

Our drinks came. I swallowed my scotch whole and banged my glass down.

"Angel, you okay?"

I half-smiled. "Sure, why?"

"I don't know. For a second there you looked scary."

"Really? Must be the scotch." Actually the last drink slipped past the tipping point so I felt a mixture of relief and high anxiety when Terry said, "Maybe we should leave."

Why the anxiety?

I loved my wife.

I had three hundred and fifty grand stashed in my backpack.

There was serious heat on Terry.

My pad belonged to a mob guy.

To make things worse Terry took my arm as we waited for a cab and her body felt soft and warm in the chill night. Yes, we had occasionally hooked up in the past, when I was blown out on booze, coke and whatever. Back then the sex was platonic, temporary shelter in the storming darkness. But now I was as nervous as a square from the suburbs – which I had become.

When we reached the pad Terry looked around appraisingly.

"Cozy, but it really isn't you somehow."

"That's because it's not mine. Get settled, I'll get us a nightcap."

"Oh my god!"

"What?"

"This bag. It's a Hermes."

"I thought it was alligator."

"Crocodile actually. This thing cost's north of sixty grand."

"A carry on?"

That gave me pause. No way Berlinski liked me that much. Then I heard a familiar tap, tap, tap.

I came back with the drinks and saw Terry cutting small white lines on a hand mirror. I started to object then realized I was a half-step unsteady. One of the properties of cocaine is its ability to absorb the effects alcohol.

I sat beside her on the couch and we toasted. Terry handed me a silver straw.

"It's top grade," she said when she saw me hesitate.

Okay one line, I told myself, just to clear my head.

That one line of primo coke was enough. A bolt of energy evaporated the leaden fumes over my brain the traveled down my spine awakening the lower chakras.

"Very nice," I said.

Terry smiled modestly. "Told you."

For a moment it was quiet

"This Georgio, he seems to be draped over you like a cheap suit. What's up."

Her smile wavered. She took a deep breath as if trying to compose herself.

"I owe him money."

"Drug debt?"

"Ransom."

The word hung in the silence.

"You're serious?"

"Serious as H.I.V."

"Ransom for what?"

"You mean who. It's my little sister Zelda. She's only seventeen."

"The bastard kidnapped her?"

Terry sighed. "My dumbass sister started fooling with heroin. She was a weekend junkie and modeling weekdays...and nights. She met Geogio at a Fashion show, and he gave her some pure heroin and that's all she wrote. Now Geogio has her locked up somewhere junked out of her brains. And he wants a hundred grand to let her go." She fished inside her bag for a tissue. "Because he likes me, he said.

"When does he want the money?" I said, suddenly sobered by the thought that my heroin was fueling these vicious scumbags.

"I've already given him fifty grand to keep her on hold. I can get the rest in a couple of days."

"Keep her on hold? What's that mean?"

She drained her glass.

"So they don't sell her."

That got the Preacher's attention. For the next few hours he paced restlessly raging helplessly while we talked, drank and did more lines until the night became a blur.

In the morning I woke up with a pounding headache and Terry lying beside me. Soggy with lover's remorse and an unforgiving hangover I staggered to the shower. When I finished the headache was down to a dull throb but the guilt and anger were on full blast.

I called Delaney and set up a meet. Before I left I pulled five stacks of money from my backpack and put it on the pillow beside Terry's head. She opened her eyes and blinked sleepily at the money. Then she gave me a suspicious stare.

"What's this for?" she demanded.

"Relax. It's for your sister. When I get back we'll talk about getting her home."

Before she could reply I headed for the door.

+        +        +

The fifty grand wouldn't be missed. The DEA would be more than pleased with what I was turning in. It was fucking blood money anyway.

Delaney was seven minutes late. Rather than stand on the corner I dropped into a small store and bought a pack of Camels. One bad habit begets another. As I gathered the change I glanced at the newspaper head-lines. Refugee children being put in cages. The thought of my little girl alone in a steel pen aroused a shitstorm of rage. It must have showed.

"Are you alright?" he said when I stepped inside his town car. "You look like you want to kill somebody."

"Berlinski and his pal Georgio are running a fucking slave market. I want you to bust his ass."

"You know I can't..."

"They're also holding a young girl for ransom."

Delaney looked away. "Kidnapping, human traffick-ing, call the FBI we're drug enforcement."

I shook my head slowly. "What happened to you Delaney? You used to give a shit."

He fixed me with a bulldog stare. "I got older and smarter. You play action hero if you want but we need solid evidence. So the next time you sell heroin to Berlinski, let me know and I'll send in the fucking troops.

And while we're on the subject of heroin, where's the money?

Seething with righteous indignation I gave him the backpack.

Delaney hefted it. "How much is in there, two hundred?"

"Two fifty."

He whistled softly. "Tho hundred and fifty thousand? He must have a high profit margin."

"He doesn't sell it. He uses the shit to keep his girls in line. Which means he might not reorder for a few months."

"Yeah well I got more bad news for you."

"Why not? I deserve it. What now?"

"Belinski and his pal Petrov have a contract with Homeland Security to operate an air charter service to fly illegals back to Mexico and Honduras. White House approved."

I slumped back in my seat, weak against the forces lined up against me, against America. All flourishing under a nakedly corrupt administration.

Delaney tossed the backpack into the front seat. "Here Bruce, scan this."

"I told you, it's two hundred fifty..."

"Not count-scan. They have tracking devices on everything these days. Even the food you eat."

"Nothing here chief."

I sat bolt upright.

"Shit!"

"What is it?"

"I fucked up. Stop the car."

"You nuts? We're in the middle of traffic."

"Just let me out here."

"Fuck it. Okay Bruce."

Before the car came to a complete stop I was out the door and sprinting for a cab. How dumb can you get, I told myself as the taxi inched downtown. Why would Berlinski give me an outrageously expensive bag unless it was bugged? And unless he expected to get it back.

The cab stalled in traffic so I threw the driver a twenty and half-trotted the rest of the way. I arrived sweating, feverish with anxiety.

When I entered my blood went cold.

A deep stillness shrouded the apartment.

I found Terry in the bedroom. She lay face up on the floor, eyes wide and mouth open in surprise, one arm extended behind her head as if doing a backstroke.

I made a quick search of the area. The money was gone, the bag was gone, and Terry was gone. Then I noticed the hand behind her head was clenched in a tight fist. As gently as possible I pried her fingers open.

In her palm was a cloth covered button.

As I started to get up the stillness exploded with thundering pain and I spun into an endless vortex.

# Chapter 19

The world was still spinning when I regained my senses.

Numbly aware somebody had wacked me I lay still trying to gather my tattered resources. There were at least two people in the room, both male. Both were discussing how to dispose of me.

"He already got a goddamn bruise by his ear. You never watch *Bones, CSI?* We got to dis-a-pear this sucker baby."

Melodic but chilling. I had the Glock in my ankle holster. Risking a fractured skull I focused through my throbbing brain and made a Zen move. I curled into fetal position and fumbled for the gun, aware of the huge shadow floating into my peripheral vision.

I yanked the Glock free and waved it at the towering figure with blonde dreads. He took a half step towards me.

I thumbed the safety and steadied the Glock.

"Don't move."

He moved.

I pulled the trigger.

The blast froze everybody.

The bullet went into the mattress.

"Next one's yours," I said, struggling to my feet. "Hands!"

King Bong and Snappy Jack lifted their hands.

"Why you kill her motherfucker," Bong blurted.

I didn't kill her but I know who did. Now why the fuck are you here?"

Snappy Jack lowered his hands, "Terry called us."

"Bullshit. She didn't have the address. I know, I took her home last night."

"Yeah? Well do you know GPS sucker?"

He was right about the sucker part. As a profession coder and cyber expert I was a bust. Apparently anybody with an iPhone and a two dollar tracker could game me.

"Why did she call you?"

The two men glanced at each other. Nobody spoke.

"About her sister Zelda maybe?"

King Bong shrugged. "Yeah. What we do know some dude gave Terry fifty grand for the ransom. Now it's gone."

For the first time they looked at me with a modicum of respect.

"Let's sit down and talk. I need ice on this ear."

We sat at the kitchen table while King Bong prepared an ice pack, half apologizing for whacking me. "I did what I had to do man," he mumbled, gently pressing the ice on my pounding ear.

Turned out Jack and Bong had helped Terry put together the first fifty grand and were working to get Zelda back safely.

"Terry called and said she had the rest of the cash. We were gonna take Zelda right to detox," Jack explained. "Then she screamed. That's when I got busy on the GPS."

"You're pretty handy with that thing."

Jack smiled, showing his custom gold teeth.

"I got skills."

"I found this in Terry's hand." I gave him the cloth covered button. "She ripped it off during the struggle."

"A button?"

"Belongs to Berlinski's boy, a goon called Andre."

"Who the fuck is Berlinski?" King Bong said.

"Georgio's boss."

King Bong slammed the table. "Motherfufcker! Let's find Georgio, get Zelda and then deal with this fucking Andre."

"I'm in," I said quietly, "but first we have to take care of Terry. Can't leave her here."

"How we suppos' to do that?" Bong demanded.

"We'll need a sleeping bag and a trunk both. Meanwhile I'll get on my computer and find Geogio's address."

"Meanwhile shit. Why we got to go shoppin'?"

"Because we're going to need a big car. Like that Escalade you got parked somewhere out there, right?"

Jack sighed. "Okay get the trunk. I'll help the man here."

"Do you have Terry's phone?" I said, taking my Mac from its case.

"No, do you?"

Bad answer. For the next ten minutes we search the bedroom without success.

"Mothafucka must of took it." Jack said.

"Maybe you can track it on your GPS," I said, popping open my Mac. "I'll hack into ConEd and trace his electric bill."

It took a while but I finally got a hit on. G. Amanti. A double hit actually. Georgio had two addresses.

Just then King Bong walked in holding a black trunk like a Christmas package.

"What you got?" he demanded..

"I got nothin'," Jack said apologetically.

"I show G. Amanti at two places."

"Dude, that's dope." Jack said.

I shrugged modestly. "I can't be sure it's the same guy."

King Bong carefully set the trunk down next to Terry's body. "We need to talk."

We solemnly discussed the best way to deal with Terry's body.

In the old day Snappy Jack and King Bong were members of a major Brooklyn street gang and they still had connections. They knew a funeral director in Fort Greene who would take care of the body for an exorbitant fee."

"Twenty K cash," Jack said, "but I only got two on me."

"I got near five," Bong said hopefully.

"This is on me," I went to the stove and withdrew the money stashed inside. "Call your man and let's do this."

It was the very least I could do.

After all, Andre had come looking for me.

We zipped Terry's body inside the sleeping bag then put her in the trunk."

"I don't know" King Bong said, "we get stopped on the route and you know the mothafuckas gonnna open this trunk."

He was right. In these divided times a white dude and two black rappers in an Escalade was guaranteed to rouse a cop's suspicion. But carrying a trunk?

Everybody out of the car and on the ground.

I decided to call Manny.

"Do you have a small truck I can borrow?"

"Sure, what for?"

"I need to haul a trunk to Brooklyn."

"Trunk huh? I be right over."

When Manny arrived he eyed my new friends, and the trunk skeptically. "What's in this thing?" he said in lieu of hello.

"You don't want to know," I said.

Manny grunted and grabbed the trunk's handle. "We got time. It's a long way to Brooklyn."

I helped Manny carry the trunk downstairs. His truck was double-parked outside, Manny's Garage emblazoned on the doors in red Gothic. It had a towing winch in the rear and plenty of room for Terry.

I rode with Manny while Snappy Jack and King Bong followed in the Escalade. It was as close to a funeral procession as Terry would get.

It was indeed a long way to Fort Greene. As we drove I told him about Georgio's human trafficking operation and Terry's murder. I also mentioned Berlinski was Georgio's boss hoping Manny had heard something."

"Berlinski?" Manny spat. "Fucking Russians are taking over New York. Vegas even. And they're all over Hollywood."

"This scumbag's got his fingers in the White House. Contracts with Homeland Security."

"Fucking politicians. They're worse than honest crooks."

Fort Greene has benefited from Brooklyn's literary gentrification. Once dreary, the avenues were bustling with specialy markets, boutiques and cafes. We turned onto a tree lined street, past rows of red brick apartment buildings, and slowed in front of a large house set apart from the tightly packed buildings. The sign in front read: Good Shepard Funeral Home, Rev. O.J. Vance Director.

There was a side entrance but as we rolled up the driveway a short stock man built like an NFL fullback came out and waved us off.

"Nobody here called for no tow."

"Delivery," Manny said casually. The man started to protest until the Escalade came up behind us, stopped and doused its lights. Manny did the same. Now in semi-darkness we emerged from the truck.

The man said something to King Bong who walked over to me.

"He wants to know who's paying."

"No problem." I walked back to the Escalade where the man was waiting and smiled. "Who am I speaking to?"

The man sized me up before he answered.

"I am Reverend Ordell Vance," he intoned with professional gravity.

"Then this is for you." I handed him a paper bag stuffed with cash. "I do insist on one thing."

"Which is?"

"You take proper care of the ashes."

Vance checked the bag then bowed. "Mr. Jack has already made that clear."

The formalities concluded Manny and I carried the trunk inside and set it down on a metal table.

"You may go now gentlemen," Vance said, "we'll take it from here."

"We appreciate this Reverend," Snappy Jack said respectfully.

"Uh Mr. Reverend..." Manny ventured.

"Yes, what is it?"

"Do you have a business card?"

"You never know when this kind of service might come in handy," Manny said as we drove back to Manhattan.

"This favor should make us even," I said.

"You kiddin'? You saved my skin, asshole. This is just a ride. So, you going after the wacko who did this?"

"Soon. First we have to get her sister free."

"Let me know if you need some muscle."

Comforting but I had a bloodless coup in mind.

+          +          +

Manny declined my offer of a drink so Snappy Jack, King Bong and I sat around the kitchen table at my place, smoking weed, sipping scotch and devising a strategy.

"Have you ever dealt with Georgio directly?" I asked.

Snappy Jack passed me the J. "Yeah, when we gave him the fifty grand. I handed him the cheese. Terry waited in the car."

"That's good. Call him and say you've got the rest of Zelda's ransom money."

"He might know Terry's dead," Bong said.

"Not likely. Terry's murder wasn't planned so chances are Georgio won't know. And Berlinski's too smart to cop to murder."

"Okay, say he takes the bait – then what?" Jack said between gritted teeth.

He exhaled a cloud of weed and started drumming his fingers on the table. "Take the bait...take the bait...saw it too late...That's dope. We can use that shit."

I cut into his creative process. "How did it go down last time?"

"Like I said, King Bong and me went out with the cash. Terry waited in the car."

"Was he alone?"

"Nah. Had some cracker with him. Big blond mothafucka."

Andre? I hoped so.

"Who took the money?"

"Georgio was sittin' in the back. I passed the swag through the window."

"They took off real quick," Bong added.

"Really? I think we can do this – one thing – can you get guns and backup?"

Jack flashed his gold teeth. "Can a dog get fleas?"

+          +          +

The plan was simple.

As he had before, Snappy Jack would leave his car, followed by King Bong and deliver a gym bag filled with cash to Georgio's waiting limo. Only this time the money was fake and the bag accompanied by a Glock 9 which Jack would push into Georgio's well-groomed face.

I stayed in the Escalade hoping Georgio would mistake me for Terry.

At first it all went on cue. Snappy Jack jabbed his gun through the back window and King Bong flourished his weapon, the Colt .45 like a Derringer in his big hand. At the same time I slipped behind the wheel and started the car.

As expected Georgio's driver stepped on the gas. Tires squealing the Limo lurched forward.

Out of nowhere a black SUV came around the corner and stopped blocking the Limo. As planned I put the Escalade in gear and sealed off the street. I got out of the car, my own Glock ready.

The limo had stopped but was racing its motor nervously, snarling like a trapped beast. As I edged closer I saw a female next to Georgio.

Then it all went sideways.

The Limo's front window shattered spraying the air with glass and noise as the driver shot at Bong and roared ahead ramming the Toyota. The occupants jumped out and suddenly the quiet street erupted into a free-fire zone.

Seconds later it was quiet again. Snappy Jack had ducked behind a fire hydrant and King Bong was down on one knee. As I edged closer to the stalled limo saw the two shooters ahead get into their Toyota and back away.

It crossed my mind that I was exposed and the driver might be lining up another shot. I pressed against the side of the vehicle and inched forward, closely followed by Jack. I yanked open the front door and the driver fell out, a ragged red hole where his nose had been.

When Jack opened the rear door I saw Georgio and a young blonde girl huddled on the floor. Georgio had the gym bag clutched against his chest.

"Zelda? It's alright girl," Jack said.

The girl didn't respond.

Snappy Jack gently patted her arm. "Zelda it's me Snap. It's alright."

Slowly, the girl half-turned and blinked at him, as if roused from a deep sleep.

"Mothafucka! That ain't Zelda."

Snappy Jack lifted his Glock in Georgio's direction. "Where the fuck is she?"

"She is good, okay," Georgio assured.

"Get them out of here before company comes," I said hurriedly. "We'll grill him later."

Jack pulled the girl to her feet and half carried her to the Escalade. I took the gym bag from Georgio and gestured with my Glock. "Up, scumbag."

He made a big show of getting out of the limo.

I should have known. The low whine of a siren rose in the night sky and I glanced up. When I looked back Geogio had a cute designer .22 automatic pointed at me.

He was only a foot away which made it easy to deflect the pistol with one hand and Glock-slap him with the other. He was bleeding profusely from his ear as I grabbed his collar and dragged him stumbling to the car.

"Shit! You ain't gonna bleed on my seats mothafuc-ka," King Bong declared.

I plucked the silk pocket square from Georgio's jacket. When I did a silver vial fell out. Georgio reached, but I snatched it up. I handed him the silk handkerchief and pushed him inside.

"Get the fuck out of here," I said as the sirens grew louder.

The sudden acceleration pressed me back in my seat.

"Yeah!" King Bong yelled over the screeching tires. "Got me five hunred horses and a racing Hemi."

We sped away leaving behind a dented limo and a dead driver.

But no Zelda.

"Where the fuck is she?" Snappy Jack shouted taking the words from my mouth.

I nudged Georgio with the Glock and pointed at the gym bag on the floor. "We had a deal," I said as if bewildered. "What's the problem?"

He sighed. "We need the girl. So we can control Terry."

"But Terry's..." King Bong blurted."

"Control Terry?"

"Yes she has many connections. A valuable asset."

Obviously he didn't know.

"Where is Zelda now?"

"Safe."

Snappy Jack lifted his gun

"Lemme smoke this fool."

"You shoot and you'll never see Zelda," Georgio said calmly.

"So what do you want?" I said, still the good cop.

The cash bag and the vial you just took from me."

"And you will...?"

"Take you to where she is staying."

King Bong parked at a deserted construction site and turned off the lights.

"No deal," I said. "Jack, ask the girl."

Georgio lunged forward. "Jan don't...!"

My backhand slap caught him full on the mouth.

"This bitch is smacked out of her brain," Jack reported.

"Do you have any coke?"

"Yeah, I'm holdin'." King Bong said. "Terry's best." He fished a silver tube from his oversized jeans.

Jan came awake when he put a tiny spoon heaped with white powder under her nose. Holding one nostril she snorted greedily. A second later the spoon was empty and Jan had perked up considerably.

"Can I have another hit?" Was the first thing she said.

I took her hand. "First tell us where we can find Zelda."

Jan's large dark eyes remained fixed on the coke in King Bong's hand. I noticed the needle marks on her pale arm.

"She's at the Club."

"What's the Club?"

"That's where we stay."

"You and Terry?"

"All of us."

"How many is that?" Snappy Jack asked.

"Six. Eight sometimes. Plus the guys."

"Who are the guys?" I said.

"Pete and Alex. Pete's the nice one. Can I have another hit now?"

I was starting to get the picture. Along the way I worked up a crude plan. A few blocks from our destination we stopped at Ray's Original Pizza where I bought two large pies. The aroma filled the car overcoming the lingering scent of weed. Georgio stared at me with hatred, one hand pressing a paper towel to his lip, the other at his bloody ear. But he was no match for the Preacher's ferocious rage roaring in my belly.

The "Club" turned out to be a three story town house on the Upper East Side. King Bong double parked a few yards away, out of sight from any cameras. I borrowed Snappy Jack's Yankee baseball cap and carried the pizza boxes to the Club's front door.

It took a few minutes and repeated rings on the door chimes to get a response. "We're closed," a gruff voice declared.

"Pizza delivery."

"Nobody ordered fucking pizza. Get lost."

I assumed he wasn't the nice one.

"Says here Pete ordered the pies."

"Fucking Pete," the man grumbled as he unlocked the door.

The man was very big, rock solid and hairy. His white, wife-beater tank top framed furry arms and shoulders. He glowered down at me.

"How much?"

"No charge." I dumped the boxes into his arms and showed him my Glock.

"Nice and easy."

He didn't seem fazed. He just stared, a wooly mammoth sizing up a mouse. I waved at King Bong and Snappy Jack in the shadows. Bong had Jan with him.

"You don't know who you're fuckin' with, the man said.

"I'm fucking with you right now – Inside!"

The first floor was dominated by a huge Art-Deco living room with a black carpet, red leather couches and a painting of nude nymphs above a full sized metal bar.

Snappy Jack whistled softly. "Dope crib."

As I noted how far we've strayed from the mother tongue, my hairy hostage became visibly enraged.

"You stupid junkie bitch, you're dead," he shouted when he saw Jan.

I tapped his ear with my gun to get his attention.

"Where's Zelda?"

"Upstairs."

We followed him to the second floor.

A man stepped into the hall. He smiled when he saw us.

"Pizza time, alright Alex..."

Pete was a good looking kid, tall and athletic but he wasn't meant to be a gangster. His smile wilted when he saw the guns as did his knees. He sagged against the wall hands chest high.

"What's up?" he said weakly.

"We want Zelda," I said quietly.

He seemed relieved. "She's back here."

There were a number of bedrooms off the long hall. As we passed I saw all were occupied by young girls who were nodding out or blankly watching TV. The rooms had the messy, strewn clothes look of a college dorm.

The University of Heroin.

Zelda's door was the only one shut. Pete fumbled with the lock then stood aside. I pushed Alex ahead of me and looked around. I saw a needle, scorched spoon and a few glassine bags stamped with a Spiderman logo on a vanity table, clothes on the floor and a young girl sprawled on the bed.

She was young, maybe seventeen, with smooth tawny skin and delicate features. Her pink tank top revealed fresh punctures on her arm. When she opened her eyes I saw they were the same startling sea blue as her sister Terry.

Without warning Alex flipped the pizza boxes into my face and lunged for my gun and the room exploded. I fired my Glock a second before the ear-shattering blast of King Bong's .45.

I missed. Bong didn't.

At that distance a .45 caliber slug does major damage where ever it hits, in this case Alex's thigh. The impact lifted him off the floor and slammed him against the wall.

He fell heavily, hot red blood spewing like lava from a fuming black volcano.

Zelda screamed. Pete threw up.

"Easy, it's okay baby. It's B and J baby. We're gonna take you home."

"Jack?" Zelda said drowsily. "Where's Terry?"

"Come on baby," King Bong said,"We out of here."

As Bong lifted Zelda to her feet I ran to the bathroom and grabbed a stack of towels and a long-handled brush. When I came back Alex's eyes were glazed and his ravaged leg was spurting jets of blood. Feverishly I made a tourniquet using a towel and the long brush.

I threw a towel at Pete. "Clean up-you're coming with me."

Jan moved to his side, "I want to go with Pete."

True romance. I covered Alex with a blanket and hustled down the stairs. Once outside I called 911. Then I called the DEA hotline. There were bound to be drugs somewhere in the house.

"Why the fuck you bring that chump?" King Bong said when he saw Pete.

"Because he's going to tell us about Mr. Berlinski. Aren't you Pete."

He nodded.

"Who's your boss?"

"Mr. Amanti."

That reminded me. "Where's Georgio?"

"Stashed his ass in the trunk," King Bong said.

I turned back to Pete, "What was your job?"

"I took care of the girls."

"With smack?"

"No, I make sure they're ready."

"Ready for what?"

"You know, parties and stuff."

"Did you recruit girls for Mr.Amanti?"

"No that's Alex. His specialty."

For a moment I regretted the tourniquet.

"Who's Andre?"

"He works for Mr. Berlinski. Scary guy," he added.

"How so?"

"He likes to break the girls in. Sometimes he gets rough."

A few more questions made it clear Pete didn't know dick from Dick Clark.

"Okay, call Andre and tell him you've got a new girl for him," I said, said, grabbing at straws.

"I don't have his number. Alex..."

"Anyway Andre will be at the party," Jan put in. "Don't you you remember?"

"Oh yeah...shit..." Pete said numbly.

"What party is that?"

"Halloween is tomorrow. So Zsa Zsa is throwing a big party." Jan said as if it was obvious. "Costumes and shit."

For a long few seconds it was quiet. King Bong, Snappy Jack and me looked at each other. We all had the same thought.

"Can I have another hit?" Jan said.

+ + +

It was near midnight but this was New York. Snappy Jack made some calls and found a place that supplied costumes for music videos twenty-four seven.

Afterwards we pulled Georgio out of the trunk and made him exchange his soiled silk suit for a spanking new striped convict outfit, complete with handcuffs. I myself had chosen a police uniform which allowed me to sport a holster for my Glock King Bong was decked out as a maharaja, a bright pink turban wrapped around his big head like a cloud of cotton candy. Looking snazzy in a Zoot Suit, Snappy Jack tugged at his chest-high pegged pants.

"This is some dope shit," he said admiring the huge-shouldered jacket that hung to his knees. He adjusted the wide-brimmed hat, "Original Gangster and the Sultan of Soul. Our next album. Like it Bong?"

"I'm down but I don't like mothafuckin' pink," Bong declared.

We all wore masks, except for Georgio who was our ticket inside.

Perhaps it was the costumes but there was a festive air in the car. The weed was being passed and Snappy Jack played their latest tracks on the speakers and Jan, dressed as Wonder Woman was shaking her skinny arms to the beat. Only Pete, wearing pirate rags and Georgio, lips bloody and swollen, seemed miserable as we rolled across town to kill Andre.

A vial of coke came my way and to my regret I partook. It helped gloss over the reality of what I was doing there.

Assassination has never been my thing. My cardinal rule is: Don't kill anyone who isn't trying to kill you first. Especially if you're already wanted for murder.

Then the Preacher reminded me; Terry was an accident.

Andre had come for my sorry ass.

Reassured but far from convinced, I let the Preacher do another line.

When we arrived at the lobby of Berlinski's penthouse the bored Door Man looked up from his magazine and pointed at the elevators.

"Thirty-fifth floor. Penthouse A."

The air inside the elevator bristled with repressed aggression. We spilled out of the cab and marched to a half-open door. I knew the layout from my previous visit and had briefed my co-defendants.

Our hostile aura must have been apparent because the bouncer in the gorilla suit stepped back as we entered.

"Georgio. What the fuck happened?"

"Just make-up," Georgio said as instructed, prompted by my Glock ,

"Please tell Andre we'll be in the side room with a surprise guest."

Extremely crude but it was all I had. On the up side, we were masked for the party, which negated the hidden cameras. Of course the coke had rocketed my confidence level way past reasonable expectations.

At the moment it all seemed easy.

We were in the house, locked and loaded.

What could go wrong?

Snappy Jack and King Bong took positions by the door. I stood in the center of the room, my gun massaging Georgio's back. Jan and Pete were edging towards the bedroom.

Andre stormed inside, resplendent as a Prussian general, his crisp white uniform sparkling with medals. A black mask did little to hide his anger.

"Georgio! You know I'm fucking busy..."

Snappy jack jammed his Glock into Andre's ribs. "Freeze mothafucka..."

Andre was good.

In one blurred spin he wrenched Jack's gun free and knocked him aside.

Georgio dropped to the floor.

Reflexively my gun followed him until I realized Andre was pointing Jack's Glock directly at me.

I glimpsed King Bong lunging just before a burning fist pounded my brain.

# Chapter 20

I must be coming up in the world, Delaney thought when his assistant told him who was on the line. This made the third call from a high government official this morning.

The first was from Section Chief of the CIA, Tip Jenkins. He didn't waste time on small talk.

"What's the status on your rogue agent Delaney?"

"Still at large Jenkins. Has the Agency come up with anything?"

"We think he may have left California. The agency has Homeland's full cooperation on this, so it's just a matter of time before we locate and execute."

*"Execute?"*

Jenkins paused. "Look Delaney, your boy killed one agent and seriously wounded another. When one of my men gets shot I shoot back. Are you with us here?"

"Sorry Tip, when one of my boys stands accused I like to get the facts before I kill him."

Prick, Delaney thought as he hung up. Max said he might be dirty. Delaney tended to believe him. What kind of name was Tip anyway?

The next call came from an old friend in Chicago. Pat Hicks. Pat was now state deputy director. In their rookie days he and Delaney had worked the streets together.

"Alvin, what's up?"

"You called me. Anything special?"

"First off congratulations on the big bust. Great work. Reminded me of the Brooklyn sting. Remember that one?"

Delaney did of course. The operation had boosted them both up the ladder.

"But there is something..."

Delaney got the drift. Here it comes, comrades in arms, for the good of the cause and all that other bull-shit they hand you to justify doing something morally wrong. He had done it himself when he had to.

"Jesus Alvin, Homeland has been all over us about this California killing. They say it's one of your guys."

"That's conjecture Pat."

"Not according to the CIA. The Agency is backing Homeland. They're turning up burecratic heat on all of us. Cutting budgets, everything. Let me help you with this. Can you give me some idea where this guy is?"

"He's undercover. That's all I can give you. You know that Pat."

"He's off the fucking reservation. This is making us all look bad Alvin."

"Like I said, conjecture."

"It's your funeral. Say hello to Grace."

"We're divorced, but thanks."

Nothing like an old pal to stick the knife in, Delaney reflected dourly.

The third call came right from the top, the new head asshole of Immigration himself.

"Yes Mr. Cuccinelli, how can I help you?"

"Actually it's how I can help you. I'm willing to of-fer all our resources to find this rogue killer agent of yours."

"Well I'm grateful."

"We need more than gratitude here. We need your cooperation."

"Uh, of course sir. Delaney braced himself, knowing Cuccinelli was about to throw him a grenade.

"We need you to open up your files, so we can cross-check this bastard. Our IT experts can..."

"Uh sir, I can't do that. It would compromise every undercover operation and our informants."

"Dammit, if we had more inter-agency cooperation we could stop the criminal cartels and bad hombres crossing the border every day. What do you say Delaney, are you with us?"

"With all due respect sir, opening our files would require a senate subpoena."

"Is that a no? Because I'll have to report back to the White House that you refused."

"Sorry sir. It's the law."

"POTUS won't like it Delaney."

"Tell him it'll take more than an Executive Order."

Did he really say bad hombres? Delaney thought, checking his texts. Is that what he calls the refugees trying to escape violence and poverty? Or the children he locks up in cages with a tin foil blanket and no water. How in God's name does he live with himself?

He made a mental note to dial up surveillance on Berlinski and friends.

Meanwhile, as of this morning, his career was hanging by a thread.

*Where the fuck was Max?*

# Chapter 21

I tried to run all the way home.

I ran through endless empty streets, wide, carpeted corridors, silent cities, long, deserted highways stretching towards a distant sunset...

I never made it.

Instead I kept circling back across ever changing landscapes, in search of lost phones, keys to forgotten rooms, guided by unanswered questions.

Faces came, faces went...Agony sliced my abdomen like a hot spear and I came to.

A dark figure loomed over me.

"Easy Angel, easy..."

Something pinched my arm and a warm blanket smothered the pain.

When I woke up again I was alone.

Except for the fucking pain.

It had decided to move in with me. It burrowed into my belly like a white-hot worm and stayed there, radiating agony.

Feverishly thirsty I started to get up until an electric jolt slammed me against the bed. I lay there for a long time my body throbbing and mouth sand dry. Then I heard a door open and a large figure bent over me. Suddenly cool water broke over my cracked lips like a spring rain.

A capsule was put in my mouth. I drank more water and swallowed. In a short time the warm blanket was back and the pain had ebbed. I looked up and saw King Bong smiling at me.

"Sorry to be late. We was cuttin' our final track."

"Thanks for the pill."

"Not me. That was my moms." He stepped aside and a woman almost as large as him beamed down at me.

"I'm a professional nurse Mr. Angel. Clarence told me how you got shot helping him."

Behind her, Bong put a finger to his lips.

I smiled weakly and nodded. "Clarence is a good friend." I saw Bong grimace.

"Well I'm going to work. I'll stop by at the end of my shift and change the bandages. You rest now."

"Clarence?" I said after she left.

King Bong frowned. "Better keep that shit down low or I lose your pain killers."

That shut me up. I looked around. I was back at Manny's place.

"So...what the fuck happened?" I asked politely.

"Your boy Andre got skills. He snatched Jack's nine and tried to smoke you. I grabbed him but he got off two rounds. One hit you. Right there it went whack. I dropped Andre but by then everybody was buggin' for the doors in these crazy costumes. I called my mom at Bellvue hospital. She works late shift. We got you out and rushed you to the E.R. Mom's had everything ready. Lucky the slug went through, didn't hit nothin'. They cleaned it out, stitched you up and then we snuck you out the next mornin' before the popo came by to visit."

"Thanks man, I owe you."

The big man shrugged. "That's how we do. Want some tea?"

"Sure, thanks. What happened to Andre and Georgio?"

"Oh they gone. Everybody gone when we hit the street. Could hear the sirens but they were far."

The news deflated my mood. Fucking Andre.

We shared some strong tea and primo weed, and Bong began reminiscing

"In our hood gangbanging is as natural as double Dutch. Only way me and Snappy Jack got out is by rappin'. Terry got out dealin' blow to rich people in the city. But you never all the way out."

I knew that only too well. Crips, Bloods, Mafia, DEA, CIA: all gangs are alike.

"How about you? Snap thinks you an ex-Seal or somethin'."

"Why?"

"Got the look, walk the walk."

"Ex-marine. Same deal. I'm going to miss Terry. She was stand up." I said, partially to change the subject.

"I got big love for Terry. She's family. Fact, we gonna do a tribute to Terry, our next album."

"I thought you working on one now."

"It drops this week. Next week we go on tour."

Snappy Jack burst into the flat, gold incisors highlighting a big grin.

He flourished a cassette tape. "The mix is dope." His smile froze when he saw me. "Whoa, you up? Been out two days."

"On vacation."

King Bong grabbed the cassette. "Let's play this bitch."

"I busted an ode to Tupac." Snappy Jack said. "You know who he is right?"

I nodded and gave him a thumbs up. I didn't know much about Hip Hop but Tupac Shakur's album *All Eyez on Me* had made an impression when I heard it. The kid was a major poet. Up there with Ginsberg, Kerouac, Bremser, and yes, maybe even Dylan. Just saying.

Ears amplified by the weed, I lay back and listened.

*You never know*
*never know when it's time to go*
*never know when the blood will flow*
*who said money talks bullshit walks*
*bullshit kills bullets talk soul walks*
*that last mile*
*never know what's behind the smile*
*it's a wheel of chance an all-nite square dance*
*cowboys and hookers saying their prayers*
*stop*
*on a dime for the rest of time*
*time crime it's all the same time is a thief*
*give you the brief count short count*
*steals it all at the end of the game*
*gold, vanity, fame top of the ladder*
*what does it matter*
*never know when it's time to go*
*who was at your side that last sweet ride*
*your bride*
*the bitch you wed spilled blood on your bed*
*you never know bro when it's time to go*
*ain't what you got but what you give*
*makes you live*
*ain't what you got but what you give*
*makes you live*

Swing band trumpets faded into a long single note.

"So Angel, what you think?" Jack said."

"Strong stuff. I like the big band samples."

"Jack does the rhymes, I do the beats and the arrangements." King Bong said. "Dre is my guru"

Snappy Jack fired up a thick joint. "It's our title track. We're callin' the album *Tupac's Tombstone.*"

A cheery message for the holiday season. Thanksgiving was closing in fast, which made me think of my family living on what seemed a distant planet.

When the weed came my way I took a big hit.

King Bong cooked up some chicken and rice that I devoured having survived on soup, tea and water for two days. Snappy Jack and Bong talked excitedly of their plans as we ate. They were going on tour in a few days which meant this would be their last visit. Bong's mom would be stopping by later to change the dressing and again tomorrow afternoon on her way to work. After that I'd be on my own. Fair enough.

The pain crept up slowly. About the size and intensity of a toothache when I first noticed, it soon progressed to a raging abscess.

"You okay Angel?" Snappy Jack said.

King Bong came closer. His blonde dreads made him seem like an oversized cherub. "Hang on, Moms be here in a half hour."

I nodded, unable to speak more than three words. Finally I managed to spit one out.

"Whiskey."

I threw down a triple shot of scotch with four Advil. The pain retreated but now I had severe heartburn. I pasted a smile on my face and held on until I heard the door open.

"You must be hurting by now," Bong's mom said. She gave me a glass of water and a pill. The nameplate on her uniform said Jenny Curry.

"Thanks Mrs. Curry."

"Your welcome baby. Now let's change this dressing."

She set about her work with practiced efficiency. When she removed my bandage I had to look away. The dressing looked like poached puke on white toast.

Mrs. Curry cleansed my ragged stitches with hot water and Neosporin, then gently replaced the bandage. By that time the pill had soothed my throbbing wound.

"I'll be back tomorrow afternoon. Did Bunny tell you I won't be able to be here after then?"

I grinned. "Bunny?"

King Bong groaned. "Aw mom."

Mrs. Curry beamed. "That's my pet name for Clarence. He's going to perform all over the country," she added proudly.

She put a small bottle on the night table. "That's as much as I could get without getting in trouble. I hope it helps."

"Your mom's a fine woman," I said after Mrs. Curry had departed.

King Bong handed me a fresh joint. "Raised me all by herself."

The boys played the tape a few more times and somewhere along the way I fell asleep. They were gone and the house was quiet at four-twenty a.m. when the pain nudged me awake. I took another pill and soon fell out again.

King Bong had left a chicken sandwich and a can of Coke on the night table along with the scotch bottle. At noon I ate half the sandwich, drained the coke and washed down another pill with a slug of scotch. I was still deep in an opioid haze when Mrs. Curry arrived later that afternoon.

I vaguely heard her cluck in disapproval when she saw my scotch, soda, and pain-pill diet. She cleaned up my environment a bit, changed my bandages and even fixed a couple of sandwiches for later. Before she left she woke me up and showed me the fresh bandages, tape and antibiotic cream on the dresser. She gave me strict instructions, wished me well and was gone.

When I woke up it was two a.m. and graveyard quiet. Even the traffic sounds outside were silent. I lay in the dark, thinking about Nina and my little girl and, as the pain slowly escalated—I made a decision. Until it became absolutely unbearable... bear it and fight back.

To this end I got out of bed. With increasing difficulty I managed to make it to the refrigerator. I sat at the kitchen table and forced down a sandwich. The pain was nearing the red zone as I grabbed the attaché case containing my electronic gear and stumbled back to bed.

I took a pill which I washed down with a beer I had retrieved from the refrigerator. As the pain reluctantly retreated I opened the case and reviewed my options.

I had my Macbook Pro, surveillance equipment, a fresh pre-paid phone, ten grand in cash and a combat knife. My Sig Sauer and an odd twenty grand were in my backpack. I couldn't locate the Glock at the moment and it would hurt too much to look. Instead I activated the burner and called Len Zane.

"Max, shit, are you alright?"

"I'm good."

"You sound weird. I can't believe this, Nina came by here this afternoon. Said she had a bad feeling."

"Do me a favor. Drive over there. Tell her I'm okay and I'll be back in two weeks, maybe ten days. Can you do that?"

"No problem. What's up?"

"Long story. I'll tell it when I see you. Look man, thanks for your help."

"My pleasure. Watch your back Max."

"Always."

I tried to sound confident but I knew Len didn't buy it.

The pain had dulled but my emotion had morphed into a rabid beast that clawed ferociously at my gut until I swallowed the rest of the pill and dove into blessed oblivion.

As soon as I awoke I called Delaney.

"Max, where the fuck are you?"

"Recovering. I got shot. Flesh wound."

"That bust you engineered got the agency a lot of good publicity. We still haven't found that bastard Georgio but we have the FBI on it."

"What about Berlinski?"

"He's in Mexico right now. I have the agency keeping tabs on him."

I realized Berlinski skipped without reporting our little home invasion. They all just walked: Andre, Georgio...

"Tabs? Make sure you keep tabs on his motherfucking government contracts."

"Max?"

"What?"

"You saved those girls. The guy you shot flipped on Georgio."

"If you ever find him."

"You did a good thing Max. Didn't you see the papers? Hero drug agent breaks human trafficking ring. That's you."

"Bullshit."

"Just remember to keep your head down. Homeland and the CIA still want you real bad. They call every day."

"Yeah right. I'll call you when I'm mobile."

"Max?"

"You're running short on tme."

I didn't know which was more depressing, being away from my family or the realization that I took a bullet for nothing.

Stay ahead of the pain, they all say. Good advice.

As the discomfort knifed through my side I took a half Oxy and set about taking a shower. The entire process, including a sloppy change of bandage took over an hour. I was not about to go back to bed, so I got dressed. I found my Glock beneath the clothes piled up on a chair. As I laboriously pulled on my pants something fell on the floor.

It was the vial I took from Georgio.

I threw on the rest of my clothes and rustled some food. As I ate I made a mental note to go shopping. Afterwards I brewed a pot of coffee.

By then the pain had made a vicious comeback and I washed down another half pill with black coffee. Resisting the impulse to lie down I paced around the apartment relearning how to walk.

I located a bag of the weed I had delivered to Manny and rolled a J. Then I sat in a lounge chair and switched on the TV news. In disbelief I watched Trump brag about the size of his crowds to the survivors of the El Paso massacre.

You can't make that shit up.

The man has the empathy of a scorpion.

Somewhere during a commercial for Designer Catheters I nodded off.

The unlit J was still between my fingers when I blinked awake.

And the news was still bad.

After firing up my joint the world got better. I switched off the TV and found Neil Young on the FM. *Harvest Moon*, a personal favorite. Inspired I put together a tuna sandwich and a beer, and devoured both.

The J and the beer slowed the oncoming pain so I started surfing my laptop to keep busy. Naturally

I gravitated from breaking news to a deep search of Berlinski's finances.

It wasn't easy.

I navigated through firewalls, around cut-out corporations, and down a series of blind alleys before I entered the maze that was Berlinski's business empire. Soon I detected a common thread the stitched everything together.

SecurEXX Tech.

The corporation was an umbrella for four other entities: Securfood, SecurCom, SecurFi, and SecurArm. At the core of this group was a single sinister enterprise.

Private prisons.

SecureFood had contracts to provide boxed dinners to fifteen hundred children being detained at a facility owned by SecurFi. A single phone call at this facility cost three bucks minimum as charged by SecurCom.

These poor refugee kids were generating a fortune for one Alex Petrov, Chairman of SecurEXX and Treasurer Zsa Zsa Berlinski.

Not to mention the air charter service provided by SecurArm.

Undocumented Latinos had become big business under Trump.

And major Russian mobsters were minding the store.

In the morning I took my starter meds, a half Oxy and two cups of coffee, and went out shopping.

I had overestimated my capacity and walked gingerly to the corner, every step aware of the hole in my love handle. Fortunately it was New York, and there were stores within walking distance.

Still, when I got back my side was on fire.

Another half Oxy later the flame dimmed to a pilot light. However there were only four pills left in the bottle.

I carefully rolled four thick joints to ease the next phase of my recovery.

I lit one up and prepared lunch, a fried egg sandwich and coffee laced with scotch. Fortified, I went back outside for a second round of serious rehab.

It took everything I had to make it to the corner cigar store and back. Too soon for an Oxy, I substituted Advil washed down with beer. But the pain was relentless. It backed away for a while then attacked full force.

Maybe I was pushing it a bit, I thought pouring a scotch. I went over to the TV and fired up another J. Halfway through the joint it was Oxy time. The agony eased but the news amplified the depression brought on by the holiday decorations outside. All I could think about was getting back to my family.

Stay ahead of the pain.

My reality had dwindled to how many pills I had left. As I dozed in front of the TV I vaguely remembered I had forgotten to eat or change my bandage.

I slept, had an Oxy breakfast, then went out to tackle the streets. I pushed it until my side was screaming. I stopped to smoke a J then dropped into a coffee shop for a short stack, scrambled eggs and three Advil.

Back at the pad I put some music on the FM and began surfing the Net. I have to confess I searched out the news story about the bust at Georgio's bordello. It mentioned the heroin, forced prostitution and an undercover agent who brought it all crashing down. They forgot to mention Snappy Jack and King Bong.

If the duo happened to read the news story my cover would be blown.

*Stay ahead of the pain.*

Another half pill, another walk. My gait was almost normal. Progress one step at a time. Patience has never been my strong suit. Depression hovered like a vulture, waiting for me to falter.

Much later I finally got around to changing my bandage but it wasn't pretty. The wound looked inflamed and it hurt like hell. Enough so I had to take a whole pill to fall out.

When I awoke my outlook was bleak. A half pill between me and agony. I swallowed the pill and went out to find a drugstore. To my surprise every store in sight was closed. No Tylenol, aspirin, Advil, not even a fucking cough drop. Feeling sorry for myself, I sat on some stairs and lit my last pre-rolled J.

The weed definitely lifted my mood but the throbbing pain in my side had me worried. The wound should have improved by now. Instead it felt inflamed. When I got back I rolled up a fresh stash, poured a scotch, and downed three Tylenol.

To make things worse I began developing signs of flu: fever, sweats, runny nose, queasy stomach, and spent the next few hours commuting to the bathroom.

The night passed fitfully, I was adrift in a cold, pitching sea. In the morning I was still up shit's creek. Breakfast consisted of Tylenol, scotch and weed. Thankfully I fell back into a bottomless sleep.

A hot spear prodded me awake. My flu and fever had worsened.

Despite the pain, my stomach couldn't handle any more alcohol, caffeine or over-the-counter chemicals. As I gathered myself to go out in search of a drugstore the front door rattled open and a large figure shuffled inside.

Manny stood there, peering at me incredulously.

"Jesus Max, what happened? You look like stir-fried shit."

I took a peek in the mirror. Pale, haggard, unshaven, tangled hair, fever-eyed: I was type casting for *Night of the Living Dead*

He lifted a shopping bag. "I brought over some left-overs from Thanksgiving Dinner. What the fuck's going on?"

I told him about our raid on Georgio's brothel and subsequent home invasion of Berlinski's Halloween Party.

"Halloween? You been recovering over three weeks? Let me see that bitch."

I realized that in my opioid haze I had lost track of real time.

When Manny saw the wound he insisted I go back to bed. Then he got on the phone and ordered various medical supplies including antibiotics.

"The damn thing looks infected," he said, unpacking the shopping bag. "Hungry?"

"Not really. "I might have the flu."

"Well don't breathe on me."

A short time later someone arrived with the supplies Manny ordered. When she came closer I saw it was Jo.

"I'm gonna need your help here," Manny said.

Jo came closer, a look of concern on her lovely face. "What's wrong with you?"

"I got the flu, better keep a safe distance."

She picked up the empty pill bottle. "Flu huh? You're kicking Max. Withdrawal symptoms."

Manny handed her a pair of surgical gloves. "Right now he might have an infection. Wash your hands and put these on."

In no position to protest, I watched Manny set up a surgical table. His preparations were worthy of a liver transplant. My anestsia consisted of three Tylenol with codeine washed down with beer. Almost instantly my flu vanished.

I tried to stay detached but I knew Manny to be an auto mechanic, not a surgeon.

"Relax Max. I done this a dozen times. The hard part is closing it up. Removing stiches is a breeze."

Maybe for him, but the rough tug of blood-crusted thread through my swollen wound, took all my will to pretend it didn't bother me. Jo stood at his side efficiently following Manny's instructions which further motivated me to grit my teeth and shut up.

Once it was over Jo set about feeding me antibiotics and forcing me to drink large glasses of water.

"As of now you're officially off alcohol. You want to get out of here? You know what to do."

Before they left Jo gave me some more Tylenol and codeine, but about four a.m. I knew it wasn't enough. My "flu" came back with a vengeance; shakes, sweats, the whole nine. There was a half-smoked J on the night table. While rummaging through my pockets for a lighter my fingers closed on a small, metallic object.

It was the vial I'd taken from Georgio. It contained over a gram of fine white powder. I took an experimental lick. The bitter taste told me it was heroin, my numbed tongue suggested it was laced with cocaine.

A speedball. The junkie's Holy Grail. A short sniff later I was a believer.

I showered, shaved, made breakfast then got busy on my computer. My depression had been displaced by a new sense of purpose. I delved deep into Berlinski's finances trying to get to most vulnerable area. The cash and where it was buried. I remained comfortable and productive for the next four hours but I still wasn't able to crack the safe.

Stay ahead of the pain, right? I took another small sniff and went out for a walk.

The morning was sunny and cold but my light jacket was enough. Heroin has a way of cloaking the user from the outside world. My depression had lifted and when I got back I changed my bandage and gulped some antibiotics. My wound would leave a Frankenstein scar but didn't seem inflamed. And it had stopped throbbing.

I was beginning to heal and functioning. A walking advert for the wonders of smack.

But after a few hours on the Mac, finding the key to the inner sanctum of Berlinski's empire still eluded me. Worse, it reminded me that my clumsy raid failed to nail Andre and put Berlinski out of reach. Not to mention getting myself shot.

They say depression is anger turned inward. So when the Preacher swung his rage my way it cut deep. By the time Manny and Jo Dropped in to check on me I was well insulated against myself.

"I'm glad to see you looking better," Jo said.

"You guys have been taking good care of me. Thanks"

"How did you get shot anyway?"

"Halloween prank."

"You go to some rough parties."

"I've never been popular."

Max is a real stand-up guy," Manny said. "Guys like him are always getting hurt."

I shrugged. "Could be I'm just stupid."

Jo gave me a wry smile. "It's a strong possibility."

She put together a meal and the three of us sat around drinking wine and talking current events. Of course the absurd antics of our president came up often. Graveyard humor. Absurd is one thing, cruel another. Miss Liberty needs to get a Restraining Order.

"This last shipment is near gone," Jo said passing a joint, "and the holiday season is here."

Manny glanced at me "I'm trying to make arrangements right now."

"Maybe I can make a few calls."

"Thanks Max." He turned to Jo. "See? Stand-up, old school."

"Not that old."

Her eyes held on mine for a long second.

I looked away. I've always been a sucker for brunettes. Especially when they have smoky blue eyes.

They left shortly after midnight. My side was starting to hurt so I took a tiny snort and went to bed. I awoke with full blown flu symptoms but a hit of Georgio's magic elixir put me on my feet. At that point snorting heroin had become routine. Stay ahead of the pain.

I went out for a long walk, pleased my body was creeping back to normal. I needed to get back into combat shape. Not until you're off the junk, a voice inside me reminded.

I ignored it.

When I returned I put in a call to my pilot pal Berto.

"Max, what's up? People are askin'."

"You coming east anytime soon?"

"Be in Chicago in a few days."

"Any passengers?"

"You interested?"

"A friend. I think you already know him."

"Okay. Yeah, things look good."

"Actually I need a ride west too."

There was a long pause. "Welcome aboard."

We agreed to finalize the details later and I hung up satisfied I had solved two problems at once. Manny and Jo would get their Holiday weed and I would finally go home.

Later that day Jo paid me a visit, "to make sure you take the antibiotics."

Although grateful she cared, I took my meds but kept my distance. Jo was young, lovely, full of life, I was in a dark place trying to crawl out.

"I made that call," I said, all business. Which means I'll be leaving soon."

She seemed disappointed. "Oh, great. Manny will be happy. I'm hungry. How about I fix us a snack?"

For a slim girl Jo could eat. I watched her devour her sandwich and polish off the rest of mine. We sat making small talk over a bottle of red wine until my growing discomfort forced me to retire to the head for a snort.

Jo was bright, lively and funny but the heroin I had ingested made it easy to stay detached.

Fucking smack separates you from the world. That's what they mean when they say, "I got off."

"So what do you do back on the coast, weed business?" Jo was saying.

"Just a sideline. Actually I'm a computer nerd."

She had a melodic laugh. "I would have guessed something different."

"Oh, like what?

"Getaway driver, or maybe a film actor."

"Film actor, you kidding?"

She refilled our glasses. "Not at all. I don't think you realize how intense you are."

"Probably a result of getting shot."

"Bullshit. You were that way when we met."

"That's because I've been shot before."

Actually grazed was more like it.

I assumed it was my turn to tell Jo how good she looked. Instead I said, "Where's Manny tonight?"

She started cleaning off the table. "He's at some meeting he can't tell me about. Have you changed your bandage today?"

"Not yet."

"Take off your shirt," she said briskly. As she efficiently cleaned the wound the touch of her cool fingers penetrated the opioid layer over my skin. Her face was very close to mine and I could smell her wine sweet breath. She leaned a little closer and so did I. Just before our lips met it occurred to me that I had managed to become a junky and a serial adulterer in a little over a month.

"Oh shit! Excuse me guys."

Manny was standing in the doorway, an embarrassed grin on his big moon face.

"Kind of late for a visit," Jo said.

I put on my shirt. "What's up?"

"Big problems. I just put my wife on a plane to Florida to visit her sister. You got a new roommate."

"Tu casa amigo. Why the rush?"

"Fat Carmine found out what I did to Nicky Melons who is his nephew. So he put out a contract. I need to lay low for a while."

"I made that call. The shipment is due in a few days. Chicago area. From there I fly back to the coast. I'm sure I can book you a seat."

Manny thought it over. "Yeah, it'll work. You and me can drive the Escalade to Chicago. But we got something else to worry about"

"What's that?"

"Whose gonna drive the weed back here?"

"I'll do it," Jo said.

*"On the mountain, more people are killed
on the descent than the ascent"*
– Doc, ***"The Ghosts of Galway"***

# Chapter 22

Within twenty-four hours we were on the road to Chicago.

Should you decide to take a long motor trip I highly recommend the Escalade. It floats along the highway like a luxury yacht and has enough room for a passenger recovering from a gunshot to stretch out. This one even had a drop down TV screen so I could follow the tragic burlesque that our White House had become. Fortunately there were plenty of movies, series and games to distract me from the depressing reality of America's fall from grace.

Not to mention my own descent into opiate hell.

I kept staving off the residual pain and increasing withdrawal symptoms, with daily snorts of heroin. But I found it took more each day just to stay even. Like any good junky I kept my jones on the down low, self -medicating in better rest rooms along the way.

My fellow passengers didn't seem to notice even though Jo had appointed herself resident nurse feeding us vitamins along with our burgers and periodily checking my wound.

She was also very big on hydrating.

"You guys don't drink enough water. Which happens to be the leading cause of senility in older men." She gave me a wicked smile and passed me a bottle. "That means you."

"Women," Manny grumbled from the driver's seat, "I thought I sent my wife to Florida."

I took a swig of water and watched Trump on TV, spraying his venom at our free press. My detachment seemed to annoy her.

"I hope you're keeping that wound clean."

"Seems to be healing fine."

Manny half turned. "Max is a tough cookie. Matter of fact it's his turn to drive." He pulled into a rest stop. "And it's my turn to eat."

"Didn't you have breakfast?" Jo said.

"You call that breakfast? I haven't had a decent meal since we left the city.

We had left the motel late that morning and were ten hours out of Chicago where we planned to rendez-vous with Berto.

I stepped out of the big SUV with difficulty and head-ed straight to the restroom for my early afternoon dose.

Smack slows time. When I entered the diner food was on the table: an omelette, bacon and a stack of pan-cakes for Manny, iced tea and salad for Jo. The drugs cut my appetite so I ordered coffee and toast.

"You seem to be moving better," Jo noted.

"Once I loosen up it's easier."

"Ah, in two weeks you won't know you got shot," Manny said, between mouthfuls.

"Let's hope." But I didn't share his confidence. Mainly because my stash of heroin would be gone in a week.

For the next few hours I took the wheel. Jo request-ed the Grateful Dead on Sirius radio, Manny voting for Sinatra. Jo won.

Later I called Berto and got the bad news.

"Our flight's been delayed. He'll be here before noon tomorrow. We'll meet at the drop spot I have the coordinates."

Manny grinned. "Great. You can get good Italian food in Chicago."

"And blues music. I know a good bar," Jo said.

My instinct was to lie low until the drop. This time I got outvoted.

So we checked into a motel, Jo using her credit card, and after a shower and short rest, we went out on the town.

It began simply enough. Deep dish pizza and a red wine toast to our short journey. Then a visit to a blues bar that served barbecued wings and scotch. That was my downfall.

I'm a sucker for the blues.

We stayed too long, had one drink too many, and were well stoned when we got back to the motel. Once inside my room I had a heroin nightcap and got ready for bed. I barely had my shoes off when I heard a knock at the door.

Instinctively I glanced at the bag where my Sig Sauer was stashed but thought better of it. When I opened the door Jo was standing there with two ponies of mini-bar scotch.

"I thought we should have a farewell toast."

By then I was out of common sense. "Why not?"

"Are you always so enthusiastic?" she said brushing past me.

I found two glasses and she filled them.

She lifted her glass. "To the most mysterious man I've never met."

"What does that mean?"

"It means you've been my guest, I've changed your bandages, we've been on a road trip and I still don't know anything about you."

"Why should you?"

She paused. "Good point, you bastard."

"Look, I'm very grateful for your hospitality, and your help."

"My pleasure but it's not what I mean."

"Which is?" My side was stiffening so I sat on the edge of the bed. Jo sat next to me.

"You're just not like any man I've ever met."

"I don't know if I should be flattered or insulted."

She flashed that wicked smile I'd come to recognize. "Well for one thing you're the only male that hasn't hit on me inside an hour."

I had to admit she looked hittable. Earlier I had watched her dance and marveled at her primal grace.

"A bullet wound gives you other things to think about."

"You weren't wounded when you showed up at my door."

I was about to tell her I was married when she leaned close and kissed me. Lightly at first then her soft lips pressed harder. Her tongue flicked against mine like a high-tension line, sparking jolts of pleasure and need down my spine. I responded hungrily. We fell back on the bed and I found myself cheating on my wife.

Again.

+    +    +

In the morning Jo was gone but guilt was there in bed with me.

A bit of smack and the guilt was gone but not forgotten.

Jo and I were quiet on the drive to the drop point, but Manny rambled on about the Yankees, packing the weed in the Escalade's custom door panels and trunk compartments, and who to call in case Jo was stopped.

He handed Jo a business card. "Jerzy Winkler, best mouthpiece in the business."

Jo laughed. "If I get stopped with two hundred pounds of weed, I'll need more than a mouthpiece."

"Don't worry Jerzy's connected. Worst case you'll get bail."

She studied the card. "Jerzy with a Z, sounds more like a rapper. By the way when do I get paid?" she said suddenly.

Manny seemed surprised by the aggressive tone in her voice. "Call Luigi, when you get to New York. He'll get you the cash and your cut of the shipment."

"Should be a merry Christmas," I said.

Mistake. Jo gave me a cold glance and I realized the aggression was directed at me.

I sank in my seat and admired the scenery.

Four young men were waiting at the drop point. They kept their distance and eyed us warily as we emerged from the SUV. All of them were about thirty, two had beards, two sported ponytails. They could have been rock and roll roadies, which they probably were when they weren't off- loading marijuana.

My side was starting to ache and I realized with a touch of anxiety there was no place to snort my H. As before, the landing strip was in the middle of a corn-field outside of Chicago. It was well past the harvest and the depleted stalks offered little in the way of privacy.

Berto was late and the crew was getting restless until we heard the buzz of the twin-engine plane come into range.

It was an efficient operation. Immediately two of the crew began taking the Escalade apart; door panels, floorboards, even the rear seats. Manny pitched in as the plane circled low, made a steep descent and landed heavily.

The off load went quickly and the Escalade was road ready in an hour.

As I watched, Berto ambled to my side. "Truck'll be here soon to pick up the rest of the load. You okay Max? You don't look so good."

"I got shot while you were away."

"Jesus, who shot you?"

"A killer called Andre."

"Did you nail him?"

"He got away."

Berto shrugged. "No wonder you look so shitty."

Deflated, I ducked into the cornfield for a bump.

+ + +

It was Manny's first flight in a small plane and he alternated between acceptance and apprehension. As we neared he shifted uncomfortably and peered down.

"Those trees look awful damn close," he said.

"Relax boy, I can fly this thing between a pair of goalposts."

"Only takes one mistake. Suppose we hit a power line?"

"Hell I flown this route fifty times. Know every tree, grid and golf course. I even filed a fucking flight plan nice and proper. You ain't carrying anything illegal are you Max? Not that it matters."

"A couple of ounces of weed, and my Sig Sauer. Oh yeah, and my Glock."

"Goin' back to start a war?"

"Just self-protection. Lots of people don't like me."

"Hell, I know lot's of people in 'Frisco think you're just fine."

"Stand up guy," Manny put in. "Hey watch out for that hill."

"If you need a place to crash, call me," I said, basking in the acclaim.

Manny winced. "Don't say that."

"Say what?"

"Crash."

Berto snorted. "Now you pissed me off. Just for that I'm going to treat you to a two-point landing."

"That ain't funny," Manny said weakly.

Adrift on my own private opioid cruise I watched the big man stiffen when Berto started to descend at his trademark steep angle which was better suited for a dive bomber.

Manny gripped the edges of his seat as the plane skimmed the tops of some trees. He groaned loudly when a wooded hill appeared directly in front of us and closed his eyes.

Cackling all the way Berto nosed up sharply, shot between two redwoods at the top of the hill, and nosed down at a forty-five degree angle. The whole plane shuddered when the wheels touched ground hard, bounced, then dropped straight down into a screeching skid for about fifty feet before it stopped.

Berto whooped. "Goal! I can set this baby on a dime!"

Marty's face was chalk white and his big jaw was clamped tight. He staggered out of the plane, wobbled a few feet, and tossed his breakfast.

Grinning sheepishly, Berto ambled to Manny's side and patted his shoulder. "Easy partner, just havin' some fun."

For a moment I thought Manny would whack him.

"You're fucking insane," he declared and stormed off.

I watched impassively. The acrobatic landing hadn't affected me one way or the other.

When you're behind heroin you don't give a flying fuck.

Anyway, Manny couldn't go far.

We had landed on an unused cow field next to a freeway.

He turned and glared at me. "Where the bumfuck are we?"

I spotted a familiar green vehicle at the base of the hill we had just vaulted.

"Need a ride?"

Berto joined us. "What, in that old-school Mercury? Shit, I got my Corvette right there. Come on Manny I'll take you in style."

Sure enough a red 'Vette was parked behind my vintage ride

"I ain't going anywhere with you, you fucking nut job," Manny said, marching back to get his bags from the plane.

I had texted our landing coordinates to Len Zane who drove the Green Ghost to the site. He was leaning against the Mercury smoking a J as we approached. He gave me a lazy smile.

"That was some landing, run out of gas?"

Manny snorted. "Pilot's a fucking adrenaline junkie."

"Len meet Manny Alfano," I said, stung by the word 'junkie.'

That was me.

Len gave me an appraising squint. "You look like hell Max."

"I just got back from there."

Actually I never left.

As soon as I slid behind the wheel I noticed the change.

On the left side of the dash was a four-button panel crowned by a glass dial that was either an alarm clock or some sort of pressure gauge.

Len looked at me with bemused pride. "I installed a little booster system, in case you needed more speed. Just flip the red switch."

"More than a buck seventy? Must be nitrous."

Manny seemed impressed. "Nitrous oxide, you a mechanic?"

"Len built this custom wreck," I told him, "from the superchargers, to the computers."

That did it. Manny launched into a long dialogue with Len on the art of customizing cars. Turns out he had done the panel work on the Escalade personally.

We dropped Manny at the Larkspur Ferry landing where his cousin Pauley was waiting. Broad shouldered, lantern jawed, balding with a fringe of greying hair, Paulie might have been Manny's brother.

A polite handshake for Paulie, a brief hug for Manny and I was out of there. I wasn't looking to make new friends.

"So what happened in New York?" Len said as we drove off.

"I got shot."

"You get the shooter?"

"No."

"Looks like he got to you Max."

Reflexively I checked myself in the rear view. Gaunt features, pinned green eyes set deep in dark hollows... the eyes of a lost soul.

# Chapter 23

After driving Len to his garage I headed directly to my safe house in Corte Madera hauling an industrial sized load of self-pity. When I arrived I spotted a bottle of scotch standing at attention on my kitchen counter and didn't hesitate.

A couple of shots, a snort of my diminishing supply of H and I was ready to collapse.

I awoke at four thirty in the morning. At first I didn't know where I was. Numbly, I showered, made some coffee, and generally tried to crawl out of the depression that felt like the bottom of a deep grave in Potter's field.

I was only a few miles from my wife and daughter but couldn't go near them. Not that I wanted them to see me in my present pathetic state.

Aware that I was nearly out of smack, I smoked some weed and got on my computer system. My home equipment is significantly more powerful than the Mac I travel with and I hoped to penetrate Berlinski's finances. I lasted less than twenty minutes. By then my side was throbbing and I was developing nasty flu symptoms: runny nose, chills, nausea.

I did a line and the flu vanished, along with my energy. For the next hour I sat in front of the TV, staring blankly at the screen until it dawned I was watching the fucking shopping network. I switched from rhinestone bracelets to the news which – if possible – was even more miserable than my wretched state.

Wretched because America, the land that I loved was morphing into a corporate Gulag. And because my heroin would be gone by tomorrow.

Sometime later I heard a knock at my door. Reflexively I glanced at the overnight bag where my Sig Sauer was packed.

Paranoid? My religion.

It was my landlord, Organic Phil. Although over eighty his thick white hair and erect bearing gave him the air of a man of sixty.

"Oh Max, you look terrible," he said, stepping inside for a closer look.

"I had a problem in New York."

"What happened?"

"Somebody shot me."

"With a gun?"

I skipped the sarcasm. "Yeah."

Suddenly he was all business. "Let me see the wound."

He examined my injured side and left. He returned with a shopping bag full of various potions, unguents and salves. After treating my wound he left again and came back with a big glass of vegetable juice.

"Now," he said, sitting across from me and clasping his hands like a priest about to hear confession, "tell me exactly what happened."

Add another mortal sin to my already crowded account.

"I was mugged in a subway. Lucky a train came along. That's all I remember."

"Lucky? An inch left and you'd be dead. Well it's healing nicely. Doctor did a good job with the stitches."

I silently thanked Nurse Jenny Curry.

"It'll leave a scar but it could be worse. What the hell have you been eating? I'm gonna go make you some Tofu."

That's Organic Phil, ever the nutrition prophet.

When he left I snorted a line.

Fortified by carrot juice and smack I settled in front of the TV.

As always Trump was tweeting himself into the headlines, blasting

Impeachment,

Immigrants

The Free Press.

By now America had become inured to the daily barrage of vitriol aimed at anybody who dared disagree with his reckless lies.

Me? Smacked out, I could give a shit.

Phil returned with a tofu salad which I dutifully ate under his watchful eye. Alone again I smoked a J and hopped on the computer.

Despite my advanced equipment and reputed skills the entrance to Berlinski's financial stronghold continued to elude me. Finally I switched on the TV and vegged out.

Phil dropped in later with some sort of power drink and buckwheat pasta. Grateful for the TLC, I consumed the bland food with forced enthusiasm.

Forced because my body was telling me it was time for another line.

"We are what we eat," Phil said solemnly.

And drink, and snort.

By now my body was demanding a line or else. I was sweating, getting the chills.

"I'm not feeling so hot. I think I'll take a nap."

Phil nodded. "Do that. I'll come back later with soup."

Alone, I tapped out a modest line on a mirror but it soon became clear it wasn't enough. Reluctantly I took stock.

Barely enough for bedtime tonight and breakfast tomorrow. After that I was on my own. I poured a stiff shot of scotch and went back to the tube.

Watched *The Lady Eve* on my favorite channel, Turner Classic Movies. A brilliant comedy with Henry Fonda and Barbara Stanwyck written and directed by Preston Sturges. Actually had me laughing.

At one time film maker Sturges was earning the highest salary in America.

Died broke.

As promised Phil came back bearing soup and something called essential grains.

To me essential grains means pizza.

Phil hung around and we talked old movies. My landlord has an encyclopedic knowledge of the Golden Age of Hollywood, due partially to his advanced years.

"Douglas Fairbanks played a detective called Coke Enneday who did cocaine like Popeye did spinach," he confided over an herbal tea. "That was back in the nineteen twenties. Silent movies."

"Every day has its decadence," I said sagely.

After all it was something I knew about.

"Maybe I'll cook up some protein pancakes tomorrow."

Phil's focus never strayed far from food. While mine honed in on heroin like a heat-seeking missile. The withdrawal jitters began to scratch my sweaty skin and my hand trembled.

After a couple of discreet yawns Phil said goodnight.

The moment I fixed, the sweats and jitters dissolved into a warm fuzzy cloud. My relief was tempered by the knowledge I was down to my final line.

To muffle my panic I downed a hefty jolt of scotch quickly followed by another.

It worked.

I was walking on a beach in Mexico when the bright California sun nudged me awake. A long shower and fresh brewed coffee failed to disperse the cobwebs. Numbly I noted my side no longer throbbed or ached. I resolved to start working out again.

Yeah right. My focus was on one thing. That last line of smack.

The plan was to stave things off as long as possible.

I lit a J and switched on the news.

Not a good way to start the day. The news that is.

The weed made our national demise tolerable, like blessing a beloved relative's funeral.

Turned to TCM and found *Shane* with Alan Ladd, a western parable of a simpler time when a good sock on the jaw and a fast draw solved all social problems.

Phil fell by with the promised protein pancakes and a vegetable drink. His concerned frown faded when he saw the screen.

"That's Alan Ladd. " Phil said. "He was very short you know."

Oh yeah?"

"He had to stand on a box sometimes."

"He was great in *This Gun For Hire*," I said, devouring the pancakes. The weed had made me hungry.

"Veronica Lake, his co-star was short too. Maybe I should have made more pancakes."

"This is just fine Phil. I appreciate your looking after me."

"That's what friends do."

I had to agree, though I tended to be a tad zealous on that front.

+     +     +

For a while I actually thought I could handle it.

A fat joint, coffee fortified with scotch, no more smack? No problem.

That lasted a whole hour.

Then second by second, crack by crack... I came apart.

It started with the sweats closely followed by the chills. I threw on a sweater and rolled another J. While rolling my hands shook. I made another Irish coffee, heavy on the Irish part and lit up.

It mellowed things for about fifteen minutes before a vicious attack of nausea drove me to the bathroom where I hurled the pancakes, health juice, coffee, scotch, and whatever was left over from the night before.

It didn't stop there.

I went through several spastic minutes of dry heaves that left me gasping for air. At the same time it seemed that all the pain I'd managed to avoid the past few weeks had congealed into a single ball like a spent star and shattered in a ferocious blast of agony.

My joints, my ribs, my wound, all hurt like hell. I lay in a cramped fetal position on the bathroom floor until the squall passed.

Greateful for the lull I took a quick shower, changed into a sweat suit and stumbled to my car, body slightly bent by cramps. At this point my brain was screaming two conflicting messages.

Go out and get some Heroin, Oxycodone, Fentanyl, Percodan, Codeine...any fucking thing. Or

Go out and get some fucking help.

The chills came back in the car. That and a runny nose made it difficult to drive. I amped up the heater but was unable to locate a Kleenex. At the toll booth I handed the attendant some damp bills and drove straight to Chinatown.

My friend Jimmy Chu lives there.

Doctor James Chu has degrees in Asian Medicine, Ayurvedic Medicine, Chiropractic Medicine, and Acupuncture. In the past he's brought my battered body back to a semblance of life. But this was different. This time my soul was dying.

Jimmy owns a medicinal herb store on Jackson Street that serves as a one-stop clinic. Finding parking in Chinatown is always a bitch and I was forced to walk three blocks to Jimmy's shop, certain everyone could tell I was a junkie by my cramped shuffle.

I put on a brave smile but Jimmy greeted my entrance with the stricken surprise of a bystander watching a car crash.

"Holy shit Max, what happened? You look awful."

That made it unanimous.

"I was shot," I said, opting for the sympathy vote.

"You better come back here," Jimmy said, closing up the shop.

I stepped behind the large lacquered screen that separated the herb store from the medical office which consisted of a padded massage table, shelves with basic medical tools, a large sink, a small stove, and an enormous mahogany bureau, about six feet high, with at least a hundred tiny drawers, all neatly labeled. I sat on the edge of the padded table while Jimmy went through his preliminary tests: blood pressure, eye check, breathe deep, the usual.

"How did you get shot?" Jimmy said as he shined a light in my eye.

Normally I would bullshit a civilian, but it so happened Jimmy was a combat buddy. Some years back we had taken on a local Tong that had kidnapped Jimmy's daughter. Jimmy also put his ass on the line to help me nail a serial killer.

"I've been on a case," I began, oddly relieved to be able to tell the truth. I told him of ICE's illicit activities in the area, including the murders of a Latino lawyer, a black cop and a Latino organizer. Ending with Terry's death.

For my part, I had shot a corrupt CIA agent and killed a particularly nasty ICE honcho.

Jimmy kept working, listening quietly to the litany of tragedies.

"Seriously Max?" he said finally.

I began to get the chills. "You think I'm making this up?"

Jimmy switched on the overhead heat lamp. "You're hiding something right?"

"Such as?"

"Max your pupils show high drug and alcohol abuse. Mainly opioid, probably heroin."

"Oh that. Yeah."

"Are you going through withdrawal now?"

"Definitely."

"Okay, strip drown to your shorts."

He went to the huge bureau and took various herbs from the small drawers. He then cooked up the herbs on the stove. An acrid smell wafted my way.

"Drink it all," he said, giving me a steaming cup of brackish brew.

It was very bitter. As he took my empty cup Jimmy looked at me hard, as if I was a stranger who resembled someone he knew.

"Have you seen Samantha lately?"

At hearing my daughter's name the air rushed from my belly.

"In this condition?" I said. "Would you?"

"Lie down, I'll be right back."

The warmth from the overhead heat lamp seemed to intensify. I began to perspire. In a few minutes I was sweating profusely, rivulets of perspiration oozing from my pores.

Jimmy returned and covered my body with a couple of large towels. He busied himself at the table while I continued to dehydrate at an alarming rate. Finally he told me to dry myself.

As I toweled off he took a roll of black silk from a lacquered box. He unrolled the cloth and I saw it contained a number of gold needles. His Acupuncture tools. He began inserting the needles in various parts of my anatomy. Somewhere during the process I dozed off.

The overhead light was off when I opened my eyes.

"Make sure you drink lots of water," Jimmy advised as I dressed. "Come back tomorrow after three."

"How many sessions do I need?"

Jimmy averted his eyes. "I'll let you know."

I got the sense he was somehow disappointed in me.

Leaving the shop I felt hollowed out, empty.

Once home I dutifully drank some water with my scotch and stared at the TV. The opioid hunger burned inside me but I managed to tamp it down with weed.

In the morning it was worse.

I managed to hold on until the afternoon and drove back to Chinatown.

Jimmy took me through the same routine: heat, bitter herb brew, excessive sweats, Acupuncture. Except this time at the finish I was famished.

After a big meal at Yuet Lee, one of my favorites, I walked to my computer shop and encountered weeks of unpaid bills.

It took about two hours to clean things up. By then I was getting jittery. I popped a bottle of overproof Herradura and poured a healthy shot. Then another.

Tequila has its tricks. A slightly psychedelic quality since it's derived from cactus. So rather than numbing my senses it put me on high alert. I walked fitfully around my shop trying not to think about going out to score some oxy.

Wouldn't take more than twenty minutes door to door.

Instead I rolled an obese joint and lit up the TV. I caught *Tequila Sunrise* and stayed there savoring the brilliant dialogue and direction of Robert Towne.

Inspired by the film I had another round or two of *Herradura* and finally fell asleep in the middle of a documentary about Hitler's rise to power.

In the morning I felt different.

Hungover, yes, beat down, perhaps–but different.

For one thing I was hungry. I took a brisk walk to Washington Square and took refuge in Mario's. Over my second Cappuccino and breakfast croissant I realized the wound in my side was no longer a factor.

It also dawned on me that Christmas was nearly here.

Mobilized by guilt I dashed out and took a cab to Union Square.

While shopping for toys, the sight of all those kids lined up for Santa unleashed a flood of memories: images of our first Christmas as a family, Samantha at two, opening her present under the tree lights... Instantly my buoyant holiday spirit disintegrated and drained into a black hole in the center of my being. A place where nothing could live but regret.

I looked for a bar where I could ease the pain with scotch. In the corner of my vision I glimpsed a flower vendor pass something to a customer.

It wasn't a rose.

I was seized by a fierce impulse to buy whatever dope he was dealing. Anything to escape the cold embrace of my despair.

Then I thought of my little girl. If I stopped to shop now I might never see her again. I kept walking. All the way to Chinatown – and Doctor Jimmy Chu.

+        +        +

"You're trying to drink this thing away," Jimmy said after a brief exam. "You're replacing one addiction with another. Doesn't work that way. The gunshot wound is healed. No more excuses. And don't give any shit about depression."

He paused and gave me that hard look again as if I might be someone else. "You know better Max. The depression goes with the withdrawal. That's the hook. Deal with it."

His little inspirational speech stayed with me during the treatment which seemed to go on longer than usual.

I kept thinking about what Jimmy said on the drive back to Marin.

This was no time to cultivate bad habits.

If I didn't nail Berlinski the CIA, ICE and probably the DEA would be hunting me for what little remained of my life. Not to mention Berlinski himself. My family would be in constant jeopardy and Andre would get away with Terry's murder.

I was painfully aware it was me he intended to kill. Which made me partially responsible.

On the way back to my safe house I did some shopping: fruit, salad, barbecued chicken, B vitamins, juices. It wouldn't pass Phil's lofty standards but it was as organic as I get.

It was still early when I arrived so in a burst of enthusiasm I went out for a jog around the hood.

I didn't get far.

Breathing hard and somewhat humbled I walked slowly back home.

The drug yearning started to itch but I stayed busy. I took a long shower, blended a fruit smoothie, and made a chicken sandwich. After dinner I brewed coffee and rolled a fat joint.

Organic Phil dropped in to check on my progress. "You look better today," he said, opening my refrigerator to deposit a fresh vegetable juice. "Keep drinking this stuff and you'll be good as new."

Of course that would never happen but I appreciated his optimism.

Despite the

New-Age Diet

Exercise

Good intentions

I was still fucked

Ready or not I had to jump back into the game.

# Chapter 24

Boutilier had a feeling he was being followed.

He kept checking his rear view mirror even though it was nearly impossible to spot a tail on the busy freeway. So he switched on the FM and continued to San Francisco.

The city was an hour from Petaluma but Police Captain Lowell wanted to meet him in the Russian Hill area. He found parking a few blocks away and used one-way streets to elude any follower.

"I chose this place for two reasons," Lowell told Boutilier when he arrived. "Number one because we're not likely to be seen, and two it's the best pizza in town."

"Is something going down?"

"ICE is sending us Zallen's replacement."

"Any idea who?"

Lowell shrugged. "Rumor is, it's a female."

"A female Zallen? There's a scary image."

"Anything on your end?"

"Nobody tells me anything. Ever since I suggested the ICE operation here might be compromised, my section chief has me on his shit list."

"Compromised? That's putting it mildly."

"He says he reported my claims to the northwest director of Homeland and it's their problem now."

"Did he really say *claims*?"

"Yeah, why?"

"Because 'claims' fall far short of charges backed by evidence."

"I have plenty of evidence. Jenkins doesn't know it yet."

"Good. Keep it that way."

"You think he's in on it?"

"Could very well be. In that case your ass is grass and he's the mower."

"How so? I've got the evidence."

"Jenkins is section chief. He can sweep your evidence under the rug and throw the whole thing onto you." Lowell paused. "How long have you been with the Company?"

Boutilier felt his face flush. "You think I'm too green to handle this?"

Lowell's flinty expression didn't waver. "I think you need to watch your back. If Jenkins is in on this he has two options: throw you under the bus or... take you off the board."

"You mean like have me transferred."

"I mean like have you killed."

The pizza arrived, filling the uncomfortable silence.

Boutilier had long suspected he was being set up but he hadn't considered the possibility that Jenkins would actually have him killed.

"Any word from Max?" he said, changing the subject.

"Not a word. I'm getting worried."

"Ever since the thing with Zallen, the ICE operation has slowed down."

"They still fly in every night."

"You think they're smuggling drugs?"

Lowell gave him a lopsided smile "What else, medical supplies? Man, this pizza is good."

"Can't we organize a raid?"

"With who, ICE or the DEA?"

Boutilier sighed. "Bad idea, great pizza."

Ever since Max killed Zallen there was a war between the two agencies. In fact he still didn't understand how the CIA was involved in a Homeland operation.

Which leaves me up the fucking creek without a clue, Boutilier reflected unhappily.

The gravity of his situation settled over Boutilier like a heavy cloak as he drove north to Petaluma. He felt hemmed in, weighed down, and for the first time, helpless. His carefully compiled evidence meant nothing. The only thing he could count on was the Glock in the glove box.

He made a mental note to start carrying the weapon.

Late the next morning Police Chief Bannon called him.

"How soon can you be here? There's somebody I want you to meet."

"Twenty minutes," Boutilier said coolly, and hung up. He disliked Bannon as much as he had Zallen.

No doubt Bannon wanted him to meet Zallen's replacement. Another ICE-hole, he thought, grinning at his little joke.

The woman standing Bannon's office was no joke.

Tall, athletically slim, with short blonde hair that framed a heart shaped face, and silver grey eyes that seemed to take in everything at once, Homeland Agent Bryce Taylor greeted Boutilier with a firm handshake then turned away, as if she had measured him at first glance and found him wanting.

"So this bastard who murdered Zallen – Who the hell is he?" Taylor demanded. Her question was directed at Bannon but took in everyone in the room, which included Captain Lowell.

Bannon spread his hands. "His name is Max LeBlue. Undercover for the DEA. That's all we have. The DEA won't release his file. Says it would compromise an ongoing investigation."

"Horseshit. This LeBlue has gone rogue and they're covering their bureaucratic ass. Zallen was one of ours."

One of yours maybe, Boutilier thought. He looked up and collided with Taylor's steel grey eyes.

"What's the Company have on this guy?"

He didn't waver. "All undercover assets work under the same rules. Otherwise they'd all be in jeopardy of being exposed. You need a court order."

Taylor pivoted to Lowell. "What about you? Anything?"

"Actually we do. The man shot along with Zallen is Luke Pardo, member of a local Motorcycle gang known as the Vandals. Pardo still hasn't told us why he was there with Zallen."

"Maybe he was there with LeBlue."

"Not likely."

"Oh, why is that Captain?"

"The Vandals have a bounty on LeBlue's head."

For the first time uncertainty flickered across her face.

"I need to interview Pardo."

"That might be difficult."

She rolled her eyes. "What now?"

"Pardo skipped bail last week."

Clearly exasperated Taylor turned to Bannon. "Can I at least see his goddamn rap sheet?"

"Of course, Lowell here will get it to you right away."

"Thank the Lord for small favors," she said, marching out of the room.

A short time later she poked her head inside the storage room Boutilier had converted to an office.

"Got some time for a coffee meeting?"

"Sure," he said, "I know a place."

Boutilier chose a small bakery located away from the main streets that served gourmet coffee and fresh pastry.

They didn't speak much on the short drive and he braced himself for some intense questions. Instead she was friendly, charming even a bit flirtatious.

"I love little places like this, how did you find it?"

"Just stumbled on it. Petaluma has lots of odd corners."

"Maybe you'll show me some."

Boutilier shrugged. "Anytime," He didn't like being played.

Taylor seemed to sense this and shifted gears.

"Word is you wrote up a complaint about my predecessor, Paul Zallen," she said flatly.

"That's correct – and classified. How did you find out?"

"Your boss passed it on to my boss. It's in our court now and the defendant is dead." She gave him a sympathetic smile. "What exactly was the problem with Zallen?"

Zallen was a corrupt, cruel, motherfucker, he wanted to say but he didn't know where Taylor stood. For all he knew she was in on the payoffs.

"He was abusing the illegals, especially the women," he said instead.

"So you think this DEA agent was justified in killing him?"

Boutilier lifted his hands in mock surrender. "That's way above my pay grade. But there's still the question of Luke Pardo. What's a member of a motorcycle gang doing with Zallen? The Vandals' headquarters are right here in town. If I were you I'd shake that tree."

"Thanks for the advice and the great coffee," Taylor said briskly. "I'll let you know when our next field operation is scheduled."

She leaned closer, jaw set and silver eyes blazing. "Just for the record, I work by the book, so put that in your next report."

"Don't worry I'll stay well out of your way – can I drop you somewhere?"

That went well, Boutilier reflected, walking to his car. The charming Agent Taylor had a spikey attitude. Thanks to Jenkins he had been outed as an informer which was both embarrassing and fucking dangerous. However it hadn't escaped his notice that Taylor launched her counterattack when he mentioned Pardo and the Vandals.

Now I understand why Lowell wanted to meet in San Francisco, Boutilier thought, dialing the police captain's mobile.

"I can't do anything without a subpoena" Lowell told him, "For some reason Chief Bannon is reluctant to go up against the Vandals."

They had agreed to meet at a small, North Beach pub called Tony Nix. The place was crowded with regulars and noisy. Lowell's partner Steve was tending bar and they were staying in town that night.

"Now that Jenkins blew my cover sure as shit Taylor won't try to buy me off the way Zallen did," Boutilier said. "No more envelopes stuffed with cash."

"Yeah but you have a clear record of past payments and the cash," Lowell reminded.

Boutilier gave him a rueful smile. "True, I've got the evidence right here." He showed Lowell the two small keys on a silver chain around his neck. "Locked up tight in a bank vault. But who can I give it to? It looks like my section chief is in on it."

"Did Taylor mention Max?"

"She tried to trap me into saying Max was justified."

"It was self-defense. Both men were armed."

"Makes no difference, they're out for blood."

"I know, Bannon even formed a little death squad. Where ever Max is holed up, he'd better stay there."

Lowell lifted his glass. "Happy holidays Max."

+    +    +

Parking in North Beach during Christmas season was non-existent and Boutilier had to leave his car near the Stockton Tunnel at the outer edge of Chinatown. He didn't mind the long walk, the city was lit up for the holiday season and the cafes and restaurants were filled.

Passing Café Greco he glanced through the window and spotted a familiar figure. Agent Bryce Taylor was hunched over a laptop, enjoying a cappuccino. She looked up and caught his eye.

He waved, intending to move on but she motioned him inside.

"Hi, I was just sending some greetings and cheers" she said, pointing at the laptop. "I always get misty this time of the year."

"Do you have family nearby?"

"Mom's dead and dad is two wives removed."

"What are you doing in North Beach?"

Her small pout made her look like a teenager. "Oh you know Petaluma. Locked up tight by ten p.m. I needed to be around people, pretty lights, that sort of thing."

Boutilier nodded. He felt the same way.

"I guess I'm a sucker for Christmas. And speaking of good will towards men, I want to apologize for the way I acted this afternoon."

He shrugged. "Considering the circumstances..."

"There's really no excuse." She pouted again. "We're supposed to be on the same side."

It was possible she knew nothing of the payoffs, he reflected. "We are," he said softly, "you ready for another cappuccino?"

Off duty Bryce, as he now called her, was animated and displayed a sharp sense of humor, especially when it came to Chief Bannon.

"Can you believe the old goat hit on me an hour after I reported? He must be sixty."

"Actually I can believe it."

"Was that supposed to be a compliment?"

His stomach tightened. "Politically incorrect?"

Her smile melted the tension. "Maybe. But socially correct. I could use a compliment right now."

"Holiday depression?"

"That and the demands of my job. I'm not sure I'm up to the challenge."

"I'm certain you can handle it."

"Wish I had your confidence. Let's talk about something else."

"Fine do you like movies?"

"I love movies, especially *Marriage Story*."

Apparently Bryce was an Adam Driver fan. Boutilier had seen the actor in the latest episode of Star Wars but was less enthusiastic than Bryce.

"Driver was pretty good in *BlackKKlansman*," he said, "lately he seems to be in everything."

She grinned. "Well this girl can't get enough."

Oddly, her personality endowed the trivial conversation with a note of import as if something of consequence were being decided.

"Guess you'll be visiting family," she said with that now familiar pout.

"No family to speak of. Just my brother, he lives in Miami."

She drummed her fingers on the table. "I think it's time I drive back to Petaluma before the coffee wears off. Can I give you a ride?"

"Actually I have my car. I'm parked over by the Tunnel in Chinatown."

"No problem. I lucked out with parking. I can drive you there."

"Sounds good."

Bryce's car was a block away. As they walked she heaved a long sigh.

"Still depressed?"

"Oh it's just that sometimes I hate my job."

"You can always quit."

She gave him a regretful smile. "In too deep."

"When's your next op?"

"Middle of January."

"I'll try to help."

"Sure, thanks."

In the car driving through the now deserted streets of Chinatown she seemed pensive.

"Want to get an eggnog or something over the weekend?"

She smiled. "We'll see."

Boutilier took it as an encouraging sign.

"This is it," he said, when they reached his car. "Thanks for the lift."

As he got behind the wheel and shut the door Bryce's Taurus rolled past and stopped just ahead of him, temporarily blocking his car.

Bryce got out and walked towards him.

"I wanted to tell you something," she said.

"Yes what?"

She looked at him with that little pout which was part regret, part mischievous teen.

"I'm really sorry."

Confused, he realized she had a gun in her hand.

It was the last thing he saw before she blew off the top of his skull.

*"This is not the end. It is not even the beginning of the
end. But it is, perhaps, the end of the beginning."*
– Winston Churchill

# Chapter 25

Christmas Eve is not for the lonely.

The jolly carols and festooned trees only highlight the empty room where St. Nick ate the milk and cookies and left a lump of coal.

I was on the cusp of a massive feeling-sorry-for-myself binge which usually preceded a massive drinking binge. Instead I rolled a fat J and brewed a pot of strong coffee. I was holed up in my Marin pad, the irony being that my wife and daughter were less than a half hour away.

However if anyone associated with

ICE

the Vandals M.C.

the DEA

the CIA

the Petaluma PD

should discover where my family lived, I had no doubt they would be slaughtered.

Paranoid? To the bone.

Halfway down my joint I had a brilliant idea.

Every time you step into a vehicle you become vulnerable to stop, search and seizure. Right?

But a bicycle is invisible – if you keep to local streets. So I stuffed the presents I'd bought into a back pack and cycled through the dark, deserted back roads of Marin to my house.

I could see the tree lights through the window as I quietly climbed the stairs and left the back pack at the front door. Nina would know who it was from.

Rolling back I felt lightheaded, a fugitive Santa returning from a stealth mission.

+    +    +

In the morning I woke up feeling refreshed.

After a healthy breakfast that would have made Organic Phil proud I decided to call Detective Lowell and find out who else was hunting me.

"Merry Christmas Bob."

"Jesus, Max."

His funereal tone was far from festive.

"What's up?"

"Our whistleblower. The kid who replaced Goldsmith."

"Boutilier?"

"I met with him last night. Two hours later somebody killed him."

"Where are you?"

"Steve's place in the Castro."

"I'll meet you at the pizza joint you like."

The problem with Christmas Day in San Francisco is that all the restaurants are closed, including ZA Pizza. Except of course for Chinese restaurants. Everything in Chinatown being jammed we wound up in a Bakery on Jackson Street. Over coconut buns and coffee Lowell told me the details of Boutilier's murder he'd gotten from the original police report.

"Pretty consistent with a robbery, wallet and phone missing. Single shot from a .38 no sign of resistance. Funny thing, his weapon was still in the glove compartment. And they found his laptop in the trunk."

"Robbery? High risk, small payoff. It stinks."

"I warned him to watch his back," Lowell said, shaking his head. "He was a good man. Even worse we're about to lose the evidence on Paul Zallen."

"Which evidence?"

"Boutilier kept records of the payoffs and stashed the cash and records in a safety deposit box. He wore the keys around his neck. I tried to get the keys this morning but SFPD won't release them without a court order. If today wasn't Christmas the CIA would already have them and buried everything along with Boutilier."

Fuck me. That evidence was the only thing that got me off the hook for shooting Goldsmith and killing Zallen.

I immediately grabbed my phone and punched Delaney's personal number.

"For god's sake Max, it's fucking Christmas!"

"Thank God it is Christmas or we'd both be fucked."

I gave him the short version of events: Boutilier's murder, the bank keys.

"The evidence in that safety deposit box clears everybody – me, you, the DEA. But we need that court order before the CIA buries it... and us."

One thing about Delaney, he was a survivor. And a quick learner.

"Alright, alright," he said hoarsely, I'll get back to you."

Three hours later he called back. By then Lowell and I were waiting it out in Mr. Bing's bar. The music made it tough to hear.

"You got your court order," Delaney announced. "Unfortunately I had to put down your name. So move fast." He gave me the details, where to pick it up, computer links, so on. The Stones flared on the jukebox as I was about to hang up but I heard something about *Berlinski*.

"Wait, it's too noisy," I said, walking outside, "what did you just say?"

"I said your boy Berlinski is up to his old tricks in Mexico. Our man there tells us he's got a stable of twenty very young girls on his compound outside Tijuana. And he's getting cozy with the local Cartel."

The Preacher suddenly rose up, his wrath pushing aside whatever vestiges of good will towards men were still floating about.

"What's wrong?" Lowell said when I returned, "you look like you're ready to eat human flesh."

I told him about Berlinski's penchant for human trafficking. "Their fucking government contracts for these ICE charter flights make it near legal; girls, guns drugs, money, whatever – fly Air Scumbag."

"Keep your eye on the ball partner," Lowell said quietly. "Let's go get our evidence."

I picked up the court order at the local DEA field office where the agent in charge eyed me suspiciously.

"Max LeBlue? We're supposed to arrest you. ICE sent us a memo..."

Since he was the only agent working the day after Christmas I assumed he was junior.

"First of all I'm undercover numbnuts so don't broadcast my fucking name which is on the court order that you've been ordered to release ASAP."

He ran a shaky hand over his crew cut. "Right away sir."

Our next stop didn't go as smoothly. The Evidence Room at San Francisco Police Headquarters was in the basement and the short, pot-bellied officer in charge looked like a gnome who lived down there permanently.

"Uh I don't know about this," Sargent Gilliam said, chewing thoughtfully on his toothpick. "We got a call from Washington D.C. to hold this evidence."

"If you'll notice this court order calls for immediate release. We're on the clock here Sargent."

He peered at me through the cage separating us. "I don't know, I got to check with the chief."

"Get him on the phone. No problem."

Gilliam suppressed a burp. "He won't be in until tomorrow."

That did it. The Preacher woke up enraged. It must have showed for just as I was about to reach through the cage for Gilliam's neck Lowell put a firm hand on my shoulder and yanked me back.

"Look Sarge," he said, dropping his ID on the counter, "I'm a cop myself and there's one thing I know. If we lose our suspects because our evidence is late you're going to have a shitload of explaining to do. You'll be filling out paperwork for years."

Having a Detective Captain as your sidekick when trying to extract evidence from the SFPD helps but even with that and a court order it still took more serious arm-twisting to get Boutilier's safety deposit keys.

"Jesus Max you need to watch your temper," Lowell said over a late breakfast, "I thought you were going to deck that dumbass sergeant."

"I know, I should brush up on my people skills. But we got the damn keys."

"Yeah but now he'll remember us clearly. And when the CIA gets here..."

"We should be long gone," I said, dropping some bills on the table. "Let's get back to Petaluma."

Boutilier's safety deposit box at the Chase Bank was crammed with bundles of cash. Each bundle had a folded sheet of paper attached, with the circumstances of the payments, including names and dates. Zallen's name appeared on all of them.

"What next?" Lowell asked, as we walked out of the bank.

"I get out of Dodge before they send in the troops. I figure by now ICE knows it's me or them."

"They'll be covering planes, trains and buses from San Diego to Vancouver."

"It'll take a few hours before they're up to speed. I'll be in Hollywood by then."

I was wrong.

Among the niceties Len had installed in the new, improved version of the Green Ghost was a police scanner and my BOLO was all over the airwaves. I noticed an inordinate amount of police vehicles on the way to LA but my aged Mercury attracted little attention.

The DEA maintains a safe house in the Hollywood Hills above Beachwood Drive. It originally belonged to a film producer who decided to finance his next project with a shipment or two of coke. He lost his job, wife, house and money in that order. The lawyers got the money and the DEA kept the house.

I phoned Delaney somewhere north of Bakersfield.

"Do you have it?" he said in lieu of hello.

"Yes. I'm heading to LA to drop it off."

"Negative. Don't do anything until I get there."

"Really boss? You're picking it up personally?"

"Fuck you Max, just shut up and sit tight."

"They're on me like wolves in a butcher shop," Delaney declared when he arrived, "ICE, the CIA, even the FBI – they all want me fired."

"They all want me dead," I reminded.

"When this breaks you'll be a hero."

"Bullshit. Those psychos at ICE will be looking for revenge. And the CIA won't forget I shot on of theirs."

"The DEA will protect you on this. Maybe even a medal. Shit boy, this is your second big bust in as many months."

"Yeah and a year from now some spook will put a bullet through that medal."

"Fortunes of war. Meanwhile I'm going to tear those bastards in Washington a new asshole."

"I'm going to need a couple of favors."

"Oh, like what?"

"Tell your boys in Tijuana to lay out the red carpet when I get there – but quietly."

Delaney's bulldog face folded into a nasty grin. He reached into his briefcase and produced two sheets of paper. "I took the liberty of bringing along a fresh ninety-day contract."

"Does it include expenses?"

He fished inside his briefcase and came up with a thick envelope.

"Fifty thousand a month – first month in advance."

I hated when Delaney was ahead of me. It usually meant he was setting me up.

"You'll have a tough time getting into Mexico without somebody noticing," he mused.

"No worries," I said, as I signed my life away.

*"He will give them death and they will love him for it."*
– Derek Jacobi, *Gladiator*

# Chapter 26

Once you're out of LA the drive to San Diego is a breeze.

At night there's very little traffic and I had to resist opening up the Green Ghost for a shakedown cruise. Despite my transaction with Delaney it would be at least a week before the death sanctions would be lifted. But at the moment there was an active police BOLO for my ass.

So I took it slow and safe, like Eastwood in *The Mule*. Just a worn down dude singing along to the radio with a load of coke in his trunk. Except I made the mistake of turning on the news.

As a combat veteran I consider Trump's outright lies, his naked corruption of our democratic institutions, and his shameful treatment of refugee children, an insult to God, man and the flag.

That our so-called leaders would allow this pompous, overfed, draft dodger to threaten decorated war heroes while the senate conducted a cynical cover up marks a sad, pathetic chapter in America's bipolar history.

I noticed my outrage was goosing the speedometer past eighty and switched to easy listening. Soon I was humming along with 'What Are You Doing New Years' and easing down to sixty five. I was still humming when a police car cruised past me.

Before I reached San Diego I punched Sidney Kingman's number.

"What's up Sidney?"

"Everything is set. She's waiting for you."

He paused. "Are you sure about this?"

"No, but I'm going to do it anyway."

"It's your funeral."

"You can give the eulogy."

I sounded cocky but my mind was a morass of damp, sticky doubts. The sane thing to do was rest on my laurels. Bask in the glory of uncovering a corrupt conspiracy and clearing my good name.

And go the fuck home.

But Berlinski was still out there holding his White House contracts – and contacts. Sooner or later the boys in black suits will come knocking on my door. And Andre would be leading the pack.

Only he wouldn't knock.

Paranoid? My New Year's resolution.

+     +     +

When I reached San Diego I went to the address Sidney Kingman had provided. Selena Suarez was waiting for me. Her dark eyes were sad but her smile was genuine.

"Welcome Max. We're so happy to see you."

"I'm sorry it has to be like this. If it's any trouble..."

She put a finger to my lips. "Please Max. I will never forget all you did for us when Fernando was killed. What do you need?"

"Just a guide and a safe place to leave my car."

"The guide has been arranged. And you may leave the car in my garage."

"I don't think anyone would want to steal this," Selena said, when she saw my vintage model Mercury.

"That's part of its charm."

A small laugh broke through her somber expression then disappeared.

"Max, I heard... Sidney old me... "

She hesitated, suddenly embarrassed.

"What did Sidney say?"

"That... you killed the man who murdered Fernando. Is it true?"

"Yes," I said quietly, it's true."

Impulsively, Selena hugged me. "We will pray for you every night. Julia and me. Every night Max."

Is it possible to feel ashamed for feeling proud? I had killed a man and was now basking in spiritual grace.

Even worse, I was going into Mexico to kill again.

The plan was simple.

1: A guide would take me across the border.

2: Once inside I would contact the local DEA for resources.

3: I would whack Andre. Maybe Berlinski too.

"I can drive you to meet Oswaldo, he'll take you across the border," Selena said.

The name stirred a cloudy memory that instantly dissolved.

"You know this man?"

"Fernando worked with him in the past."

The professional guides known as "Coyotes" transport illegals on both sides of the border. Migrant workers and refugees fleeing to America – and criminals like me who needed to enter Mexico without signing in.

Coyotes have a horrendous reputation. Leaving migrants to die in the desert is the least of their crimes. Even the honest guides are forced to pay homage to the Cartels.

It ain't like Siddhartha ferrying good people across the water.

However I had prepared for the long hike which included a pocket GPS, a combat knife in my boot and a .45 caliber Taurus tucked in my pocket.

Better paranoid than dead.

Selena drove me to a diner at the edge of a Latino neighborhood.

"I'll introduce you and then I must leave," Selena said, almost apologetically. "Julia..."

"No worries. You've done more than enough already."

There were seven people inside the diner. Nine with waitress and short order cook. Two men sat at the counter, a colorfully tattooed young couple occupied a corner booth, and three large men were stuffed in another booth. The large men were also sporting heavy ink

Selena led me to the corner booth. Up close the couple was not as young as I first thought. The man's tank top did nothing to conceal a sizable gut and there were grey streaks in his van dyke beard. The only thing youthful about him was his upper torso; wide, well-defined deltoids and biceps the size of pineapples.

The female also had a well-formed upper body, half of which was spilling out of her tank top. The word Santa was inscribed on one breast, Bruja on the other. Her lips were blazing red. Like her boyfriend she wore shades.

"Oswaldo this in Max."

He nodded slightly. "Sure. Sit down, relax."

"I must go. My daughter's alone."

"She's probably asleep honey," the girl said but Selena was already walking away.

I slid into the booth. "So what's good here?"

"Nada." Oswaldo removed his shades. "We ain't here for dinner gringo."

I met his fierce stare. "When do we leave?"

"Now, tonight. You bring the cash?"

"Five grand right?"

"Make it six." He shrugged and spread his palms. "Inflation."

"It was bullshit and I had already counted out the money. Oswaldo was starting to piss me off. I leaned forward and lowered my voice.

"There's five in my pocket *esse*. You get me there and you get another five."

He blinked. "Let me see the money."

"Outside. You have a car?"

We made the exchange in Oswaldo's red '73 Pontiac Catalina, me in the back, his lady friend Brenda in front blasting the radio while he counted the cash.

"Turn that fucking thing down," Oswaldo said finally. He gave me that hard stare intended to intimidate. Probably practiced in his bathroom mirror.

"We get to Tijuana. I get another five. Guaranteed."

"No problem."

Brenda poked the backpack beside me. "What you carrying baby, drugs, guns or money?"

I smiled. "Water, protein bars and a laptop." I forgot to mention the forty five grand and .40 caliber Sig Sauer P226 in there.

"What else you packing gringo?" Oswaldo said slowly.

I kept smiling. "A great big can of none of your fucking business."

Brenda laughed. "He's funny."

Oswaldo started the car. "Yeah hilarious."

He drove to a deserted mall and parked near a black van. Four men emerged from the shadows of a darkened Walmart. Darkened or not I knew there were security cameras everywhere so I pulled up my hoodie, and kept my head down.

"Everybody here?" Oswaldo said.

A man wearing a Chargers football jersey grunted something in Spanish.

"Okay, everybody in the van."

The man in the football jersey slid open the side panel and we clambered inside. The Charger fan shut the door behind us and took the driver's seat. Oswaldo rode shotgun.

There were four of us in the rear. As my eyes adjusted I realized one was a female. I noticed two of my fellow travelers were checking me out. I nodded and they looked away.

It was a short trip. Twenty minutes later the van stopped at a semi-deserted beach. We walked across the sand in groups of three, spaced five minutes apart.

A pair of sleek aluminum boats with large outboard motors were waiting at water's edge their silver skins bright in the moonlight. Oswaldo directed us to board one of the boats. Then he pushed the boat into the surf and jumped in. I heard the other boat's engine cough awake and within moments we were knifing across the waves headed for open sea.

Once past the surf line the ocean was relatively calm. We continued for about twenty minutes then made a left turn well beyond Trump's futile wall.

I glanced back and saw Oswaldo gazing intently at something.

A low cluster of lights flickered dimly on the distant horizon like a glowworm. He kept his eyes fixed on the smudge of light as we raced past, the light craft skimming the water.

Oswaldo proved to be a skillful navigator. As soon as the lights were out of sight he cut the throttle and turned toward shore.

"You ever run into the coast guard out here?" I asked.

He shrugged. "They mind their own fucking business."

Alerted by the vague threat in his tone I patted the Taurus Compact in my pocket. The feel on the rubber grip was reassuring.

We rode the low surf onto the beach and Oswaldo cut the engine. When we debarked he pulled the light boat onto the sand. Door to door the trip had taken less than ninety minutes.

Clouds had obscured the moon and I couldn't see the other boat, or much else. Oswaldo led the way across the darkened beach to a concrete lot where three vans were parked. He paused, not sure which van was his and called out in a hoarse whisper.

"Yo, Chu Chu."

"Yo Exxon over here."

Where had I heard that name before? I couldn't place it. I was still rifling my mental files when we reached the van at the far end of the lot. This one had a rear door, which was open. Inside was a mattress covered by a rumpled blanket.

"Get in," Oswaldo said.

The girl hesitated, so I started to board.

"Not you."

"This isn't Tijuana."

"It's as far as you go gringo."

The moon came out of hiding and I saw two things:

The fear on the girl's face

The gun in Oswaldo's fist

"Now get in baby, we got big plans for you."

She froze, nearly hysterical. Oswaldo reached out and shoved her.

The blast from my Taurus ripped a flaming hole through my jacket and slammed Oswaldo to the concrete. I figured Chu Chu was likely armed and would come out shooting so I crouched behind the rear wheel.

I was wrong.

Chu Chu bolted out of the van like a fullback charging the line and didn't stop. He stumbled when he hit the ground but his legs kept churning until he was out of sight.

In the silence that followed I heard the sound of labored breathing. It was the girl. She was sobbing.

"Tranquillo," I said softly. "Where do want to go? Donde va?"

"Madre mia," she said between sobs.

"¿Donde va?" I repeated in my best mangled Spanish.

She produced an index card with an address. There was no town attached to the street name and number but when I consulted my GPS it confirmed the address was in Tijuana which was about ten miles north.

The sound of voices drifted in the distance. Chu Chu had left the keys in the ignition. I picked up Oswaldo's phone, motioned the girl into the van and drove north along the beach.

During the brief trip I tried to talk to the still frightened girl but all I got was her name, Oliva. She couldn't have been more than thirteen. Oliva started shivering so I gave her what was left of my jacket.

Tijuana is a tawdry strip of bars, discos, titty clubs, bordello's, drugstores, liquor stores, souvenir stalls, street dealers, strolling hookers, stone killers and bone stupid college boys, all strung together like a cheap necklace. The address Oliva gave me was on a darkened street within shouting distance of the action.

As I stepped out of the van a burly man in a white wife-beater appeared at the front gate. He jabbered at me in Spanish too rapid for me to understand. The only two words I got were chinga and pendajo. Finally Oliva came around and said something to the effect that I was a friend.

The man stepped back behind the gate. "Lucia!"

A tall woman with gaunt, tired, features came out of the house. When she saw Oliva her face came alive. Laughing and weeping at the same time the two women embraced.

Lucia welcomed me inside and I followed them into a small room furnished with a table and four chairs. As soon a she sat down Oliva launched into a long, impassioned monologue. Lucia kept nodding her head and murmuring sympathetically. So smiled at me when Oliva's voice faded in a fresh round of tears.

Lucia spoke passable English as opposed to my impassable Spanish.

"Please would you like Tea? Something to eat?"

I shook my head. The burly man went to fetch a blanket for Oliva who was still shivering.

"Poor child, she's only twelve years. All this trouble..."

"Why did she have to cross illegally?" I said.

"Her bag was stolen at the bus stop, with her phone, money, ID, everything. Oliva's mother is in hospital. Oliva call me from San Diego and say this man is taking her home. He'll find her job so she can pay him. I tell her no don't do it but she all alone and scared for her mother."

The burly man came into the room with a bottle of Mescal and two glasses. He filled them both and set one in front of me.

How could I refuse the hospitality? After a silent toast I drained the glass. The burly man refilled it. By this time the fiery liquid had burned its way down to my belly and settled like red hot coals in a furnace, spreading warmth across my stiff, battle-cramped body.

I smiled at my hosts. "You speak good English," I said to Lucia.

"I work in souvenir shop."

I nodded and sipped my Mescal. "The man who offered to take Oliva home is probably the same man who stole her bag," I said. "It's a trick to trap young girls."

Lucia turned to the heavy man who was pouring his third drink. She said something about Oliva. I presumed she was repeating what I said. The man knocked down his Mescal and slapped his palm on the table. He began ranting in high speed Spanish in which the words chinga and gracias appeared frequently.

Lucia gave me an embarrassed smile. "He says that you did the right thing. We all thank you."

I realized Oliva must have told them about the shooting. It was my cue to split. Before I left I dipped into my backpack and took out the five grand I had agreed to pay Oswaldo. I handed the cash to Lucia. "Take care of Oliva and her mother."

She pressed my hand and thanked me tearfully. "We will pray for you at mass. And we will never betray you."

As I drove off I realized I hadn't really thought about what I'd done back at that beach. Oswaldo was now another notch in my tattered soul.

Suddenly I felt tired. What was I trying to do by playing Robin Hood?

Help a poor, honest family – or secure a room in Heaven's retirement home?

Was I really trying to bribe God?

+    +    +

The DEA occupied a safe house on the better side of town. I had no doubt that every dealer in Tijuana knew its exact location. For that reason I left the van a few blocks away and walked.

Two senior agents ran the station, Harry Singer and Gil Moreno. They were expecting me.

"Welcome to Fort Apache," Singer said. He was a portly dude with fading hair and wise eyes. "This bruiser here is Gil Moreno."

"Did Delaney brief you?"

The two men exchanged a quick glance.

"In detail," Singer said with a wry smile.

"He said you're a wild card," Moreno added. He wasn't smiling.

'Bruiser' was an apt description of Moreno. He had the short, thick legs and heavy torso of a wrestler, and a face to match.

But butting heads with a man fresh from the kill is never wise. The Preacher blinked awake.

"You got a problem with wild cards?"

Singer got the memo and half-stepped between us. "Gil's got a problem with everybody. There's a reason we call this Fort Apache."

I took a deep breath and managed a smile. After all I would need their help. "Everybody's stressed on this gig." I said softening my tone. "Us and them."

Moreno folded his big hands. "Thing is, them just murdered one of our guys last week"

"Well I'm here to take them out."

That seemed to mollify Moreno.

"You want something to eat?" he asked casually, as if we'd been watching a ball game.

"Yeah, now that you mention it."

Singer nuked some tacos and Moreno popped a few bottles of Corona.

"We keep it simple around here, no cook, no housekeeper." Singer explained. "Thank god for the microwave."

"Budget?"

"Fucking Cartel. They've got the whole town on their payroll. Cops, federales, housekeepers, everybody"

"What kind of cover do you have?"

"We're art dealers," Moreno said between mouthfuls, He waved his hand around the dining area. "But nobody believes it."

Indeed the walls were hung with boldly colored paintings, mostly primitive, mostly bad.

"Your guy, what happened to him?"

The question sobered the mood. Modena drained his beer.

"Her actually, name of Angela Carson. Worked undercover dancing at a high-end club."

"She was a stripper?"

"You know a better cover?"

He had me there. Angela had access to both management and brand new drug cowboys with loose lips.

Singer left the room and came back with a framed photo. It was a picture of a young couple, faces pressed together, smiling at the camera. The guy was clean cut, tennis player handsome, the girl had dark sensual eyes and a vivid smile .

"It's the only thing she left behind. We don't even know who to send it to," Singer said.

"What's name of the club she was working?" I asked.

"Brillianti," Modena said. "We know they move drugs through there. Mainly retail, but lots of Cartel boys spend time and money there."

"Who runs the place?"

"Dude called Philippe Brillo." I can give you a print out of his profile."

"Can you roust the joint, see what shakes out?"

"He's totally protected by the police."

"Then why was Angela working there?"

"A month ago one of the dancers was murdered. Someone strangled her. She was sixteen. Angela decided to go in and find out who killed her. It became like a cause for her."

Singer shook his head. "Go figure."

I could, and so could the Preacher who had begun to stir in empathy.

"What happened?"

"She was dancing three times a week, and reporting back. One night she disappeared. Days later they found her in an alley. Strangled just like the other one."

"Same killer?"

"We'll never know," Modena growled. "The local cops didn't make the connection."

Strangled.

All through the sleepless night my adrenaline addled brain kept flashing pictures of Terry's bulging, death-surprised eyes.

+      +      +

I woke up late, made my own breakfast, then hit the computer. I began by delving into SecurEXX, Berlinski's corporate empire. Aside for some new contracts for SecurFOOD and SecurFI there was nothing I could use. But when I turned my attention to my new target, Philippe Brillo, I made an immediate connection.

Seems the gentleman's club Brillianti had availed itself of the services of SecurARM, Zsa Zsa Berlinski's transport company.

It was all I needed.

Singer and Modena returned from their morning rounds. Over lunch I asked them about Berlinski.

Mouth stuffed with burrito Singer nodded. "He's on our radar."

"He's got a compound a few miles from town," Modena added. "So far all we have on him is his posse."

"Posse?"

"He's got an entourage everywhere he goes. Couple of cartel boys, military officers, politicians, lots of young girls."

"Yeah, a regular Jeffrey Epstein."

"Does he ever go to Brilliani?"

Modena snorted. "Only every night. " He gave me a knowing grin. "Why?"

I shrugged, "Routine surveillance"

That night I packed up my meagre belongings and left the safe house. I had given Singer a shopping list and when I fell out I was wearing black jeans, a fringed leather jacket, cowboy boots, a moustache, a badly fitting toupee and blue shades. I looked ridiculous but harmless. Just another aging john out to get laid. Except I had my Taurus tucked in one boot and a combat knife in the other

The first thing I did when I left the safe house was get a room at a hotel that took cash. I stashed the Sig Sauer in the bathroom air vent and went for a walk.

It was a busy night. Tourists from everywhere out to celebrate the holidays in wide-open Tijuana. The hookers were strolling, the dealers hissing, the hustlers hawking, the suckers gawking. The music leaking from the bars flowed into the blare from the street musicians enhancing the carnival atmosphere.

I joined the parade, slowly making my way to Club Brillianti.

It was impressive.

A three-level palace at the end of a long driveway, its sparkling white façade gleaming in the spotlights arrayed at its base.

The usual two gorillas stood on either side of the red velvet rope across the entrance. They wore identical powder blue tuxedos and unhappy expressions.

"Members only," one said in perfect English.

I held up two hundreds. "Mr. Franklin recommended me."

He snatched the bills and unhooked the velvet rope. "Inside to the right."

Just beyond the glass doors was stunning blonde woman seated at a table. She smiled as if she actually meant it.

"Would you like to purchase a membership?"

"Sure, what's the dues?"

"One hundred American for lounge privileges, six hundred for our VIP room."

I counted out six more Franklins from my roll.

Her smile grew warmer. "Good choice. Your card includes a complimentary bottle of champagne."

Quite an operation. I had already dropped eight hundred before I stepped inside. When I did, I saw why the place was full of eager customers.

The décor was Early Miami Tacky, lots of glass and gold, with a raised six-pole stripper stage in the lower lounge level and a dimly-lit balcony area that hung over the proceedings which included cocktail waitresses dressed as harem girls, and six dancers on stage undulating to heavy-bass rock pounding from an incredible sound system.

A transparent elevator hauled me up to the VIP room. A harem girl met me at the door. I slipped her a hundred and she seated me in a red leather booth with a good view of the floor below. My champagne arrived promptly, bucket and all.

The harem girl who greeted me, came over to pour. "If you'd like a lap dance from one of our performers," she inclined her head at the stage below, "I'll be happy to fetch her for you."

Sex Slavery Lite.

I toasted her and watched the strippers below. They were enthusiastic but a bit awkward. Perhaps because at their tender age they were better suited to be cheerleaders.

My attention was distracted by a flurry of activity at the elevator. Two of the harem girls and a bald bodybuilder in a black tux had gathered at the glass door. When the door slid open two men stepped out. One was a clone of the bodybuilder, the other – resplendent in a silver grey Gotti suit with cloth covered buttons – was Andre.

## Chapter 27

"*Once a philosopher, twice a pervert.*"
— Norman Mailer

# Chapter 27

Andre was easy enough to find. Killing him would be more complicated. As I mused over possible methods the bald bodybuilder came to my table, phone pressed against his ear.

"I'm sorry sir, you'll have to check your weapon."

"What?"

He pointed to his phone. "Boss says our scanner detected a gun in your boot."

Before I could protest he placed a numbered chip on the table.

"No worries. Present this on your way out and we return your weapon."

Reluctantly I passed him my Taurus under the table.

"Thank you for your discretion sir," he said politely, and was gone.

I had to admire the efficiency. But I was pissed. Downsized from assassination to mere surveillance. Not exactly tough duty when drinking champagne in a strip club but the Preacher was revved up.

However I realized the management knew precisely where every customer sat. No doubt they had Vegas-style cameras all over the place. I made sure to turn my attention to the dancers below.

From time to time I would take an occasional peek over my shoulder. Andre lounged in one of three large booths on a raised tier in the rear of the large room. He had a harem girl on each side. Nobody was smiling. The looked like they were in the waiting room of a bus depot.

To maintain my cover I decided to take my hostesses offer of a lap dance. I scanned the stage and decided on a lithe brunette. I motioned for my hostess who was only too happy to oblige.

A few hundred dollars later the girl came upstairs. She was about eighteen and her performance was energetic but joyless. Half way through I occurred to me that my choice wasn't random. The girl bore a strong resemblance to my wife Nina.

Depression fell over me like cold rain. My self-pity was diverted by a crowd of people at the elevator. When I saw Berlinski enter the room my depression morphed to icy fury. If I had been packing at that moment I would have done something stupid.

"Did you like?"

My lap dancer was smiling anxiously at me. I tipped her a hundred.

"Very nice."

The girl slipped close beside me. "You're cute."

I caught my reflection in one of the many mirrors. Bad wig, ratty moustache, Sleaze City.

"Thanks darlin' so are you. What's your name."

"Bambi."

Lovely name. I'm Barry. Have a drink."

Bambi's presence enabled me to watch Berlinski without being conspicuous.

Andre and his girls were now animated, all smiles as they welcomed Berlinski and his entourage who filled all three booths on the upper tier.

Berlinski appeared to be entertaining two men who looked like classic Latino drug lords; barrel chested, Zapata facial hair, custom western suits. And six girls who were barely sixteen. Moments later they were joined by a tall, slender man with long white hair who I recognized as Phillipe Brillo from his DEA profile.

My private dancer smiled at me hopefully.

"We could have lots of fun later," she confided.

"As much fun as they're having?"

Bambi shrugged. "Oh them, that's Phillipe the padrone, and his friend Zsa Zsa. They love to party."

"Maybe we should join the party."

She giggled, half drunk. "I don't think so. Very tough guys. Especially the tall blonde one."

I signaled for more champagne. "In that case we'll party right here."

"You're cute Barry."

Right, cute as Andre's cloth button. Not wanting to seem anxious, I waited until the wine arrived. "You're a good dancer," I lied. "You been doing it long?"

She smiled. "Seven months. Soon as I turned eighteen. You really like it?"

I filled her glass. "Sensational."

Across the crowded floor I saw a harem girl draw a glittering sky blue curtain across the upper tier. So much for surveillance.

My simmering anger was further stoked by frustration. It had become clear that stalking Andre wouldn't work.

As I stared at the gleaming curtain I slowly understood.

I had to get Andre to stalk me.

"You're cute" Bambi repeated. Maybe to convince herself.

I was about to call it a wrap when Andre appeared through an opening in the curtain and strutted to a double door.

I gave Bambi a big smile. "Where's the men's room honey?"

She pointed to the double door. Trying to look casual I followed Andre. Problem was, I had no idea what I would do.

The men's room was a garish affair that included a gilded sitting room and a state of the art head. Andre was standing at a urinal shaped like an oyster shell. I shuffled over to the oyster next to his, acting a bit looped, and glanced at him.

I snorted and shook my head as if I had seen something offensive.

Without looking I could tell that had annoyed him. An electric cloud of tension gusted behind me. The old attendant had a stricken expression. Still shaking my head I made a production of washing my hands. A moment later a tall, blond man loomed up in the mirror.

Andre had me by three inches and fifty pounds, none of it fat.

"You got a problem?"

The attendant rushed with a towel as if to defuse the situation.

I tipped him a hundred and smirked at Andre.

"Not me pal. You."

"Yeah? What's my problem?"

"That suit's a real problem, who gave it to you – Elton John?"

I laughed and turned my back on him.

Half expecting the axe to fall I swaggered drunkenly to the door. I could feel the heat on my back all the way to my table.

Bambi felt it too. She looked scared.

"Hello darlin' miss me?"

"Oh yeah Barry. Hey are those guys staring at us?"

Sure enough the two heavies in western suits were standing in front of the curtain, hands folded, dark eyes fixed on our booth.

"Fuck 'em, let's have more champagne."

"Uh look Barry I've got to go on stage. I'll be back in ten minutes okay?"

Without waiting for an answer she hurried to the elevator.

Smart girl.

I hung around for a bit, ignoring the attention, then made for the elevator. On the way down I wondered if I had overplayed my hand.

I was certain I had when I went to checkroom. My Taurus was returned – minus the bullets. A bad sign. However I was still angry and slightly drunk. So I decided to up the ante.

"Is this some kinda gay club?"

The young lady behind the counter looked flustered.

"Of course not senor. What do you mean?"

"Some tall, Nazi-looking blond dude hit on me in the fucking bathroom up there. Can you believe that shit?"

As I strolled to the exit I saw the girl's reflection in the mirrored door. She was jabbering excitedly into the house phone. When in Mexico you mess with a man's macho at your own peril. It's a capitol crime.

Once outside I quickened my step, pausing only to take the combat knife from my boot. Ten yards down the curved driveway I heard the cough of a motorcycle and knew it was him. The Preacher rose up from his grave.

Never bring a knife to a gunfight. At best the blade would give me a few minutes to run. But I couldn't outrun the oncoming bike, or the car a short distance behind it.

Andre came swerving up next to me, spraying pebbles and dirt everywhere.

Tactical error. Too close.

As he tried to pull his weapon I sliced him above the eyes.

I'm no Ninja but a horizontal cut across the forehead causes immediate bleeding. Your opponent will be blinded by a curtain of blood.

He was straddling the motorcycle which also made him vulnerable to the short, hard chop below his chin, and he toppled, the bike still churning up debris.

I yanked the bike from underneath him, hopped on and scrambled away from the car behind me. A bullet snapped past my ear and I opened the throttle. The front wheel rose up, back wheel spinning until the edge caught traction and I shot forward, wobbling all the way.

The bike was a Suzuki crotch rocket, light, quick, but with a top speed of maybe eighty, far less than the Mercedes bearing down on me.

However it was nimble. Once in the street I was able to weave around cars, turn onto a one-way boulevard and duck into an alley. As soon as the Mercedes was out of sight I dropped the bike, tore off my toupee, moustache, and fringed jacket and hurried back to the loaded Sig Sauer stashed at my hotel.

Pausing only long enough to crack a tequila from the mini bar, I called Harry Singer.

"Not now," he said tersely, "the goddamn town's on fire."

I poured another Herradura and switched on the TV.

There was Trump on CNN, patting himself on the back as usual, actually taking credit for Christmas, and scoffing at intelligence warnings of a new virus in China, calling it a "hoax." His favorite word.

In Trump's world everything is a
fraud
fake

hoax.

Still raging on high levels of adrenaline I switched to a nice, honest cage fight.

Without warning my adrenaline plummeted, leaving me in a bleak pit of abject depression as I realized I had accomplished nothing. In fact Berlinski and Andre would now be on high alert.

Singer called back an hour later. "Seven a.m. – in front." Was all he said.

After a sleepless night I went downstairs at seven and saw Singer waiting in a Ford Fusion. We joined the slow line of commuter traffic and after forty five minutes stopped off at a small restaurant for a spicy breakfast.

"Things got really nuts last night," Singer said between mouthfuls of omelet. "We were on the horn to Washington, Mexico City, every fucking body. We might have a cartel war on our hands."

"What happened?"

"Our inside asset was murdered, and then some asshole attacked one of Berlinski's boys with a knife. Colombian style."

"That would be me."

Singer stopped eating. "Who, the asshole?"

"Both of them."

He stared at me, food in mid-air.

"Oswaldo was feeding you false intel," I said.

"So you shot him?"

I shrugged. "He had a gun pointed at my head, and he was about to kidnap a twelve-year-old girl."

"And the other guy?"

"I fucked up."

"How?"

"I came here to kill him."

Singer's chubby features hardened as he tried to decide if I was a dedicated agent or a stone psycho. I didn't know the answer myself.

"Well at least we don't have a cartel war to worry about," Singer said, digging into his food. "Just you."

"By the way, I picked up Oswaldo's phone."

"Open it?"

"Not yet. I thought I'd do it at your place."

Singer looked uncomfortable. "I'm going to have to sneak you back in."

"Why?"

"Like I said, this town's crawling with heat, looking to burn your dumb ass. And it's a small town."

Singer dropped me a few blocks from the safe house and as instructed I made my way to the delivery entrance carrying a McDonald's bag.

"Even if it doesn't fool anybody watching, I can use the burgers," Singer explained.

It didn't take long to unlock Oswaldo's phone. There were lots of pictures, mainly girls but three stood out.

The first two had been taken some months ago, and attached to messages. Both were head shots of Singer and Modena.

The third was recent, also attached to a message.

It was me.

I was walking into the diner where I met Oswaldo. Fortunately Selena was out of the frame.

"Exxon you motherfucker," Modena said when I showed him the pictures.

"Notice anything?"

"No, what?"

"They all went to the same number."

I went back to the computer and soon came up with a name.

"Phone number is registered to one Irving Berlin. Probably Belinski's alias."

"What makes you so sure?"

"Irving Berlin is the guy who wrote *God Bless America*. Do you have a blueprint of Berlinski's compound? I need to get in there.'"

Singer's eyes went wide. "Are you fucking crazy? I told you, cops, cartel, local citizens – they're all hunting for you."

"Anyway," Modena said quietly. "It won't do you any good."

"Why is that?" I said, a tad belligerent.

He folded his arms. "My informants tell me that Berlinski and his entourage are flying out of here tomorrow."

"Where to?"

"Northern California somewhere. He's throwing a big New Year's party."

"Just as well," Singer said.

Something in his tone prodded me.

"Oh yeah, why?"

"Because we don't need some lone gun, running wild around here, blowing our operation."

I tossed Oswaldo's phone on the table.

"Exxon blew your fucking operation months ago. Those are your faces he sent to Berlinski."

Singer shook his head. "You don't get it do you?"

"Fuck no I don't get it," I said, trying to keep my voice down. "They know you're DEA – game over."

"They know because we want it that way," Singer went on calmly. "There are three other stations like this."

"Used to be five until the White House cut our budget," Modena put in. "Fucking Homeland bastards. They're recruiting border agents off the street."

Singer nodded wearily. "While the bad guys are busy watching us, the other three stations are under deep cover. We're like the sacrificial goats they put out to bait fucking lions."

"So give us a break and let us do our job," Modena added, voice edged with scorn. "We got the intel on Berlinski's party because we have a man inside. And we need to keep it that way."

Chastened but still seething with frustration I retreated to what I do best, the computer. At least there I exercise a modicum of control.

I dug into SecurARM, which held Berlinski's air charter contracts (at two hundred fifty grand per flight) and found one of their planes was scheduled to land at Petaluma Airport the day before New Year's Eve and haul a load of illegals back to a detention camp outside Tijuana.

Feliz Anno Amigo.

I gave Singer and Modena the good news.

"If I leave today, I can meet that flight tomorrow."

They both seemed visibly relieved.

"Oh, there is one thing though," I said, trying to sound presidential.

They exchanged a distressed glance.

"What the fuck is it now?" Modena growled.

"I crossed the border illegally, and I'll be packing weapons when I go back."

"I can't believe this shit," Modena muttered, stalking out of the room.

Singer shrugged in resignation. "This will take a while. You want coffee or something?"

"You done?" I said, when Modena joined us in the kitchen, "what time tonight do I leave?"

He glared at me. "Not tonight, tomorrow. Fifteen hundred hours. Any coffee left?"

"Tomorrow? Why the fuck so late?"

"Look Braveheart, I had to pull some favors to slip you past the Mexican side – and our side. There's a fat contract out on you."

I wanted to say get in line but instead I lifted my hands in surrender and kept my voice steady.

"Goddammit okay, I'm a psycho pain in the ass. Agreed. But Andre the scumbag strangled a good friend, trying to get at me. And most likely did your Angela the same way. So cut me some motherfucking slack."

"Max, Max," Singer said, "we get it, It's just that, you know..."

"Say it Harry."

"You're uh, not much of a team player."

I almost laughed. "Tell that to Angela."

I kept to myself after that, nose to the computer. Just to piss Modena off, I smoked a little weed while I worked.

The plane from Tijuana was due at 2330 hours. With luck, I could be back in Petaluma a few hours before Berlinski's party landed. To that end I contacted Bob Lowell and asked him to round up anybody he trusted. Then I called Delaney.

He wasn't friendly.

The afterglow sparked by my recent coup had faded fast.

"They're pushing back hard on Boutilier's evidence."

"The Company?"

"The White House, that fat fuck Barr is involved now."

"Barr, the AG?"

He paused. "Are we encrypted?"

"Times three."

"Barr's trying to prove, the evidence was illegally obtained."

"Son of a bitch, so he's Berlinski's lawyer now."

"What's up in Tijuana?"

"I'll be back north tomorrow. Berlinski has a party plane due to land in Petaluma. A routine search is sure to turn up something, guns, drugs, whatever."

"Call me back."

Frustration stoked my anger. Protect the scumbag, pollute the evidence. How's that for teamwork Harry.

But underneath was the numbing realization that I'd fucked up.

Twice.

Andre 2, Max zero.

*"There's very few mistakes in life that
can't be corrected–if you  have the guts."*
– Ellen Barkin, *"Sea of Love"*

# Chapter 28

My dark mood fouled the interior of the Ford like sulfuric fumes from some alien bowel. Even Modena, who was driving – and far from sensitive – noticed the noxious atmosphere.

"Let's hope you catch up to the bastard," he offered. I grunted.

"Guess everybody's coming this way."

It was true. There was a thick mass of traffic flowing into Mexico. Families, tourists, college kids, eager to celebrate the New Year. Me, I would be dancing with the devil.

We passed smoothly through the various border checkpoints. Modena tried to make small talk but I was having none of it. Finally, safely in San Diego I decided to throw him a bone.

"That went well. Thanks."

He hesitated. "You know, Delaney told us your one of his best."

"Did he mention I'm crazy?"

A smile cracked Modena's dour expression.

"That too. But I didn't believe it."

"Thin line between crazy and stupid."

He gave me a hard look. "Don't get down on yourself Max. We're in a crazy business. Half the time it's pure luck when an op goes right."

I was starting to like this stalwart soldier in America's war on reason but it didn't disperse the sense of failure wrapping me like the moldering arms of a corpse.

"Uh, wanna get some tacos?" He said.

Anticipating a long, straight drive to the Bay Area, I decided to accept. Berlinski's plane was due to land at 11:30 p.m. which gave me time. Modena knew a good down-home place that served draft beer and after our late lunch he dropped me at Selena Suarez's home, where my Mercury was parked.

Along the way I told him how Oswaldo aka Exxon had falsely accused Selena's late husband of cooking meth, giving him up at the behest of Homeland Security.

"Fernando Suarez was actually a brilliant lawyer with the ACLU, who set up clinics for immigrant rights. Somebody at Homeland set him up."

"Fucking bastards. I've seen how they treat people. Like cattle at the slaughterhouse. Used to be a lot better."

"Do me a favor, look out for this woman. We owe her."

"I hear you Max." He wrote a number on the back of his card. "My personal phone."

I didn't linger when we arrived at Selena's home, staying only long enough to thank her for taking care of the Green Ghost, and to warn her against future contact with any of Oswaldo's friends.

I told her Oswaldo was dead and gave her Gil Modena's number should she need anything.

Once I got on 101 north, anticipation scattered my depression. Aware that the Highway Patrol was out in full force to nab holiday drunk drivers I switched on my radar detector, police radio scanner and my computer so I could pinpoint their exact location.

Anxious to get there early to coordinate with Lowell and whoever he managed to recruit, I kept a heavy foot on the accelerator trusting technology to avoid the authorities. Nearing Bakersfield I let the beast loose, reveling in the four-fifty V8's power.

A shrill electronic whistle slowed my down. As I neared the Bay Area there were more warnings, which was just as well. My old Mercury was supposed to be invisible. So I turned on KPOO F.M. and relaxed, rolling smoothly to great music that ranged from old Blues to R&B. I perked up when I heard the DJ

"Today we have the new joint from Snappy Jack and King Bong, *Tupac's Tombstone,* and don't forget they are appearing in a special bashorama at the Oakland Paramount tomorrow night New Year's Eve."

For some stupid reason the now familiar Hip Hop ode eased my tension and I began to construct a plan. On the way to Petaluma I stopped at my place in Corte Madera to pick up some equipment including extra clips for my weapons.

I met Lowell at Graziano's in Petaluma. The Italian restaurant was festooned for the holidays but the two men with Lowell greeted me with somber expressions. One was Lieutenant Jake Boone, the other his young assistant patrolman Tim Ferris. They looked like they'd rather be somewhere else.

"Good to see you Max," Lowell said, "I think you know Jake and Tim."

I nodded. "Thanks for coming, but you may not want to stay."

"Maybe we should order first," Lowell suggested, signaling the waiter.

We ordered the usual, pizza and a round of beers.

"So what's the deal?" Jake said when the waiter departed.

"If you go in on this you stand a good chance of being fired or killed."

"Is that the good news or the bad?" Jake said.

"The good news is we're outnumbered and have no legal backup."

Jake grinned. "You make it sound like a walk in the park."

Tim Ferris looked seasick.

Just as the beers arrived my phone rang. It was Delaney.

"Okay, you got back up. He'll be at the Petaluma airport. The diner there."

"Is he holding a warrant?"

"Just his Glock. Sorry."

"Thank God for small favors," I said, switching off. "At least we have DEA back up."

Tim brightened. "How many?"

"One."

"Is that all?"

I shrugged. "There's only one plane."

"If anybody wants to sit out this dance I fully understand," I added. "There's very little upside."

Tim looked around the table, then sat back.

"What time does the plane land?" Jake said.

+      +      +

There were four customers in the Two-Niner Diner when I entered. A uniformed patrolman, a slim, well-tailored blonde and a balding man in a rumpled blue suit sat at a booth, and a heavy-set bearded man with a ball cap was at the counter reading a newspaper.

The trio in the booth looked up as I stepped inside, the bearded man didn't. I took a spot at the counter and ordered coffee.

When the waitress returned the bearded man signaled for a refill. He gave me a curt nod and returned to his paper.

A few minutes later the cook came out with a large bag and passed it to the waitress who took the bag to the booth. The blond woman paid and the trio left the diner.

The bearded man glanced my way.

"Quiet bunch."

True. They hadn't said a word.

"Silence is golden."

"Max?"

"I hear that."

He moved his coffee cup closer.

"Ben Fleeman. Delaney said you needed help."

"Could have used a warrant."

"Will an UZI do?"

"Always. Been here long?"

"Long enough to eat a good burger—and get a line on those three."

He waggled his phone and handed it to me.

"The guy in the bad suit works for ICE. Names Harvey Platt. The nifty blond is a Company girl, Bryce Taylor. Cop's name is Gibson."

Sure enough they were all there on the small screen. I was impressed.

Fleeman's dark, inquisitive eyes bore into mine. "What's the drill Max?" he said calmly but I knew he meant business. Two to one he'd walk when I told him.

"A charter from Tijuana lands at 23:30, less than an hour. We're going to roust it."

"Without a search warrant."

"Exactly. I want to know who's on board and where they're going. It's New Years. They're bound to have some party drugs. That will make it official DEA business."

"Pretty thin."

"Thin is all I got. You in?"

"Any back up?"

"Petaluma police captain and two assistants."

"I'm in."

"One more thing. Don't call me Max."

"Why's that?"

"The CIA and ICE have orders to shoot me on sight."

He grinned. "This only gets better. One thing though. Why do they need all that food they just took out?"

"That's for the poor bastards they're deporting on the return flight."

I gave him a quick overview of Berlinski's operation.

"Slimy motherfuckers," was his only comment. "So how does this roust go down?"

"You take point. Captain Lowell and Lieutenant Boone will be your back up. Don't let anybody off the plane. Get pictures, make them fucking nervous."

"Where will you be?"

"Me and Tim Ferris will be out of sight, setting tracking devises on their vehicles."

"What about the ICE patrol?"

"They'll be busy with their illegals. Hopefully they won't notice until you have a chance to board the plane."

"Where do I find my back up?"

"They'll find you. Follow me out when I leave."

Once outside, I walked quickly to where I'd left my car with Ferris in it. He was sitting there fiddling with the buttons on my dashboard when I opened the door."

"What the fuck are you doing Tim?"

"Man, this is a damn nice ride. What is it a custom job, like James Bond?"

"More like Dom Torretto. We can admire the car later. You clear on your assignment?"

"When the plane lands you plant trackers on the vehicles that meet the passengers. And I watch your back."

"And...?"

"No shooting unless I have to."

"Let's hope you don't." I checked my watch. "Why did you volunteer for this anyway? Sure won't be good for your career."

He snorted. "My career? Zallen and Platt took care of that."

"How so?"

"I was along on an ICE raid, when Agent Zallen shot a man called Canseco in his own home. It looked deliberate. When I wouldn't falsify my report Zallen and Platt claimed I bugged out when the shooting started. Accused me of cowardice."

"Motherfuckers, what happened?"

"I'm on suspension while they review my case."

It was easy to see the frustration and pain on his face. I had been there too often.

"Cowards are the guys who falsify reports," I said.

"Thanks."

"Don't thank me yet, this thing may put you on a wanted poster."

The plane landed on time.

I watched Lowell, Fleeman and Boone hurry onto the tarmac which was my cue to leave the car and slip behind the hangers where the detainees were stored.

Waiting for Berlinski's guests were three stretch limos and two choppers. Problem was I only had three tracking devices.

I decided to tag two of the limos and one motorcycle. I was heading back to the car when I heard excited voices.

Four people were running across the tarmac to the plane. The trio in the diner Fleeman Identified, plus another uniformed cop. I sprinted back to my car and fished a pair of powerful binoculars from my backpack. I saw the four board the plane and waited.

Ferris got in the car. "What's happening?"

"Don't know yet."

"Should we go help?"

"We can't help. It's in Fleeman's lap now."

+    +    +

Ben Fleeman had always been a good bullshitter.

When he boarded the plane he had an UZI in one hand and a smudged copy of an old warrant in the other. Lowell and Boone were right behind him.

"Everybody stay right where you are," he said calmly. "Just a routine customs inspection."

"Where's agent Platt?" A tall, Nordic man blustered. "You have no right here."

Fleeman smiled. "Agent Platt is ICE. I'm DEA and this search warrant gives me the right. Let's start with you – ID please."

The Nordic man turned out to be Max's target, Andre, who was traveling with a Russian passport. Unfortunately he was clean, no drugs no weapon.

Working in tandem, Fleeman and Lowell quickly checked almost all the male passengers. Lowell was cuffing a biker type who was carrying a bag of meth when Agent Platt burst in, followed by a uniformed cop.

"What the hell are you assholes doing?"

"Our job," Fleeman said waving the phony warrant. "DEA. We have just found drugs aboard the plane, which gives us probable cause. Now who the fuck are you?"

"Platt, Immigration and Customs, which gives us jurisdiction here. This plane is chartered by Homeland Security."

Fleeman thought fast. If anybody checked his false warrant the whole op was blown. He decided to beat a graceful retreat with the little he'd gained.

"What the fuck is he doing?" Platt yelled when he saw Boone quietly taking pictures with his mobile.

"Half these girls don't have visas," Fleeman said. "Two of them are only fifteen years old."

"They're old enough to fly. The visas are my problem. Now stand down."

Fleeman played his last card. "Alright, but this asshole comes with us." He pointed to the cuffed biker. "Meth is my problem."

They had a ten second stare-down, then Platt relented.

"Get the fuck off. Make sure he's properly booked. I'll be right behind you."

Boone took charge of the biker when they debarked. As the trio hustled the prisoner to their unmarked car a young blond woman approached them. She lifted her wallet as if waving a flag.

"Why are you people here?"

Fleeman flashed his ID. "DEA m'am. We got a tip there were drugs on that plane. But..."

"But what?"

"Why are you here? You're CIA right?"

She didn't answer. Instead she attacked.

"Why didn't you inform the authorities of this raid?"

Lowell stepped forward. "Captain Robert Lowell Petaluma PD. And my associate Lieutenant Boone. Agent Platt coordinated with us. We had to keep it on a need to know basis. You understand."

Lowell's polite, respectful tone totally deflected Taylor's self-righteous bluster. Fleeman had to struggle to suppress a grin as the young, blond agent lifted her hands in exasperation and stalked off.

"Nice work," Fleeman said.

Boone hefted his prisoner erect, who seemed to have difficulty walking. "Let's get this asshole booked before she comes back."

Fleeman half turned. "You guys go ahead. I"ll see how Max is doing."

Abruptly the biker straightened up.

"Max? That's the motherfucker shot me."

Boone shook him hard. "Which means you're Luke Pardo, the motherfucker who jumped bail."

Pardo grinned defiantly. "He's got two hundred fifty big ones on his head. Once the word's out Max is a dead man."

As Boone and Lowell escorted Pardo to jail Fleeman stood watching them, his small victory erased by the knowledge that he was the one who let the word out.

*"I'm getting very close to the cashier
on the check-out line."*
–Frank Lauria

Frank Lauria

# Chapter 29

I couldn't believe what I was seeing.

I kept the binoculars pressed against my face as I watched the passengers straggle towards the waiting vehicles.

They were all there.

Andre, his forehead bandaged, Berlinski, Phillipe Brillo looking like the high-end pimp he was, even Georgio, sporting a black nose guard had managed to join the group. They were followed by a string of young girls and two heavily tattooed thugs wearing armless leather jackets bearing the Vandals' colors. A third biker had been arrested earlier.

But it wasn't until I noticed the bag Andre carried that the Preacher sat bolt upright.

The fucking Hermes.

The one that led Andre to my pad. Where he strangled Terry as his consolation trophy.

Body rigid with repressed rage I stared until they were out of sight. I struggled to keep the Preacher from shooting Andre right there.

"What now?"

"Now we fucking wait."

A thick silence filled the car and I realized I had almost snapped the kid's head off.

"We see who escorts the illegals onto the plane," I said quietly. "Then we track the limos."

Moments later a ragged line of forlorn men trudged to the plane herded by ICE agent Platt, Gibson and another police officer. Platt and Gibson boarded with the deportees. The uniformed cop walked away as the plane revved its engines began to taxi to the runway.

I started my own engine and drove slowly to where Fleeman was waiting.

I handed him an iPad. "Use this to track the chopper. I'll call you later."

"I have to be back at the station to book the asshole biker you shot."

I paused. As far as I knew he was the only Vandal who could ID me. "Okay, make sure he stays booked."

"Bail jumper? He's not going anywhere soon."

Ferris seemed impressed when the two computer screens fanned out from my dashboard but he didn't speak. I assumed he was still pissed off.

It was no trouble following the limos electronic trail. They headed north into the wine country. Meanwhile the Preacher was twitching like a crack addict. I had to keep reminding myself this was merely reconnaissance.

"Everything okay?" Ferris said.

I gripped the wheel tighter. "Yeah why?"

"Because my ass is on the line and you're acting weird."

The kid had a point. I took a deep breath and tried to relax.

"Just don't want this to fuck up. It's personal."

"So is my ass personal."

My short laugh broke the tension.

"No worries, I'll cover you. Anyway the action won't start until next year."

It took a second before he got the joke.

"Corny Max."

He was quiet for a few minutes.

"Jesus, where are they going?"

Good question. The limos were heading into Land Rover country, undeveloped forest land in the hills above Healdsburg. Large swatches of terrain were still recovering from the big blaze two years earlier. The narrow country roads made it impossible for fire trucks.

There were few lights. Len had installed dimmers on the car's headlamps which made us hard to spot, but also made it difficult to see.

"Max?"

"Yeah?"

"You watching the screen?"

"Sure, the limos are still ahead."

"The other one. The motorcycle. It's behind us."

"It's just following the limos."

Then I saw something that worried me.

One of the limos had turned around and was heading our way.

I shut the lights. "They've been tracking us. Look for a gap in the trees."

We found a narrow gap and squeezed between two trees. They blocked the doors but we managed to wriggle out.

I bent and checked the underside of my car.

"Watch the road."

"What are you doing?"

I held up the small magnetic tracking device I had found behind the rear fender.

"Looking for this."

There were no lights but we could hear the distant rumble of motorcycles. I trotted ten yards up the road and tossed the tracker into the dense vegetation. Then I drew my Glock and took a position across from Ferris.

"Wait until they pass," I said in a hoarse whisper.

Ferris gave me a thumbs up. In the dim light I glimpsed the service .38 in his hand. As I wondered if he had enough fire power the steady growl of cruising motorcycles came closer.

Lights loomed and they slowly passed us, the lead biker intent on an electronic device in his hand. They paused at the point where I'd tossed the magnetic tracker.

A dense quiet draped the darkness when they shut down their bikes and dismounted. They lifted their weapons and the silence shattered into noisy fragments: the flat clatter of assault weapns, bullets chewing on trees, limbs crashing to earth, whining ricochets.

Abruptly it was quiet again. Some vegetation was in flames and the air was thick with gun smoke.

Then Ferris did something stupid.

He stepped into the open.

"Police! Drop the weapons!"

Maybe he thought their clips were empty. Before I could shout him back the bikers half-turned and fired.

Ferris spun hard and fell out of sight.

As the bikers moved forward to deliver the kill shot I squeezed off four quick rounds.

One of them fell, the other dove for cover.

A flurry of bullets chopped at a tree trunk above drenching me in splinters. From the size of the chunks I assumed they were .45 caliber slugs, and from their distinct sewing machine chatter I judged my hunters were packing Uzi pistols which carried thirty round magazines. Twice my capacity.

To make things worse the dude I hit started shooting and suddenly I was stuck in a crossfire.

I blindly fired in the direction of the fallen biker while crawling through damp leaves.

The return volleys ferociously ate up any available cover and I was trapped behind a tree that was rapidly becoming firewood.

Anyone who thinks a tree will stop a bullet is in for a nasty surprise. My nose flattened against the roots as the trunk above me was drilled with .45 caliber holes as big as my fist.

I rolled, pumped six shots at the gun flashes and heard a loud grunt. Another barrage drove me face down in the dirt where I stayed, frozen. Despite the chill mountain air my shirt was soaked with sweat. I peered through the smoky gloom, scanning anxiously for my attackers but the only things visible were the choppers parked in the road. On impulse I took a shot at them and one motorcycle toppled over.

"Motherfucker!"

I fired at the outraged voice and an answering burst plowed the ground nearby.

"Cover me!"

Two words that meant I had a minute to live.

One biker laid down suppressing fire while I lay suppressed by panic watching a pair of muddy engineer boots coming toward me. I lifted my Glock in the air and took a wild shot.

Nothing happened. Empty clip.

The boots stopped.

Assuming he had a bead on me, I gathered myself for a final charge.

A light swooped across the road. A car came into view.

Abruptly everything went quiet. I lifted my head and saw the boots turn.

A short burst of gunfire riddled the silence.

The boots sprang into the air.

The biker hit the ground face first and lay there.

"Cisco!"

The cry was accompanied by a long volley that dug trenches into the road. One headlight blinked off in a spray of glass.

After some struggle I finally gripped the Taurus at the small of my back and rolled into shooting position. I had five little rounds left.

Then I saw a shadow separate from the car.

A barrage of sound and fire erupted. When it stopped the shadow was gone.

For the next long minutes a deep silence hung suspended over the forest like the thick cordite haze fogging the single headlight.

"You there?"

The voice was familiar but I couldn't quite place it.

"Who?" I said.

"You know damn well who. Give me a name asshole."

I finally placed it.

"Fleeman, it's me."

"Fuck you Max. You hit?"

"Negative." I half stood and looked around. One biker was sprawled on the road. I could see a pair of legs in the foliage.

"Tim? Yo Tim!"

"Over here."

My empty Glock in one hand, Taurus in the other, I crept towards the sound of his voice. I found him pressed against a tree holding his bloody arm.

Both bikers were dead. I had wounded the one going for Tim. Fleeman had finished him.

"These wounds in his leg look like nine millimeter," Fleeman said after a quick exam with his phone flashlight. "The forty fives took his face off."

"How did you get here?" I said numbly.

Fleeman stroked his beard. "I was tracking the bikers, hanging back. You okay?"

"Dandy. Let's get Tim into your car. Take him to the nearest hospital. One of their limos is coming this way. I'll head them off."

"How?"

"My problem. Let's go."

Tim was woozy but mobile. We hustled him into the car and Fleeman sped him back to town.

One of the choppers stood parked nearby. A helmet hung neatly on the backrest. It slipped easily over my head. Bad fit but fine for my purpose. The keys hung from the ignition. I fired up the chopper and rode to head off the oncoming limo before anybody saw the damage.

Less than a mile up the road I spotted the lights approaching. I stopped and slid the visor over my face. As the limo came into view I lifted my arms.

The limo stopped and a man leaned out the window. "What's up?"

I gave him a thumb's up. "It's all good. We took care of it.""

"Then why the fuck you call? Asshole."

The limo had difficulty turning around on the narrow country road. I watched patiently, aware I was packing nothing but a five-shot .45. When they were on their way I followed.

Berlinski's compound was another fifteen miles of bad road up the hill.

The place was remote and surrounded by a seven foot spike-topped fence. When we arrived the limo stopped for the gates to open.

The recent gun battle had left the Preacher loaded with hostile adrenaline but I managed to wrestle him back, reminding him we only had five shots before we'd be shredded into a bloody hamburger.

So I waited until the limo cleared the gate, which gave me a good look at my target. I paused long enough to take in the two guards at the entrance, the interior roving guards walking Dobermans, then waved and turned back.

When I got to the crime scene the biker's body was still there, just another roadkill. I dragged him into the foliage near his partner. It took a bit of effort to lift the heavy chopper off the ground and roll it out of sight. My adrenaline jag plummeted like a meteor and cratered, leaving me shaking with exhaustion.

Gratefully I climbed into the protective shell of the Green Ghost.

My hands were still trembling when I got back home.

It took a half bottle of scotch before they calmed down enough to roll a J. I fell out right there at the kitchen table.

*"America is a country of entertainers.
Even the fascists have to be entertaining."*
– Arthur Miller

# Chapter 30

A hangover is no way to prepare for combat.

Neither is sleeping in a kitchen chair. That, and thrashing wildly in the woods, tweaked every injury I'd suffered since puberty.

Fortunately it was early.

I called Fleeman who assured me Tim Ferris was resting comfortably at Healdsburg District Hospital. I yearned to be there myself.

"Leaves us a little short-handed," he observed, "Only Lowell, Boone, you and me."

"We were short-handed up front," I said, recalling the roving guards with their dogs. "I'll see what I can do."

But I had nothing.

After the call I forced myself to get on the floor and stretch my limbs into some semblance of order. Then onto a long, hot shower and breakfast.

Over coffee I checked my arsenal.

I reminded myself that no matter how well prepared, we were outnumbered by professional killers. On their fucking turf.

I needed more than a plan.

I opened my computer and googled Berlinski's compound in the woods. With NASA's help Google Earth provided me with a virtual tour of the premises.

Basically there was a big house with a smaller house attached, both set in a V shape, a short distance away was a wide, two-story structure with triple doors, probably a garage.

Which meant we needed three teams. Nine men at the very least.

I turned on the FM which was pumping out high energy sounds for the impending New Year's celebrations. Inspired by the beat I smoked a fat J, and let my consciousness flow back to the basics.

The fundamental principle in the martial arts is spiritual focus, which can conquer superior force. From there my body followed into simples katas blended with Tai Chi.

Be like water, said Bruce Lee. The opposing pole of the Preacher's rock-blind aggression. While executing the deliberate moves of *Kung Fu*, it became clear I had to stay detached in order to survive.

When I finished my body was fluid and my brain lubricated. I also had an idea.

"Who the fuck is this?" Manny said when he answered the phone.

"It's Max. You still on the left coast?"

"Yeah, sure it's great out here. Hey look, we're havin' a party. Come on over."

"Actually I called to invite you to an after-hours party."

Manny paused. "Yeah? What's the deal?"

"I'm having a problem with the guest list."

"I see. I'll be with some people tonight. You know, New Years."

"Bring them along if they're good friends."

Again he paused. "Okay Max, you got it. Give me a time and place."

My next call was more complicated.

"Mrs. Curry, It's Max. Do you remember? I'm a friend of Clarence. I was shot."

"Of course dear. Are you alright?"

"Yes. Thanks to you. But I'd like to speak to Clarence."

"Oh, he isn't here. He's on tour now. In Oakland. They're doing the big New Year's show," she added proudly.

"Can you give me a number where I can reach him?"

She could, and I called him immediately.

"Oh man, that's hard Max, you know we got this monster gig . Be rockin' all night."

"No worries, just remember to give Terry a shout out."

"Terry? This about Terry?"

"Same dudes, different party."

"You got shot last time."

"Might get killed this time."

There was a now familiar pause. "I'll call you. This number good?"

My final call was to Sidney Kingman.

At first he was reluctant. But when I pressed him about the innocent lives at stake, he agreed to be ready.

I felt far from confident. At the moment my assets had increased by only one. If nothing else I could depend on Manny's old school code of honor which left me with a five-man delta force. Barely enough to take on the guard dogs.

So much for my big idea.

+    +    +

We met at Lowell's home in Petaluma. It occurred to me that 2020 was something of an anniversary.

September eleventh would mark twenty years since I officially died.

Lowell and Boone were there when I arrived. Fleeman came a bit later with a surprise guest, Tim Ferris, his arm in a sling.

"They just winged me,' he said. "I can still shoot."

"We'll see. Right now let's go over the layout."

"Jesus, that's like a few football fields," Boone said when I showed them the print-outs from Google Earth.

"Berlinski's got twenty acres. Owned by one of his companies. All courtesy of Uncle Sam."

I had brought along a large screen MacBook Pro that showed us the compound in real time.

Earlier I had managed to hack into NASA's satellite.

"How the hell did you get in there Max?" Fleeman said, visibly amazed. "That shit's highly classified."

I shrugged. "I have a particular set of skills."

We took a virtual tour of the grounds. There was the large main house which was lit up, the smaller dwelling next door, also well lit. And a short distance to one side, a four car garage.

"Actually we only have these three areas to worry about." I said, "We break up into teams and hit them when they're drunk and tired."

"Teams?" Boone put in. "Do the math Max. With Tim, we got five. Somebody has to be a one-man team."

I spread my hands. "It's still early. Game kicks off at two a.m. I'm expecting reserve players by then."

But as 2020 came and 2019 went, the mood around the kitchen table was subdued. The Zen calm I'd briefly acquired had evaporated with the Preacher's mounting anxiety. Launch hour marched closer and my phone remained dead silent.

"We do have a dog problem," I said lamely, "Dobermans, maybe pit bulls. Any ideas?"

Lowell lifted his hand. "Tazers work. I've got a couple"

"Yeah I've got one," Boone said. "Tranquilizer gun too. People saw a Puma wandering around town."

It seemed like a good time for a weapons check. Anything to lift our sagging morale.

Fortunately we all had Kevlar vests. After that the armory was spare: a few Tazers, a shotgun, Fleeman's UZI, three Glocks, my Sig, my back up Taurus, assorted .38s. An added touch were Lowell's flash bang grenades.

"Almost zero hour," I said, "still time to come to your senses."

Nobody answered.

"Okay Tim, I know you can shoot with one hand. But how are your text skills?"

"Fastest thumb in the west."

"Good. You're our spotter. You ID a target and send it via text. Pictures too."

"I like it. Let's coordinate our phones."

In the middle of our tech conference, my phone rang.

"Where the fuck are you?" Manny shouted. "I've been circling this bumfuck town for twenty minutes. Happy new year."

+       +       +

Manny showed up a bit tipsy, with two other men who looked like larger versions of himself.

"These are my cousins, Vinny and Mikey," he said expansively. "Why is everybody so depressed?"

Our new allies sobered up when I explained our objective and the resistance we were likely to encounter.

"Good thing we got our own vests," Vinny said, "these here wouldn't fit us."

"Do you guys have weapons?" Lowell asked. "We have some extra police specials."

They looked at each other and grinned.

"We brought along some Heckler forty fives," Manny explained.

"Make sure you don't hit the girls we're trying to liberate." I said.

Mikey waved a huge hand. "No worries, we got laser sights."

I was impressed. Heckler & Koch machine guns spew forty five caliber slugs at the rate of seven hundred rounds per minute. Our odds had improved considerably.

"Lets go over it again. I figure four body guards, eight house guards for Berlinski. Another eight from his Cartel pals. At least twelve members of the Vandals motorcycle club, which gives us thirty two armed men to subdue and zip up while Fleeman, Lowell and Boone toss the premises for drugs and arrest everybody."

"That's nuts," Manny blurted, "even if we do it, the charges will never stick."

"True, but the girls are mostly underage, victims of sex trafficking, we round them up, hustle them out. They're our key witnesses – and those charges will fucking stick."

Manny seemed unconvinced. "And suppose we get them out what the hell do we do with all these girls?"

"I've already made arrangements. A place they'll be safe. I'm going to give you all an address. If you have one girl or ten, take them there."

I looked around the table. "We ready to do this?"

My phone rang.

"What up? We here. Don't go nowhere." King Bong said.

A few minutes later King Bong and Snappy Jack swaggered inside, still in stage clothes and make-up. Bong in a gold-trimmed purple jump suit. Jack in leather and silver.

"We killed it Max!" Jack announced triumphantly. "And we gave Terry a special shout out."

At the mention of Terry I struggled to control the Preacher's fury. I still had a personal objective, Andre.

"What's a shout out?" Vinny said.

Snappy Jack gave him a sympathetic smile like a priest addressing a sinner. "Be like a show business thing. We entertainers."

At that moment a flicker of inspiration wiggled through my anger.

"Change of plan gentlemen."

*"It is fatal to enter war without the will to win."*
– Gen Douglas Macarthur

# Chapter 31

King Bong's signature Escalade led our three-vehicle caravan along the misty country road to Berlinski's compound. We were an hour off schedule which worried me. But then again so did this entire operation.

If we weren't killed we stood a good chance at significant jail time. The authorities frown on home invasions. However I had figured out a way to get past the guards.

Vinny was driving an F650, a massive, off-road pickup truck, that towered over the oversized Escalade. I was third in line, my computers watching the compound via satellite. Fleeman rode shotgun. Behind us were Lowell, Boone and Ferris in an unmarked police car.

Before we reached our destination we stopped. I parked the Green Ghost well off the road and got into the Escalade, Fleeman right behind me. The rest of the crew Lowell, Boone and Ferris climbed into the F650.

"If this doesn't work bull this bus through or we're all sitting ducks," I said by way of encouragement.

Snappy Jack grinned "Don't worry baby, we've done this before."

He stopped in front of the gates and blinked the headlights.

Long minutes later the gates opened wide enough to let one man through. He had an AK47 on his shoulder.

"Yo, we're the band," Jack said amiably.

"The band? You're a little late ain't you?"

"We got lost getting' here."

I stuck my head out the window. "Check with Mr. Berlinski."

I was counting on Berlinski being otherwise occupied.

"What's that behind you?

"That's our equipment."

Actually that was true.

The guard opened the gate further. "Alright come on through," he said wearily.

"Where do want us to unload?"

"Front entrance. When you get inside take the second door on the left. That's the ball room."

We rolled slowly to the large, well-lit house. There was a row of motorcycles in front of the smaller building next door. When we stopped Manny's mammoth pick-up seemed to swallow the parking area.

Fleeman, King Bong and myself went over to the F650 and helped Manny unload two trunks. We had taken the old trunks from Lowell's garage. Led by Snappy Jack we carried the trunks through the entrance into a large hall. Before we could go further two guards scanned us with metal detectors looking for weapons.

As directed we hauled the trunks into an immense ballroom with a stage. At the moment the stage was occupied by a DJ and his turntables. The party was still in gear. People were dancing, drinking, inhaling various substances, all to the mellow beat of Michael Jackson promising to rock with me all night.

While I helped carry the trunk I sized up the competition. There were about ten couples on the dance floor. Half the males had pony tails and gold earrings, Cartel style. The others were biker types or slick suited bodyguards.

On one side of the dance floor a large table was occupied by a group of bikers. Further down a trio of Cartel boys were making merry.

Everybody celebrating but it wasn't quite festive.

The girls seemed tired, all of them wearing expensive clothes and too much make up. There was an air of resignation about their grim smiles and blank eyes.

The DJ was dressed in a gold lame' robe and oversized shades with rhinestone frames. Lost in his groove he didn't deign to acknowledge our presence as we unpacked our trunks behind him. Shielded from view by the upraised lids we quickly slipped on our Kevlar vests, before helping ourselves to the weapons hidden inside the trunks. Minutes later the five of us were armed and ready.

Nobody noticed.

Hunched over his turntables the DJ rocked back and forth to some hypnotic house beat. I motioned to Fleeman and waited until he was in position to cover the tables. Then I nudged the DJ with my Sig.

He jerked upright, half startled half annoyed

"Pull the plug," I told him.

For a moment he stood dumbfounded.

I pulled off his ridiculous shades and jabbed him hard.

"Turn it the fuck off."

He flicked a switch and silence dropped like a lead curtain. The entire room stopped short. Everyone motionless, as if doing a group vogue.

King Bong took the mike.

"Alright, alright the party's on!" He proclaimed in his big bass voice, ever the pro. Then he came up with a brilliant stratagem.

"For this one we gonna get you boys on one side of the dance floor, and you ladies on the other. Oh yeah!"

As the guests separated into two groups Bong turned to the DJ and pressed a Glock into his groin. "Play Grandmaster Flash – *Don't Push Me*. Got it?"

"I got it man. I got it."

The appreciative murmur that accompanied the Grandmaster's classic rap turned sour when Fleeman announced it was a bust.

"DEA, everybody freeze," he shouted, and with Manny's help, he immediately began cuffing the males, one to another, into a well-dressed chain gang.

It was all going well.

And then it wasn't.

An unruly male lunged at Fleeman who swatted at him with the UZI.

Fleeman missed, the male grabbed the UZI which went off, a girl screamed, Manny clubbed the attacker, and the Preacher blasted out of prison.

"Round up the girls!" I shouted as I hurried to the entrance to head off the guards – and find Andre.

Adrenaline flooded my body as I shot the lead guard and I veered toward the stairway. Before I could get there two more guards burst inside. I fired blindly. One guard dropped, the other kept coming shooting all the way.

As I ducked a nearby mirror shattered. Reflexively I shut my eyes against the sharp glass shards flying everywhere. When I opened them again the shooter stood five feet away carefully aiming a cannon-sized revolver at my face.

Fast-forward impressions skipped through my brain. Shouts, acrid smoke, gunfire chattering outside, Grandmaster Flash rapping 'don't push me, I'm close to the edge', someone scrambling down the stairs, the looming barrel of the.45 Magnum about to blow me away.

A loud blast stuffed my ears.

Magically the gun barrel vanished beneath the slowly folding body of its owner.

I looked back and saw King Bong smile, his Glock still fuming. The man on the stairs stopped to stare at the three bodies on the blood-splashed marble floor. Then he turned and scurried back upstairs.

Not before I glimpsed his black nose guard.

Fucking Georgio.

Which meant Andre wasn't far.

"Go!" I yelled to nobody in particular and ran after him.

Georgio had disappeared in one of the many rooms upstairs but the Preacher didn't care. By now his ferocious appetite for vengeance had devoured all reason or caution.

As I reached the landing a shirtless man popped out wildly waving an automatic. Ignoring the bullets fracking the walls and ceiling, I clipped him on the run and he went down holding his broken shin. When I went through the open door a naked girl screamed and ran past me.

Before I followed her out I scanned the hall wondering how many guns were behind the still closed doors. I didn't have to wait long for an answer.

One half step and the walls on both sides exploded, showering me with plaster shrapnel. I had blundered into a fucking crossfire.

I had an angle on one gunman, but when I leaned out to take my shot a heavy fist punched the air from my lungs. I staggered back and hugged the wall unable to catch my breath. Fortunately my vest had caught the bullet. Unfortunately there'd be more slugs coming.

I slid down to the floor and rolled to the door. Still struggling to breathe I pointed my Sig in the general direction of the shooter and fired a quick burst, aware a second gun was lurking on my blind side.

"Fuck!" someone yelled but I couldn't tell if he was hit or just annoyed. The hailstorm of bullets raining debris on my head gave me the answer. I finally recovered enough to be mobile, got into a crouch, started shooting, and did a belly flop into the hall. When I hit the floor I rolled and fired in the other direction.

Like an actor padding his death scene, the man on my blind side, swayed and slowly collapsed. A gust of splintered wood stung my ear. Reflexively I jackknifed, twisted and sprayed bullets at the other shooter.

A familiar figure staggered ghost-like through the gun smoke fogging the hall, and fell.

R.I.P. Georgio.

Andre however, was still around somewhere. But as battle-crazed as was the Preacher at the moment, he couldn't kill everyone still hiding behind the closed doors. The shouts and gunfire outside had escalated which meant our op had to go into third gear soon.

I started to trot along the hall opening doors at random. One was empty the next two were occupied by half clad couples. Both times the males were too stoned to fight. I motioned the girls out and told them to go downstairs.

Manny shouted something from the entrance below and I heard a metallic crack. Phase two had begun. Torn between retreat and attack I tried a final door.

Locked.

Without hesitation the Preacher blew it open, kicked what was left of the door aside then did a NBA step-back as a stream of bullets poured into the hall.

I scooped up a fragment of broken mirror and used it to peek inside. The splintered image showed a tall blond man with a muscular torso holding a Thompson machine gun. A pair of young girls were huddled on the bed behind him.

It was Andre all right, looking like a movie poster. I tossed a flash bang and charged when it detonated.

To avoid hitting the girls I held my fire a moment.

Polite, but dangerous.

As I jumped inside I ran head on into Andre. He was still shaky from the blast but had enough left to blindly swing his Thompson my way. I ducked and fired. The Thompson leaped out of his hands. Lucky shot. He roared and rushed me Sasquatch style. I swept his leg Bruce Lee style and he went down – taking me with him.

Fatal error.

On the floor I was at a distinct disadvantage. Andre was heavier, with longer arms and had landed squarely on my chest.

The vest protected my ribs but his huge hand clamped my throat and squeezed.

And kept squeezing while his free hand wrestled for my gun.

Hoping I wouldn't shoot myself I pulled the trigger. It fired into the ceiling.

Still squeezing Andre somehow snatched the gun and tossed it aside. Suddenly both hands were around my neck. One knee had me pinned while ten steely fingers methodically crushed my trachea.

His face loomed over me, features twisted in a grimace of triumph infused with raw hate. He slammed my head against the rug and leaned on my neck. Black holes danced in my fading vision. I felt blood vessels bursting behind my eyes. Thrashing from side to side I chopped at him with my fists but the pressure was relentless. My awareness began sliding into a yawning chasm.

I was dying.

A white-hot spark of primal rage pulled me back.

Frantically I clawed at my ankle. My fingers pulled my pant cuff aside, exposing the combat knife holstered there. It felt like my last official act before checking out. Everything had shrunk down to a tiny point of light, like a doomed star about to go supernova.

The Preacher wouldn't have it.

I found Andre's groin and gripped hard. With a ferocious effort of will I jerked the serrated knife free, yanked Andre's scrotum down – and sliced.

Andre's scream would have awakened Snow White.

He clutched his bloody crotch with both hands freeing my windpipe.

Even before gulping a full breath the Preacher struck like a maddened Black Mamba. Repeatedly my knife punched angry red holes in Andre's exposed torso long after the big man went limp.

For long moments my hoarse gasps were the only sound in the battle fogged room. I heard a whimper and turned.

The two girls were huddled on the bed, sobbing. I found my gun and motioned for them to follow me. Unsteadily I led them through the wreckage in the hall to the stairway.

Sure enough Fleeman and King Bong had nearly finished loading the remaining girls into the Escalade that blocked the entrance.

"Two more!" I yelled.

One of the girls behind me said something in Spanish but it was drowned out by an eruption of gunfire outside. Bong tried to help the girls into the Escalade but one held back. Tearfully she kept repeating something in rapid Spanish while pointing to the upper floor.

"We need to bug out!" Manny yelled. His shout was punctuated by a sustained barrage. I stepped outside and saw him leaning over the hood pouring suppressive fire at the small house. Fleeman was beside him snapping a fresh clip into his UZI.

"They're holed up inside the other house," Manny said hoarsely.

Bong came up behind me. "Max, that girl sayin' her baby sister still upstairs."

Baby sister? The girl looked fourteen. It was enough to reenergize the Preacher.

"Where is she?"

"She say the man with a scar took her."

Fucking Berlinski.

I inserted a new clip in my Sig. "Hold them off."

I bolted up the stairs. Andre's room was at the end of the hall so Berlinski's was likely to be nearby. I spotted a double door and blasted the lock. The doors swung partially open and there was the scumbag himself.

Berlinski had been in the process of retreating from his suite when I intruded. He stood frozen at the door of the inner bedroom one arm around the neck of a terrified young girl he was using as a shield. He was clutching the fucking alligator bag with his free hand and with the other held a baby automatic to the girl's chin.

"Get back or she's dead!" he shouted moving further into the bedroom.

To slow him down I pumped a couple of bullets into the bag.

He dropped the bag, shoved the girl straight at me and fired a flurry of shots, one of which connected.

The tiny caliber slug had a negligible effect on my vest but it did send me stumbling backwards. When I recovered my balance and dashed into the bedroom, Berlinski was gone. Instinctively I started after him then remembered the girl. On my way out I saw a Rolex, jeweled ring, and a wallet on a dresser. I put the wallet in my pocket and went out to help the girl get out of there. Along the way I picked up the alligator bag thinking it might contain evidence.

They were waiting nervously when we got downstairs. Manny and Fleeman were laying down a withering wall of automatic fire but the group of young girls cowering inside the Escalade were in serious danger of becoming collateral damage.

King Bong helped the girl inside and started to shut the rear panel. I handed him the alligator bag. "Take care of this."

"Ain't you comin' ?"

"You got a packed house. I'll cover you."

"How you getting' out?"

"Split now," I said, unable to answer.

"I'll stay," Fleeman said, his eyes battle glazed.

"No damnit!" I snapped. "You make this fucking op legal. Get them to the meeting place."

He handed me his UZI and two clips. "You got less than a hundred rounds. Mazeltov."

"I'll help you cover these guys." Manny shouted, "You're gonna need Hector here."

He was right. The Heckler & Koch. Submarine gun is a fierce weapon. Don't leave home without it. As the Escalade pulled away Manny laid down a blistering line of fire that chewed up large chunks of real estate and kept the guards at bay.

"Come on!" Manny said, jumping into the open. "Follow the car!"

Wrong move. As soon as he left cover he went down.

Immediately I tossed a flash bang and ran to the closest motorcycle which was lying on its side.

No luck there. I threw my last flash bomb and duck walked to a Harley which miraculously had remained standing.

The key was in the ignition.

Spewing fire from my new UZI I started the bike and spurted over to Manny's side. I grabbed his collar and pulled him to his feet.

"Get the fuck on!" I yelled.

By now the guards had regrouped and their bullets began tearing up fountains of dirt and stone. Manny climbed on the bike backwards and we roared off. We were back to back speeding through the gate and, as Manny delivered a devastating hailstorm of fire, I could feel the heavy recoil from his weapon.

Manny kept firing into the darkness Long minutes after we cleared the compound. Abruptly he stopped shooting and I felt his body slump.

When we got to the spot where I'd stashed my car I helped him off the bike. With great difficulty I half dragged him and got him inside the back seat. He was losing blood fast.

Expecting armed pursuers any second I dug some towels from my trunk and hurriedly wrapped a crude tourniquet around his thigh.

"Try to keep that tight," I muttered as I pulled onto the road and hauled ass, tires squealing.

My phone dinged. It was a text from Ferris.

Trouble ahead, with a couple of pictures. They showed about six or seven bikers on their way to Berlinski's compound.

"Can you still handle the Heckler?" I said.

"Are you fucking kidding?" Manny said. "What's up?"

"Some bikers coming."

"Let 'em come."

Brave words from a man slipping in and out of focus. Still, should Manny pass out my UZI could hold
them off. As it happened the Green Ghost was armored.
Len Zane had customized the interior with Kevlar. So I
concentrated on getting Manny to an emergency room.

"Stay with me back there. Keep that towel tight."

"Yeah...tight," he said weakly.

I pressed the accelerator and opened the windows
hoping the cold damp air would revive him.

I checked the time. Twenty-Twenty was five hours
old. Our surprise assault had taken less than forty minutes. We had pulled the fucking thing off.

At the very least a lot of young girls were free.

At the very worst Manny would bleed to death.

I went a bit faster, cursing the narrow curves. A low,
drumming sound alerted me. At first I worried that it
was my engine. But as the deep rumble loomed louder,
worry became panic.

Dead ahead, at the end of a long, dark stretch, a
wall of light was advancing toward me. The six bikers
on Ferris' text had swelled to a phalanx of armed men
about forty strong, riding wheel to wheel, shoulder to
shoulder, choking off the road.

I glanced at the rear view and saw the bobbing lights
of our pursuers. No way back. Kevlar be damned, we
were about to be shredded.

Desperate, I stomped the pedal but there wasn't
enough space to rev up some real momentum. I might
damage the first row before being swallowed by the
rest.

Then I remembered the nitrous oxide system Len
had installed and flipped the red switch.

A giant hand drove me back against the seat as the
car shot forward with lung-crushing speed. The bikers had a split second to swerve before I rammed the

center of the formation, hurling bodies into the air like bloody confetti.

A bearded thug with hoop earrings landed flat on the hood and stayed there while I plowed through the mass of flesh and steel. I heard shots and hoped they didn't hit the tires. Bullets peppered our retreat fracturing my rear window as the Green Ghost powered free and sped away engine shrieking.

My human hood ornament slid off somewhere and suddenly it was quiet.

+      +      +

I made it to the hospital without being attacked or arrested and arrived just in time to give Manny a pint of my blood.

"Bullet nicked a small artery," the doctor told me, "he should be okay." Doctor Zane Bryan was a typical California surfer type: killer smile, athletic build, positive attitude.

"What the hell is going on tonight?"

I opened my eyes. Doctor Bryan wasn't smiling.

"What do mean?"

"We have a police detective shot, report of a major accident just north – it's mayhem out there."

"Police detective? From Petaluma?"

"How did you know?

"Is his name Lowell?"

"Boone. But Lowell brought him in."

"Can I see him?"

Lowell and Boone were in a small treatment room. Boone was shirtless, sporting a fresh bandage on his bicep. Both men were on the phone.

"That was Fleeman," Lowell said, "he's with your lawyer friend Kingman and the girls we pulled out of there. He says Agent Platt from ICE is on his way."

"Platt? How the fuck did ICE...?"

"I don't know. I'm going there now."

"I'll drive."

Sidney Kingman had turned his house into a refugee camp. There were two women, including Mrs Canseco who I'd met earlier, and three lawyers, one of them female, taking care of the girls we'd rescued.

They were doing a good job. The girls were in small groups, most wrapped in blankets against the morning chill, some drinking tea, while the lawyers gathered their names and vital information.

"The oldest are sixteen, those two are barely thirteen," Kingman said.

I recognized the two he pointed out as the pair who were with Andre. Any residual guilt still hovering disappeared. King Bong came over to join us.

"We takin' off Max. Happy New Year." He lowered his voice. "What you want me to do with the bag?"

"What bag?"

"The 'gator bag you told me to hold."

Then I remembered. Berlinski's fucking designer bag.

"What's in it, a laptop?" I said hopefully.

Bong glanced at Kingman

"Money."

"How much money?"

"I lost count at four hundred grand."

"I'll leave you gentlemen to settle this," Kingman said. He went over to join Fleeman who was taking to one of the lawyers.

I was tired, in the throes of an adrenaline comedown and in no condition for wise decisions. So I punted.

"I'll take the bag for now. Slice off fifty K each for expenses. And thanks, I owe you."

King Bong put a huge, jeweled hand to his chest.

"For Terry bro."

It helped dispel the darkness closing in on me.

Cars began to arrive. My cue to disappear. As I walked away I paused to tell Kingman and Fleeman.

"I'll call you. I have to leave before ICE gets here."

"They're already here."

"From Petaluma? How...?"

"Platt took a fucking copter. He's all heated up, claims he's got jurisdiction."

"Don't worry," Kingman added, "this is one time our legal team is working with the DEA. The girls are safe."

Trying to look inconspicuous, I trudged to my car. The Green Ghost needed a lot of body work but the engine's throaty rumble reassured me it was still a contender.

Dawn was spraying gold and pink graffiti across the murky sky as I left Healdsburg. At the edge of town I saw a man setting up a roadside produce stand.

Thinking I might pick up some food I slowed down.

A female voice behind me said, "Don't stop. Keep going."

And I felt the gun against my skull.

# Chapter 32

For a few moments I struggled to comprehend. I was
   exhausted
   damaged
   totally blindsided.

"Who the hell are you?" I said finally.

"Just keep driving."

I glanced in the rear view and saw a flash of blonde
hair.

"Where are we going?"

"Eyes on the road."

Slowly, too slowly, my brain shifted from shut down
mode into some semblance of functional. I prodded my
memory. Blonde... female...

"You were with Platt at the airport last night."

"Very good Max.'

"Who?"

"Forget it. You're blown Max. It's over."

"I suppose Jenkins sent you. CIA right?"

Her assured manner didn't waver

"The Company and the DHS want you for Zallen's
murder."

"So you're arresting me?"

"Something like that."

"Whatever that means."

"You'll find out. Take this next turn."

The road was sparsely populated, a few houses separated by small vineyards or farms.

I didn't like where this was going.

"What do you want to know?" I ventured, stalling for time.

"Clever Max. You read my mind. What did Boutilier tell you before he was mugged?"

"Assassinated you mean."

"Not the point. What did he tell you?"

Sparse had become remote, farms and houses giving way to undeveloped tracts. I'd vanish, like Jimmy Hoffa,

"I heard Zallen was taking payoffs, and Boutilier had evidence."

"Old news Max. What else did you hear?"

"I hear better without a gun in my ear."

"I'll talk louder. What else?"

"His boss wasn't interested."

"You'll have to be more specific."

"Jenkins. He's in on it."

"Turn in there."

Adrenaline squirted though my tired veins. She had pointed out a construction site. Somebody was building a McMansion in the middle of nowhere. Situated at the end of an unpaved driveway stood the skeleton of a monstrous dwelling, as well as a number of trenches intended for pipes, generators and cables.

Or a fresh corpse.

By now my nerves were buzzing like a hive of killer bees, primed for that final suicide sting. I had no doubt she intended to kill me but I was determined to exact a heavy price.

Somehow.

At the moment all I could do was drive. The gun at my head hadn't yielded an inch. The bitch had a steady hand. A consummate pro.

"Stop here."

The moment of truth.

"You haven't asked me about Goldsmith."

I heard her exhale.

The gun stayed firm but something changed.

"What about Goldsmith?"

"After I shot him he gave it up."

"Like what specifically?"

"Names, dates, numbers. He was covering his ass. Like Boutilier."

It was bullshit of course. Anything to squirm out of having my brains redecorate the dashboard.

"And where is all this evidence?"

"You're Bryce right?" I said, dredging up the name from my swampy memory.

The gun didn't budge.

"Irrelevant Max. Tell me where – now."

"He told me he had a safety deposit box in San Francisco."

"Which bank?"

I got the sense it would be the last question I'd answer.

"What's in it for me?"

"We can drop the charges to accidental homicide."

"I can live with that."

"Now. Which bank?"

"Wells Fargo but..."

She sighed heavily. "But what?"

"He used a fake ID."

The moment I said it, I knew I'd made a mistake. If Goldsmith had used a phony name the evidence could be buried.

Along with me.

Time paused while she processed the information.

I reached for the glove compartment. "Okay if I smoke?"

"No."

I had stopped the car with the engine still running. My hand was an inch away from the nitrous system. Hoping there was something left in the tank I took my foot off the brake and flipped the red switch.

The car came alive.

It squealed ahead six feet, smacked a steel pillar, and came to a wrenching stop. I was ready. She was not.

She hit the back seat hard and bounced, leaving her slightly dazed.

I didn't bother going for her gun. Instead I pulled the Taurus tucked in my waistband and pressed it against her face before she could recover.

"Easy," I said hoarsely.

She froze.

"Very slowly, drop the weapon on the front seat."

She did. A standard issue Glock.

I opened my door.

"Now, very slowly, out of the car."

The morning chill was refreshing after all those long, sweaty minutes of waiting for the shot I'd never hear.

"You're making things worse," she said calmly. "Take the deal and you walk."

"If I can trust you."

"We'll put it in writing, that work for you?"

She had a great smile. I almost believed her.

"What about Goldsmith?"

"Goldsmith?"

"He's still alive."

She shrugged. "He'll be no problem."

As we talked I tried to decide what to do about her. My first choice was drive away and let her walk home. However that left me completely exposed. The Company would focus all their resources on hunting me down, and eventually they'd succeed. It would also compromise our case against ICE. And render Boutilier's death meaningless.

My second choice was to pretend to go along, take the deal and hope for the best.

Seriously?

Choice two would have the same result as choice one.

Unfortunately choice three wasn't in my playbook. It was in hers.

"You'll need to sanction Goldsmith."

"Not my decision."

"Who decided to kill Boutilier?"

She looked away, as if bored by the whole affair.

"Jenkins. His section chief."

"He's in D.C. Somebody here took the contract. Who do you suppose it was."

Her hard blue eyes met mine.

"Had to be done. He gave us no choice."

At the moment I was knee-deep in choices, so I had little sympathy for bureaucratic logic.

"Take the deal Max," she persisted in a smooth, day-care voice. "You can't fight the world. The Vandals have a price on your head. We can protect you. If you don't care about yourself think about Nina. What happens to her?"

At the mention of Nina's name the Preacher snapped awake.

Until that moment I'd been under the delusion Nina wasn't on their wish list. The fact that she was, severely limited my choices.

Bryce took my silence for assent.

She reached out to gently push my gun aside.

"We can protect you Max."

I squeezed the trigger.

The sky exploded with frightened birds.

# Chapter 33

*"In the depth of winter, I finally learned that within me there is an invincible summer."*
– Albert Camus

# Chapter 33

It took me two full days before I was fit to go home.

When I did Nina's fierce embrace was a jolt of healing energy amped past infinity by my daughter's squeals of delight. After a few euphoric hours playing with Samantha and her new Christmas presents, Nina put her to bed and opened a bottle of Pinot.

"I wish you could have seen her Christmas morning, "Nina said showing me the pictures on her phone. "She was so excited."

Nina took a thoughtful sip of wine. "Couldn't you have come in for an hour? I was awake all night, hoping you'd show up."

The raw memory of Bryce dampened my spirits. I kissed her gently. "Sorry baby. But as it turned out it was the right thing to not do."

She insisted on inspecting my latest battle scars while I recounted a heavily edited version of my misadventures.

"I'm glad I didn't know you were shot," she said softly, "I would have gone crazy."

Then she sat up and gave me a suspicious stare. "Who took care of you anyhow?"

I was ready for that one. "King Bong's mom is a nurse. Mrs. Curry."

She settled back against my chest.

"You did a wonderful thing for all those girls. But Max...?"

"What baby?"

"Promise me you won't go after that Russian."

For a moment I thought she meant Andre.

"Russian?"

"The one with all the White House connections."

"Berlinski? He's probably in the Bahamas by now, checking his bank account."

"Promise me?"

I kissed her. "Anything you say."

"Ready for bed?" she whispered.

"Born ready." I drained my wine glass and started to stand.

An ear-stinging slap sat me back down.

Stunned, I rubbed my burning face.

"What the hell was that?"

She smiled. "That's for everything you didn't tell me."

I followed her meekly to our bedroom.

+      +      +

Sidney Kingman contacted a friend at the *New York Times* and the story broke big.

The whole corrupt mess: sweetheart contracts for White House cronies, payoffs to ICE Agents, human trafficking, drug smuggling, conspiring with the Cartels, and other abuses enabled by Homeland Security – all went viral and stayed there.

There were enthusiastic denials by the administration and calls for a congressional investigation. The Petaluma Police chief Bannon, is under state investigation and when they get around to checking his computer they'll uncover the child porn he tried to plant on Lowell.

Delaney and the DEA came up smelling like roses for 'heroic devotion to duty.' I was cleared in absentia for Paul Zallen's death and received a healthy bonus for my services.

The money bag I liberated from Berlinski contained close to nine hundred grand. I gave a hundred K to Manny for his medical expenses and kept a taste to restore my severely battered Green Ghost. I also took care of Lieutenant Boone who had been wounded in the assault.

Captain Lowell and Agent Fleeman, true to their oaths refused to take a cent – so I donated the bulk of the money to Sidney Kingman to pay for the rehabilitation of the young girls we rescued, and his continuing work as advocate for the Latino community.

At this point, two weeks into 2020, no one seems to have discovered Bryce's body and her Section Chief Jenkins is too busy fending off charges to investigate. Or so my sources tell me.

Funny thing, the most crucial bit of evidence I discovered was tucked in the wallet I swiped from Berlinski's dresser.

A credit card from an obscure bank in Iceland.

Using the information on his driver's license and that credit card I finally – after fruitless months – tracked down Berlinski's virtual fortune.

Eleven million dollars in bit coins.

Untraceable and easily transferred from country to country.

I managed to siphon off nine million dollars before they shut down the account.

The money went to various charities like Head Start, the ACLU and Doctors without Borders. The buzz on the dark web is that there's a contract out for a mysterious hacker in Germany known as Wasp.

In the process I remembered Carlos Canseco's dying words about 'bite money' and discovered he had over one hundred thousand in crypto currency stashed. I cashed out and sent it to Rosa Canseco.

As for me, I'm perfectly happy to be permanently off the clock and hunkered down with my family. Nina and I are even planning a vacation, maybe a cruise.

After all that went down at the end of 2019, I'm looking forward to a long, lazy, stretch of boredom.

I mean seriously, what else could happen?

# Acknoldedgements

This book could not be written without the extraordinary kindness, generosity, and friendship of the following: Sam W. Anderson, Chris Barideaux, David Baskin, Jerry Boxley, John Calella, Al Chan, Ellora Ong, Rob Cohen, Avi Emanuel, Gregory Fleeman, Philip Lederer, Rick Levine, Glenn Peckman, Lucy Phillips, John Hanford, John Iddings, Ellyn Lazarus, Christine Roth, Dianne Roxas, Linda Rude, Ellen Smith, Glen Scantlebury, Craig Wolfson, Jack Wright, Louise Wright...You're listed in alphabetical order but you're all number one in my book. FL